Forging the Blade

When the Student is Ready, the Magus Arrives

A Pre-Arthurian Novel in Five Cantos

A.J. Campbell

Forging the Blade

The *Tyrfing* Saga, Volume I

ISBN 978-0-61559-609-9

Aryante

There is tale my people tell of a great warrior priestess—Giver of the Sword—who lived long ago at the Warm Lake. She could view the Old and far ahead to the New, her armor built from countless scales of shimmering gold. At her last breath, they built a mount, shining white, chambered rich and deep for endless repose. Some claim she died, but I know she rode to Dreamland on a holy stag. Such a ride did she earn! She only sleeps between worlds—and someday she will return to correct virtue's loss. And I, alone, await to affirm her.

Merjands the Proclaimer

Prelude: Dreamland

A cold autumn eve in Anno 339

A harsh wind held no peace for rough men never tasting sweets of knowledge. It simply pushed wood-smoke through their beards. On another crest—leagues beyond their darkened mount—a fairer breeze held secrets never questioned. So bright was Dreamland! And upon this night, three elder men forged a blade, each in his own way.

* * *

Crickets chirped not at all yet Othar pondered when they did, far to the north. *No sound in this place, except from the knowing owl. Life stills in the Wasteland, shrinks from lack of substance as the moon hangs lost, fearing to crack its foolish smile. And cruel laughs are gone from the girl's bleeding ears, for the man's death wrought a hard joke when the whole camp plunged to Hell. How might I soothe her?—if I spoke like I do in flawless dreams?*

He mused to flames, scratched aged hairs, while peering to chilled stars, not crisp ones of younger days but like melting snow in an empty field. He scanned the far trees, dropping his gaze to the wrecked mound, smoke joining the night a full week after the explosion. And at his side, Vainamon grunted. *He rips flesh with poorly teeth. Waiting and lusting.*

Othar's eyes flicked to the girl squatting across the fire, then swung to view all the shadows of his sins. The stumps ran barren... *far as a man can see...* rolling up the mount in a giant swath. With his back to the night, he felt a dead man's hand brush his furrowed nape. He jumped!—and his hand twitched not from age, almost dropping his venison piece to the coals' warmth.

Ten years he worked here, coming down from North Farm with Vainamon to pull the saw... to watch hardwoods fall. *Wasted it is. Not a thing remains for the girl.* He scratched his beard in longer thought. *More than ten years. Eleven, ja.*

He found a bitter grin and shook his head, for the youngermen broke the charcoal man's arka with not a gleam left by the time his brother pawed the chest. Vainamon picked teeth with a black hand, spitting gristle to the flames. Othar chewed his piece of doe, only a shadow away, eying his good tunic upon the young one. *Fears the darkness, she does.* Tonight he would gift the balsam doll's comfort.

The owl called again, out beyond the Wasteland. *No place to be here. For the charcoal man remains... skulking to regain what he lost.* And the owl knew. Mice lived under dead branches, more mice than he could count!—but the owl stayed clear.

Vainamon gnawed the deer-bone again, squatting with elbows to knees and leering at the charcoal man's daughter. She hunkered to warmth, knowing what he wanted. He elbowed Othar with tight eyes, "The youngermen took the gleam, the draughts and wagons, all but the nag. How do we cross the Frozen Sea?—no gleam to pay our way, stuck here in Bairgs-ahei, this Trans Sylvania."

"We go south. Take the girl to her kin," scowled Othar.

"Nay! We sell her," demanded Vainamon, "Brusts not small! Fullnan now. She be a woman-child. Sai!" and he nodded toward the girl.

She sat facing them with hair of liquid flame, her eyes piercing every word. *Ja, she can hear again*, Othar knew full well, "Mind what ye say. She better now, no longer daufs. What be her worth? Her bloma gone!—like water down a rushing flodus. We take her to far-baurgs where her uncle lives."

Vainamon jumped to his feet, veins in his neck pulsing as he tossed the bone to flames, "I say we sell her in near-baurgs! She must have some worth. Then we have gleam to reach North Farm."

"Gleam!" cried Othar, "Say gleam one more time, I cut ye tongue out." He stood tall to face his kin, wiping grease from lips with the back of a hand, "Begone! Take the nag and go from this realm of death."

Vainamon growled like a wolf to clench tight fists, shaking them in mighty rage, for the quarrel always fell to Othar's view. In a quick move he pulled the knife from his belt, thrusting it to Othar's ribs, lips twisting, "Nay. I sell her!"

They fought to the ground!—rolled through flames— the girl running off with green eyes wide. Arms twisted. And they wrenched hard, until the knife found Vainamon's chest, stabbed by his own blade, and he lay unmoving as hair burned to acrid curls. Othar rolled from the stench of it to crawl like a dying badger as he fell to elbows, burying his face in barren dirt. And he lunged to one knee, finally standing in confusion to stumble this way and that, unable to see clearly as the world streamed a great blur. He tossed brush to flames, covering his brother where he lay. And he wiped ash from his eyes, to clutch a bloody tunic still smoking and charred, trying to see clearer while peering to the charcoal man's yurt, the girl within it frightened like a deer.

She chews barley crust and tendons, no goodness in her life, the only child in a camp gone mad. What will she have? The chest holds no more than her winter smock! Cold time is here and she should wear the wool, not my good tunic. And he glanced back to the fire. *He melts like wax, he does. Never did have substance. Gleam. Gleam. Gleam! For the thought of wealth he died—to sell a child?—only ebilsmen do it, ebils like her father. The charcoal man paid his wicked price, a death fiery and quick... just like Vainamon's.* Othar reached to his wound, blood no longer seeping through linen. Grabbing more branches, he dropped them to his brother's pyre.

He strode to his tent, forcing eyes to focus. *Now I see worse than ever, like a mole in the summer sun.* And he sat in a future world of darkness, fingering the balsam doll and checking knots for strength. For a week—the whole time the girl was deaf—he tried to keep order while the youngermen laughed as he fashioned a human shape from balsam fronds, no easy task, not a sawyer's work. Yet when finished the doll looked like a man, green and smelling good.

He closed gritted lids, seeing the girl's birth, her mother dying upon that day. Her father grieved for the wrong life and cared not for the little one. He took her to a brook to let her die in the water's palm, not the worth of maleness. Yet what good might a girl-child do? Who would she become? So Othar pulled her from death and wrapped her in a blanket. And he scaled mounts to the Quadi, buying a she-goat with hard-earned gleam, milk for a child who grew up wanting in a world too wild. She became *Thulia*... named for an isle in the Bairgs of Ice, a bitter land where life thrives by threads. The name seemed right.

Her father was a second-born noble, good in blood yet poor in coin. Even less in probity. What could he offer a second bride?—his birchen stool or oaken arka? She would laugh! So the man raised Thulia alone and in rough fashion.

He worked hard between drink, and so she raised herself. Othar could not help; he and Vainamon had to saw the logs!

She grew up wild without a guide, an untended Taifala. Long ago, out upon the Great Steppe, her people became the Taifali from the blood of Alans and Amazons. *She will remain dark like her mother was, yet such beautiful eyes and hair*. Othar clutched the balsam doll and stepped outside, glancing to the ruined charcoal mound. When the coal gas exploded, he was sawing logs half a mile away. *Blew her to trees, it did! Like lightening of the Thunder God*.

He walked to the girl's yurt, finding her crouched at the far side, knees folded to chest and hands tucked to stomach, her legs together. He pointed to the pallet, "Go to bed, girl. Sleepan now." She stood and walked to it, crawling beneath wolf furs. He knelt beside her, gifting the doll, "Othar not foolish. He know things… so ye be sleepan with balsammon. Smell fresh and clean. Make ye better, ja?"

The girl nodded and took the doll, pulling it under the furs.

Othar tried to smile yet hurting within, from the wound and burning eyes, from killing his only brother and watching her live as she did. Sadness within him caused his hands to shake. *Lost the only worth she had… here in the Wasteland, mountains full of dread, no meadow or rolling fen, no warbling of a love-struck thrush*. He screwed up his mouth, clawed at his beard, to view his fleeting, final age—no son to provide for his last years, no brother to hold the saw's far end. He was an oldamon now and wished to die at North Farm. And the poor child? Othar began to weep, tears filling cracks of age as he leaned to the girl and pulled furs round her neck. She looked to him. Her own eyes watered.

Yet he found words to sooth her, "Vainamon took the Journey, like ye father. Ye be free, girl, like the Amazon ye wants to be. Bringan ye down from these mounts. On the dawn we take the nag to far-baurgs, to your uncle Cannabas. Now ye sleepan, ja? Go to Dreamland."

She nodded and Othar stood, stepping outside to eye the ruined mound. He would find a way to get the girl to her uncle before snow fell, yet he knew not where the man lived or the time needed to get there—somewhere down in Gothia. Pushing the flap again, he smiled back to the girl, as good a one as he could muster. He knew she held the doll tight even in darkness.

He tipped his face to endless stars, to himina-gards— the upper house—knowing he would never see North Farm again, too poor to get back there; but if he could atone for destroying these woods, maybe the gods would let him reach a better place. He paused, closing lids to see beyond the Wasteland; for he could make dreams in his head, make them seem real. Only in Dreamland did the world seem right.

He sat at the long bench singing a song, all the swords before him, their owners gone. Above him, the hardwoods shined anew! Othar looked across a garden, plants so ripe and tall. In a meadow stood a cow and goat; he had a bucket for the milk.

On the far side, there formed a deep-green lake. A fat trout jumped, and he held a line and hook. And there she was—at water's edge—the one pure heart.

He saw the girl wear plaits of silk, gold bracelets on her wrists, garb her form in a blue dress... to sit upon a gleaming boulder, not a waif but a strong maiden eating honey from a marbled jar.

It glowed a fine dream. No better dream could an oldamon have.

* * *

At the Warm Lake, a last train of camels passed hours since, vending down the trade road—strewn hard with endless rocks—from Issyk Kul to the Jade Gate. And not far from the lake stood the kurgan. It no longer gleamed white, now covered with brown grass half nibbled by tan goats. A mud-brick house, built low and small, sat upon a hummock between the road and man-made mount as winds swept down from the Tien Shan, colder now than a week before. To the Proclaimer, the house was not a home but an abode, temporal for a few months before he again walked his wanderings. Perhaps this time he would return to the land of Qin and converse with Liang the Wise Priest, and eat a golden pear, sweet and tasty as juice dripped from hairs of an aged chin.

His wanderings took him to all the shrines built by men to honor gods, yet his wanting soul never found a scrid of peace. He simply waited to affirm her. When would she ride back upon a holy stag? Years passed beyond burden; and to conserve his limited animus, the Proclaimer slept, webbed halfway between a profane world and a land of dreams. In his low-roofed house, he stretched upon a hard bed (hay compacted by endless waiting) and pulled the Sogdian blanket to his chin, tucking his cinnabar beard and hoping for warmth that never came. His flesh clung to old bones!—no meat upon them.

Yet something beyond chill haunted the Proclaimer's nights. Subliminal wrenching, never connective, plagued sleep for months. Random segments of thought. *Another Giver of the Sword calls, new and young and perhaps a child, for she gleans nothing of a right world.* And now after months of solitude, his mind finally sank deep in a nocturne of recall, floating the expanse to reach the old her, to feel an essence oft blocked by aged encasement....

Aryante, can you hear me? Someone calls between worlds.

Merjands. Is it you?

Oh, heavenly yes! Of course, my dear. Who else endures time's weir?—waiting and trapped, the curse of the forever old. You are finally returning... with all things good and wise... for you stir in sleep, bridling your stag for the journey. Is she really you?

Yes, and protected by an Old Bear upon a mount, distant to the west. Do you still have my sword?

Of course. I predicted you would return about this time, but where? No great distance I hope, for I grow no younger and riding cracks my spine.

You must leave the lake and travel far westward...

Heavens no! I'm too old...

Merjands, what have you prepared for?—years of study with Greeks and Magi, all your time below the Kush and in the land of Qin? Your knowledge holds no aid if you remain where you are. All your patience will be needed. She is stubborn and wild, the worst student you could ever teach, but she is me and has my strength, the blood of Alanus.

What joy might I find in the west? They have no animus and little sense of Godhead.

You recall me with fondness, the years we had?

Of course, my dear, the very reason I came back to Warm Lake. I love you no less through time's wear.

Take heart; I'm riding back. But I'll be brazen and wild. What you found in me, you will love in her. Pack your books, cork your potions, and travel west to Gothia where twin rivers join above the Danube. There you will find me.

He awoke as the connection snapped, raising to elbows and peeling the Sogdian blanket. He arose to his feet! And like a man far younger, he ran from the mud-brick hut wearing no more than trousers to greet the endless cosmos. Forever he waited, refusing to succumb to a finality that took friends and colleagues, priests and thinkers, down to a withered pit. *There is no end, only a cycle, perhaps longer than it should be.* Steadfast and alone he believed in the gift of Dreamland, and he alone would nurture and guide it—the ultimate rebirth.

Oh, glorious night! Unshakable and singular, he clung to hope... to find life sprouting anew, yet countless leagues westward. *The Sword shall arise in a new hand.* Valor, probity, faith, dignity, forgiveness, all would return to this invidious world. *A champion of correctness.* He inhaled the excitement of it and flashed eyes skyward. The stars gleamed brighter than they ever did, and the night held wonders beyond all others. He raised arms above his head, lifting palms to guided perfection. *Yes! She rides back... after all these years.*

Canto One

VALOR

Anno 346

Seven years later

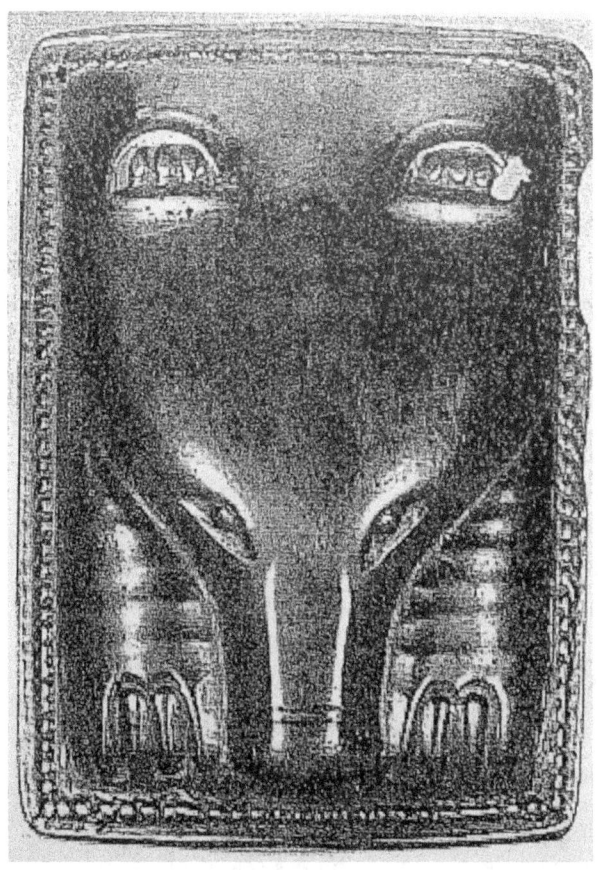

Chapter 1: Rites of Spring

Threisbaurg—"triple-town" between Twin Rivers,
The first day of Maius, Anno 346

The emerging sun greeted Old Hempstalk far too rough. *Eye-piercing, like a flame devouring tinder.* He winced and closed lids, snapped his head back to pull a deep breath, letting it escape as a heavy sigh. Beyond his doorway he paced to the awaiting mare, cinching the saddle in tautness required to support his hefty frame; for the mare had been readied by Cow Eyes, weak in sinew and mind. *A useless drone stumbling through boyhood like a three-legged goat.*

The last mares foaled a month ago and Old Hempstalk needed a count of fresh geldings from Pigfoot the conservator. This would be no pleasant visit. *Probably another confrontation.* Accordingly, he refrained from a hair of the dog, his usual morning cups of wine; and even more important, he avoided using his favored mount—the white-spotted gelding—the one horse he loved, yet the catalyst of great alienation, compounded by animosity; not that he feared his niece, but she was bigger than most and punched a hard knuckle. He swung to the saddle with a grunt and urged the mare toward the trade road, halting near the ferry to survey tribal lands.

To the west beyond the flodus Ilomata, the steppe unfurled as rolling hills across Walachia for seventy miles. All of it sprouted green as an endless sea of grass. Not a hill upon it rose above the height of ten men. And Old Hempstalk could picture the river beyond, the mile-wide Danube coursing its way to the Pontic Sea.

The ferry was operating again. *And the bullock team drops dung exactly where you step,* he mused from the safe height of his saddle, knowing exactly how soft-a-load gray bullocks dropped. He reined his mount from the river and rode east, smoothing his moustache with a deft hand as he gazed north to high peaks scratching clouds, the fearsome Bairgsahei. Creatures of nightmare lived there, hiding in places wild, gold-guarding griffins and the one-eyed man. There were specters far worse!—nameless and evil. *Things that were once men. Only fools go up there. Better to ride in sunlight and view what lies before you.* Those who lived in the mounts found misfortune, the Quadi—*the four-legged ones*—and the Gepids, *the dark-thought ones*. Transylvania claimed his brother's wife and then his brother, leaving Old Hempstalk to raise Thulia alone. *A hard bitch that one.*

The trade road through Threisbaurg remained muddy between hills, another fortnight before totally dry. He finished rites of spring, ten lambs butchered upon the Stone to praise Freyr and Freyja, the meat distributed to vassals. He was hetmon of the Taifali, blood of the Alans but now the Tyrfingi's clients and heavy horse—cataphracts armored from head to toe. Called Old Hempstalk by Thulia and the king's sons, Cannabas was not old. *Simply gray at the temples, perhaps a little overweight. And the wine?—all her fault, not mine!*

The sun warmed his face as he reached the eastern edge of the Taifali village. Before him, the conservator's house stood small and decrepit, its thatched roof uneven. *I'm not rich myself, but this place stands in shame.*

He closed eyes in humiliation, for his niece lived within its rotting walls... her wretched existence his fault.

Thulia arrived in his life as an uncontrollable child—drove him to drink—and he bartered her to Pigfoot the conservator when she turned fifteen, the legal age of marriage. He couldn't handle her defiance one more day! She was born wild to the charcoal burners, her early years spent in a yurt up in Transylvania. They constantly moved to virgin stands, felling hardwood in clear-cuts, leaving miles of stumps—the Wasteland. Thulia learned to swing an axe and pack dirt, never viewing civilized ways. Her father's crew stacked logs in huge mounds, covering them with earth and coal dust. A burning lasted for weeks, the charcoal then sold to Gothia's blacksmiths, the essence of all that was forged, chisels and horse bitts, fish hooks and plow shares, and the costly sword. To allow hardwood to char completely, her father opened vent holes to let air in.

One day he thumped the mound to make a vent and the coal gas exploded. Blew him to four winds! Thulia had been standing well behind her sire, found charcoal-black yet alive.

When Othar brought her to Threisbaurg, she was beyond the age of ten. The first words she uttered—*"I made Papa disappear"*—sounded strange to Old Hempstalk. The girl had nightmares from the experience. She arrived right after the reiks died in battle, his sons left parentless, their mother passing a few years back. As the deceased king's duce, Old Hempstalk spent too much time overseeing the boys and neglected the girl. Before he knew it, she was riding his best gelding, claiming to be an Amazon. Simply too vexing. Even a strapping with a belt proved no deterrent. (The belt was early in the game… before she strapped him back.)

According to Merjands, the girl wanted to be one of the boys, rejecting her gender's softness. People laughed at first, but no-one in Threisbaurg considered her foolish.

Merjands, in his wisdom, claimed, *"She simply has a wild imagination. Let us humor her and find something positive in her behavior."* Humor her? Apparently humor was the "last resort" in dealing with the undealable. Amazon? Old Hempstalk knew full well the last Amazon died centuries ago... or did she? He could only smile. That was seven years ago. Strong-willed, Thulia was almost eighteen and had grown to an Amazon's stature, nearly six feet tall and broad-shouldered, her limbs strong. *Maybe she is an Amazon.* She came from the right blood, about as Alanic as a woman could get, robust in features. *Just like her aunt, bless her memory.*

"Well, if it isn't the hetmon," shot a hard voice beyond Old Hempstalk's thoughts. He snapped straight in the saddle!—for he sat dreaming of a good wife lost to the pox. Before him, Pigfoot lurched through the doorway, lips warped to a sneer as Old Hempstalk slid from his mount to clear his throat, "Heh-hem. Well, now. I need a count of this spring's geldings. We get thirty for every hundred, the Alans twenty...."

"And the Tyrfingi retain the other half," the conservator spat. He stood weaving before his door-stoop, eyes attempting to focus through a mass of red veins, "The split always favors Aoric and that puke son of his... and those frigging snots, the king's sons," and then he puffed, "But to me it matters not. I always keep the best two each year as part of my wage."

"Like the *best two* I got from you three years ago?" Old Hempstalk thought it judicious to say no more, for it was unwise to raise Pigfoot's ire. The man could forever hold a grudge, seething inside for months, even years, as if bloated by evil dropsy. And truth was, he stank, giving an aura of raw leeks which he ate by the handful with bad teeth... and so the combination of inner bile and outer stench afforded the signum

Pigfoot. Of course, no one called him Pigfoot to his face, reserving it for offensive stories concerning his family's lack of prowess; for the entire Pigfoot gens had fallen to debilitation, neither riding fast in a skirmish nor fleet enough on foot to garner the proper amount of booty needed to sustain them in a style befitting good Gothic nobility; nor were they lovers, not ugly yet never handsome or virile; and this combination of slowness, bad breath, and physical mediocrity had taken its toll over several generations, leaving—alas!—the one remaining Pigfoot, a man given the responsibility of conservator of the horse herd, not too difficult an occupation or particularly rewarding... other than first choice of two yearly geldings.

Changing the subject to pleasantries, Hempstalk blurted, "Nice warm day. So then, how goes the count?" involuntarily wiping lips with fingers and thumb, for he was suddenly very dry, "I'm parched from the ride. This day is too hot for Maius first."

The conservator turned for the cabin's entrance, stumbling over the stoop to catch his balance by grabbing the door casing, "You come here to drink a poor man's wine?" he muttered, trolling bloodshot eyes back to the Taifalus, "Come inside but don't expect much. It's Greek and cheap and tastes like shit."

Old Hempstalk hesitated, "My niece isn't in there, is she?"

With a twist of lips, Pigfoot spat, "She's off to the market fair, the big-titted whore. Took that mute daughter with her... so this be your lucky day."

Old Hempstalk grabbed the man's arm with a broad hand, "Don't call her a whore."

The conservator's eyelids closed and snapped open, "I apologize. Everyone knows she never charges."

On the seventh day of each week, the open market brought people together from all three villages, yet this event was far larger, a spring fair with additional booths, plus music by an aged citharist and a woman who played two flutes at once. Every item under the sun would be bartered or sold: black pots from Samos, dried dates from Tunis, oil from groves of Sicilia, and rare fineries carted from exotic places, wares from Aetheopia, India, and the far land of Qin.

Arriving at the fair early, Thulia paced slowly, drinking in the sights and smells. Triple notes danced in ears and someone was brazing fish, trout from the aroma. *Almost like fried mushrooms.* Cradling Sesca in her left arm, she stopped at a silversmith's booth and lowered her daughter, "Look, my sweet. A wristlet inlaid with Indic garnets. Isn't it pretty?" She tucked Sesca higher, giving a broad grin, "When you grow up, would you like a silver wristlet?" The girl nodded and imitated her mother's smile.

Thulia continued through the crowd, "What else can we find? Oh, look!—a deft jongler in a fool's hat." She squeezed along a maze of mothers and children to stand before him. Sesca's lips parted in wonder, eyes bulging huge. The man was small and slight, and he sat upon a wagon bed, legs crossed and withered as he tossed three wooden balls, one green, another yellow, and the third bright red.

Eying Sesca, the man let the red ball drop to one hand. He continued jongling the other two as he held it out to her, "Please help me with this one," he begged. Sesca clutched the ball tight, lifting it up and down with both hands—for she did not want to drop it—and Thulia laughed a good one. Then Sesca leaned out, handing it back. Without missing a beat, the jongler added it to the others. "Thank you," he winked, "I couldn't keep them up without your help. My hand gets tired, so a little girl or boy must aid me."

"Sesca thanks you," purred Thulia.

"More than welcome," claimed the jongler as he switched rotation of the balls, "Got two, myself. One older than two years, about like yours, and another pushing five, both girls."

He has no sons, nor can he walk! Thulia reached into her tunic and withdrew a purse. Its leather was stained and aged, a small pouch gifted by Old Othar, good Othar the Finnermon; and she pawed for a single bronze ass.

"No, no!" cried the jongler, "Buy something for the girl."

Thulia stood straight, a little taller, and nodded she would. Then she leaned toward him, purring, "Wave farewell to the nice man," secretly placing the coin on rough boards of his wagon bed. And she left him to other mothers as she strode toward the butcher's stall.

*   *   *

At his market-booth, the Roman trader displayed household wares for Threisbaurg's locals, the Tyrfingi, Alans, and Taifali. His items were functional and needed: raw Colchian linen and red skeins of Peloponnesian wool, iron razors and needles from smiths of Brixia, plated dinner-ware from the tinners of Gaul, and famed Ulmenian spoons and bowls.

He manned the booth once a month from spring to autumn, coming up from the Stone Bridge at the twin Drobetas, stopping at Ulmenia to replenish his wooden-ware. Rarely did he travel further north toward Tyras, although he ventured to Hospice twice a year, trading with Bishop Wulfilas and the Christians at the river Hierasus.

With a keen eye for women, the Trader rearranged wares while studying Thulia the buxom Taifala. She walked along the butcher's stall holding her daughter to bosom. He knew her history, as did every red-blooded male. She came from a poor family, gave her virginity away, and married poorer. Pulling his gaze from Thulia, he found Heldrid the widower looking her way. He knew the man retired years ago, once a successful trader yet no longer venturing beyond Threisbaurg. The Roman grinned a big one, "Quite the figure. Might you agree?"

"Indeed," noted Heldrid, "Bronze hair like the setting sun, emerald green eyes. Handsome young woman," repeating himself, "Handsome." He fumbled through the Roman's tinnery, "Fine stannum plates. Alesian, no doubt," his gaze again shifting to Thulia.

"Aye," the Roman touted, "The best Gaul offers; thick silver plating."

"I'll take all four," Heldrid confirmed, still watching Thulia, "A gift for the conservator. Do you know him?"

"Her husband, the horse conservator? Not really. Only his reputation, an acute judge of horseflesh. I know all the good looking women, though," then nodding with a shift of eyes, "There's the Alan leader's daughter. Pretty girl, very young and due to drop her first child. Married a little early into the highest Tyrfingi family, the wife of Selenas the Balth."

Lilia turned her back to the Roman and Heldrid, knowing they were discussing her condition, and walked toward the butcher's stall. She became pregnant a year under marriageable age, the magistrate thinking she was older, her father conveniently silent as she caught Threisbaurg's most eligible male. She skirted the stall, almost bumping into Thulia, a woman she knew through gossip, and she blushed at the thought of such wicked tales. Yet in a way, she and Thulia were alike. She was the daughter of the Alan hetmon, and Thulia was raised by the Taifali hetmon. As she brushed past Thulia, she smiled, trying to look pleasant.

Thulia peered down and cracked, "Ah, Selenas is so good at it. To beget a child from a child." And a dozen women chuckled.

What a cheap thing to throw my way. Lilia ignored the slur and moved away, *The woman is coarse, tastelessly flaunting grotesque brusts, seething in envy and married to a wretch.* She knew the Taifala's reputation—the Trollop of Threisbaurg, Queen of the Horse Barns. Thulia's nights were filled with rustling straw, young men coming and going like weasels in a woodpile. Selenas avoided the Taifala for good reason, a disgrace to the community. No decent young man would speak to her. *What did I ever do to raise her ire?*

Perhaps wishing to lighten the tone, Thulia added, "Lilia is beyond full term. She'll drop the baby in her market basket." Again the women laughed.

Lilia found no humor in Thulia's statement, her stomach huge and the small of her back aching. Away from the woman and her speechless child, Lilia found a booth with a stack of Gallic soap, far better than the homemade variety Thulia used. She purchased two chunks with silver coin, making sure the Taifala noticed the soap while she paced for the Roman's wares.

The trader was slipping stannum plates back to linen bags, handing them to Heldrid as Lilia noticed a magnificent tunic reposing upon his table. *It must be expensive, purple-dyed from sea-snail's blood.* At sleeve-end and the tunic's collar, a beauteous zigzag hatch was sewn from real gold thread. *Selenas would love it, a regal garment for the future reiks.*

Seeing her interest, the trader boasted, "The work of an artisan in Adrianople. The last one I have."

She raised the tunic to examine it, making sure other women viewed its workmanship. Not even knowing its price, Lilia replied, "I'll take it. A gift to my husband for a special occasion."

Lilia was envied for wedding into the highest Tyrfingi family—the Balths. She lived in a house built for a reiks, its logs debarked to fine smoothness, the timbers chinked with lime. Its floor was tamped smooth, liberally watered, and tamped smooth again, the result covered with Sassanian rugs. Brighter rugs hung bold along the walls, partitions extending outward from a central hearth. A great house it was, the second best in Threisbaurg, only exceeded by Heldrid's. She had never seen the interior of the Villa Heldridus Constantinus, yet doubted it could be much better than the one built for the Tyrfingi king.

She searched her embroidered purse for a gold coin, handing it to the Roman trader. After folding the garment to her basket she approached Thulia, still at the butcher's stall clutching her mute child. Thulia purchased not a ham or cut of beef, not even a freshly hung fowl, but a pair of sheep hocks. *The cheapest fare, gristle and fat, only eaten by the unfree*, "Do you cook them with dried peas or beans?" smiled Lilia, fluffing the purple tunic.

Thulia's brows lowered. She snapped around, a gaze no less sharp than her tongue, "I feed them to dogs and a certain Pig. Would you care for one?"

What a rude slut! She left Thulia behind in an awkward pace, but once the baby arrived she would be slim again, the perfection of noble womanhood, auburn hair over flawless youth. Beyond the village square, she found clean grass and lowered the basket to sit beside it. Closing eyes to the sun's warmth, Lilia pondered her station in life. She had found the correct man—Selenas the young Balth, son of a dead reiks and destined to be the next tribal king.

*　　*　　*

As townsfolk prepared to celebrate at the gardens, a band of Quadi warriors swung horses from the trade road, slipping quietly into a stand of larch, a little shade to hide intent. The Leader dismounted and squatted, calling the dozen horsemen to a circle around him. He scratched soil with a hardwood stick, using it to draw a map. "We are here, about two miles east of the Prahova ferry. Ahead of us—right here— is the Alan village. On the other side of the river, the larger Tyrfingi settlement extends along the trade road west until it passes Four Corners. The Taifali village is just beyond the intersection and built on both sides of the flodus Ilomata. Understand?"

The Quadi acknowledged with grunts while the Leader continued, "We'll not have a better day: one in a hundred thousand. The seventh day of the week, their market day. It's also the first of Maius—Fertility Day. Not a soul laboring in the fields or horse barns. Some will be at the market fair, while good pagans are congregating—right down here—at the communal gardens to watch the Virgin ride the Phallus Wagon, the rites of spring."

"The Alan village will be deserted, everyone across the river at these functions," the Bold One agreed.

The Leader nodded, again drawing with his stick, "Exactly. Just to the north of us on the other side of the Prahova are the horse barns and pasturage. The river runs slow here, easy enough to swim our mounts across. We need a dozen pack horses with strong shoulders. The Alan grain is right here… stored above the village and close to where we are now. We get the horses, then empty grain sacks just enough to tie them in pairs, two sacks for each horse." He looked up to his men, "The tribe is depending on us. Our corn supply will be exhausted in less than two months, and the Alan stores are essential for our survival."

"Why not ask the Alans for it?—or the Christians at the flodus Hierasus?—and offer to return an equal amount at harvest time," quizzed the Honest One.

They glared at him, and the Leader growled, "Because we cannot afford to take no for an answer."

Chapter 2: Always in the Dreams

Thulia bought a loaf of black bread at the market-fair. Its aroma made her mouth water—sweet from oven brick and sour from rye—but it wasn't hers to eat. She stuffed it to the hempen sack with the sheep hocks; and carrying Sesca in her other arm, she trekked to the home of Pigfoot's sister. The woman enjoyed Sesca and would take care of the girl for the rest of the morning.

She finally reached Four Corners, the road south leading to communal gardens and Tyrfingi grain barns. In another hour or so, this year's virgin would clutch the wooden phallus as the wagon bounced through furrows plowed and ready for seed. The phallus was carved from aged pine, and it would wobble from side to side when strapped upright in the wagon bed. Thulia stopped for a moment, looking down the garden road. She conjured a thin smile. *I was the most memorable fake virgin of them all.* Priests had no idea of what took place at the horse barns under rolling stars.

She turned a heel to look west, her home a quarter-mile down the trade road. She kicked a rock with her toe, watching it bounce to a ditch, and she paced north on the road to the horse barns. The walk was always soothing, the road vending through trimmed birch; and beyond them stood the marvelous Villa Heldridus Constantinus, the home of Threisbaurg's richest noble, yet a man with no airs of pretense. Heldrid gave her an early morning ride to the communal well, not once or twice but often, as she sat on the wagon seat—not in the back with his freewoman. *There are a few good men left, like Othar and old Heldrid the widower... and the crippled jongler.*

The north road ended at the horse barns, about a mile from Othar's cabin in the oak grove. At the barns she would saddle the white-spotted gelding and deliver the bread to Othar. The gelding was Old Hempstalk's prized horse, trained for the steppe dance. He loved it as something priceless—as if a carnelian ring or lapis brooch. And to spite him, to make him fall to another stupor, Thulia rode the gelding whenever she could, even using his saddle. She took a famed deep breath, grinned a wry one, and began the trek afresh.

*   *   *

Rustan sat upon the banks of the Prahova discussing Lilia's condition with Selenas, the baby due any day. As a diversion, they fished for tench since early dawn, their boots soaking with dew when they walked from the wagon. Now they sat waiting for midmorning bite. The Prahova rolled deep and slow below the tribal gardens, the soil tilled and waiting for the fertility ritual scheduled at noon. All three tribes within the kunja hoped for another bountiful season, the past one excellent. Rustan smiled content as the Alan hetmon. The previous year's harvest filled his tribal barns, mostly wheat with a small amount of millet and rye.

The morning was so quiet Rustan could hear the tow-cable groaning upriver, the bullocks' plodding, even the ferryman shouting. He seldom fished with his son-in-law, usually coming to the river with Fritigern the younger brother. Frit was a real fisherman, an angler extraordinaire. Water swirled torpid in a pool where tench reached two pounds; and on a light rod, they were a brute to catch. In the wagon at their backs, Rustan kept a "tench tub" with a circular lid. Earlier, the fishing was fast with Rustan catching the first one as Selenas rushed to fill the tub with a bucket. Once tossed in, the fish circled the perimeter, a good sign it would survive. In two hours they caught nearly twenty fish, all big enough to split and broil. The tench would be held in the tub for three days, feeding upon pieces of bread. They tasted sweeter that way.

"I wonder why Frit didn't come. He missed a good bite this morning," claimed Rustan, "It gets no better than this."

"Truthfully, I wouldn't know. Frit's the fishing expert, not me," Selenas admitted, "He's practicing lancing up at the horse barns, or so he claims."

Rustan raised his rod to check the bait. The grub remained on the hook, and he lowered it back to the flodus, lifting an eyebrow, "What's that supposed to mean?"

The young Balth twitched his pole to make the bait move, "He probably wants to be alone. The Fertility Rite conjures an old heartache. At the time he discovered manhood, Frit had a big crush on Thulia. He always figured they would marry. Then, Old Hempstalk—our acting guardian—made a deal with the conservator. It practically killed Frit... if a kid could die from a broken heart. Took him a long time to get over it, and maybe he never did."

"Must have been three years ago, the spring she rode as Freyja's Virgin."

"Uh, huh. He was thirteen when she reached wedding age. They were close, growing up together. I was a little older. Didn't think much of her."

"So this is Frit's day to celebrate loss. We'll fish until the sun swings high and then go watch the ride of the Phallus and Virgin. I doubt the priests have found a maiden as ripe as Thulia was. Quite the ride through furrows that year. She was so top-heavy, the wagon flipped." Rustan chuckled, his rod twitching from it.

Selenas rolled his eyes, "You actually believe that?"

"Believe what?"

"Her stature tipped the wagon? I wasn't there, but that's a hard tale to swallow."

"Let me tell you something," avowed Rustan, "That pine phallus is seven generations old. At least a hundred-fifty virgins bounced through the gardens with it. Right?"

"What's that got to do with Thulia tipping the wagon?"

"Everything! That phallus is always stored in the horse barn rafters. It's cracked from drying out and weighs less than years ago. But—as everyone saw—the extra weight of Thulia's endowments flipped the whole thing in one of the greatest shows the kunja ever saw. The crowd cheered until freemen got things going again. The drought horses were spooky but finished circling the fields."

"Thulia was just bigger than your average virgin, that's all."

"Perhaps, but every tribe in the Barbaricon heard of it. The wagon never flipped before, and Thulia was what?— almost fifteen? Two weeks later, a gang of ruffians came down from Tyras just to '*check her out,*' I think the expression was. We all know what they really wanted and they probably got it. As far as I can tell, she's still growing. Seen her lately?"

Selenas flushed to dark scarlet and stammered, "Well, ah… no… not for some time."

* * *

Othar visualized his two-man saw. He knew it stood bent to a corner of his cabin, its blade orange rust. If he had flax-seed oil, he could wipe it clean. *A good saw, it was. Cut more logs than a man might count.*

He sat at bed-edge, leaning slowly to find the ash-wood staff, feeling at his feet to grasp it, then pulling the staff upright to raise himself. He remembered when he stood tall, *A bigamon, ja... with arms like a bear.* Now he stooped in final age. Othar thumped his way to a sliver of light, cracking the door to greet a day not unlike the one before and the one before that. Days of darkness. He would milk the goat, not sure what he might do after, perhaps sit in the sun at grove's edge and feel its warmth. Blinking eyes, he could see a lighter green beyond the oak grove's darker shade. Ja, he could picture all the horses and Tyrfingi barns, the way they stood long and low. Even up close, he could not view his own wood pile, his eyes milk-white.

Tapping the staff before him, he walked until feeling chunks of green wood, all birch and oak. By autumn, the pile would be dry and ready for the hearth. He shook his head, for another man cut it, bringing it here through Hempstalk's grace. For long moments he tapped the hardwood staff to the ground. He didn't need it to walk, only as his eyes. He tapped it again as time passed to moments long and possibly lost, for he was unsure of each one's length. The moment had passed, now hardly remembered. He was going to do something but forgot.

Hearing a noise, he couldn't tell what it was or its direction. *Maybe down from the Bairgs-ahei, down from the Wasteland.* "Vainamon! Is that you? Get away from this place. Go back to the pyre where ye belong." The noise came closer and he raised his staff to beat Vainamon off. Othar looked to his right, the visage moving; a horse he thought. The image stopped and split apart, half of it coming toward him.

"Othar," the girl cooed, hugging him, "I have a loaf of black bread, enough for today and tomorrow. When the tribal catchermon brings the hare, I'll cook it for you. Have you milked the goat?"

He shook his head, not sure where the goat was.

"Let me milk it for you. I'm big now, remember?— strong of hand and limb."

"Nay!" Othar affirmed, his voice resolute, "If ye milks it, girl, what shall I do? Not a thing to bide me time."

She took his arm, leading him to the left, "The goat's right here. I'll bring the bread inside and get your milking stool. To your right is the old stump. You can sit if you like."

"Tell me, girl. How far to North Farm from this dark place?"

"Too far for even me to walk," she claimed, her voice further away, "You sit and I'll be right back."

He nodded his ja, standing still to wait; but he would not sit like an oldamon, for he still had strong legs.

Thulia entered the moss-chinked shack to wretched darkness, setting her bag on the table to pull his bread from it. Her sheep hocks had changed its aroma but Othar wouldn't notice. She'd get water and a rag, wipe the table clean; and she pressed the bread to chest, clutching it tightly. From all the havoc in her life, she couldn't smile to a man who loved her. *He would not have seen it, anyway.* She was losing him! The gods were punishing her for taking the wicked path. Thulia turned to the open door, the old man standing patiently beyond it. *He's going to die!* She could feel spirits of Death creeping down from the mountains, hovering in the grove, waiting for his final breath. In another week or month he would be gone.

Othar saved her life, not once but twice! If the gods could steal his respect, turn him into her uncle's ward, if they could blind his eyes and still his hand—if they could do that to such a pure man—then what was her value to the gods? Every deity sat in the lower house, no better than demons they kissed. *Damn them all, every one, for striking goodness down.* She knew the truth—gods were malicious, bent on revenge, not at all what priests claimed.

She set the bread to the table, her eyes misting, yet an Amazon would not weep. Her girlhood declaration killed the stigma of abasement, as she learned to ride and wield a lance better than most men, a training owed to Old Hempstalk. From her stature, people still called her the Amazon, yet she lost her way. In childhood dreams, she was going to slay evil and save the good. Instead, she became the priests' fake virgin. Each night, young men arrived at the horse barns in droves, far too many to appease at once. If she refused, Thulia feared what they might do. She should have screamed, "Enough!" Yet she took them on, two at a time, until she found the right young man.

She closed eyes in recollection.

She pulled the latch-string quietly, yet the bar clicked. Old Hempstalk heard it as she entered. He snapped erect sitting behind the table, slamming his chair backward as the sudden move tipped the wine flask. It rolled and bounced to the floor. Giving a hard stare, he brushed lips with a hand and smoothed his gray moustache.

Thulia shut the door as her eyes met his. She was totally disheveled, out of breath with hair tangled in snippets of hay. Of Gothia's women, only she wore men's clothes; and he knew where she had been, her tunic far too loose as more straw clung to her trousers. In no great hurry, Thulia wrapped the tunic tighter, studying her uncle for an instant. Then she raised her chin and headed for bed.

Old Hempstalk no longer shouted, not a scolding word. Clearing his throat he remarked, "I suppose hay needed tending in the horse barns."

"You're drunk," she hissed, spinning back to him.

He stood quickly, the chair falling rearward as he mastered his balance. "We're a good Taifali family, eh? A slut and a drunk."

"I'm not a slut!" she snapped, her eyes fiery, "He's a good young man from a noble family."

Old Hempstalk leaned, placing hands to the table, palm down, "That's fine but he isn't going to marry you, is he. Just like the rest."

"How do you know he isn't?" She demanded, pacing long strides to him.

"Well, it doesn't matter. Earlier this eve I sealed a bargain with your future husband. No more rolls in the hay. Your vulgar career is over."

"How dare you!" she spat, raising a hand to slap him.

"Don't do it!—be a lady. You've got exactly a fortnight to practice."

"Marrying me off on my birth-date? You couldn't wait one day beyond," she gasped, lowering her arm, shocked by it.

He stood straight, weaving a little, "I'm sorry, but my trials must end. I cannot stay up all night—eve after eve—worrying about my niece... wondering if she's been raped or laying dead somewhere."

She spun about in a fury, long legs carrying her to the cupboard. Taking the wax tablet and stylus, she scratched upon it. Pacing back to Old Hempstalk she threw the tablet on the table and walked for her bed.

Thulia opened her eyes, staring at the bread on Othar's table. *"I shall never speak to you again,"* the note claimed in rough Latin, a well-kept promise, not a word to him since that night. She carried an unborn child into her marriage with the conservator, and now she was pregnant again... by the same young noble! What a fool she was, mistaking his lust for love. Old Hempstalk was correct. She wasn't an Amazon but a slut!—falling from her dream and left with the wraith, a man's voice soothing the night, a honeyed coo disguising evil intent.

So much for girlhood dreams. She grabbed the milking stool, took a deep breath, and stepped out to Othar's dark world.

*   *   *

Fritigern slid from his white gelding at the horse barns. Just for the fun of it, he tossed the contus with an overhand throw. The twelve foot shaft flew its perfect arc, hitting the straw-man target at mid chest. Frit grinned a broad one, *Not much left to it*. Twine holding straw together had been severed by too many lancings, and the target looked like an upright pile of hay.

He mused upon his talent or lack thereof, and it seemed he was better when using a contus as a javelin, able to make an accurate toss. Frit had an eye for it. Someday he would get a Sarmatian bow, laminated from horn, sinew, and wood, the perfect weapon for a man with a good eye. Pacing to the target, he pulled the lance, tossed it to the ground, and began repairing the twine. As he knotted broken strands, he eyed the white-spotted gelding as it galloped uphill from the oak grove. *Thulia!* He tied more loose ends and stepped back, checking artistic handiwork. The straw-man looked better yet stood as a sad figure. Frit swung around as Thulia dropped from her mount, their eyes meeting.

"How long have you been here?" she asked with a curl of lips, "I didn't see you when I saddled-up this morning."

"A couple of hours, but I circled the herds to see how many new males had been knifed by the gelder. We probably missed each other in coming and going." He grinned all the broader, iron eyes atwinkle, "You look incredibly good. A little bigger, I think."

Thulia guffawed, knowing what he meant, "So are you. Taller this year and more muscled." She paced to him, face to face, "As tall as the Amazon now. Amazing how a person can change in eight or nine months; I think it's been that long, not since last summer." He shrugged and leaned to retrieve his lance. Thulia studied his mount, her voice just

32

above a whisper, "The white horse. How long have you had it now?"

"Three years to the month. I stole the coins from father's Jove-wood arka and Selenas thrashed me for it, but it was too late. The Alan noble refused to return the money." He stepped to the gelding and ran a hand along its neck, flashing a grin, "It was your fault. You goaded me with the great promise. I was trying to fulfill requirements, perhaps not as honest as I should have been... but then again, I was the bad boy, as you were the bad girl. We were the perfect pair."

She turned from him, not wanting him to see her reaction, and she mumbled, "Yes. The demands of a girl to a younger boy—'I don't come free. The man I marry shall ride a white horse and live in a castle halfway up a mountain.' You corrected me, claiming castles were built on mountain tops, and I told you I feared high places. We were so romantic, not even knowing it." She faced him again, wiping a hand to eyes, the sob drowned by her laugh.

Painful moments lingered, so Frit stepped to the other side of his mount, distancing himself from her while pretending to cinch the saddle tighter. It was still there, the intenseness of their dream, almost five years and going back to when he was twelve. He wished to make light of it, to lift her spirits, "Well, I just came up here for a short practice, trying to be more proficient and equal the Amazon's talent. I have trouble with penetration even though I've a straight lance," and he laughed nervously.

Thulia wheeled on a toe, all smiles, "Oh, really? I searched for a good one but never found it, waited for you to reach manhood, but then came the arranged...," and she stopped short, an explanation no longer necessary, "Are you approaching the target with the contus held parallel to the ground? No angling downward. It keeps thrust from deep penetration," she chuckled uneasily.

Leaning arms over his saddle, Frit looked beyond her, watching activity in the fields below, "I thought this was a holiday. I avoided going to the rites of spring because nothing could equal your ride; but it's not a holiday for everyone. Look down toward the river. The gelder's crew is still roping horses."

Thulia snapped around, raising a hand to her forehead, "Gelding was completed last week, and those are not young of the year but older animals. Look! They're already swimming four pairs across the river." She snapped a gaze to him and demanded, "Give me the contus."

"Certainly not," resolved Frit as he swung to his mount, "Stay here. I'll put a stop to this." And then he dug heels to his white horse.

"You're going to get yourself killed!" she screamed after him, yet knowing he was too stubborn to listen. *A weapon! I need something sharp.* Thinking fast, she ran into the nearest horse barn and grabbed a pitch-fork from the stack leaning against the back wall. *Wooden tines are better than nothing.* In quick time, she reined the white-spotted gelding down the hill, crossing fields and reaching the Prahova to find four remaining thieves at the river bank. One of them brandished a spear, while another flashed a sword-blade, both fighting Frit. Beyond them, the other two thieves guided a pair of geldings into the water.

They were taking the biggest horses not claimed by tribal leaders! Thulia glanced back to Frit as she chased them, hoping he'd hold his own against the first two rustlers. She witnessed perfect execution. Frit kept his contus level, holding it double-handed as he skewered one of the strangers. Two feet of shaft protruded from the thief's back!—the man propelled backward from an empty saddle. Frit couldn't withdraw his lance, too much of it within his victim, and he released his grip while leaping from his horse to regain the weapon.

Turning her gaze, Thulia's attention fell to the two men in the river. Water splashed high, soaking her as the white-spotted gelding plowed through it. Hearing her approach, one of the thieves twisted in his saddle, trying to pull his sword from its scabbard. He never found the time! Leaning forward, she thrust the pitch-fork deep to his ribs, snapping tines as the man fell sideways into the Prahova. The current washed him downstream, arms chopping the surface in a vain attempt to swim; yet his flailing ceased, the water coloring pink to mix with silty brown, a dead man drowning. For an instant his hand pushed above the surface, closing upon itself, trying to re-grasp a fleeting, escapable life.

The other thief was too far out in the river, guiding misbegotten booty to Alan territory. She gave up the chase, reining back toward shore. Frit was down, rolling to his side!—as the surviving thief turned his horse for another pass. Thulia dug heels to the gelding's ribs, and the horse knew her intent. In mere moments, quick instants, the mount carried her to intercept the last stranger. Yet she had the poorest excuse for a weapon—a tineless fork, a skinny club. And undeterred, she slapped the broken pitch-fork hard to his face.

The man went down!—rolling in the field to regain his feet, then searching to find his sword as he ran in a feverish circle. With haste gained from an unknown urge, perhaps a need for requite love—wanting to keep Frit alive for another day, another time, when they could seal a childhood vow—she jumped from her mount, landing upon the assailant as they fell spread-eagle to tender shoots of an interrupted spring. She jumped to her feet! And using the broken fork as a club, Thulia waylaid the man in a shower of hits, again and again, to his neck and face. The thief never regained his posture, sinking lower in the field; and finally he lay motionless, his expression no longer threatening but a visage terminally calm.

At the moment when she sensed life's flight, Thulia turned from the raider and dropped the shaft to the soil of Gothia, discovering that only she remained standing. Frit lay crumpled twenty paces away. *He cannot be dead!* She froze, afraid to move or even breathe. He was always there, perhaps not in person but always in the dreams. He was her prince, her soul's other half, once too young to be a lover but never unloving or unloved. All the good—the correct and rightful thoughts in her deepest pith—trembled in fear. If she could not save him, who would save her in the end?—when the world finally turned right. Who?

Chapter 3: With a Stick

Athanaric squinted from the hill watching the action in the fields. At first he wondered what to think; but when ropers began toppling to the ground and splashing in the river, he realized the gelders were fighting one another. The river was a long way off and he had trouble seeing anything in bright sunlight. His pupils were small, his eyes beady and strained, the reason everyone called him the Squinter.

Wanting to miss the excitement, he rode downhill at a moderate speed, keeping his horse at a pace that assured his arrival *after* blood-letting was over. *"Be judicious, my son,"* claimed his father the magistrate, sound advice from the most important man in the kunja, now that the king was dead.

For the past few weeks, the only men around the horse barns, other than himself, were the conservator and the gelding team. *Perhaps they got into an argument over the conservator's wife and a melee began. Things like that happen, just a joke, then a small blade, then a sword, then a friend stepping in, then the other man's friend, then the uncle and cousin. And before you know it? A minor Gothic war, with bodies strewn all over the field.* And it seemed to be a fine day for a small war, no great carnage. *Quite balmy and warm, and I think there's only one survivor, rather hard to discern at this distance.* Athanaric could smell those blue and yellow flowers blanketing the steppe in Maius, nameless as far as he knew; but then again, he was not much at recalling flowery names. He was too manly a man for that sort of thing.

Ah, yes. One survivor. A woman, I believe, or a man with extremely long hair. Perfect day for a ride if not for an overly bright sun. And he supposed that someone would have to report this to his father, the entire gelding team killed by one of their own. *Must have been a fierce argument.*

"Never insult a gelder or he'll cut your nuts off," his father always claimed. And he rode leisurely down the slope to approach the river. By now Athanaric was reasonably sure whoever was going to die had done so. *Gods forbid! I think the conservator's wife is smothering the last gelder in her bosom,* and it seemed a strange way to kill anyone, although rather unique.

* * *

Frit came to full consciousness as Thulia clutched him overly tight, his head squashed in luxuriant cleavage. The best thing he could do was forget ringing in his ears, the lump on his temple, and pretend he was still unconscious. He had fallen upon his back, yet she raised his torso, holding him tight, kneeling while rocking him back and forth, mumbling over and over, "Please, don't die. Don't die." He wasn't planning on it, reclosing eyes and trying not to give himself away with an involuntary grin.

Suddenly, Thulia realized he was awake and unhurt. She released him with a jump, regaining her feet as he fell to the ground upon elbows. "Well!" she huffed, discovering her tunic was loose, "Pretending you're dead, eh? I ought to run you through like the rest," then interrupted by an approaching horseman.

The Squinter jumped from his mount with sword in hand, yelling, "Drop your weapon and stand back. You've had your killing spree. Who is it, anyway? Oh! Young Fritigern, eh. I thought he was one of the gelding team."

"What weapon?" barked Thulia, pacing back while adjusting cleavage.

"The one you slayed them with," he accused her, "I saw you do it from the hill-top. Why would you want to kill the gelder and his ropers? They're just doing their job, and you—of all people—should have known it."

Propping himself higher, Frit rolled eyes to the sky, "Hey, Plato... or is it Aristotle? Take a squint at the dead. Two of them carry the Quadi Venus, their mother goddess. And if Thulia hadn't stopped them, we'd be missing more than eight horses they stole."

"Oh! Well, that's different then," admitted the Squinter, "I suppose I should apologize for the accusation. I thought it odd the conservator's wife would be killing gelders. You know what I mean?"

* * *

The day after the Quadi raid, Aoric sat stiff upon his wagon-seat listening to the hum of the ferry-rope. He hated ferry rides, perhaps because he couldn't swim. He should've learned in childhood, as most children did, but he feared water. His son Athanaric stood upon the ferry deck, one hand secure upon a harness, just in case the team bolted into the Prahova taking Aoric with them. The ferry thumped the east bank, and the magistrate's wagon lurched as Athanaric was yanked by the momentum.

"Hold the damned team," snapped Aoric, "Or they'll gallop for Tyras before that idiot positions the off-loading planks. These fancy spokes will snap at the hub if they slam from this conveyance. Ruin an expensive vehicle." *And fact is, this wagon is too delicate for the Barbaricon, made for downtown Marcianopolis or some such place, but I'll be damned if I admit its purchase as poor judgment. I'm the judge!*

Aoric remained in a sour mood after arriving at the Alan village, the closest scene to the crime. He snapped at Athanaric, his son trying to help him down from the wagon. Aoric's leg was bothering him again, usually a sign of impending rain; and the combination of lameness, moisture, and reluctant duty, pitched his mood straight down a bottomless well.

At the Alan grain barns, they all gathered around, every wronged person, not counting the entire Alan tribe, especially growing children who needed good nourishment. Aoric's first act was designed to alleviate concern, and he promised that both the Tyrfingi and Taifali would contribute grain if the Alans exhausted their supply before harvest time. After addressing the Alans, the magistrate limped into the largest grain barn, along with hetmen and witnesses. The story unfolded. Quadi raiders made off with over a ton of grain. They stole a dozen geldings, all at least five years old and worth more than the grain itself.

Within the barn's shadows, Aoric listened to witnesses, Fritigern the Balth and the conservator's wife. Why they were together at the horse barns was immaterial. This was not a moral judgment. Yet Aoric noticed the conservator sulking in the rear, glaring at his spouse, with Fritigern standing well from them.

He shook his head, his countenance serious, "Fritigern, son of Thiudebalth, killed one of the thieves with a contus. And two other miscreants were slain by a woman, one of them beaten to death with a stick. Do my ears hear correctly—a stick?"

"Actually, it was a broken pitch-fork," explained Thulia.

"Well, that's still a stick," Aoric insisted, "And when the Quadi hear of this—a woman from the Tyrfingi kunja killing two of their warriors… with a stick… well, it can only bode well for our side. A good advantage. And I suppose a commendation is in order, even though I don't approve of women using weapons. No good shall ever come of it. Mark my word. They have a fine place in the home next to the hearth, cooking or spinning wool, but it seems you wish to revert to old tribal ways. I shan't condemn or condone it. As a Taifala springing from Alani, your steppe tradition sways above all, an Amazon's prerogative. In saying that, I acknowledge your lineage, your determination, and your valor and strength," shaking his head again and mumbling, "With a stick."

The subject then turned to a retaliatory raid, hopefully to get the grain back. Aoric disliked this type of assignment. It forced him to draft warriors. The best he hoped for was an all-Alanic contingent; and with some tact he tried to absolve the other two tribes of responsibility, "Seven generations ago, we Tyrfingi and the Taifali entered into a foedus. Then it was modified in this generation when you Alans arrived from east of Greutungia. You are the minority tribe yet you receive equal protection under the treaty. Nonetheless, the treaty states that all three tribes can only retaliate against a common foe, not against an isolated raid like the Quadi's."

From his corner, Frit held seeds in a hand, pushing them with a finger, "I'd rather not argue but that's poor rhetoric. The Quadi are an enemy by the corn's origin. They stole common seeds, grown by all of us. When the grain was in the chaff, who owned it?"

"Well, it was all of ours," huffed Aoric, "And I don't need an upstart like you to remind me. I came here knowing we have no time for tribal councils to chew the fat. It matters not whose grain it was; and a raiding party led jointly by my son and Rustan's son-in-law—Athanaric and Selenas—can certainly get volunteers without resorting to conscriptions." And then he added, "But Thulia stays here, if for no other reason than to guard the herds with her deadly stick."

* * *

That night, Thulia sniffed her soup at the hearth. The rankness of sheep hocks pinched her nostrils as it permeated the deepest corners of the conservator's cabin. *What can I do? This sheep died too long ago.* If she had some pepper, the strength of its bite would cut the foulness, but only rich nobles could afford it. Pepper and silk, the fragrance of amber and frankincense, were not in her world. She stood from the hearth to find Sesca grimacing; and with a fake smile, Thulia resigned, "I have made tastier bean and lentil soups, but this will do. It's filling." Patting Sesca on the head, she went to the oaken cupboard and grabbed the lard crock, spooning out a wad of it. Returning to the hearth she stirred the lard into the soup pot, watching liquid globules float to the boiling surface. *There! That shall disguise the odor.*

Unfortunately, the conservator entered the house a little too soon, wrinkling his nose to leave the door open, "This place needs fresh air. It stinks in here."

No worse than you do, Pigfoot. "When the beans soften, they will release a pleasanter smell. The soup will be ready before sunset," then she added, "I was thinking that perhaps after dinner we could go to the east hill and watch the ceremony, the Sword in the Stones. The Shaman will be there, for he is well again."

"That old fart?" the conservator snarled, "He's a hundred years old if a day. The man speaks gibberish. Who can understand him?"

"Merjands the Proclaimer can," she asserted, "The Shaman is wise, even in old age. He once said that someday I would wield a sword."

The conservator's jaw tightened as lines around his eyes furrowed deeper, "Do not speak of it! I'll hear none of that Amazon shit. And never touch my family sword again. It stays in the arka where it belongs."

Thulia jammed the spoon hard to the soup, swung around and took a stride to him, her face close to his as she looked down to his eyes, "What if I do? What might you accomplish to hurt me? Call me names, more names? Slut? Whore?" Her eyes flared hotter than flames, "Find something original." She caught Sesca's movement in the corner of an eye, the girl retreating from them, her feet scuffing rearward as she slid behind the open door.

Suddenly, a man's voice came from outside, pleasant and lively, "Hailog, I say! Anyone home?"

Heldrid's words. Thulia brushed past the conservator, lifting Sesca to her, "I'm sorry, my sweet, for raising my voice. We have a visitor." She entered late afternoon sunlight to find the aged trader slipping from his light wagon to plant feet carefully to earth.

He paced to the wagon bed, all smiles while lifting a weighty bucket, swinging it to the ground as water sloshed upon buckled shoes, "Ah, Thulia, where is the conservator? I have extra fish."

Pigfoot rushed from behind her and scowled, "Extra fish? How did you come by them?"

"Rustan and Selenas caught too many for his live-tub. He gave me a half dozen; but you know I eat alone, sometimes with Maura my cook for a little company, but how many can we eat?" He waved a hand to the bucket, "Here are three extras. Oh, they are fat tench, over a pound each." He turned quickly, as if to retreat, pulling himself up to the wagon seat and grabbing the reins, "Broil them tonight. I'll stop for the bucket in a few days." And then he was off down the trade road, slapping reins as an inhaled "ghic, ghic, ghic" commanded his long-legged mare.

*   *   *

The east hill's crest appeared as a field of stumps, old and rotting, seemingly unidentifiable, yet he—Ufar Gudja—knew they were birch, as did anyone with faithful memory. Although Chief Priest, he felt nettled to the bone, having neither the Proclaimer's wisdom nor intellect; but Merjands had disappeared as he often did. *Poof!—gone to who knows where.* There seemed little sense in scouring him out, for the man held lairs in secret places. And so this ceremony fell to him, not really an intellectual, and neither young nor old in androgyny.

Squatting low, Ufar finished the circle of stones, each the size of a human heart and placed to fill the circle's volume. The last circle had been formed awhile ago, back when the Tyrfingi and Taifali warred upon Vandals, the battle that took the king's life.

Ah yes, Thiudebalth the Good. In the old days, the king humored Ufar's eccentricities, giving him an earring that *"once belonged to the Great Alexander,"* a claim in jest. The priest stood erect, fingering his prized earring, hoping he could remember the ceremony. He glanced down to notice a rock out of place. *Well, we cannot have a concentric circle!—gods forbid.* And so he dropped to a knee, realigning the stone to make the circle perfect.

Regaining his feet, Ufar studied four assistant priests hovering together. They stood in their own circle, the two youngest quite attractive, one of them arching a thumb toward the Shaman's felt tent, a small structure twenty paces away and only three feet tall. They were probably discussing shamanism, almost a lost art. The Gothic shaman died centuries ago, and the little tent held the last holy man of the

Alans (not counting Merjands who was more like a philosopher-medicus). Rumors claimed Huns still had knowledgeable shamans, but they were foreigners, the "others." *And not particularly handsome, either.*

Catching an assistant's eye, Ufar motioned to the tent, and swept his gaze to the fifty warriors. They stood about the crest, two here and two there, most with a foot upon a stump, each posed to look rather manly. He turned his head, pretending to cough while chuckling uncontrollably. *Warriors! Each with a prick bigger than his brain, and a good thing I guess.* Spinning around, he almost bumped into the sword-bearer. The young man was stunning—*a beautiful nose*—almost a priest, another year to go, and he held the sword outstretched.

Ufar unwrapped the material while quizzing, "Why do we store *Tyrfing* in woolen cloth?"

"Because wool contains oils, keeping the sword from rusting," claimed the assistant.

"Ah, very good. Oils are *Tyrfing's* unguents. They make him happy. He is shorter than the old one, yet impressive when planted as the incarnation of Tyr. Most important, he is the axis mundi, the link between heaven and earth, between us—all these not-quite-perfect stones—and the gods. Understand?"

The assistant nodded as Ufar pulled the weapon from the wool, and he asked, "Why do we not use the older sword, the one Merjands likes?"

"Merjands hides it," claimed Ufar, "And he is off someplace."

"Is it his?" wondered the assistant.

"It belonged to the Last Warrior Priestess of the Alani. She lived long ago because the sword is very old. Merjands is its keeper. When he returns you can ask him more about it."

And he better come back because I hate singular responsibility. Returning to the circle, he pushed *Tyrfing* into the center, then stacking a few stones upward and along the blade, "He must be just right, not leaning to one side or the other and directly in the middle. Tell me, what do the *others* call him?"

The novice hesitated and murmured as if speaking blasphemy, "The Romans call him the Sword of Mars... Ares by the Greeks."

"Very good, my boy," purred Ufar, "But we are Tyrfingi—People of the Sword of Tyr. Foreign gods live somewhere else. Now run along and fetch the bowl of goat blood. I'll get the ceremony started." The novice scampered off and Ufar clapped hands, "Come now. All horsemen gather around. Attention horsemen! Let us begin," clap, clap, clap. The warriors sauntered in from the stumps and formed a large circle, each man equidistant from *Tyrfing* as all eyes looked across the hill to study the shaman's tent. Three assistants leaned in unison to grab the bottom seam, pulling the tent straight up to expose the shaman as a cloud of rank smoke billowed high to approaching dusk.

The holy man remained crouched with legs crossed, sitting before dying coals of cannabis buds. Stalks and leaves held no potency yet the buds had great power as the cannabis raised the shaman to a plane of wondrous wisdom. Carefully, the assistants lifted him from where he sat, clutching his arms to guide him to the horsemen. The formation opened, allowing the shaman into the circle as the guides released his arms.

The old man fell!—flopping around like a wounded seamew. And the guides ran to him, returning him to a standing position. He tottered this way and that, his steps uncontrolled. His eyes focused on nothing in particular as spittle ran from a corner of his mouth. He fell again!—but the guides pulled him upright as he mumbled, "Ah, yah... eh, die Gudas... nay a slahan, qeh... qeh," and he rambled on, stumbling toward Athanaric while saying, "Qeh... ein dwafs en fielden... una stelen... Bladen!... die flayen... susta Artur en dwafs gifja doofs!"

Athanaric stood immobile, not sure what to do, and Ufar enunciated slowly, "He says, *a Mouse hides in tall grass to steal the Bear's food. Then the Mouse gifts to the Dove.*"

Again the holy man tottered about, flopping here and there, aided to his feet until facing Selenas to make another utterance, translated as, "*The Owl strikes in forests dark, the Eagle in sunlight. Beware of the Mouse but welcome the Dove.*" Ufar's heart thumped atwitter, for he was not sure his interpretation was entirely correct. *I'm an artist, not the Proclaimer.*

The shaman staggered back to the Sword in the Stones. He looked skyward, waving hands with fingers wide, "Qeh! Qeh! Ah na Quadis. Qeh! Qeh! Ah na roves, najif da jaben da Monta—da Monta Gepeh!"

Then he crumpled, twitching before them. The guides rushed to him, cradling him gently in their arms; and the circle opened, the old shaman placed to the ground amid stumps far younger than he was. "*Beware!*" warned Ufar, "*Beware of Four-legged Ones. Stay clear of the Bairg of Dark Thoughts.*"

The shaman had warned them all to be careful of the Quadi and avoid the dark mount of the Gepids. *Positively chilling*, as Ufar tried to lighten the tone, clapping hands thrice, "All right now, horsemen. Horsemen! It's almost fun time. I want you virile riders to line up. That's it! Single file and no talking. Now—one at a time—kneel to *Tyrfing*, dip your thumb in the blood and draw a line across your forehead. That's it. Wait a moment! None of that! You, there, in the green tunic. Go back to the end of the line. I know everyone's in a hurry to get drunk and hump your wives, but kneel correctly, honor *Tyrfing* but—for Gods' sake!—touch him not. Only the Chosen touch his divinity. That's it. Now run along and release whatever you deem important upon this eve before leaving for the Bairgs-ahei."

The riders dispersed, each brimming with resolve to regain the grain. Ufar watched them stride downhill, waiting until they were beyond ear-shot to turn back to his assistants, all hovering around the stricken. "That dear shaman. Took a load of cannabis for a man his age, but I think he'll make it." And then he closed eyes. *I hope our warriors fare as well... but I have my doubts. Not a soul, not one, ever fared well in Transylvania.*

Chapter 4: Like a Snake in Agony

Above the Alan village a small flodus was known as "the stream" and nothing more, its winding course entering the Prahova from the east bank. A clear pool lay near its origin, remote and catching the tumble of a diminutive waterfall, a place where people could meet beyond respective tribes. Water swirled to a slow depth of three feet, just enough to bathe in. The sun reached the south bank, the north shaded, and soft green were the rocks about it. The thickness of moss, a certain rock's smoothness, made a bed of sweetness where two lovers might kiss or even more. Lilia sat upon the rock, feeling even bigger with child, the very rock where the child was conceived.

She hoped her husband was unhurt and safe, now a week after the raid. Selenas and Athanaric were up in Transylvania with fifty horsemen including young Frit. *Perhaps they have already fought the Quadi and are returning with our tribe's grain.* She watched eddies swirl, clear bubbles floating above tannic brown, and she mused upon past innocence... *at this very place.*

"My name is Lilia," she proclaimed, *her eyes raised to his.*

"I know," he returned as he stood from the rock, his own eyes smiling, *"Your father and mine became friends when you were a child."*

"I have grown, have I not?" she returned proudly. For certain she had.

They stood close yet apart, and he waxed phrases men used in either lust or truth. "Your eyes have depth in their darkness, like that of an endless night, the hint of love upon your lips. What then, if I should steal a kiss?"

Her face flushed red! Wearing a kaftan of Sogdian make, white and clean as if for a special occasion, she had trouble breathing. Yet she had courage and warmth, tilting her head up to his to close her eyes and whisper, "Only one."

Lilia snapped back to the present and her worries about Selenas and the grain. If he could not retrieve it, the Alans would eat mostly meat until harvest. Her father might have to ask the Taifali and Tyrfingi for corn. *Selenas will get it back and show the Quadi how a Goth fights.* She pictured him tall in the saddle as he led horsemen north, a long-sword belted to his waist. In bearing and stature Selenas rode as her hero— the avenger who would make things right. *He will be a king someday, and all the Tyrfingi and Alans will look up to him.*

*   *   *

In high Transylvania the road writhed its slow descent like a snake in agony. Trees waved a mirage of false movement, rippling in the midday heat. What was real or not in this land of hot-sharp iron? The old ones always said, *"No more than death in the dark mounts."* They were right. Upon a tired horse, Selenas followed dust of those ahead, only to fall back further, alone to review a short life.

Darker than her hair, her eyes looked up to his, marvelous lips in a purr, "Soon we shall have a child." Her voice wisped beyond a distant hill, or was it a mountain? Her fingers tickled his cheek. And as he looked at Lilia she seemed blurred, her features beyond cohesion.

Suddenly he entered the earth-world, road dust caking nostrils and corners of his mouth. Under his nose, the gelding's mane swept his focus, not the caress of Lilia but the hair of a horse. The wound was huge, the spear entering below ribs and exiting his back. No longer feeling pain, he existed in ethereal lightness. Selenas removed his left hand from the lesion, fingers dried brown, yet his palm remained red wet. Was Hector's end or that of Achilles any worse?—a dark crimson spilling life behind him, down his leg, along the road taken, going back to the moment he felt the Quadi spear.

He no longer viewed his brother's horse or the rest. *Too far ahead. I shall meet the earth far from the woman I love. What a place to die!—here in the land of four-legged ones.* Slumping to the horse's neck, digging heels to ribs, he urged his mount ahead, yet after a quarter mile his gelding slowed to a trot. Someone was coming back, hoof-beats approaching as men and mounts blurred together.

His horse stopped. Selenas pitched forward, leaving a stain along the mount's withers as he toppled to the ground. Upon his back, he viewed the sun red through closed eyelids, then a shadow cooling it gray. He whispered, "Lilia came to me, but I'll not see my child."

Kneeling to him, Frit answered, "I never should've pulled the spearhead. It bleeds much worse."

Fading to the other realm he opened lids to find iron gray eyes, the blonde hair that marked his father, "You will be the last son of Thiudebalth, little brother. Take care of Lilia."

"You must keep riding," gritted Frit, trying to pull Selenas to a sitting position, "Athanaric and I will reseat you in the saddle. You will live! The Quadi are far behind and I think they no longer follow. Another ten miles and we'll leave Transylvania."

"Let me rest and save yourselves," murmured Selenas, then addressing the horseman behind Frit, "Is that you, Athanaric?"

"Aye, but we have no time," urged the Squinter, "You must remount. Tonight will find the moon bright, and the Quadi will change into wolves! They turn at full moon and then become men again. You have heard what elders say!" the recounting making beady eyes wide.

Selenas knew he would soon be under the earth, a soldier to the Sword of Mars. Tales of old wives meant nothing—change into wolves? He would not view the moon's rise.

Down the narrow road, trees crowded strange forms approaching, perhaps men or now creatures on the trail of fresh blood. At the sight of it, Frit's eyes feared, "They are coming, for dust rises from many hooves."

"Leave me be," gasped Selenas, a last order on an ill-fated mission.

Turning to the Squinter, the youngest son of Thiudebalth vowed, "I will stay with him, but you must lead the rest back to Threisbaurg."

Athanaric looked down to Selenas, then to Frit, "They will kill you both."

"Better to die in honor than the shame of an old man's bed." *That's what Old Hempstalk would say if he were here.*

Eight months into his sixteenth year, this was Frit's initial ride to foreign soil, his introduction to the Realm of Death. He excelled at hunting roebuck, but this was a darker kind of blood—soberingly human. He would always remember this day, carry it with him, never to forget the smell of it, a dying man's essence on the palm of his hand.

Twice he pushed Selenas back to the saddle, relieving his brother's thirst and his own. The taste of spring water couldn't drown the scent, for it permeated his nostrils, an alchemy of iron and flesh. It would not wash away; and the fear that arose within? The bravest hero could not dismiss it.

In every man, young or old, there must be this drive to survive. I want to live a longer life, to hunt and fish, maybe find a woman like Thulia... have sons, carry on the bloodline. Yet I must stand with him. He had no choice, simple as that. Frit glanced up the road to a short future, dropping his gaze to study his brother.

Lying in Frit's shadow, Selenas' eyes again met his, "Go with them."

"No!"

With Fritigern's statement, Athanaric paced to his horse. Spinning around, he warned, "You're a fool to stay here."

The youth stood tall, stanced firm to the road, "He is my blood. Would you do any less?"

Yes I would. This is your first raid, son of Thiudebalth. Standing at his gelding's side, Athanaric shook his head. *You punched holes in a straw-man. This is not practice. It's the real world. I have myself and thirty men to lead back to safety.* He peered back to Frit, the sun too bright, "One man against many makes a poor battle." He had quoted his father, a sensible man, and his gaze met the curve of his saddle's crown, not wood but bronze polished to a sheen giving the appearance of gold. Someday his crown would be the real thing and all that came with it.

Athanaric mounted his horse. Taking his reins, he turned from the brothers and rode for the lowlands. As the magistrate's only son he could never understand them, not even back in childhood. *Let them die in Transylvania if they wish.* One man's death could be another's gain, especially with the two brothers gone. Selenas would leave a widow, the woman he desired. They were sons of a deceased reiks; and upon their deaths and that of his father, the tribal primacy would pass to him, Athanaric the Squinter. He was a Balth, the same high blood flowing through his veins, and someday he would be magistrate, possibly the reiks, and perhaps he would even have Lilia. Oh yes. The right death was very good.

* * *

The cloud of dust approached ever slowly. With it came an incredible noise, the rumbling of thunder! Frit stood by his stricken brother fingering his sword, shifting it to the left hand, wiping his right along his trousers. Removing excess sweat, he wanted the best grip possible. He would fight to the end when attacked.

The huge amount of dust rolled toward him, perspiration salting his eyes as he tried to discern the foe. He had never heard such a ruckus. Then came relief!—for the end of his world could wait. He breathed steadier as cramped fingers relaxed upon his sword-hilt. The Quadi horde materialized as a giant magnum drawn by four brown bullocks, its thick wheels built solid. The huge Sarmatian wagon rumbled to a stop, the man in charge jumping to the ground.

In his mid thirties, the stranger carried a beard above long features, even his nose at some length. His tunic and trousers were plain yet clean, like those of a husbandman. The dust still rose from the road as two more men landed at his heels, each wearing summer white. Not one carried a weapon, and the wagon seemed loaded with Tyrfingi and Alans who fell in the fray, all packed between hempen sacks of grain, one bandaged and still alive, others a dead gray. The strange men gave Frit no heed, although his sword remained in hand, pushing beyond him to reach Selenas.

"Lord in Heaven! Is he dead?" the leader asked in East Gothic, the accent of the Greutungi.

"Near death enough," snapped Frit stepping back, recognizing oddness in the man's expression, "Please help my brother. You are a Christian, from your speech?"

54

"He is our brother, too. We must act quickly," claimed their leader as the two men helped lift Selenas to the vehicle.

Frit resented the statement. They didn't know Selenas or what blood he came from… certainly not his name! He was no relation of theirs, for they were gasts—the Others!—and Christians to boot. An odd sect, foolish in postulations; and they could never be Selenas' brothers by any stretch of imagination.

"Hurry! Not a moment to lose," commanded the long-faced leader. With Selenas crushed between warriors, the stranger took the reins and brought the magnum up to speed as the bullocks plodded through unseasonable heat. "The hottest spring I can remember," claimed the leader.

Wagon sides rattled, as massive wheels crushed pebbles to dust, and the conveyance seemed ready to explode as the team pulled with all its might. Frit guided his horse close-by as they slammed down the road, "Where are you taking him? To a medicus?"

"To the upper house, if he lives to reach the ford in the stream."

Soon enough they stopped where a brook cut the road, the leader jumping to water licking knees, again issuing instructions, "We'll take him first." They slid the young Balth from the wagon, two men at his shoulders, the leader grabbing Selenas' legs. Then, to Frit's surprise, they pushed his brother completely underwater, raising him quickly. Even Selenas' eyes were open! Studying Frit upon his horse, the leader asked, "His nomen?"

"Selenas, son of Thiudebalth."

"Good. I will introduce him to the Son of God." Looking down, the strange man quizzed, "Do you want to live again?"

Rightfully knowing his end, Selenas whispered, "Yes. I have a wife big with child."

They raised him back to the wagon bed, and the leader gazed straight to his eyes, "Then forsake the Sword of Mars and accept the true God and his son Xristos."

"If I do," Selenas mumbled, "will I live?"

"You must believe in here with all your heart," the man claimed as he tapped a hand to chest.

"Then I accept your single God."

"Good," the stranger replied; and placing a wet hand upon the Balth's head, he pronounced, "I baptize thee, Selenas, in the name of the Father, the Son, and the Holy Ghost. Welcome to the Gothic Church." Turning to his aides, the leader quipped, "So much for him. Grab the second before he expires. I'll not have the whole damned lot go to Hell."

The same procedure began for an Alan from Lilia's village. An odd process. Dunking wounded men held no curative powers. Usually they were washed with urine, then sewn with an iron needle and boiled horse hair. Rituals concluded, the giant wagon continued rumbling down the road, turning south to a wider via. As Frit matched pace, the leader kept turning to him, yelling words over the wagon's noise, "You are all Tyrfingi, am I correct?"

"Mostly. A few Taifali and Alans."

"He lived by it and shall die by it," the bearded one shouted over to him.

"Lived by what?"

"The sword!"

Frit made no answer, for the hero wields a sword.

Hearing no response, the leader claimed, "Worry not. He'll be buried in a Christian grave."

Frit was appalled! They tricked Selenas, to die in disgrace—not as a good pagan. Riding in his first year of manhood, Fritigern had few worldly experiences to judge people by, especially Christians, and he tried to fathom their intentions. Were they trying to help his brother, or was Selenas a victim of their strange rites? Again he said nothing in return.

The long-faced man continued, "I followed the blood. Twenty miles worth. The other one may live, but your brother has lost a barrel-full, maybe an entire cistern's worth."

Hearing what could only be jocularism, Frit moved his mount closer to the wagon, "You make fun of a dying man? Who are you?—to be so callous about death." His voice quavered and he was close to tears, but he could not accept the unwanted, unmanly... not even upon this, the worst day of his life. With his brother's impending death, who would he have? Not even Thulia. She was lost to Pigfoot!

"I'm stating fact in the lightest way I know," the leader claimed, "I would like to stop and sew him up, but I'm dirty, he's dirty, and I have not the materials or circumstance."

"He is going to die!" yelled Frit as he began to weep, "Don't you understand? Death is the end. The end!"

The man looked to Frit, eyes intense, "You have it wrong. Death is the beginning." He ceased speaking as the magnum slammed hard, the wounded and sacks bouncing while those in the rear tried to comfort the dying. Then he added, "I'm Wulfilas, Bishop of Gothia. I'd like to save every man I meet, body and soul. That's my great prayer. If I can save one in six, it's a start, is it not? All my life, I've been out here in the Barbaricon, watching them kill one another. For what? Glory? Greed? Revenge?—or any of the other seven sins?" Wulfilas turned to the wagon bed, studying the dying young. He shook his head, looked straight ahead, speaking so low Frit could hardly hear his words, "We must accept facts. He has stopped bleeding, my young friend, because he has no blood left. So he will die before I get him to Hospice."

Chapter 5: Tines Like a Lance

Travel was slow with a number of wounded. Five days after the road companions left Transylvania they crossed the Prahova on the ferrymon's barge, entering Threisbaurg just before sunset. Most horsemen jumped to good earth while their surviving leader remained saddled. Among relatives or the curious, Lilia arrived at the village square searching for her husband. Athanaric rode through the crowd, his mouth tight with news he wished not to utter. He was not much for rhetoric, proudly illiterate, Gothic law committed to memory from the word, not from books. Reining the mount before his tribesman's wife, he blurted, "Selenas is dead. He died upon the road, wounded by the Quadi... and Fritigern is probably dead as well. I'm sorry, especially with you heavy with child."

He had no other way of saying it. Although wanting to console her, the correct verbiage escaped him; and being ill at ease he turned his horse before Lilia grasped the words. Athanaric avoided the sight of weeping, hating the notion of it, not at ease with women. Even with a slew of sisters, he stood uncomfortable in their gaze. From their peering at him in that distinct way, he felt self-conscious long after puberty, perhaps due to unpleasant features—his lips too thin, eyes spaced close together, giving his face an overly broad appearance. Sunlight watered his eyes, and he was only comfortable in shade and known as the Squinter from boyhood. He became used to it. Averting his gaze from the woman before him, he departed for his father's house in a timely manner.

*   *   *

Thulia strode quick, her long legs carrying her before him, her weight halting the Squinter's horse as she grabbed his reins with one hand. She did not ask but declared, "Of all those who could die, they were the brothers. Is that it?"

He was unnerved by her tone, the way she pulled him to a stop. She could read it in his face as he answered, "They were not alone. Sixteen men perished. We were overwhelmed, lost a third of our men in less than an hour. Now stand aside."

Thulia released his reins, "Yet *you* lived. It must have been *fauratani*—white magic saved you. Is that it? A man blessed by the gods, to become ranking commander of the kunja. Fortuna cannot smile any broader."

"Yes," he returned, not catching her implication, "I am fortunate to be alive." Backing a step, she let him go. Athanaric could never figure her out because he was slower than she was. *Close to an idiot in backward thinking. Again he rides for home to drop reins to a freeman and enter Papa's nest to hide.* Thulia stood tall for a time, watching his horse push through relatives of lost men, not hearing comments upon the abortive raid but lost in thought. *Gods make poor choices in who they abandon.* Anger seethed between contempt and sorrow, and her eyes calmed to a sting yet she would drop no tears, for she was the Amazon.

Mounting her own horse, Thulia rode from them all, heading north for the largest horse barn. The day became all the warmer, stifling, for she could not remember her breath arriving with more labor. Reaching the barn, she slipped from the saddle with the swing of a leg. Again she stood motionless, eying the hay, thinking of its softness, moments of pleasure forever gone. Finally she left the horse behind her. Heat hovered under the low pitched roof and clumps of fallen straw lay strewn upon the floor, not tossed back upon the piles when freemen fed the prized geldings. *The shiftless drones.*

Searching the stack of pitchforks, she chose one with sharp tines. Already she was beginning to perspire.

She walked to low hay piles, the aroma sweet; and stabbing the fork to dead grass, she removed her tunic as if it were her real burden, tossing it over the saddle log. Naked to the waist, she began pitching fork-load after fork-load atop the pile. *The way it should be.* And she stabbed hard, her thrusts quick, using tines like a lance—her contus of grief. One stab was a Quadi and the next Athanaric, until sweat flowed from her neck, running down her torso, soaking trousers below.

Her jaw ached as she clenched teeth, yet arm muscles tired not. Selenas never fathomed her needs and pushed her below his dignity, yet she had memories of a better man, even as a boy.

With eyes blurred, she could view Frit before her. Other than little Sesca and aged Othar, he was all she had! *No one else understood me enough to reach my well-spring.* He created something deep within her yet unaware of what he wrought, a rapture beyond anything felt before. If love existed, he was its essence. After all her trials—the selfish users, a foul-mouthed husband, a silent daughter, and poverty lower than the unfree—Frit would not be there for the ending. The girl's dream, never quite dying and growing to a woman's, had vanished.

Damn those who destroy! The good were gone, leaving all the fat-lickers and flesh mongers behind, a world full of greedy and oafish men. The heat in the horse barn increased and every inch of her body—even her soul!— seemed flooded by the boiling of an unknown and foreign liquid. Her face ran flush, muscles quivering, and Thulia could no longer see what she was doing, blinded by liquid. *It's sweat! Just sweat and nothing else. Certainly not tears.* And she stopped pitching hay to run a forearm over closed eyes, the sting of it burning forever deep. *Not tears!*

*   *   *

The crowd hushed to silence after Athanaric's announcement, some families guiding a widow home. Others looked toward Lilia then departed, having many things to do. Cauldrons required scrubbing, and seedlings needed planting. And all these terribly important chores needed doing immediately, as villagers left the Balth's widow deserted to herself. The Gothic clearing became lifeless, void of all humanness; and for the first time, Lilia understood. She befriended not a single Tyrfingi woman, pushing them lower than they already were. She had been too aloof, too proud of her station within the tribes. They were not jealous. They simply didn't like her... or worse.

She was alone. Only then did Athanaric's words fully reach her. *Selenas is dead*, a singular blot in an otherwise perfect life. Not a woman consoled her as she stood in the shadows of a day, a life, and a husband gone. And not just alone, but alone with child and a widow at the age of fifteen. At first she made no sound, her lips quivering, tears rolling. Her hands shook like those of an old woman and all strength failed her; and she fell to knees, staring at hoof-prints of those who abandoned her husband's body.

Yet in guilt, they were not alone. She herself, more than anyone else, was responsible for the rude end of her own happiness; for without Selenas each day would pass without a hint of joy. He died the death of a brave commander, exactly what she wished him to be. With girlish indiscretion she encouraged it, glorifying deeds of great leaders, wanting him to be such a man, urging him to fight back against the Quadi, her words no more than a fortnight old—*"Your rightful legacy is a vanquished foe."* She had spoken like a child. That's what

61

she still was, only visualizing a hero's sword, difficult to think like a woman at her age, now far too late to recall words. She had mimicked the elders, her own father, all the men who praised death upon the field of glory, a convention to braveness. His true legacy was to raise a son or daughter and grow old in her arms.

At day's end, the sun rolled behind trees, to die in approaching darkness. And kneeling in the dust, she finally became a woman, for Lilia earned the right to wail. She had seen it as a young girl; and now her own hands clawed dirt to spread upon her clothes and hair. She knew the filthy truth, the secret of the universal widow. *You weep more for yourself than you do for him.* And in the end?—her tears shrank barren, used-up, as was the light in her soul.

Chapter 6: A Few Warm Afternoons

Day twenty three of the fifth month

Thulia paced resolute up the hill. She alone dug Othar's grave and gently laid him in it, a peaceful spot at the oak grove not far from his moss-chinked shack. At his side, she placed bread and cup of goat's milk. That would sustain him until he reached himina-gards, yet she knew not how a blind man could walk to the stars, especially one that old. The journey seemed impossible.

A rider came down toward her from the horse barns and she stopped pace, dropping shovel from shoulder. *The white-spotted gelding.* She swung the spade up again and continued walking, looking beyond the rider, for she had nothing to say.

Old Hempstalk reined to a halt, extending palms up, "I'm sorry. Othar was a good man. I never thought of him enough; should have bid farewell."

She looked to the white-spotted gelding, "Tell your owner he's too damned late," striding past them and pacing uphill for the barns.

"I'm sorry. I truly am. I woke up too late," explained the voice behind her.

Thulia wouldn't lower herself, break a vow. Never would she address the man again, her legs taking longer strides, putting him further behind her. Why should she speak to him after all this time? For saying, *I'm sorry?* Not much chance of it. Sorry for what? Being a selfish bastard? *Let him go to the lower house and burn.*

Stopping her stride, she inhaled deep, not a bold breath but slow and quavering. With palms soiled, Thulia wiped cheeks with the back of a hand. Not tears, just excess moisture. *He has to go to the upper house. Where else could a good man go?* In less than a fortnight her loved ones were gone, Frit first and then Othar. She reserved a special place for Selenas, not quite loved and hard to hate, just difficult to forgive. Thulia knew Othar was dying months ago, believing she prepared for his death. Perhaps she had. Anger overwhelmed grief, and she walked in churning sarcasm.

Again Thulia started toward the horse barns, shifting the spade to her other shoulder. She made no offerings, gave no sacrifice for the old man's soul. *As if I could afford one*, she snarled. The wealthier a noble was, the more offerings given. That's what priests called them—offerings—but she knew the truth. Offerings were bribes. The gods were so vain, so frigging dishonest, they had to be bribed like a Roman tax collector. She never offered a bribe; and the gods could not have done a better job, wrapping love up neatly, tossing it to the dung heap. It seemed best to acknowledge their support, to find something appropriate for all they had done. She stopped her pace, wadding spittle in the hollow of her tongue. With a turn of her head, she spat a fat lunger. *Thank you gods. I'll give a bigger offering the next time I squat.*

*   *   *

At mid day, the magistrate and son stepped outside the house to speak beyond women's ears. The sun bathed the structure in light intense, reflecting from circular walls, wattled clear to a thatched roof. Aoric viewed harsh light wrecking havoc upon his son's eyes, for Athanaric's squinting increased with each new season. *He suffers from it, suffers deeply, and he might have been blessed with better intellect. My father had no such maladies, so they must come from Brida's side. What a woman brings to marriage you never know, like too many near-sighted daughters.*

"The clients are sinking the Circle of Posts tonight and the priests will plant *Tyrfing*. We will pay homage to those lost against the four-legged ones," claimed the Squinter.

"An old and correct observance," the magistrate sighed, "Around the Sword of Mars, we can honor the memory of a fallen leader. Selenas was brave, was he not?"

"Aye, but he tried to save too many lives when we were ambushed. Got himself killed for it."

The magistrate hobbled further from the house, distancing himself from thin walls and his wife and daughters, each spinning wool and gabbing. Distaffs moved slower than their lips, for they lived for rumor and juicy news. *One cannot be too careful. A man's conversation is certainly not for women to hear.* Soon enough they were under the oak, a big tree and old, planted by the giants in a time long gone. Aoric curled a lip, "Ah, you are judicious and wary. Fine attributes for a future judge," then postulating, "Mistakes lead to death. They say his widow came from her house yesterday. With the brothers dead, she carries the last blood of Thiudebalth. I'm sure an intelligent man, a compassionate man, will take her to wife. Yet it seems unfair to have the grandchild of a reiks live in the house of a lesser noble."

Aoric limped to a bald spot, burned white by horse manure yet surrounded by fresh grass. *Tall and ready for the scythe, an early season.* With practiced fingers he reached for a stem, sliding the green top from it, bringing the tender shoot to his mouth. In so doing he let his son grasp his words. He would not order Athanaric to do anything, yet he knew his son was a creature of ambition.

The widow Lilia? Athanaric mulled his father's words, formulating options. He would proceed carefully, picturing several variations of fate. She could drop a daughter, a child of little consequence. But if a male, he would be grandson of a reiks, perhaps the future king himself. *A good stepfather would have comprehensive power, at least until the child reaches majority. Such a prudent man would hold sway over the entire kunja for many years...* and he would have Lilia. Pacing from shade to where his father stood, the Squinter opined, "She could die in childbed or bear a daughter, both a shame to posterity. We shall see, but I think it wise for me to step forward at the widow's lottery."

*   *   *

Beyond pity's stare and her father's sighs, Lilia took the lover's path. The forest remained green year around. Trees were mostly firs and spruce, a sequestered place, the only sounds arriving from birds or the quick tailing of a surprised trout. There were no whispers, no benign statements falling from the concerned.

With her birthing time near, Lilia walked slowly to the stream where she and Selenas met so often. Along the way, the day's heat recalled hours of love. Yet upon reaching tall firs, their shade cooled memories seeming far in the past.

She sat upon the same rock that once spawned love, running fingers over its carpet of moss. Droplets rolled down cheeks, her stomach huge, the baby overdue. In her young life she had seen tribal widows rock back and forth, watched them beat their chests with clenched fists, and now she wept her own lament, never to see him again or feel his loving touch. Once in a reflective mood, she wondered what Selenas would look like as an elder man. He had fine hair, the color of sand and thinning, perhaps balding in old age. His eyes knew some great secret of inner joy, but how could he discern such things at nineteen years?—yet she knew those eyes would have made him a wonderful father.

Thoughts of him would not diminish. She wept all the harder, sobs coming from deep within, the pain of his death transposed from heart to eyes. At the same time she realized that part of this great pain was the result of contractions. They had come before, not so pronounced, the time between them now much shorter. Besieged by fear, she was far from the village, a half mile in the woods! What would she do? This was her first child, not the second or third. Rolling to her side, she gained her feet, yet standing upright was impossible. She could not even walk!

She could only crouch! And she knew the baby was coming, to be born without the presence of a midwife. Agony increased, each contraction stronger as she sat back upon the rock. In her girlhood she had seen birthing, clearly remembering the delivery of her brother Safrax when she was eight. Yet she was alone in the woods; and leaning back upon her elbows, she pushed and pushed. Even under the shade of the firs she was hot!—perspiration following a trail of tears to soak her peplos. Time dragged its heavy burden, and she could only push all the more, no longer able to weep, her arms beginning to knot as muscles reached exhaustion.

Incredibly frightened, Lilia pictured her own death added to that of Selenas, the fate of the child inside, unable to reach air of life. Push… push!... push! And with each push, she screamed at all the weak gods who had forsaken her. She cursed them!—each and every god who allowed a good man to perish, who punished her unto death for the harpy she was.

Then the baby was out and yelling with her!—a small wrinkled child sliding down the rock, and it was alive. Moving upon her side, she reached for her newborn, the umbilical cord keeping it from rolling to the water below. And she could not believe the small amount of blood flowing down the rock to stain the pool a pale pink. The stream bubbled below the falls, and its color seemed like a rainbow.

Yes, a rainbow child. A boy in throws of madness!— crying to the leaves and trees. She pictured birds in hurried flight, winging their way from the terrible sound of him, the deer racing to quieter glades. And for the first time since his father's death she smiled. She—Lilia the Alana, widow of a Goth—would live, and so would her son. She wept and laughed all at once, knowing this child, this boy, would become a good man... for he was the son of Selenas. Lilia held him to her, and he screamed like a warrior, mad and loud!

*   *   *

The eve remained too warm for the end of Maius, no breeze to cool memories. Thulia had prepared a simple meal, flat bread and mutton plus a few eggs, the type of food Pigfoot hated. *"Can't you cook a stew with decent beef?"* She only replied, *"We have no beef; and now I work at the barns and have less creative time."* There would have been more to the rebuttal, but she noticed her daughter's eyes widening. Leaving half his dinner in the bowl, the man walked outside where it was cooler to have his wine and repair a harness in fading light.

In the small house, Sesca scratched an X upon the wax tablet, her new stylus of hardwood. When the little girl broke the old stylus, it was she—Thulia—who replaced it, carving a new one from apple-wood. She, not him, wanted her daughter to read and write. Sesca was too young to know what the letters meant, but teaching Roman numbers was a start, an X, an I, and V. The C would come much later.

Finished drawing, the child went to her bed, a small pallet no wider than two feet. Thulia extinguished the single lamp and sat at the hearth. She thought of Othar and how he always called her *"girl."* He never viewed her as she was now, far beyond girl stage. She smiled, for he could do that, always make her smile with gifts he carved for her. He had a special tone, stern yet loving, *"Ye sleepan, now,"* and she would fall asleep and not have the nightmare. He had that kind of voice.

How could she live without Othar and Frit? No-one to love, to banter with. Little Sesca no longer spoke, never said a thing. Over two years old and mute. Thulia was alone again, right back where she was in childhood. If only she had a chance to do something worthwhile. She mused upon girlhood dreams that wrought the Amazon—to slay an evil giant, earn the love of a prince. She would be fulfilled!

Such foolishness. There were no giants; and all the young men were gone. Three years ago they rode miles to bed the Amazon, some talented, others dross. She had the pick of the crop yet forced to marry an aging woman hater, not a decent word from him. One by one, the dreams vanished. She brandished a pitchfork instead of a lance. Old Hempstalk looked the other way when she passed him on the road, and she hadn't spoken to him or entered his house since he bartered her off. Whatever he meant by *"I'm sorry"* came far too late. The only man to speak decently to her was old Heldrid the trader. Sitting pensively she recalled his kindness.

Spring rains passed, the Prahova coursing slow as the saltamon arrived upon his initial float of the year. He always made an early trip downriver from Saltsbaurg, appeasing Gothic neighbors to the south. Then he would continue down to the main river and the Roman fortress at Noviodunum. Thulia used the last of her salt months ago, and now she ran to the riverbank with the other women, each anxious to procure a new supply.

The saltamon was a cagy Dacian who spoke Gothic and Latin. He owned a mine upriver, in his family for generations and worked by the unfree, his product slightly bitter. He stood at the boat's stern while leaning to a sweep oar and shouting to his rowers, four handsome youths in their teens, probably his slaves and what not else, "Paddle back, now fast aft. Aye, me beauties!" The square-sterned boat slammed to the flodus bank as he and his boys all pitched rearward. Squat barrels of salt remained where they sat, heavy and brim full. Regaining his balance, the saltamon pulled the oar inboard, took a deep swig from a jug of mead, and yelled a practiced refrain:

> "Salt! Salt!
> Salt for your meat,
> taste for your fish.
> Salt! Salt!
> Salt for your taste,
> taste for your pinch."

With the boat secured to a post upon the bank, each woman stood in line to purchase his product. Thulia moved forward—one step at a time as each woman's terra-cotta jar was filled—until she faced the youth doling salt, his eyes burning a hole in her tunic, his jaw aslack.

The saltamon caught his stare, "None o' that, now. You're mine and she's someone else's, so pat down your snake and turn yer mind to business."

Thulia couldn't help it, an action ingrained too deep as she took a deep breath to give the young man a fleeting glimpse of himina-gards, something wondrous to remember her by, perhaps worth more of a scoop than she could afford. Three bronze asses fell from her palm. They were all she had, and the youth poured a level scoop-full into her jar, not a salt-grain more. She was losing appeal!

Then came a command from the rear, "Fill that jar. What, I ask, is the price of salt?—more than a hardworking woman's need?"

She turned, and Heldrid Constantinus jumped carefully from his wagon to pace toward the boat. He tossed a silver coin to the saltamon, then turned to study her eyes while addressing requisites, certainly not her desires, "Let her return home with all she needs." He was a kind man, a rich man, perhaps alluring in the past, but fifty years beyond prime and far too old for good sport at the horse barns.

If not for Heldrid's grace, she would have come home to this sad house with a near empty jar. Hard to remember what a gold-piece looked like, beef and sausages escaped the hearth. In this dark shack, she only heard complaints. She ran from it at winter's end and had a short affair, a few warm afternoons. They humped in melting snow, a rutting buck and doe in heat. *How could I have done it?* Yet she knew the answer, a deep need for a loving touch.

Thulia stood from the hearth and walked outside. Pigfoot sat upon a stool, leaning back to the cabin. A goat-skin of wine lay at his feet and the harness reposed in his lap, unrepaired. He said nothing, eyes remaining closed, either in a stupor or simply wishing not to converse. She paced long strides, putting herself between him and the setting sun. He opened lids and reached for the goat-skin. "I'm sorry for being a poor wife," she admitted, "The mutton was overdone, but I wanted to cook it thoroughly so we wouldn't get the trots."

He glared up to her, "I could not chew it, burned to a crisp. You know I have few teeth yet turned it to charcoal. What a trade I made with that uncle of yours, eh? Hempstalk complained. Said one of the geldings was downright stupid. I was the dumb one."

"I never could have been the virgin you expected. Fate held it otherwise."

He gave a cruel laugh, "You were fated to be a slut. Is that it?"

Thulia let the insult pass, "Before we were married, I had my nights. But for two years I slept alone, not a man's touch for the frailest instant. I cannot live in a void, and not long ago I had a short affair. Now I'm carrying a child."

Pigfoot leaned and retrieved the wine-skin, turning to spit on her feet, "I could have you burned at the stake for this."

"But you will not," she shot back with clenched fists, "It would prove what an impotent man you are… then your position of conservator will go to someone younger."

He sat back to pull a long draught and wiped lips, speaking not so much in a twisted smile but a promise, "Perhaps so, but mark my word. The child will die."

Chapter 7: The Widows' Lottery

The Christian settlement held the anomaly of being called Hospice, vexing to the Roman Trader. Anything north of the Danube was less than hospitable, yet he had to admit the Gothic bishop had a pleasant villa, the store-house bright and airy. He hoped to conclude business before noon, his first trip of the year into deeper Scythia. The Trader's slaves were outside waiting, each a loyal and strong eunuch, and the mules were packed. He wanted to get upon the trade road and back to Threisbaurg for weekly bazaar day. Then he would head up to Ulmenia for wooden wares and travel south for the Stone Bridge at the twin Drobetas. Below the river, he had another eighty miles before reaching home, the busy port of Tomis. The Trader had taken a young bride and wondered how she occupied nights. His attention returned to Bishop Wulfilas. Upset over some crisis, the bishop's own mind seemed elsewhere.

The entire trade ran poorly as he pictured his wife's escapades in a multitude of beds, while the bishop thought of whatever else, and the goods? He couldn't accept the wool; and to sour the trade even further he had to foist poor vellum on the man. So the Trader had to be explicitly honest, "It's discolored vellum, but perhaps good enough for your purpose. The Armenian linen is superb, as good as anything from Egypt. And figs are figs—always sweet to the taste. I must be going, the boys waiting, my horse chafing at the bit."

"I appreciate your candor. Not every trader admits inferior goods."

"Such a man trades with a customer but once. I'll return this way in autumn but not again until spring. I prefer mules over wagons, faster, better for perishables. But mules hate the cold of winter."

"I know," replied Wulfilas, "That's why the Sogdian traders arrived here when the weather warmed."

"You-He and Oxartes? They came through early."

"A week ago. Heading up to the mounts for Gepid amber."

The Trader's eyes rolled, "Let them do it. Not me! I want to live a few more years."

"What's so terrible about Transylvania?"

"My good bishop, there are stories—old wives' tales, yes—but the four-legged ones? The head-hunting man? I want to keep my head upon my shoulders, not on a pole."

Wulfilas studied the trader, mulling rumor's flames, "Ah, the four-legged ones," leaning to the hardwood table and feeling the linen's texture, each piece three feet by six and made on an upright loom, "Exactly what I want, a tunic from each one."

"A good tight weft," noted the Roman, "After a few washings, it will become tighter, keeping out the cold. I realize you're still burdened with raw wool, but I cannot move it, every Scythian tribe flooding the market. What time is it?" To answer his own question, he stepped to the door, checking the sun's height. "Later than I thought," he winced, "I'm going back near empty. Hate doing that. Could you part with a few sacks of that grain?"

"I cannot," the bishop replied, "It's not mine to trade."

The Roman paced back from the doorway and clasped wrists. "You've got it, the best I could do."

"God Speed," the bishop returned with a smile.

The Trader paused, uneasy with the bishop's expression, "Yes. Of course." Leaving the bishop to his own thoughts, he mounted his horse to lead the pack train. "See you in September," and he departed, knowing his occupation was hardly conducive to a young wife's chastity.

To the last mule, Wulfilas watched them go. *Scythians,* he mused, *That's what Romans still call us. He had no idea I'm a Greutungus, one of those barbaric Scythians... like that young man.*

Snapping from his thoughts, he paced to the main house. Entering the humble villa's kitchen, Wulfilas approached his wife, a delicate woman dedicated to his mission. Helena smiled, her eyes all aglow, "Figs, my dear. How thoughtful of you." And then she leaned, kissing his cheek, the beard tickling her lips.

He wished to smile but couldn't, long features accented by sober thought. *That poor young man, to fight for life through a fortnight, even more!—and then perish.* Picking a couple of figs from the basket, he turned from his spouse, silent for a moment, then presenting a somber tone, "He died just before noon as I gave last rites; then the trader came. All I could do was close his eyes."

He knew her own heart was torn by it, an endless stream of death, a far cry from the city court she matured in. Yet Helena married not a Roman but a man raised in the red hills of the Crimea. She moved to him, fingers running along the side of his back, "You cannot save the whole world. They are so naïve yet they kill each other with impunity."

* * *

A month after the Quadi raid, the Tyrfingi council and candidates gathered for the traditional lottery of widows. Beyond plans of men and at the house called Thiudgards, the youngest widow sat at bed-edge nursing the son of Selenas.

She would never forget him, the way he smiled to relate some wondrous tale. He spoke of far places where Greeks and Romans lived, told stories of ancient heroines—mighty Amazons who fought at Troy or Tomyris the Sarmatian queen who killed the mighty Cyrus. Selenas chose tales a woman liked. He would bring her flowers, small and wilted, but she knew they came from the heart, his true wealth. And the way he kissed? Oh, he was so very good at it, his lips opening hers, tongues playing chases, hands cupping her breasts or sliding up her leg. He had so many fingers she could never say "No!"

Unpinning her other brooch, Lilia dropped the peplos and continued nursing the infant. Nearly asleep, his eyes were closed. Her thoughts wandered from the touch of Selenas to the words of her father.

"The time has come, my daughter, for the council to meet at the east hill, the widows' names submitted to those who wish a wife."

"But why must I remarry?" she pleaded, *"I have the chest of Thiudebalth, enough wealth to sustain me and Waldrid."*

Rustan tried a smile through failing countenance, "The draft is the law. And a young man with a good future has offered to step forward."

Lilia looked down to her child, now asleep. *A young man with a good future.* She knew exactly who he was, and he was certainly not conducive to *her* good future.

She felt a chill, bringing the peplos up to her shoulder, fingers searching for the fibula on the coverlet. His very name—Athanaric—turned her mouth to bile. Lilia knew he could not even read, referring to books as "abominations." He trusted no one, always looked for dissension and plots. Physically he wasn't ugly, tall and striding with good carriage, but his wide face was short of handsome. And that damned squint!

She disliked his very nature, a complete refusal to believe anything beyond what the Singers claimed. Songs of deeds long gone held little for the real future. He held to old ways, ancient beliefs not for Waldrid. She wanted her son to see another world, brighter with less death—the burning hope of every mother. No, Athanaric was paled by the tenor of Selenas; for the son of Thiudebalth presumed hope, never despair, never the dark brooding of one who saw trolls in each cave, evil behind each tree. *"These are modern times,"* Selenas would say.

She gained her feet quietly. Walking across the room, she placed her son in the osier basket once holding laundry. She would get a bigger one from the wicker woman, the old crone who lived near the marsh, and he would have a new bed. With gentle fingers she wrapped the small blanket round him, its wool from the land of the Medes, soft and right for a child. She leaned back, her mind returning to wedlock: exactly what it would be, locked in marriage to a tactless fathead. She wanted her son to grow up fighting the very type of man Athanaric was.

Lilia lowered her gaze to Waldrid, for she liked the name—*man of the wood*—picturing him tall like his father, a man who knew books and nature. She walked over to the great arka of Thiudebalth, bending to open the lid. There they were! Gifts from the Greeks—Herodotus, Strabo, Homer, people like that. They wrote of wondrous things and places, and Waldrid would learn about the great world of Others.

*   *   *

On the hillside before them Aoric cleared his throat, leaning his weight upon his good leg, early-day sun at his back as he surveyed his audience. With arms folded, Rustan stood at the fore of the Alan delegation, nobles assigned from each tribe. Just over the hill, they could hear occasional bleating of sheep, disconcerting to the magistrate. "We all have things to tend, especially a certain shepherd, so I'll make it short," he promised, "Then we can go about our business. Good men have been lost and widows have wailed. Now it's time to go on, for a widow has no income and an uncertain future."

"That is true," an old warrior noted.

The magistrate continued, "Each respective hetmon has the names. A free woman shall be assigned to a freeman, a noblewoman to a man of equal or better lineage, the woman's dowry is hers to keep," he took a breath, continuing a well-memorized rote, "The former husband's worth and rank belongs to her eldest son upon majority. His father's chair is his chair. His father's horse is his horse, and so on and so forth. If she be childless or has daughters, then all is hers to own or give as she wishes, according to customary Gothic law… which prevails in all fairness."

"That is correct," the old warrior added.

Aoric paused for a moment, eying the man with contempt, knowing full well he was correct, being a magistrate for fifteen years, and he wanted very much for the old warrior to drop dead! But!—he controlled limited patience and continued, trying to make the process sound pleasant, "We are fortunate. Only seven brave men left widows, the others unmarried. Each hetmon has asked an unmarried man to step forward, to treat this woman with kindness, to care for her children and raise them as his own. If any man has knowledge that such a union is unfair to widow or child, let him step forward to give argument."

"That is the law," the old warrior noted.

Again Aoric glared at the man, "Do you think I do not know?" promptly clearing his throat, "Well, then. Let those who were loved be loved again. And let them be supported in kindness in the absence of a king. So it falls to me, your enduring judge, to be impartial and brief."

A buzz swept through the gathering, various candidates moving to the front, some men nodding, a few shaking heads in knowledge that the "impartial" magistrate's son was among the aspirants. When order again reigned, Aoric gave the first name, "Balthea, age twenty seven, widow of Hermaneric."

In his early thirties, a short Balth took a step to raise his hand, "I—Sigeric—offer my house to Balthea, widow of Hermaneric."

No one contested the union; and with the choice settled, Aoric stated, "You are a good man, a just man, and a wealthy one; for you may take the hand of Balthea who has two sons but only one daughter." The distribution of gender was far better than his own, for he was saddled with three daughters, all nearsighted and lacking in beauty.

Again the crowd mumbled this and that, more than a few knowing Sigeric was the father of Balthea's two youngest, all water under the bridge, seeds sown in another man's field and now rightfully legitimate. The sun rose over the hill, sheep bleating, the magistrate a little sharp, his leg bothering him, a sword-wound inflicted by a dead brother whose widow he married (grounds for eternal gossip!), as he now tried to foist off the son of his shady union. In the least concerting way he could, Aoric brought the name of the youngest widow to his tongue.

Directly in front of the magistrate, Rustan stood in great disappointment. He grew fond of Selenas, dismissing the Balth's conceit and unrealistic concepts. The young man was intelligent, learned, and had a capacity for quick humor, not quite Fritigern's but quick enough. Rustan liked humor, well-spoken rhetoric droll enough to fly over heads of the dross. It was an art and could save a sour situation.

As prearranged, his daughter's new husband would be Athanaric. The magistrate's son had some wealth, a slew of clients, and possessed a good future within the kunja. Yet there was something missing within the Squinter. He was untrusting and humorless, causing great uneasiness in Lilia's father. While a small point in the great scheme of things, this lack of humor seemed a portent of something darker. Rustan could not pinpoint the exact problem, and he would not contest the candidate, but he knew Athanaric was not the best young man for his daughter, only the most eligible.

"Lilia, age fifteen...," began the magistrate.

* * *

Saba walked among his hillside flock, the road to who-knows-where below him, a dusty thoroughfare leading to places beyond. He had never ventured to another settlement. Within the tribe he had no standing although a free man, free to tend sheep, help his mother, and carry his father out to the sun. For these reasons Saba seldom smiled. Believed by many as simple, he knew little except the ways of nature, mostly the nature of ewes and lambs, and all things sheepish. Almost thirty, he remained unmarried, as were his sisters, the youngest crippled in early childhood. His family became too large, the cabin too small, with food always scarce. He was a small man, had neither sword nor spear, yet in his youth he once carried the reiks' shield. The king pointed to him and said, *"You, there! Fetch my buckler, and quick about it."*

He smiled at the thought of it, to have been addressed by the king. He—Saba, a youth of no consequence! And so he picked up the shield and carried it. They went some place far away, across a river and then to another one. There must have been other towns near these waterways, but he did not see them. He walked the whole way, for he was a good walker—the shield so bright it shone in the sun. At that far river they met Asding Vandals in a great battle and Thiudebalth died. That was the end of it. He had no king to carry the shield for.

Lost in his reverie of glorious youth, Saba raised eyes to see a vehicle coming along the trade road below him. *That's a big wagon, for it has wheels taller than a man.* He studied the vehicle carefully, for such things entertained his mind. *Wagons are all different,* he mused while tugging an untrimmed beard, *some hardly bigger than a cart, others with spoked wheels and tyres of iron. But this one is an old Sarmatian magnum, built for capacity with solid wheels and high sides for heavy loads.* He watched the bullock wagon approach, finally noticing a horse tethered behind. *That's a nice horse, too,* he admitted, *I would like a horse like that if I knew how to ride; but I do not, so the horse would just eat grass my sheep need. Yet it's a pretty horse, totally white, not just partially white, a rare horse in these parts, the only one like it being Fritigern's.*

Suddenly it hit him like a hammer on the head. CLANG! *That must be Fritigern's horse. There is no other like it.* Saba stood puzzled upon the hillside, turning to see if someone else noticed this huge wagon towing Fritigern's mount, then turning in another direction, looking for anyone. *Where is everybody? This is important, I think! Maybe this wagon-driver knows something about the death of Fritigern and Selenas. Perhaps he is Fritigern!* Very excited, Saba walked one way for a moment, then another, turning his head this way and that... and suddenly he remembered the judge and bachelors were on the other side of the hill. *I will tell them!—for they should know.*

Saba hurried up the hill and along its crest, avoiding a multitude of old stumps; and down he went on the other side, breathing heavily, for he seldom ran for extended periods of time. He was the walking type, could pace himself all day long, walk around the largest flocks, always hoping to catch a ram coupled to a ewe, visual proof that family holdings might increase, one small lamb at a time. *There's Aoric right below me!*

The magistrate was saying, "Lilia, age fifteen, widow of...."

"A wagon is coming!" yelled the shepherd; and Aoric turned from the throng to stare up the incline while Saba added, "It's a magnum of Sarmatian design, big as a house and pulled by two pair of bullocks."

Panting like a mid-summer dog, Saba reached the first noble who ran up the hill, the man asking, "What is so excitable about a magnum?" a perfectly legitimate question. And a second man laughed, "Is it attacking us?" Many were the guffaws and chortles.

"You think me a fool?" Saba returned, knowing they believed he was, so he added his second observation, "It's a great wagon and tows Fritigern's horse. See for yourselves."

Several men reached the east hill's crest, the trade road clearly visible, sheep scattering in all directions. Indeed, a gigantic Sarmatian wagon came rumbling toward Threisbaurg towing Fritigern's horse.

Chapter 8: The Dead Returned

What is this?—half the nobles of Threisbaurg? Frit began waving as they ran down the hill, still able to smile after four days of traveling through Gothia at a bullock's pace. Reining the team to a halt, he jumped from the magnum to land upon friendly ground. Some vassal could inherit the bruising seat. He grinned all the more as the crowd hurried to him, and he whooped out, "Greetings from a ghost of battles past, back from the gates of Hades, and Selenas lives!"

Sigeric panted, "What of the others?"

Frit softened his tone, the smile disappearing, "Buried by the Christians. A week ago Ruteric died at their village, killed by the red line of death."

"Yet Selenas lives?" cried Rustan, leaning hands to knees and puffing, then finding more words, "How can that be? Athanaric said he was dead."

Fritigern's mien hardened, his eyes to murderous thoughts, "He did, eh?"

They viewed the glare of sharp iron and not one spoke, expecting him to say more. They knew he would. Frit had a silver tongue, poured from the crucible of the Greek. Eyes of one man met those of the next, and those eyes looked to another's.

"Athanaric got it wrong," Frit averred, "He fled, not knowing the vengeance of the Quadi—the slathering of hungry wolves—was actually this old Sarmatian wagon."

The crowd surrounded the wagon, one of the Alan vassals leaping to the cargo bed, "This is our grain, but how? The Quadi stole it!"

"And what is this?" another man quizzed, opening ties to an unfamiliar sack.

"Figs for the children," replied Frit, not pleased with the idea.

"There are sacks of them, at least two hundred pounds or more," returned the man as he retied the hempen bag.

"A couple for each kunja child, a *gift*"—and he spat the word—"from Little Wolf, Bishop of Gothia."

"Not my bishop," yelled a mid-aged warrior, "and I'll not have my daughter eat figs touched by a Christian."

"That's your choice. You can explain why she'll not partake in a child's delight," claimed Frit in a moment of fine verbiage, "Each child of Threisbaurg will have the opportunity to eat something he or she will not see again for years. I made a promise and shall honor it."

Limping to the fore, Aoric raised the hand of authority, "You will not! Dump them on the ground and let them rot."

Frit stepped to the iron foothold, swinging himself to the cargo bed. Standing upon sacks and drawing his sword, he yelled, "I cannot break a vow. These figs shall go to the children, just as grain returns to the Alans. Who wishes to die for figs? Come!"

"I am the judge!" screamed Aoric, his eyes turning up to Frit's, "What I say is law. You recite smooth words learned from a Greek, that tutor of yours and your brother. But you are hardly more than a boy, and the wisdom of elders shall prevail."

Frit flashed his sword as he grabbed a sack of grain, pulling it upright, "Without a weapon, Little Wolf and two other Christians went to the Quadi. They heard about the grain; the Barbaricon wags many tongues. Here's half of it, returned by their chief to the bishop."

"Without a weapon?" spat a freeman, "Either brave or foolish."

An old Alan noble gripped the wagon's side. He shook his head and turned to Aoric, his voice seasoned, "What, then, must we do? Shall this youth die for figs? Who will draw the sword? You, Sigeric? You, Theordrid?" He glanced back at Aoric, "I no longer ride but I still have a voice. And so I ask— if one gift is forbidden, is not the other? Shall we spill grain to the road? Sacrifice to Hunger? What is wrong or what is right; does Hunger know one from the other? No! Hunger is emptiness, for it feels neither wisdom nor valor. It only aches."

Aoric stared at him. What could he say? For the old noble had spoken wisely... and with no less than truth.

* * *

A single figure amid bald stumps, Athanaric knew exactly who owned the white horse. In the trade road below him, Frit jumped from the magnum, a crowd of shouting Alans taking his place on the cargo bed. Mounting his horse the brother of Selenas rode for the house of Thiudebalth and the young woman therein. The Squinter stood upon the hill's crest, not another soul upon it. Even Saba's sheep were gone. He would not dignify the base turn of events, appear before the dead-returned. This was some vile trick begat by evil spirits— the witches!—the filthy hags. How else could a dead man still be alive? Frit could not have survived the approaching Quadi horsemen without the help of some powerful specter.

He knew exactly what lay within the magnum. Alan grain, all of it. The glory of its return would go to a boy!—a brat and his damned white horse—not to those who gave their lives trying to regain it, nor to those who led the survivors home in one piece—but to a Greek-tongued, spoiled rich boy. Teeth clenched by spasms of his jaw, he stood there watching the whole sordid scene, the reveling Alans and dancing clients, the women arriving from houses and cabins along the west hill. He had never seen anything like it, despicable in its shamefulness, everyone reveling like... like Christians. Like Judeans. Like damned Greeks! He had never seen the Others, but he knew what they were not. How could a gast be as good, yes as brave, as a Goth?

And where was Selenas and his dark horse? Yes, for certain he was dead, his mount under the groin of a Quadi or eaten by wolves they turned into. Good riddance! For Selenas was just like Thiudebalth, forever trying to sway the people toward Greek and Roman ways. What good would come of it? They were degenerates! Every good Goth knew they performed foul acts with boys, slept with their mothers, and married first cousins. Perversions!

He pondered the vileness of it, grinding his teeth, and he wanted to cry out and scream!—but the Squinter would not satisfy the element who disliked him, those who uttered besmirchments behind his back and his father's. Not one of them would have contested his marrying Lilia. The whole thing happened so fast he never even stepped forward. But Selenas was surely dead, and Lilia and her son were his because only he—Athanaric, son of the magistrate—had the ability to guide the child's future with good sense.

Below the hill, the big wagon rolled down the road like the monster it was, filled with grain that should have been returned by a better Goth. Men and women began to disperse, the road emptying. *They go back to their homes thinking this a great day, but it's not! Evil flies about. And it recurs with the king's son.* Coming up his way, Aoric moved slowly, limping. *He is a good man, a wise and just one. And he should not have to walk up this hill.* The Squinter unclenched fists, tilted his head back for a moment, relieving the pain of tension, and then he began his descent.

*   *   *

Frit reached the horse-path leading home, only a hundred paces to a surprised Lilia. Yet he reined his mount short and paused upon the road. It vanished beyond the bend, curving to the tribal well and another mile to Four Corners. Pigfoot's house sat a distance beyond and just before the Ilomata ferry. For a moment he mulled a visage lost, the stream at the oak grove where Thulia taught him to use his tongue. Young he was, more like twelve than thirteen. Three weeks later she was given to the horse-keeper, their woodland dream shattered. The maiden was gone and the prince occupied himself fishing. They never met one another except occasionally at the horse barns. Then came the day of the Quadi raid and Thulia was back in his world, slaying two bandits intent on carving him up. She was exactly what she professed to be as a young girl—an Amazon. Did she realize who she was and what she could accomplish? He doubted it.

Not entirely lost, just a setback. Perhaps our time will come. He still had his brother. Selenas would be strong enough to return home in a few weeks, to continue leading the Balths, *perhaps become a reiks like Father was.* As the second-born, Frit had no such ambitions. He disdained tribal affairs, all politics and palm greasing. Days would roll into summer and he would fish for tench until the trees emptied. Then leaves would crunch underfoot, a perfect time for hunting. He could hound the boars or stalk roe-buck and eat like a king. But to be king? That would be his brother's burden.

Frit's thoughts went round the bend again. Many a noble married at his age, but he found no appeal in noble maidens, not his type, a little too nice, no fire in their eyes, no hair ablaze. Good girls were boring, but not the Amazon. She was unique, the gods tossing their knives after whittling her. *Probably didn't dare carve another like her but it was too late, Thulia released upon mankind.* He would await the right time to continue the dream.

With a pull of his reins, Frit turned for a house too big for a shrinking family. After his father died, the Greek stayed on to teach ciphers and rhetoric. He hated reading, especially dry shit like Plato's *Dialogues* and the seemingly numberless books of Pliny the Volcano Gawker. Only Herodotus could grip his attention. When Frit reached sixteen, the Greek slipped his books into their canisters, headed down to Tomis, and sailed back to Athens. Frit's formal education was finished. He grinned a wide one, for he would run from studies to join Selenas and Thulia while they rode under Old Hempstalk's tutelage. Too young, he forever dipped the contus as it caught in the grass and tore from his hand. Riding instruction had advantages as he leered at Thulia's consummate build. Ah, the thought of it; and Frit shook his head and guided his white gelding up the path to Thiudgards.

*   *   *

While the baby slept, Lilia continued rummaging through the great Jove-wood arka. At the very bottom she found a heavy gold torc, a wild rider formed at each end. They were barbarians, fierce beards and long hair, mounted on horses, and all in miniature. The neck ring was fashioned long ago, for nobody looked like that anymore, at least no anyone she knew. *It must have great worth*, she knew, tucking it back where it was, covering it with Selenas' purple tunic.

Lovingly, she ran fingers over gold thread. *I bought it for him and will always cherish it. Athanaric cannot make me throw it away, and he shall never wear it.* Then she replaced the leather pouch of coins, each one stamped with some

Caesar, this Caesar and that one, all dead probably. Caesars never lived very long. They died in all kinds of ways—poisoned by their mothers, smothered by younger brothers, but mostly they were stabbed by their own armies—only to be replaced by another Caesar. *Why would anybody want to be one? You could never sleep!*

She adjusted the fur-cuffed coat, trying to fold it back the way it was. As she fussed at the old chest, Lilia heard a noise down the knoll a bit. Closing the lid she looked toward little Waldrid. He was still sleeping. Then someone called her name. Instantly she thought it was Selenas, her heart beating fast as she jumped to her feet! *There it is again. Fritigern?*

* * *

At the horse barns Stefan squatted before his fire while rotating two branding irons in the flames, one carrying the conservator's tamga, the other having the family mark of Aoric. Next to him, Stefan's helper turned two more irons, those of Hempstalk and Rustan. Each tamga was burned upon a gelding's left shoulder, except for Old Hempstalk's, the man preferring his mark on the right haunch. Dark clouds spun overhead, the wind turbulent up high, and Stefan wanted to brand another twenty geldings before it rained.

Not far away, Pigfoot's wife examined the new stock in a temporary holding pen, each stake chest-high and roped to the next. She turned and her eyes fell to his fire. He studied her build—as he did every breaking season—elbowing his assistant, "Goten the bigaones, ja?" And the helper added, "Flippen the vaggon." They guffawed a loud one, slapping their knees until noticing she overheard the crass remarks. *Be takin' this iron up me dark place!*

At her approach, Stefan rolled eyes, waiting for his due. She could slam a mean pitchfork, but no worse than his broken shoulder, the cracked ribs, and every other bone in his body at one time or another. He was a wiry Greutungus from the far shore of Maotis, married into the Alans, now bucked and tossed for thirty years. At the age of ten he had bow-legs; and when reaching sixteen, he was the ugliest youth in three tribes. But he had a special talent that raised him to brikanmeister—*"the horsebreaker" to them what hails me*. His scars were legion and he gained a deserved reputation as the toughest rider in Threisbaurg. *And nay a deadamon yet.*

The woman stopped two paces from where he sat, put hands to hips and huffed, "You like bigaones, eh?"

"On a right wairths queins?" he shot back, "Faur triut I plaed."

She turned, watching Pigfoot hover at the barn; and in a flash, she swung around to boast, "Each year, you miss the best part. I strip to the waist when tossing hay." And with a grin, she loosened her sash, unwrapped the kaftan, and took a famed deep breath. A proud woman she was!—to have brusts like that.

Stefan's eyes bulged to the scope of the fullest moon, "Gudas verboden! Bind 'em up before Pigfoot sees."

She laughed a good one, stuffing their abundance with difficulty and retying the sash. Then everyone heard shouting as a faraway chant. Out in the pasturage, each horseman stopped wrangling, the most distant first, as they cupped hands to mouth and yelled out the news.

Sliding his coiled lasso round an arm, the closest rider bellowed, "Fritigern is back. Selenas is alive. With the Christians."

The words passed beyond the horse barns and faded into the distance, yet realization lingered. Stefan crooked his neck toward Pigfoot at the barn, "Be splittin the Balth's share a bit thinner. Half now go to kinsmen." He winked to his cohort, for he liked Frit's dry humor. Then he noticed Pigfoot's wife.

Going to faint, I faur think. She looked sallow, putting a hand to chest and taking quick breaths. He jumped from the fire to catch her, yet she regained composure as her face brightened. She ran for the nearest horseman, evidently wanting to hear more, then stopped midstride to return to the fire, eying Pigfoot.

I saw that, the conservator noted, *Your noble lover is still alive.* He had no idea which one, yet the brothers were suspect above the rest. After wedding her, it took one night to find out. There was no nuptial blood! It was long gone, the big-titted whore. She couldn't even fake it, spread a little chicken blood on the mattress. And now she was pregnant again by some noble bastard. He watched Thulia stride back toward the horsebreaker, racking his brain, trying to ascertain who the father was. *Not Stefan, a little too ugly. Fritigern?* She liked the young Balth above others. He recalled Fritigern riding along the road minding his own business. That's when she did it, lifting a foot to a rock and raising her skirt. The young man got a close view of that bronze bush of hers. When she saw him watching her too, that skirt came down faster than a hawk drops on a hare! *"I was retying a boot lace,"* she claimed. What a whore. Fritigern had to be the father, although he never caught the youth with her. But he could tell. Fritigern always stared at her, undressing her with his gaze.

The thought of it made the conservator's blood boil. She wouldn't let him touch her. Where was the trust of husband and wife? *She gives it away for free, just for the pleasure of it.* If she charged a bronze coin for each throw, they could buy a palace in Rome! The conservator had her work with him at the horse barns just to keep an eye on her. Otherwise, she'd be home with a line of studs waiting in the road, the line going for miles, vending from village to village... all the way to Constantinople. His careful surveillance did little good, but he had a plan, a fine justice waiting for the right time.

*   *   *

At a long morning's end, father and son strode toward home as clouds moved down from the north, covering the sun. The rain began, at first a sprinkle then steady in its fall, wetting their tunics to cold dampness as mud formed in the road. Their house was close, a half mile or less, its thatched roof tight, its hearth warm, a solace in its comfort, yet events drowned the light in their hearts, especially the Squinter's. They paced slow in silence, chords of speech elusive. His old wound inflamed by the weather, Aoric finally moaned, "My leg becomes worse, stiff it is. Your uncle laughs, he does. In the lower house, not Valhalla, the bastard grins. Soon I'll need a walking stick. Then I shall retire, but I have two or three good years left."

The son walked slower to accommodate his sire, his mood black, grinding deep within as the entire wagon episode settled like bile. He had not expected the news his father gave him. *Selenas lives*—two sorry words falling to darkness of his soul. Fortune spit in his face! No man could live after taking a spear like that, yet the eldest son of Thiudebalth did. Athanaric would not stoop to give Christians credit, or their singular god, but some unknown spirit caused it. *Perhaps the witches have come back.*

Seeing Athanaric's dour expression, Aoric spoke in feigned assurance, "Alas, bad things happen in this sorry world. Demons laugh at the good, they do. The man who holds to sinew and tradition will ultimately win. This shall pass, my son, and you will take your place at the head of the confederation in another way. You have inner strength and must weather the storm."

"Perhaps so," Athanaric returned, droplets falling from his nose, eyes squinting straight down the road to a fading dream, seeing the essence of Lilia in the increasing distance, a graceful shade almost gained. She danced before his eyes as if she were really there, her arms white, ankles thin, auburn hair flowing in the wind. But Selenas wooed her first and claimed her. Again they walked in silence, the Squinter knowing he almost gained the peak of tribal status. He could wield a sword with the greatest strength. He could ride like a Hun. Yet this was a different kind of battle, he knew. The road would be far longer than this one trod.

At the end of his worst day Athanaric strode heavy with his father, each avoiding deeper puddles as they stepped through increasing mud, their pace seemingly a retreat. Yet a better day would come, when Selenas would be no more than a faint and irksome memory.

Canto Two
PROBITY
Anno 348
Two years later

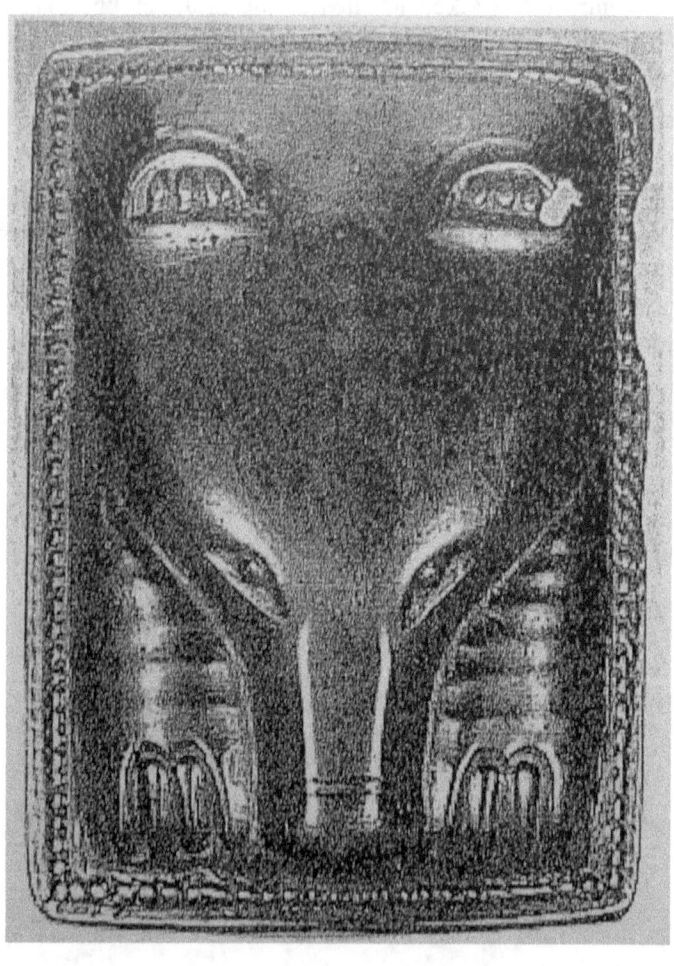

Chapter 9: The Sound of Fury

Early in the ninth month of Anno 348

The fields lay brown under a colorless sky, yet the day held warmth. At a slow pace the bullock team approached the Tyrfingi village from the Prahova ferry, the hands of Selenas at the reins. His clients and those of his brother welcomed a man who almost seemed foreign. He scanned the faces, each in turn gazing his way along both sides of the trade road. After his two year absence, people looked remarkably similar. Saba waved in excitement, for the shepherd loved a big wagon. The sisters Heldiga and Heldigard beamed as mirror images, born on the same day and daughters of the old crone who lived near the swamp, basket-makers themselves. And almost hidden in the crowd, Seno smiled a toothless grin, still alive as the Tyrfingi's eldest man.

Among them was Thulia with her classic wasp waist, skin overly tanned, and hair flaming to hips. He wondered if she still claimed Amazon blood, straddling a horse to aid her husband. Selenas looked her way, Thulia's gaze piercing. Astride her gelding she took a famed deep breath. Even two years ago, the gesture seemed fruitless. The Amazon grew less than gorgeous, more like primal, eyes the color of Indian emerald, flawed in their depth. *She will always be obscene.* Unable to discern Thulia's features at a distance, he remembered her as coarse, her cheekbones high, nostrils small, the bridge of her nose rising to a slight hump. Her lips were too lavish, that knowing smile always lewd, her mouth parting as she tongued her upper lip. *How incredibly vulgar she was!* He closed his eyes, seeing her overly ripe back in her second year of marriage.

"Are you alright?" his wife asked, sitting next to him. He snapped to where he was, his face reddening. Perched on a pillow, Lilia crooked his elbow in hers while grasping Waldrid with her other arm. Old enough to run some distance before falling, the boy was a terror. "We are home, my husband. Who could dream in a thousand years you would enter the Arian ministry?"

Amazing how his world changed. He went from lector to deacon, finally ordained presbyter by Wulfilas. Months went quick, the rote easy. He already knew Greek and studied the Bible until quoting it in his sleep. All of it was due to no less than a miracle. Wulfilas said it best, *"Everything about your wound spelled death—the loss of blood, a hole large enough to push a fist through, then a burning caldor, enough to kill the other young man; and you lived because you had true faith."*

Selenas resolved to return to the tribe and spread the good word, *"The Tyrfingi will come to one of their own."* Little Wolf was amenable to it, probably his design all along. To his great pride, Lilia was baptized immediately after her arrival at Hospice. She seemed intent upon creating another Christian in all due haste, their nights spent in throes of passion, what she termed procreation. *"Oh, Selenas, you can procreate so good."* Not yet showing, she was pregnant again. Meanwhile, little Waldrid's hands reached for all to be had. Everything they owned required hanging above the boy's touch. During the two years, Fritigern visited Selenas a few times, not really comfortable at Hospice or resigned to the Arian cannon. Although impressed with a Christian community in the thousands, he would "wait awhile."

From the seat of the old wagon, Selenas noted his brother and Rustan, each straddling a horse upon the hill-slope. With the presbyter's face toward him, Frit gave a grin, raising palms up as if making an offering. Then he tilted his head, nodding in the other direction.

Selenas looked across the trade road from his brother. Standing on the other hillside, two noble Balths stared in his direction, one with a walking stick, the other squinting. They looked his way, neither moving, no raise of a hand or nod of recognition. The presbyter knew exactly where everybody stood.

*   *   *

Less than a fortnight later, Selenas surveyed the cleared knoll above the stream where little Waldrid was born. Before him stood the finished house, two clients still on the roof tucking the last thatching in place. Not a great house, its mud-daubed walls would chase winter's chill. Being mid September, one day warm, the next cool, it was completed just in time. That night would be their first in it. Well furnished, the new house had a bath made from the bottom third of a vintner's tonna; and the bed was huge, its thick mattress coming up from Durostorum with the Roman Trader. Ordered months ago, the cadurcum finally reached journey's end, cargoed from Aquitania up the Rhone, then down the Danube.

In the interim he and Lilia lived in the old house of his father, but Frit seemed restless, wondering when the new dwelling would be completed. On one occasion after visiting clients, they reentered Thiudgards to find Waldrid dragging Frit's sword across the floor, luckily still sheathed. *"Big knife,"* the child said. The weapon pried from his grip, little Waldrid bawled, the entire episode not impressing Frit at all, *"I think I'll wait awhile before having children."*

During those first weeks home, Selenas had no trouble converting his clients, at first wondering what the Gothic Church was all about, a God, a Son, and a Holy Ghost. Yet soon enough, they thought it better than the Sword of Mars—*Tyrfing*, as Merjands and Ufar called it—which seemed more like a thing than an entity. No more Selena the moon goddess, his own namesake. Some freemen came over easy, including the entire family of Saba. The old man and youngest daughter, both crippled, betook the Lord first. Saba followed next, having a talent unknown to everyone, able to remember scriptures with amazing accuracy. Needing a lector, Selenas would give him the honor, although he wasn't literally a reader of psalms. Finally Saba would be somebody.

At least I have a semblance of a congregation. The two clients finished thatching the roof and climbed down the ladder. Lilia came out from within, offering them cider, just beginning to perk with a little "bite" to it. While the wooden cups were filled from her big earthen pitcher, Selenas paced a short furlong to the second building site, the stumps already pulled by bullocks. He pictured the first church of the kunja. Selenas had built his house upon a knoll at forest edge; and here would be the church, away from the old ways, the old gods and all they encompassed. There would be no complaints about "those Christians" moving into Threisbaurg. He was building at a distance.

In periphery of thought, the clients waved to him as they departed. He hailed back. Short moments later Lilia came down the path, Waldrid running after her. Having changed into fresh clothes, she had an air of clean beauty. Walking close together at day's end, they continued down the path to the place where it all began, soon to be the baptismal pool. Brushing his body with hers, she remained silent for a moment, studying eddies circling deep, and she whispered,

"Sonja and I filled the mattress with the sweetest grass we could find. It is very soft."

*   *   *

My Thulia, why can't you sleep tonight? She awoke with a start to sit up straight, not a sound from her throat. She never screamed, no longer crying from the nightmare, a specter with no form, just a kindly voice. Once again, she couldn't get back to sleep, fearing to close eyes. *It must be close to dawn, perhaps an hour or so. Time to visit the morning man, the one who chases wraiths to make the world seem right.*

To the east, the first hint of passing night came as a tinge of rose. Thulia strode briskly down the road, bucket in hand. She needed it, that peerless touch, driving the fear and pain of childhood back to where it hid. He was her light—that talented Bad Boy, yet so very good. Oh how he had the touch, strong and gentle all at once; no other man like him. Her very timbre melted to his fingers, his tongue trained to her entire frame. He understood her deepest needs like no other lover did. When the time came, she prayed to die in his arms.

He grew handsome beyond her wildest dreams, with hair dark blonde, his moustache trimmed upon a clean-shaven face. She knew he trimmed it every day with a small pair of iron shears. His countenance remained boyish, yet his jaw sat firm upon a manly face. And his eyes? They were like a brook!—clear and toned to the color of a sword blade.

Suddenly she jumped in surprise!—her thoughts squelched by the crow of a nearby cock. He hailed the dawn only yards away, yet it sounded like he was scolding her, a rough call from the depths of his throat, "what-you-doing-there!" Leaving the rooster behind, she answered his question mentally, *I'm walking in guilt, walking in need. And it's none of your damned business.* Thulia swerved from the road, her steps hurrying up the path. She couldn't wait! His servants left each eve for their own abodes, and he was all hers to ride hard. She paced all the faster, unloosening her tunic belt, dropping the bucket in the path as it bounced in the increasing distance.

She stopped at the door, leaning back to it, breathing hard to view the coming day. *I must compose myself, at least a little bit.* But she couldn't! The deepest part of her, beyond the body itself, needed him, craved him beyond reason. How strange it was to love him that much, wondering if he returned a part of it. He loved the act itself, the way she rode him hard, and he appreciated her body, even overripe globes. But what of real love?

Quietly she entered, dropping her skirt to the floor as she ran to his bed, tearing her tunic as it caught at her shoulders. And then she was upon him, his eyes opening. No phantasm this! He said not a word, reaching, fondling her softness, his hands like those of an artisan. Thulia pressed to him, their bodies tight, like two trees growing from a singular stump. Their kiss was so passionate their teeth clicked!—each tongue working deep and quick. *May the gods help me,* her thoughts screamed, for she loved and needed him for all he was. *I could ride you forever, my handsome morning man.* Some day it would end, she knew full well. *But not upon this dawn.*

*   *   *

An Alan raised by good Sarmatian tradition, Rustan the hetmon distanced himself from the presbyter's early sermons. The One God was too new, the message simple. Yet when it came to raising the church, Rustan stepped forward; "man's work," he claimed. With Oktobre approaching, the congregation needed a structure with some warmth, nobody wishing to praise the Lord with cold feet. When finished, the log building was forty feet in length with an angled roof, one side for the women to stand, the other for the men. Thatching arrived from the swamp in thirty wagon loads, the roof to be finished after the "Sabbath," a new word and day in their vocabulary. In the church's rear, a large hearth stood big enough to hold three foot logs. Substantial, not elaborate, the structure was built for and by the kunja.

With Rustan in the congregation, albeit not baptized, other Alan families came forward to receive the good news, one third of the flock children. Lilia's brother Safrax had reached his ninth birth-date, not quite so little, his hair turning fiery blonde, the hues of reddish gold mixed to saffron. Hanging around their house, even when he was supposed to be home, he had a million questions for Selenas.

"Where does God live? Up in the sky?" he quizzed, his hair falling in his face, a thousand freckles under a boyish tan.

"He lives everywhere," replied Selenas, "even in here." And he tapped his chest, indicating the body.

"Oh no!" cried Safrax, "He may not be in me anymore."

"What do you mean?" besought Lilia, trying to keep Waldrid from pulling raw wool from a tall wicker container.

Safrax looked worried, "This morning I ate too many green apples."

"And so?" quipped Selenas, waiting for the rest of it.

"I threw up!" the boy exclaimed, "God is out in the bushes next to the leaning pine."

* * *

A throng lined the east hill upon the Sabbath, all listening to the man preach. Thulia stood at the rear, inconspicuous as she wished, seeing her uncle near the front. They called themselves laity, Selenas not a priest but a presbyter. The previous day most of the men in the group worked on the church, even that haughty bitch's father, the Alan hetmon. Now they had the structure almost completed. Again Thulia listened to the man's sermon, the verbiage of Arianism perplexing yet a message plain enough. The son of God sacrificed himself so that she could gain eternal life. But to enter the upper house, she had to admit her sins.

She attended the first sermon in curiosity, but now Thulia was moved to shame. She knew it before, always knew it, breaking moral and tribal laws calling for her death if caught. Now it seemed much worse, to forever burn in the lower house! And once again Selenas gave the Commandments, "Honor thy father and mother. Thou shalt not kill…." Hearing each a third time, she practically knew them by heart. Old Hempstalk was her only blood, yet she could not honor him; and every night of her life she wished to kill her husband. Selenas was no less tainted, speaking Xristos' words as if he were so damned pure. *What a hypocrite, a stance so humble, telling the wronged to turn a cheek.* And that supposedly pure wife of his?—Lilia entered wedlock no more a virgin than she did.

How could Thulia forgive those who trespassed against her? She wanted to, but the anger burned too deep. She wished to reach himina-gards, to see Othar, to comfort his trembling hand. He had to be there, for they couldn't steal the Journey from him. In his own guilt he had foreseen it, *"I go to the verms, girl. Killed me brother. For me, only the verms."*

Those were his last words. *The worms!* She turned from the congregation, tears forming. Not the gods, the tribe— not even her uncle!—cared about the old man. He was just a gast, one of the Others, from a northern place. He was gone, the warmth she craved left to Frit's arms, as near to love as need might get. *"Thou shalt not commit adultery."* Yes, adultery, the one decent thing in her indecent life.

The service ended and she hurried from the crowd. Pacing fast she began to bawl like a wanting child; for Xristos, the son of God, gave his life for a wretch like her. Thulia slept in sin, divorced herself from her own flesh and blood, and knew that Othar was nowhere at all. There was no Journey. He laid with the worms! The truth was no less strong than the phantasm in her nights; and she felt guiltier than ever, trying to reject this new God. He was too real and right. How could she ever redeem herself, get Othar to himinims? And the sound!

It simply grew louder, her beating heart or something else? Hoof-beats, yes. They shook the ground beneath her feet, like a landslide!—and right before her, the white stallion stopped, a great horse with dark-flamed eyes. Its rider glowed, a man dressed in silver armor, a man of light! He was difficult to view through all the tears, for he seemed to be here or there all at once. She could swear he smiled. "You *can* forgive, can you not?" he plainly said, "And now you know the Lord— inside thyself, where Othar is," and his voice reverberated, deep and loud, "Prepare you then! The quest begins."

He reined his steed around, both man and horse blurring to a bright whirlwind. She opened her mouth, wishing to ask, *Who are you? What quest?* But he was gone in a wink!—and the hoof-beats subsided. She stood there, immovable, unaware if people paced by her, or perhaps there were no people at all.

* * *

With the church finished, Selenas strode toward Thiudgards in early light, jays scolding him for scuffling leaves. His wool coat chased the morning's chill, tan grass still glossed with the previous night's dew. Here and there, a woman or older girl walked to the well for a new day's water. Some would smile to speak his name, others moving aside as if he were a leper. *Their conversion won't be easy; old ways die hard.*

In two days time he would lead a hunting party to the far side of the swamp, hopefully to find a half dozen boars. He wiped his bow with flaxseed oil, hoping it wouldn't break. The moth-chewn arrows would arc straight enough to kill a pig once dogs stopped it. To be served with boiled vegetables—squash, turnips, beets, carrots, and the like—the boars would be spitted early on the Sabbath, all roasted when services were over, a delicious reward to those who built the church and stood at its first observance. He wished to invite his brother although doubting Frit would attend, a reticence extending back to the very day they raided the Quadi. Upon that road to his own baptism, Wulfilas offended his brother, struck him the wrong way. The bishop's resolve was searing—*"You have it wrong."* Frit never could accept a sermon. He was too stubborn; and resentment lay deep in his gut, the distance between Christian and pagan. Yet Selenas hoped he would join them for the feast. What man could refuse good roast pork?

Selenas turned from the road, taking the path toward the house where he and Frit were born, where their mother died of fever. In his childhood, its logs glistened a yellow-white, now weathered to dull silver. The house had original thatching, still a tight roof, a good one lasting a lifetime. No smoke rose above the ridge pole, the hearth down to embers from the previous eve.

He's still asleep, Selenas mused, *the lazy wastrel.* With a smile, he formulated a plan to wake his brother—he would quietly lift the latch-string, sneak to Frit's bed and grab his feet. He had to think of something clever to say, otherwise Frit might jump to the floor and clobber him.

With stealth he opened the door, his eyes suddenly huge as he beheld the sight. On Frit's bed—upon Frit himself!—she was mounted, her thighs apart, head tilted back yet facing the doorway. With lids closed, she rode in quick rhythm, her brusts slamming up and down. Then, sensing another person in the house, she opened eyes to meet his.

He knew her!—he and Frit grew up with her.

Instantly, her jaw dropped as Selenas turned and made a quick exit. He stood outside, blood rushing to his head. How was he to know? Who would have guessed it?—so early in the morn. *Heaven forbid. It's Thulia!* Pacing quick he distanced himself from the house, moving down the path. Suddenly he heard the door open to his back.

"What were you thinking? Couldn't you tap first?" snapped Frit as he held up trousers, belt still unbuckled.

Spinning upon his heel, Selenas returned, "I'm sorry. How was I to know? For Heaven's sake, she's married! She has a daughter and husband."

Frit was furious, his eyes casting fire, "Her husband wasn't quite good enough, and you dare speak of propriety," and he spat it, "You?—a man who robbed the baby basket."

"What are you implying?"

"The whole damned tribe knows. They can count. You knocked her up when she was still thirteen, no more than a child."

Selenas' face turned crimson, lips unable to find a reply.

"So you like nubiles," added Frit, his voice firm, "If that's your penchant, then well enough. But don't preach probity to me."

Blood still racing, Selenas managed to find his tongue, "You don't mince words, do you. But what of her husband? He's the head conservator of the herds."

"Not anymore. At winter-end he got wined up, fell from his horse and landed on a stump. With a broken back, he lays unable to move from the waist down. I give them food, anonymously, just as Father would. She won't accept a fowl-leg from Old Hempstalk."

Having no idea of the accident, Selenas looked back to the door. Frit continued, "She's in there scared to death. If he were to find out, Pigfoot would condemn her to the stake. She comes here before getting water. That's her excuse," he pointed to the bucket near the door.

Probitas fought the demon's world, tricing up the lost, yet Selenas found no right to profess it. He could only ask a secular question, "How long before she burns? A week, a month? If I found out, someone else will."

*   *   *

Down at the Stone Bridge, Roman guards changed watch at the mid-hour between dusk and dawn; and further north, the moon arced over a nameless stream, dark trees framing it, not far from the rivers. A fleeting shadow crossed the stream just below the baptismal pool, working its way through spruce to enter the newly cleared field. An owl, once hoping for a mouse or shrew, unfolded wings to retreat further back into the wood. The noise startled the shadow, splitting it to four immobile strands as arms and legs froze. *A full moon and infernal creatures*, bethought the shadow, casting a black figure, sweeping past remains of immature spruce cut to clear the land. *And a full moon leads to no good. The witches are out.*

Skirting the edge of the tree line, the shadow found a path, well worn by someone or perhaps deer that once drank from the stream. Following the path up the knoll, the shadow moved off to one side, slipping through trampled grass to reach the back side of the new Arian church. *Not a breath of wind.* The light of the moon, the ultimate quietness, seemed ominous, as if someone were watching. Could they hear it?—

the quick pulse of guilt? Kneeling to the ground, the shadow opened the tinder bag, feeling the striker and fluff. But kindling would be needed, something to burn long enough for logs to catch, something to bring flames up to the thatching.

Dropping the bag, the shadow re-crossed the field to wood-edge and grabbed some brush—*freshly cut firs!*—plenty of pitch and needles to flame a good burning fire. The shadow dragged brush to the rear wall, stuffing it tightly against the church. Then it went back to striking tinder. A single spark touched the fluff, then another, until it smoked to ignition. Quickly the shadow pulled spruce to increase the flames, the fire sputtering as needles burned. Breaking an entire branch, the shadow held it over the small fire until it began to crackle, then reaching it high to the thatched roof.

Oh, yes. Very good! The thatching burns very quickly, and soon the abomination will be nothing more than charred embers. Its work done, the shadow moved over the clearing to enter the woods, to tarry there under dark firs… for it liked to watch.

Dried reeds began their swelling roar. The sound of fury.

Chapter 10: A Fading Breeze

Upon the next eve the council met under clear skies, the moon coursing its arc to the other side of the earth. The star called Vesper began its glow, as if signaling others to journey across heaven's blue vault; yet the mind of man was far from wonders of the cosmos.

Aoric turned from the council, the meeting unresolved. The nobles raised hands equally in aye and nay, as if it were planned. Too many were sympathizing with either the Christians or their leader and nobody wanted the responsibility of banishing them, yet a legitimate and final solution had to be made, their church torched by someone, for Aoric knew it was no accident of nature. *First arson, and what next? An altercation? A knifing? Murder?* They had to go, every last Christian, and as far away as he could lawfully send them. Then peace and order would prevail.

It must be lawful, for the law is above all. Searching his memory for anything to use in his favor, he thought of old steppe traditions. *Yes!* His mind screamed, *That is it!—a Ride of the Duces.* But he had to make himself look and sound impartial. After all, he was the judge. With a push of his walking stick, he turned back to the crowd, "It must be settled. They go or stay, but only through the law. You stand in stalemate, so it falls to the judge. I declare a ride— *Cataphractum gallante*," and then he added, "*Convivae duce*. They shall ride a fortnight from tomorrow at the Willows. No more shall be said."

A few nobles yelled dissent, but Aoric would hear none of it as he waved them off like bothersome flies. The matter was settled and nothing could change it.

Turning from them, he limped toward his wagon, his son following to help him climb upon it. He twisted, refusing Athanaric's help as he seated himself, "Arson repeats itself, and I shall not have a young woman and boy killed by it. That young man is a disgrace, coming back here as a Christian priest. Gods in himinims! His father rolls over in his grave! Upon the dawn, send an envoy to Tyras with a good purse. We shall hire King Baduil's duce."

Athanaric's eyes bulged wide!—"The Mordwine?"

"Aye, the Mordwine. Never gamble, my son. Always buy a sure win."

*   *   *

In the crowd of nobles, Selenas eyed his brother, "A Ride of the Duces? Are we settling a feud? Nobody has made the lance ride since when?"

"Our childhood," claimed Frit, "the last intertribal war. He called for two high cataphracts, table companions of the King—*convivae duce*. The old bastard is smart. You can bet they'll find the best lancer this side of the Huns. All he has to be is a pagan."

They moved quickly from the buzz of the crowd, and with a few quick strides Lilia's father reached them, "Aoric is picturing the first dead Christian of the tribe. Your choice is limited," he resigned, "I never was a cataphract, too light for it, but I'll ride if I must." And then he left, shaking his head.

As they distanced themselves further from the others, Frit spoke tightly, "Every new day you place me in a more intolerable position, and why? Because you gave away your birthright, tossed it aside to the favor of Wulfilas. And you dumped it on me." He gritted, eyes narrow, "You should be leading the Balths. Not me! And I cannot stop this sham without losing their support. This is politics and I hate it with a passion. Do you understand?" His brother studied the ground as Frit snapped, "Look at me! You cannot avoid this one, you son of a bitch."

Selenas was slow to reply, his voice halting, "I know, I know. But I was chosen; not my choice, but God's. Please, I need your help in finding a champion."

And so the younger brother is forced to care for the flock, to watch it split into factions. It's not what I want or need. What damned champion? There is no Christian gallantus, yet Frit calmed, "You only have two duces among your Arians. Rustan speaks the truth, too small a man."

"That leaves Old Hempstalk, I fear."

"A great lancer he is—fifty years old and overweight. What a gallantus, eh? The old fart couldn't stay on a horse if he were sober."

"He's not that much overweight," claimed Selenas, "All I can come up with, if he accepts. Have you forgotten your instructor's merits?"

"He was the best, but where is he tonight? In his cups? Hempstalk is a decade older and he'll be a dead man riding," returned Frit, stopping to grab his brother's shoulder, turning him, "The pagans have a dozen lancers to choose from and you have one. As your brother I'll not offer a pagan rider, but they'll find a husky killer on their own."

"Then perhaps I should start packing," resigned Selenas, his voice sharp.

Frit hated hearing the whine of defeat. *You ride in here like a conqueror and leave like a beggar. Is that it?* He despised the position he was in, thinking of better things to do than cleaning up his brother's mess, standing before his peers trying to unseat a wedge splitting the kunja right down the middle. Yet Selenas had greater troubles, all compounded by himself and his new god. Frit guarded his tongue, searching deep for a supportive statement, "What? Give up the fight? I'll talk to Old Hempstalk, feel him out. Maybe he's on a hard binge. If that's the case, I'll find someone who can call himself an Arian for the short ride needed to punch a hole in Aoric's design."

"What can I do in the meantime?"

"I don't know. Go home, kiss your wife good-eve, and try to get some sleep. We have two full weeks before the contest at the Willows."

*　*　*

Sesca knelt upon the flat rock imitating her mother, scrubbing her little smock after soaping it. In the morning's second hour they reached the river first, even before the presbyter's wife. Thulia glanced toward Lilia, noting how the Alana found another section of riffles. *What's the matter? Afraid you might catch poverty? It's not contagious, you snooty bitch.* Immediately she felt guilty. Not exactly a Godly thought. Yet wasn't Lilia supposed to act like a Christian too? After all, she was *his* wife. Thulia pretended to enjoy herself, peering down to Sesca, "Is washing fun, my sweet?"

The child looked up to her, smiled and nodded. Thulia turned, kissing her daughter's hair while rinsing Pigfoot's tunic, the garment now too large for him. Evidently the men in her life were shrinking.

A little less than the best of lances this morning. And quiet he was.

"Are you feeling alright," she whispered to her morning man.

"Yes," he returned, raising to elbows.

The real answer was No. She rode like a whirlwind, trying to get him excited. Usually he imitated the Spring Rite

Phallus. But not this morning. In the end, he brought her to fulfillment the hard way, as he did when a boy. She thanked God he cared enough to attempt it. No other man did.

She had to give him up, guilt tearing at her. Snapping back to where she was, Thulia leaned to the river, watching eddies. *You gave your son to save my soul. Could you not let my daughter speak? She's just a child, small in her needs. It would be your grace to hear her words. Blessed are the children, are they not?* She studied the conservator's tunic, suds floating off like soft gray clouds; and closing her eyes she confessed, *I hate the man. Is that why you silenced my child? Or was it to punish an adulteress?* Opening her eyes again, she met Lilia's stare. The presbyter's wife swung her head quickly, returning to her own clothes.

*   *   *

"The damned thing caved in sometime last night," Old Hempstalk resigned, "Don't know what's crushed and lost. A whole rack of eggs in there, salt tripe and butter, a hundred pounds of blood sausage and head cheese. Just for starters, not counting the perking cabbage. I can't remember what else, but a shit load."

They walked above the root cellar, soil and turf concave below them, as Frit studied the noble's slow pace, the way he puffed after climbing the small rise. *He doesn't have it in him anymore. Way beyond his prime.* "Probably rotting timbers."

"Framed up awhile ago, I don't know exactly, maybe twenty five years. Before you were born," Old Hempstalk admitted, smoothing his moustache in recollection.

Four Taifali freemen were digging at it, working carefully as they reached inside the entrance; and hopefully they could salvage a portion of the winter supply. Not the only Taifali root cellar, it was Old Hempstalk's favorite, his private stash. Frit knew he was a perked cabbage and blood sausage man, watching the aging hetmon down it through the years. Not his choice of food, sour and tart. It probably tasted much like the man's cheap wine.

He studied Old Hempstalk's blurred eyes, a red nose covered with a net of blue veins. Frit tried to pinpoint when the Taifalus started going downhill in hurry. Shortly after Thulia wedded, as he recalled. Having explained the situation he finally asked, "Can you make the ride?"

Old Hempstalk sucked in his gut to meet his barrel chest. When he did, the man looked solid, a continuous girth of beef as he grinned broadly, "With the best! I still have it all—my armor, the same for my horse, good iron plate—and I've got two weeks to practice. You can count on me, Frit." Then he whirled around quickly, as if looking for a sign of his glorious past. "Where is it?" he quizzed.

Back in your days of yore, Frit mulled yet asked, "Where's what?"

"My white-spotted gelding," the man shot back, just realizing he hadn't ridden it to where he was.

"Thulia has it, I think."

"Shit!' the elder man spat, "She took over my best old one. With that son of a bitch dead, she rides the good one I bartered her...." He stopped midsentence.

"What was that?"

"Nothing," claimed the Taifali hetmon, "Nothing at all."

* * *

Frit rode beyond Four Corners, heading north for open ground. He needed space to think; yet all he could see was the man's niece, forever in his vision, so incredibly attractive yet failing to grasp her great worth. No woman labored harder, more than most men. She had strength beyond muscle—

pigheaded determination. He liked a strong woman and a good hearted one although she projected herself as the hardnosed type, yet he knew she was concerned about her daughter, even the tribe. Oh, yes. She had soft moments between fiery outbursts.

Between thoughts of Thulia, he checked clients, noting his own root cellars were full. Frit hated the serious part of autumn, no fresh grass for cows as their milk dried up, and hens stopped laying eggs. In the afternoon he supervised the burning of bones, all from slaughtered cows and sheep too old to survive winter; and by day's end he needed a fresh breath of air and something heavy, soft, and malleable.

Reaching the hilltop, Frit viewed the horse barns below him, the sun hovering along the western tree line, the oak grove shining brown. Halfway down the hill, he stopped his mount to survey the barns, the largest nearly a quarter mile long, open on three sides yet protected from north winds by a singular solid wall. The sixteen barns stretched across barren slopes to grove-edge, the largest structures of the kunja, each containing enough hay to feed two hundred prized horses. The rest of the animals would forage, dig up snow with their hooves to find hay of a season past.

In rolling fields beyond, the horses spread out in bunches, prides of this stallion or that, mares and young of the year almost the same size. Only geldings reached fourteen hands or higher. Perfect for cataphracts they were easy to handle, learning to rush another horse, pass inches from it, and charge a column of stationary men. The entire herd and horse barns fell to the accountability of the conservator—a dying man. For three-quarters of a year since his accident, Thulia supervised the operation, the scything of hay at early summer and again in the fall, the gelding of male foals and upkeep of the barns. On the previous eve, he planned on asking the council to appoint her as conservator, her husband no longer able. Frit knew the request would spark argument. *What? A woman as conservator of the herd? A woman's place is at the hearth.* Exactly what some would have said, but he never got the chance to bring the subject up. The burning of the church took precedence.

Coming down onto the road, he passed a number of freemen as they strode for home. "Is Thulia still here?" he asked the first man he met, a young worker recently married. As family generosus, Frit had given his betrothed a gold solidus for her dowry.

Turning slightly in his tracks, the freeman pointed to the largest barn, "She's over there, my lord, counting forks."

"Thank you," returned Frit, "Give my regards to your wife."

He found her exactly where the man said, in the aroma of hay, pungent and invitingly sweet; nothing else smelled like it. As her last chore of the day, she counted and stacked pitchforks against the north wall's interior. Each fork came from an ash or willow, its tines natural growth, steamed and shaped to a slight curve, then sharpened with a knife. Hay forks had value, for not every tree could yield one, the correct shape a gift of nature or the gods.

Sliding confidently from his saddle, the Balth strode into the long structure as she stood upright to glance his way, her hands pressing her back to relieve the ache. Thulia was the first person to arrive at the barns in the morning, the last to leave at day's end; yet it was her choice, her preference. She loved horses, each of her days counted with them.

Neither acknowledged the other. With her back to him Frit moved hot-bronze hair aside to kiss her neck. Tilting her head, she sighed. Not a word, but a sigh. He kissed her neck a second time, fingers slipping round her shoulder and through her tunic, sliding down her cleavage. Suddenly, she tore from him, pulling his hand away! Turning with lightening speed, the Amazon cuffed him hard to the side of the head, "You want it this moment? Right here in the hay?"

His ear ringing from the blow, Frit stood surprised, not having an answer.

"I'm tired!" she snapped, "Like a slave I work. And you come riding in here thinking I'll rip my clothes off and hop on your lance. That's it, is it not? Well, grow up and think again."

His face flushed and he finally said, "I'm sorry. You're too good a woman for this—working all day in the sun and supervising a large crew—yet you live for it and take the bad with the good. My day has also been a poor one, my thoughts amiss."

She turned and continued her count, not saying a word. With the sun hanging low, shadows crept their way from the forest to spread twilight across the fields. There seemed to be an extra chill to it, not simply the final approach of Naubaimbar but a coolness reaching his depths. Fritigern watched her finish her chore, quietly trying to fathom the gender. He had limited experience with women, actually just Thulia. As this whole Christian madness fell upon the kunja, she was the only person he wanted to deal with, even when she was like this.

What exactly does he want? A tumble in the straw? Thulia stacked hay forks in a fury, wooden tines clattering together. She always wondered if he loved her or her big bosom. There was more to life than sex, and he had no idea of her circumstances. It wasn't for him to know. She dreaded day's end, for she would retrieve Sesca from Pigfoot's sister and then walk home in late twilight. The conservator would be there, waiting and blaming her for every bad turn of events.

She poured no wine down his throat or pulled him from the horse, but he could make it seem that way. Not one civil word would come from his mouth, only bile as verbal abuse.

Her thoughts returned to Frit, two years her junior with no wraiths to haunt his nights, no eating sheep-hocks, no water bucket to rebind. *And he came here in broad daylight! Half the freemen saw him and they'll talk it up. He threw aside caution for lust!—and it must end. I'll not burn like a witch, not even for love.* Finishing her chores, she strode back to Frit, her expression stony, "Sometimes I think it can be no more than these," and she lifted the great weight of her brusts, "You love them beyond reason, but they are not me, only part of me." Thulia paused, waiting for a reply. Not hearing she added, "Then it's over."

"No!" he returned quickly, "You're a fine woman with a good heart; I enjoy your company, our closeness. My silence comes from distress, my brother and Old Hempstalk, that's all. I have a lot on my mind, yet I would take you to wife in a heartbeat is such a day might come."

Take me to wife? She stood surprised before him, her eyes intent, judging his. True, he wanted it—that great momentary rapture they shared—but he also wanted her. Marriage? A fine compliment, but a dream. She had her station within her own tribe and the kunja, a woman good enough to oversee freemen yet far below the spouse of a prince. What of the other reality? If he took her to wife, the bloodline would die! After losing her second child she no longer conceived, riding Frit like a wild woman. She would have been pregnant months ago. Certainly she couldn't wed him yet he kindled her deepest emotions, sometimes stormy and other times loving. No other man had done it, not even close, and he had always been honest with her.

In Judea they would stone me for what I'm doing.
Thulia would burn in Hell yet she reached to him, pressing hands where he wished them. She knew about Selenas' troubles, but what did Frit mean about her uncle? *The old asshole.* With a smile, she feigned a lighter tone, "What distress does my talented lancer have?"

They walked toward her horse, Fritigern explaining how Hempstalk would ride as the Christian champion. Now she had much on her mind, as much as he did, the Christians' plight falling to unlikely quarters. As he fitted the saddle to her gelding, she thought of the man who raised all three of them to young adulthood. Old Hempstalk drank every day, joining the Church as a last chance for redemption. She was his great guilt, traded in marriage to Pigfoot for two geldings, one a dud. For over four years she avoided him. Beyond Sesca, he was her only flesh and blood.

She knew a lance ride would kill him, perhaps what he wanted—to ride into death pretending to be the hero he once was.

Then her thoughts turned to Selenas, for she knew him well enough. Thulia always had a way of statement, her greatest declaration a deep breath, yet when she made a comment she never minced words. "Your brother will be leaving," she said. Frit cinched the saddle and swung to face her. She gripped his hand as he passed the reins, wishing not to let go; the only man she could ever love. He pulled her to him, their bodies pressing tight as his voice came as a mere whisper, "You are unique in a world of the meek, the good, and the spineless."

She heard the words oft enough, his way of complimenting who she was. Thulia knew he loved to think it—his bad girl, unpolished and vulgar, still the lascivious Squeezy Melons of waning childhood. Six years passed since she first tried to seduce him. Things had changed. He grew to magnificent manhood. And now the younger brother, who cared little beyond a moment's pleasure, was strapped with the welfare of Good Boy.

He hugged her tight, then tearing from her to pace for his own mount. She stood watching his stride. He seemed opaque as if a ghost, her fingertips reaching for him, not grasping, trying to feel a fading breeze.

How might it end?—to sacrifice happiness to save a soul, to trade this life for the next. The distance increased, his body and hers. They would ride in different directions... each to where they had to go.

Chapter 11: The Mordwine

The Greutungi long hall at Tyras was the largest south of Kieva, spanning a hundred feet with rafters peaking at thirty. Immense hearths flamed at each end as smoke billowed roofward to hover as a dense cloud. And the Long Table stood between them, large enough to seat fifty nobles. Each one spoke to the next or raised his voice to address a friend seated further down the bench. They all pursued trades once controlled by the seaport's Greeks, especially the herring fishery with its multitude of drying flakes covering the shoreline.

Tethering extra mounts for his ride, Aoric's envoy reached Tyras upon his third horse. He was welcomed by Old King Baduil as if a lost relative. Before he arrived, the Greutungi prepared a sumptuous banquet, the exact cause for celebration he knew not, but he was sitting just below the king and opposite the princess, a plump girl fair of hair and perhaps a healthy fourteen. Evidently the queen had expired not long ago, likely from one of a thousand maladies that claimed either gender, leaving the princess rather attached to her father.

King Baduil was obese and pushing eighty, waddling when he walked and aided by two clients. He sighted through a lazy left eye, its lid drooping, the right eye normal. And extra folds of skin hung from his chin, wobbling like a cock's wattle when he talked. Able to perform only the simplest of manly feats, Baduil assigned the more virile acts to his duce, "more than qualified" as the king expressed it. And that was the stark truth.

Aoric's man studied the aged king carefully, for he was a professional envoy with hair tied in a perfect top-knot, neat in dress, the epitome of good taste. (To his pride he once stood in the Court of Emperor Constantius... roughly about two moments while someone ran off to fetch the Chamberlain.) He always spoke in pleasantries, elusive words that escaped your average Gothic envoy. He smiled in a pleasant manner, keeping an eye discreetly from the princess except for occasional glances, while hoping Baduil would accept Aoric's plea. It seemed well past sundown. Iron torch-wells burned to their rear, each one filled with high-grade charcoal; and the flickering light cast shadows of those sitting at the rough table, projecting them to log walls as animate cameos.

Aoric's purse nestled between the king's stannum plate and his drinking horn, courteously eyed but not yet opened. Client servers strode briskly, one after the other, refilling goblets or horns with potent and dark ale. The princess drank milk. Time passed, the Tyrfingi envoy stared at an empty plate, and the king became half mulled before bestowing an utterance, his lazy eye drooping, "My duce is always late, his prerogative. He prefers to start drinking before we do, get a gallon or two as a head start. With the bulk of three men, it takes him longer."

"Ah, yes. I understand, sire," returned the envoy, "Bigger men require more of everything. I hope the purse is sufficient. And of course, there is the time factor. It took me four days to get here, which makes ten remaining."

Baduil emptied his horn as ale spilled down the front of his kaftan. He swiped the back of a hand across lips and reached down to heft the purse, then replacing it, "The Tyrfingi are a poor people these days?"

"We cannot compete with you or the High King, sire. Tyrfingi Gothia is a small place tucked between empires."

A serving woman refilled the king's horn, backing off quickly as Baduil continued, "I only control lands up to the Hypanis," he resigned, trying to sound humble, "But the High King has conquered east and west, aye, and far to the north—the Estoni, the Sclaveni, and of course, the Mordwines along the Volga and Samara, right to the Urals. At the center, Ermaneric has raised Kieva to a great trading center. All that comes and goes upon the flodus Borysthenes is taxed. Me? I am a small king who stinks of fish."

He picked up the purse to shake it, "Ah, gold. Not silver. Perhaps you Tyrfingi are richer than I thought. Let me set you at ease. The Mordwine will make the lance ride." And he grabbed his horn, downing great swallows as excess slopped to his lap. His countenance brightened, "Ah. Here he is!" and he raised his horn, ale splashing across his plate and that of the princess and envoy.

The Mordwine ducked low, passing through the Great Hall's entrance to stand straight again, his face unsmiling. With a drop of his jaw, the envoy stared at the man (if that's what he was), for the Mordwine stood seven feet tall, perhaps more, and carried a bulk of at least three hundred fifty pound-weight. He was dark haired, like most Volga Fenni, and a long scar marred almost good looks. The envoy knew his deeds, for the Mordwine had ridden as the High King's duce for several years, enabling him to subjugate northern tribes with little resistance. Only fools challenged a giant; and Ermaneric passed the Mordwine to Baduil as a "handy" gift to an aging client.

Pacing to his chair, the Mordwine sat to glance left and right, then pulling his dagger to slam its pommel hard to pine, "Where boar? Gif boar, now."

"He's SO entertaining," the king prided, all aglow.

The envoy nodded, trying to be civilized, cutting boar meat with his dagger and using the knife-tip to lift turnip cubes to famished lips. He re-caught Old King Baduil's attention, "What are you celebrating, if I might ask?"

"The Mordwine's one-hundredth kill."

"Ah, I understand, sire. Upon the lance ride?"

"No. A single bare hand. Raised him high and snapped his neck like an Indic chicken. Quite the show. Insulted the Mordwine about something."

"Yes, of course," agreed the envoy, eating all the more carefully.

The banquet ran pleasant for some time, and then varied discussions ceased in the blink of an eye. You could hear a squash drop! The Mordwine stood from his chair, yanking a server to him by her smock, running his finger along the side of her face as he growled, "Raven's feet. How old?"

As he softened his grip, she murmured, "Six and fifty." And she certainly looked it, although attractive in matronly build.

"Many childrens, Ja?

"Five," she breathed.

With his free hand, he ripped her smock to the waist, grabbing a flaccid teat, rolling the nipple between finger and thumb until it glistened of pig grease. "Wery goot," and he released her, leaning to sweep his plate and platter onto the floor. The squash remained where it fell, but the boar skittered upon its own fat, twirling once before thumping hard to a torch stand. In a quick swipe, he tore the smock further as it fell to her ankles. She stepped from it as he lifted her to table-end, knowing her fate as the Mordwine frantically tore at his belt and trousers.

The envoy stared in shock! King Baduil craned his neck, and the princess washed a big mouthful, lowering the goblet to order, "More milk," priding a white crescent above her upper lip. The nobles went back to feasting, conversing about flake yards, net mending, and the pros and cons of smoked herring versus salted herring. The hall filled with the aroma of smoke and pork. And at the far end, the Mordwine had the woman pinned upon her back, her legs splayed upon his shoulders, as he slammed away, causing the huge table to shake with each whomp, whomp, whomp.

Finally the milk came, and the king slid his own chair back as the princess climbed into his lap. She took another gulp, wiped her upper lip with her lower one, and tried to sit taller, cocking her head sideways while studying the Mordwine's physical attributes. "He's very big," she said.

The king guided a hand through her dress-top, his eyes looking roofward. She squirmed this way and that, her grin larger as she sighed, "Oh, Baduil. Not now."

In total confusion, the envoy knew not what to think! The Tyrfingi were not prudes, yet there was a limit to openness and family relationships, and the Greutungi had exceeded it. He feared to stare at anything or anyone, thinking it best to study his plate. It jumped to the whomp, whomp, whomps, as he tried spearing the last chunk of turnip with his dagger-tip.

Perhaps catching his embarrassment, the king asked, "Forgive me for being rude. Did I introduce you to my wife?"

"No, you did not, sire. I was told you were a widower," the envoy blurted in half relief.

"I am," Baduil leered, "Three times a widower, gods bless their souls. Gurda, here, is my fourth wife. Lovely girl. Loves goat milk. Good for a girl her age... but of course, you never outgrow your taste for milk... if you get my drift."

"How true," claimed the envoy in complete agreement, "A most lovely queen. Big boned. You are fortunate indeed, and I drink milk myself, when not drinking ale," then adding, "The lance ride will be at the Willows upon the first day of Naubaimbar."

Baduil leaned, watching the Mordwine, "Yes, of course. At the Willows on the first of the month," then explaining, "He likes to rape the older ones. Most consider it a compliment, but a few complain. Then we fine him, make him sacrifice a lamb or two. Amazing man. Great duce. He does everything for me... doesn't he dear?" as he winked to young Gurda.

So went the Great Hall's eve. The nobles discussed weather and herring, the Long Table shuddered to each slam, Old King Baduil reached deeper, and the princess-queen— whichever she was—grinned broadly, taking ever larger slugs of milk.

*   *   *

Five days later, the envoy arrived back in Threisbaurg, giving news of success at Aoric's home. They had their pagan champion. The magistrate tapped a finger to lips, motioning the envoy to follow him as he gimped to the ancient oak planted by the giants. "No need for women or anyone else to hear of it. You keep this quiet, understand?"

The envoy nodded, "I shall. He has agreed to arrive upon the eve before the ride. What about Athanaric?"

"I shall tell him myself, but no one else. We need not tip our advantage. You and Athanaric can intercept the giant before he gets to the Alan village. We can sequester him in a tent and treat him like a king. Bring in some old women or whatever it takes." He clamped his jaw, slamming his walking stick to the aged oak, hitting it again as if punishing the tree, and then spat, "I paid a fortune for this killer, but I claim no pride in it. The Mordwine is a disgrace to humanity, no more than an animal. Yet he fills a basic need and shall win at the Willows. I want these Christians gone, and if we must resort to hiring beasts, then so be it."

Chapter 12: A Good Day to Die

The first day of Naubaimbar

She walked at half-light, bucket in hand, much on her mind. The light wagon approached from behind, empty water buckets clattering in the rear. Thulia knew which one it was, although she hadn't heard it for six months. As in the past, she stepped aside waiting for his invitation.

"Good morning, Thulia," old Heldrid greeted, "A fine day it shall be. Let us hope the Christians prevail, for the world needs their sort. Come aboard."

An odd statement for a pagan. She knew him superficially, but sensed a decent man for one so incredibly rich. Through the years he gave the conservator several gifts, a hardwood table, larger cauldron, and four stannum plates—odd things for a man to receive, but they made life easier, as did his gifts of salt and fish. His woman jumped to the rear as Thulia climbed to take her place beside the noble. Like former times, old Heldrid passed at the crack of dawn on his way to the well, his companion a house servant, the woman filling ten buckets of water each morning. Thulia had never been inside his villa, a structure rambling in hugeness, yet she knew the rumors. It was nearly a palace. *Why do they need all that water? He's a widower and suffers from palsy.* Heldrid prodded the pair of mares and they went along their way, only a mile really, and Thulia waited for his question, never an important one and usually mundane.

"Do you still work at the horse barns, Thulia?" he wondered.

Usually it's about Pigfoot. "Yes. I enjoy horses," she returned politely.

"I hope you labor not too hard, for you oft do a man's work. A woman should not have to labor like you do."

She studied him curiously, for why should he care?

He allowed her non-answer to pass; and after a moment claimed, "You have resolve."

"Thank you," she replied, "How is your health, for I know you were feeling poorly," then adding, "I missed you." *It's always safe to discuss maladies. They come and go like woodcock.*

"Oh, I had a time of it. Thank the gods for your friend Merjands. He does wonders, absolute wonders, good doctor for these parts. So few knowledgeable healers out here in the Barbaricon. It seems he can do anything! Where he acquired so many talents, I have no idea."

"He's from the East."

"Yes, of course, but why would he come to a baurg like this?—out in the middle of nowhere? The man could teach medicine or philosophy at the University of Athens. And look at his position here. The Proclaimer. What is that? Ufar Gudja takes stock in his every word, yet still a waste of talent," he paused, shook his head, "But if he had been elsewhere, I would have taken the Journey. All well and good." They passed two girls heading for the well, and Heldrid stopped talking. Once beyond them, he studied her carefully and changed the subject, "Ah, the sun is up. It turns your hair copper. Most beauteous, like that of a goddess."

Thulia flushed and had no answer. *He is just odd and old.* Heldrid differed from most men, for he seemed to enjoy beauty, even when he couldn't find it. *Hair like a goddess?*

Compliments like that embarrassed her, for he always found a way of telling her she was attractive. In her silence, she liked the notion of it. His talent raised her spirit, even after a bad night with Pigfoot. That's why she always listened for his light wagon.

*   *   *

His eyes opened to another dawn as the conservator swore the same oath murmured each morning. *I shall eat nothing and finally die.* Raising himself upon elbows, he glanced at the child's bed to see her sleeping; then he studied the bed of his wife, seeing it empty.

He fell back to the mattress and closed eyes to wait. *She is out there*, he knew, *but not at the well.* Time passed slowly whether she was there or not, and after awhile he could hear Sesca slipping on her clothes at hearth-side. "Put a log to the coals," he mumbled, turning his face to the wall. Moments later Thulia arrived with water, and he knew she had been to the well and no place else. She could not have had time for it. Twisting his neck, he stated, "You are back early."

"Yes. There was little to talk about this morning."

Opening his eyes, he noted caustically, "That is strange. Women talk. And today they ride at the Willows. Would you women not find something in that? Who shall win? Your uncle?"

"I did speak with Heldrid. He is finally out and about again."

You find nothing to say about your uncle? Let him die, then. "Heldrid? What can you speak to him about?" not a question, a statement framed like a question.

"Nothing, really," she returned, "He just gave me a ride to the well and back."

He pushed himself to his elbows, "I told you not to accept rides from that man or talk to him. He has strange ideas."

"Really?"

"He went from this place, lived in Africa or thereabouts, and returned with Roman notions. That weak wife and fancy house. She couldn't last ten years out here."

"Heldrid has purchased three mares from you, given you gifts. Why would you speak of him like that?"

"Useless shit," he snapped, ending his words concerning the trader.

Thulia dipped a gourd ladle to the bucket, bringing water to him, "Here. Have some while it remains cold."

Turning to the wall, he answered with resolve, "No."

"You must have water and food."

"No!"

She looked to her daughter's eyes, the child affected by this constant argument. Sesca never spoke, always remaining silent. Even Pigfoot's sister tried to get her to talk, for that's where she spent most of her time, pretending to be a woman, working the spindle. "Sesca," she asked, "Would you take a blanket out to the oak?"

The child nodded, grabbing a folded wool blanket, then walking outside. Thulia turned back to her husband, lifting the gourd again as she demanded, "I want you to drink." Twisting from his bed, Pigfoot knocked the gourd from her grasp, water flying toward the hearth, making the fire hiss. Taking a step, she leaned to the empty ladle, dropping it to the bucket. Closing her eyes, she found no more than a whisper, "You make your Hell mine."

"Then go back to him," he hissed.

"Who?" she replied, her eyes wild.

"I don't know, but kill me first!" he demanded, "I'd kill you in a heartbeat, but you hide them—every last knife—where I can't reach them."

She looked down to him, expressionless, "I wish I could but no longer can."

"Why not? I beg to die!"

"I'm now a Christian, and it's forbidden."

He turned from her again. She went to the doorway, standing in early morning light, an unseasonably warm day that would become much like summer. "I'm taking you to the oak. It's too good a day to lie in darkness," then pacing back. He said nothing as she cradled him like a child in her arms. In a time seemingly distant, he weighed more than she did. Beyond the threshold, the sun hit his wasted body; and as she carried him, the conservator closed his eyes and grimaced.

"Why do you always shut your eyes?" she asked, laying him upon the blanket, her daughter standing to one side.

"So I'll not see anyone watching a man being carried by a woman."

She stood silent for the longest time, a dog barking somewhere, children laughing in the distance, a beautiful day for someone else. She pictured her uncle. *The great Christian lancer. They'll be digging his grave at sunset.* Thulia was unsure of what to stare at or think about, anything to drive the thoughts from her mind. *I cannot live like this anymore.* With her eyes watering, unwanted tears formed, and she could only think, *I must stop, or someone will see the Amazon weep.* She surveyed Pigfoot's expression, hoping to find a hint of acknowledgment under a sheet of rebuke. It was not there for either her or Sesca, just self-pity and hate. Taking her daughter's hand she walked from him toward the home of his sister, yet she paused long enough to take a deep breath.

"I'll not be back," she said.

Thulia reached the horse barns before the freemen arrived, knowing Pigfoot would die before day's end. In her departure she damned him, feeding the only emotions he knew. God could not save him, for he was a pagan. As for herself? Her anger stole the best of her, making her say it—*I'll not be back.* Too oft her temper ruled her tongue, yet she found no remorse in her declaration of autonomy. God punished the unrepentant and she would burn in Hell for it, but finally she was free of the man who murdered her unborn child.

She entered the white-spotted gelding's stall, dropping oats in the trough. The horse lunged forward, nudging with his muzzle, and she returned the gesture by running a slow hand along his neck. Thulia studied him closely, "Who were you in a previous life, which rider of the steppe? Did you make hard hooves dance?" The gelding's ears pricked with the word "dance;" and he stared at her, sensing her troubles as he nudged her again. She forced a wry grin, "You were my worth."

Old Hempstalk never told Pigfoot she wasn't a virgin, a marriage doomed from the start. The next day the man confronted her uncle, *"You swapped spoiled goods and never told me."*

"What? You didn't know what took place in your own stable?" Resentment increased, the conservator thinking she and her uncle were in collusion, her denial falling to deaf ears. Who could be blamed for the Hell in life, if not all three?—the white-spotted gelding the only innocent party, unaware of lust, desire and greed. Old Hempstalk rode the horse far less than she did, no longer attempting to discourage her. Thulia studied the animal, knowing the truth; her uncle was no worse than herself, for she coveted his prized gelding! She watched him practice the past few days. Now he would mount it one last

time, for a man his age could not survive a younger opponent. Only a miracle could save him.

The previous eve, she went to the home of Merjands, round and wattled; but he had vanished and it was fruitless to search him out. No one would know where he went. She tipped his door-latch and stepped inside, only to find his table dusty in fading light. Apparently he had been gone for weeks; and now when she craved his advice, he was elsewhere.

She stood in the horse barn in great guilt for the men and morals she abandoned. Soon the boy called Cow Eyes would arrive to fetch the gelding. Muscles around Thulia's eyes twitched as she smoothed oats along the trough. *The great Christian gallantus. Damned old fool.*

* * *

With the sun peering through the tree tops, Old Hempstalk closed his door, brightness of the day a little overwhelming. Yes indeed, this was his day to die like an aged hero should. He knew whomever the pagans chose, the man would be stronger and more agile. The opponent would have a good horse but he doubted it could be better than his. He trained the gelding from ten hands high, back when it was hardly bigger than a foal. It moved upon voice command, a whisper in its ear. Only two of three Taifali horsemen had the ability to control it, secret words from an age now gone.

He bent to the birchen arka, flipping the lid to view his pride—armor worn by the king's duce, back where battles were fought and won by real cataphracts. He pulled out his iron-covered trousers, scales treated to resist rain. He tossed his leather tunic to the table, the garment's scales clinking. Farther in the chest he lifted the huge horse blanket, entirely covered with iron scale and ninety-pound weight. Then came the mount's head piece and his own helmet, a death-mask designed to scare mortal man. *Yes, this shall be my great day in the sun. A good day to die*, hoping his big gut could still fit in the armor. The old lancer mused upon past glories—for he had grown with his name, Hempstalk, tough and sinewy, hard to cut, a little portly—and it seemed right and fitting to have just one drink. Not much, perhaps a half portion.

"Boy!" he shouted, "Bring my cup." He could hear the boy scrambling to dress on the other side of the partition. *One useless dunce. Cow Eyes! Just like a cow, he is.* While the boy went someplace as he always did, Old Hempstalk poured yesterday's water in the basin, scooping drowned flies aside. *If I still had a woman, this filthy basin would be clean. But those were the good old days. Built like her niece, she was. A fine figure of a woman.* He took a deep breath and pushed his face deep, pulling up quick to sputter, "Boy! My towel!" *Where is that damned boy? Never where you want him; always someplace else, out in the bushes taking a leak, over at that girl's house mooning big cow eyes. If he were free, the useless dud would starve to death, in a week!*

Eyes half open and blurred Old Hempstalk felt along the bench, finding yesterday's towel, or was it from the day before? Then he went to the oak barrel for a cupful. *Let idiots buy it by the amphora. What economy is that? Buy it by the barrel, cheap as you can get. It's only wine!—for God sake.* He stood straight, tipped cup to lips and drank quick, the morning's first taste always sour, "Gaah! *No sense to waste time, either. Time fleets. Where's my tunic?* And he smoothed his moustache, "Boy! My tunic!" Such a great day. He would ride into Hell like a gallantus, not in the failure of past attempts. He unsheathed his sword oft enough, wishing to fall upon it, to end the shame of his great mistake… but he never found the courage.

He was going to Hell; even God would not absolve him. What other man forced his only blood into a wretched life?—and all through covetousness. Thulia never entered his house, always turned at his approach, not one word from her lips in all these years. He tossed her out, banished her for want of a good horse.

Hempstalk scratched his groin. *Not bad wine for Crimean. A little tart, but what can you expect? Where is that bird-brained idiot, anyway.* "Boy!" he screamed, "My trousers." *That boy is off someplace again. Well, I'll have another small cupful. After all, this will be my great day.*

* * *

Selenas sat by the stream below the pool, tossing pebbles to the current while thinking of his parish, and he stood to flip one last rock into a special place. Leaving the stream to creatures therein, he paced up the hill, surveying charred timbers. The chances of him rebuilding were nil. Old Hempstalk couldn't possibly unseat the magistrate's champion. By day's end, he and Lilia would pack again, preparing the old wagon for another journey. Seemingly, all he worked for came to no good end, and now he would lead clients and congregation into the wilderness. By the stream, he asked God for a small place upon this orb. The shepherd had a flock, but the weight of responsibility crushed his breath. Where would they go?

He inhaled afresh, resolving to not let it show. As Wulfilas did, he would smile in assurance to every new convert of the Gothic Church. To present less than a vital spark would leave them unsure of their own new life. That could not and would not happen.

Beyond the house, Lilia played with little Waldrid. Yes, laughter, a sound that should have been foreign. She giggled like a girl as the boy chased her in circles, a stick in his hand. She looked over to him and smiled. *How can she possibly do that?* Checking the angle of the sun, his mind turned to the Willows and his brother. His position as presbyter heaved a strain upon their relationship, envy in Frit's eyes. In truth he did abdicate at that moment of baptism, laying responsibility for his father's clients in Frit's lap, pinning his brother's position as leader of the Balths at the age of sixteen. Frit might have a good future if he applied himself. Selenas knew his brother well enough, a young man with a far-roving mind, certainly not anchored in tribal affairs. At most council meetings he was absent, out hunting or fishing. *And now he has Thulia distracting him. A shame. Aoric is the judge, but Frit holds higher blood.*

*   *   *

The sun swept brightness across the fields, morning shadows cooling the river. Rustam and Frit stood outside Old Hempstalk's house, neither man having faith in the old cataphract's boast. Hempstalk meant well, stayed sober on the Sabbath, but they knew the man for what he was. At last the boy answered the door to step aside with eyes cast down.

The two men entered to find the Taifalus sitting before his armor, some of it on the table, the rest on the floor. Slamming his cup to wood, the old duce stood, teetering one way and the other as he declared, "A great day! Great day."

In disappointment Frit leaned to the inside wall, eyes to his boots, listening to the old cataphract. Rustan seated himself upon the bed, folding hands across knees. He stared first at Old Hempstalk, then to Frit while shaking his head.

"I shall ride like the wind! Punch a hole in that son-of-a-bitch as big as a buckler. Who is it anyway? No matter. He'll either topple me or I'll him," and then he turned this way and that, "Where is my lance? That's the whole point. Right?"

Frit raised his eyes roofward, "Something like that."

Rustan fell back upon the bed, scratched his chin and said nothing.

"You can count on me; I shall do it—cheap obligations falling to a hair of the dog," murmured Frit.

The house went silent. In his quiet manner, the boy slid out the door, closing it quietly. Old Hempstalk looked over to Rustan, then down to his cup, raised his eyes to Frit's, and finally dropped his gaze to the table. As he rolled the empty vessel in his hands he began to weep, at first slowly, then to a point where mucus dripped from his nostrils, wetting his moustache. "I'm sorry," he wept as he fell to the chair.

Frit turned his eyes from the man and those of Rustan, intently searching chinks of old walls. He was incredibly uncomfortable, never recalling Hempstalk in such mental straits. Imbibed yes, but never unhinged. Quietude expanded and floated across the room, each man hearing others breathing, so quiet that a dried pea would resound if dropped upon the dirt floor.

Suddenly, from beyond the door, a woman's voice scolded the boy, "What do you mean?—'He's drunk.' He can't be drunk because he must ride at noon!"

The door opened with a force almost parting hinges! Her face was livid and she walked past Frit without uttering a word, just like she'd never met him. Stepping before her uncle, Thulia spat, "Look at yourself. Not just you, but the whole damned lot—feeling sorry for yourselves, a bunch of little boys! A good woman weeps far less than what my eyes have seen this morning."

Only then did she acknowledge Frit and Rustan. Slipping off her light coat, she tossed it to Rustan, yet facing the man who was her lover, "Leave him be. I'll have the boy run for cold water. This is woman's work."

Frit pulled a hand from the wall, standing straight. Rarely did she admit being a woman, at least the domestic kind, yet more woman than most. "How will you sober him up in time? What is this?—the day's third hour? In three more he must be at the Willows."

Rustan swung from the bed, dropping her coat to it, "Perhaps she can. I say we leave."

"And what?" returned Frit, "Simply pretend that a great champion will ride to my brother's defense?" He stared at the open door, seeing the boy reach for a bucket, and tried to think positive. There had to be one good statement to help turn the morning's catastrophe around. This was his family, partially denied yet no less close to him than Selenas, perhaps closer—this feisty flame and portly drunkard.

Spinning back to Lilia's father, he admitted, "You're right. If anyone can save a day, it would be this woman," and he cracked an abashed grin, "In dealing with men, she's more capable than most."

*   *   *

Aryante! It took me forever to reach you. Folds of time have passed, and all is blackness. Are you weaker?

No, I am stronger because more of me wells forth. We are drifting further apart yet ever closer as she accepts me and all her trials. She fights everything, even what is true and right.

Have I been a poor teacher? She knows what is correct, but she remains headstrong.

You have done well enough. I wither beyond the bone and exist by weak thoughts, the sign of your success. Give her more of me, my mirror or akinakes, and waste no time in the past. Let me go.

I cannot! Memories sweep through my heart.

Oh, Merjands the all-wise! If you cannot understand our problem, who might? Let... me... go.

All was quiet. *Aryante? Are you still with me?* Silence was broken by the "tsit, tsit" of a yellowhammer scraping its song directly above. He opened eyes to peer up to gnarled branches as nostrils filled with mildew's must. Laying supine, he moved an arm, then the other. *Well, I'm still alive.*

He pushed elbows back to almost sit upright, viewing his torso, yet his legs seemed replaced by oak leaves. Again a "tsit, tsit" from the brazen bird. Just to check reality, he moved a leg as the brittle coverlet slid aside. With a grunt, a second and third, he arose to unsteady feet beneath the oak tree, brushing dried leaves from his black robe. The yellowhammer squawked again and he looked up to see where it was, checking the angle of the sun. *Ah, mid morning. Now where's my staff?*

Merjands studied the oak grove's layer, autumn leaves covering fronds once sparse yet green; and toadstools, no longer here or there, now lived in earthworm's dreams. A yellowhammer? They never arrived at the Pontic until late Oktobre or Naubaimbar. He tugged his cinnabar and muttered, "Gods forbid! I've been here two months! No wonder I'm hungry," his voice scaring the yellowhammer into flight. "Good riddance. They always were nasty birds."

He scuffed leaves, dragging a foot in a circle, "Ah, ha! My staff." With a creak, he bent a leg and fell to knee, retrieving his cambutta from its solace. *These hermitages are becoming more and more difficult, especially when you sleep too long.* And he was sure the young woman probably needed him for something important. She usually did. (He could feel it in his bones.) *Probably another family emergency. If anyone could whip up a good crisis, Thulia can.*

Chapter 13: At the Willows

The sun reached the height of its arc, seemingly too bright for Naubaimbar first, and soon enough the ride would commence. Selenas stood beside Frit wearing his robe of the sacraments, for he'd not hide in secular clothes upon this day and wanted the other side to know his colors. He believed his own flock would respect him for it.

"You cannot stand there as an intelligent man and not know why the judge proclaimed this contest," hissed Frit, perhaps thinking the black habit out of place. Hearing no rebuttal he continued, "The life—the very existence of the kunja—lies in the Sword of Tyr. It shines as the symbol of courage. To *Tyrfing* clings the strong man who leads the people; and to him come Others from ends of the earth. They kneel to pledge their own swords. In this gathering of tribes, the Whole remains strong. And Christianity will tear it down."

Aye, the Gothic creed, thought Selenas, *and well said. But Tyr is a dying god, like the tribe itself.* "It keeps them from the true path to God."

"What true path?—the path to the grave? Only in death will a Christian find redemption," snapped Frit, "That's what you teach; and the poor ones, the unfree, all see this as their final escape. It's a fantasy, designed for the weak."

"No!" the presbyter returned, "You have it wrong. The path leads to eternal life. Many are the rich who see this truth. From Syria to Rome, even the best families come to the Church."

"Well, you have no ch…," Frit stopped mid-sentence, noticing the pagan rider approach along the Willows.

The brothers stood along an incline, lost in a crowd of five thousand or more. Twenty people deep, it lined the hillside a quarter mile long, fathers setting a daughter or son upon their shoulder, women in the front. The plain ran before them flat and narrow, hay cut, with the cattle moved beyond. Before them stood the Willows, a line of trees buffering the river.

Far up the field came a singular rider, Aoric's choice. He paced his mount along the Willow's shade to reach center plain, a bronze Gothic helm upon his head. Draped to his knees with armor, he reined his black horse to a stop; a man so huge that his toes swung a foot below the mount's belly. The armor was heavy, rawhide thick, iron plates shining in the sun. Any cataphract laboring under its burden could only sweat, and so he was also called a clibinarius—an oven man. With quick hand movements, the lancer turned his horse to the right, then swinging left, finally steering his mount forward again. He did it to let them see him, for he was proud of his reputation and size. With no eye or nose piece, his spangenhelm came to a conical point with iron flaps hinged down over his cheeks. He wanted the crowd to view his face, the bite of his glare, the scar running from temple to chin. Almost dying once, he would not live forever. But this was too good a day to meet the earth.

Oh, my God! breathed Selenas, *It's the Mordwine.* Yes, a man huge at seven feet, never defeated upon the ride even when wounded by a lance head. A full giant of a man, he was foul of deed, tried more than once for rape, paying cows and sheep beyond number. Rumors claimed that one victim was his own mother, and he once slit a man's throat for rebuking his penchant.

Halfway down the line, the magistrate sat upon his wagon, having no intention of watching the contest upon a game leg. "Now there be a lancer!" he shouted down to his son.

With a grin, Athanaric raised a clenched fist to yell, "The Mordwine!" and half the crowd echoed his gesture, shouting the man's signum over and over again. Glancing back to his father, he proclaimed, "This is just the beginning."

Pushing through the crowd, warriors ran from the hillside, crossing the narrow plain to line up along the Willows. Drawing long-swords and holding bucklers to the sun, they slammed sword to shield, chanting at every third beat. Thump. Thump. Thump. "Mordwine!"

Not far from Selenas, a woman moaned, "This be a sad day for Christians." His heart froze at the chill of her statement, with his own champion nowhere in sight. Turning to Frit, he mumbled, "They shall win by default."

"I was afraid this would happen. You can never trust a wine-bibber."

Across the field, warriors continued their chant, the people looking, waiting. Suddenly the canto stopped. From the other direction came a second rider, sitting tall, straight, and barrel-chested. He wore old armor, iron scales browned by urine and boiled eggs, not shining yet draped upon a hero of battles past. He held the Taifali standard high—a Sarmatian draco—blood red, hollow and filled with air, its dragon mouth eating the wind. His horse rode under the weight of its master, its own armor reaching its knees. The mount's mask covered its head from nose to ears, affixed with an iron horn and bronze-studded straps. Yet the horse had a royal presence, its neck bent with the grace of a great gelding. The crowd could only stare.

At the forefront of the Alans, Rustan murmured to Stefan the horsebreaker, "Who would believe it? Tenacious as his name." He recognized the lazy-man's armor, browned to rust in simple utility. And that evil helm!—formed by an ancient smith. *Old Hempstalk has sinew beyond mine. He wants to end it correctly, die as a man should, on the field of courage.* The Taifalus rode as an aged veteran, the Mordwine twenty years younger and a huge man in full prime.

The crowd hushed to silence as Old Hempstalk approached to face them, the highest of royal lancers; for he once sat at the Great Bench to quaff mead with Thiudebalth—the Bold Lord. Children (who never knew him beyond old tales) pointed to his helm in awe, the mask of death!—wrought upon a forge in a time now gone—eyes staring black, as if no real eyes were behind them. Yes, a demon's mask reaching his chin. Side-guards swept down to protect his cheeks and ears, and a web of mail circled down the nape of his neck.

He began the horse ride, the age-old dance of mount and man. No one had seen it for a generation! It came from the oldest memory, far off across the steppe—the great *djerid!*—the artistic ride of the ancient nomad.

The mount was a white-spotted gelding, a cataphract's greatest pride, the Pale Horse of Biblical fame. Raising a foreleg to a graceful curve, he pranced but once, head bowing to the crowd to quickly rise. Then the horse did likewise with his other foreleg, alternating as he danced before them. Hempstalk swung his mount and paced it to Aoric; and with every step the gelding paused, holding a forefoot high without movement. Not one person could utter a word upon this day of the dance. Turning his mount, the old rider came back up the line of people, stopping before Selenas and Frit. He spiked the dragon pennant to the ground and raised arms to his sides, palms open to face them.

Rustan felt a buzz along his neck, *He's imitating the cross!* thinking of his own talents when younger, a horseman of repute yet not a lancer, and knowing he could not equal the dejerid before him. He watched the cataphract lean forward and whisper to his horse. Instantly, the mount fell to knees and bowed. *Never—in all the days of the tribe—has anyone seen a dance like this. It comes from the heart of a great rider.*

*   *   *

In a leap, the horse came to all fours!—and the cataphract guided it back to the field, reining to face his foe. The two riders positioned themselves facing each other. Of the two, the elder had an edge, the sun to his back. From under the Willows, two young warriors ran out with lances, each shaft twelve feet long, thick as a man's wrist. With a blue pennant behind an twelve-inch head, the first contus was given to the Mordwine. He held it high, the crowd yelling as he shook it to the sun. Likewise, a white pennant lance was given to Old Hempstalk, a cross embroidered upon it. The lancers faced the people and then rode further apart. Turning to each other, they held lances vertical, ready for the ride. Each knew what was expected. He had to topple his opponent to the ground, not necessarily kill him. Once unseated from his saddle, that man was either dead or wounded, but he could not remount.

Standing upon his wagon the judge held up an empty scabbard, "Let the sword of victory go to the winner." As the signal to ride, he tossed the scabbard to the field. Digging heels to mounts the riders charged, their horses galloping two feet apart as they passed. Continuing a distance they stopped and turned, the sun now to the younger man's back. They were feeling each other out, looking for "soft spots" in the opponent's armor, noticing how the other man controlled his horse.

Again they rode at full speed, both lances remaining vertical as geldings almost touched in the pass. They turned once more, each pausing. The crowd began to murmur, then a heavy buzz, each comment drowning those of the next. Moments passed, the riders and mounts like statues, no movement except a breeze upon their pennants.

In unison the cataphracts dug heels a third time, the distance closing as both horses gained speed. Then in one quick movement, the Mordwine dropped his reins, couched his lance to a doubled grip, and aimed for his opponent's chest, the lance hitting so hard it cracked like pine to a bolt of lightning!

Almost torn from his saddle, Old Hempstalk held to the reins, his mount wheeling from the impact as his master dropped his lance. With difficulty the Taifalus regained his composure, rubbing his chest to find no blood. His mask of death turned to Selenas and nodded.

Again the crowd yelled their names, both men riding back a hundred paces as young men ran to them with new weapons. For a moment Old Hempstalk let his lance-tip rest upon the ground, then lifted it to ready. Upon the fourth pass, both riders adjusted the balance of their shafts, neither looking for blood. They turned to face each other again—the last ride, and they both knew it. Old Hempstalk leaned to his gelding's ear, whispering. The mount nodded yes as it pawed earth with a fore-hoof. A hundred paces away, the Mordwine's horse seemed unnerved, moving to one side as his master fought to control him.

The Taifali rider thought beyond the lance, knowing there was more to the ride than sharp iron and the advantage of weight. *The Mordwine is the heavier, stronger rider. He rides for power, not accuracy; and he chose his mount for size, a gelding large enough to carry all that weight. The horse appears not well trained, neither smart nor steady. Look at it! Skittish. Now is the time to make my move—to do one right thing in my life—to topple Aoric's pagan design.*

Before the Mordwine's horse calmed, Old Hempstalk dug heels to ribs, the mount galloping in a fury. For once, in the heat and burden of the day, the Taifalus had an edge. In a flash of a ride long gone, the Mordwine saw the lance-tip aimed high, not at his chest but at his face! Who knows what he thought?—how the scar got there or who inflicted it, for the scar was the only part that remained.

Unnerved, the giant aimed square for his opponent's body so he couldn't miss, trying to move his head sideways just before lance tips met. Yet Old Hempstalk's weapon pierced his neck, snapping it, driving him from the saddle. At the same moment, the pagan's contus found its mark, slamming hard to the Christian's right shoulder as he toppled to the field.

The ground shook!—as both riders hit the hard earth. And dust flew in a brown cloud. People waited, yet neither cataphract moved. As dust settled, the magistrate stood in shock, his thoughts screaming. *It cannot end like this, with no winner!* The crowd around him spoke not a word, all surprised at the outcome. Both down and dead?

Silence reigned. Then an old man stepped from the crowd to the field, "What kind of gods watch us? Could not *Tyrfing* defeat this new one? Nay! Each god disappoints his own, for they hide in the bed of impotence. There are no gods, only men who mold gods from dreams." A woman began to sob and fell to knees, her husband reaching to comfort her. They would make the trek as exiles. Again silence was followed by a hail of doubts, until someone shouted, "One of them lives!"

*   *   *

Lying on his back, the surviving lancer bent one leg, arching it and trying to roll over as his left arm moved from side to side. Old Hempstalk was alive yet wounded, perhaps mortally. Selenas broke from the throng and ran for the downed lancer, accompanied by young Safrax.

Fritigern tried to remain at the sideline, one half of him wanting to divorce himself from the Christian presence, the other half worried for his mentor. More than anything, he wished the old lancer might recover, to sit again—if only in reverie—at his king's side. Yet blood seeped between scales of thick armor. Frit found his legs moving across the field as his brother and Safrax fell to their knees beside the injured. Selenas pulled the demonic helmet from the cataphract as bronze hair tumbled from it; and Safrax blurted, "It's Thulia."

"In Heaven's name," gasped Selenas, "What has she done?"

Oblivious to the wounded or those concerned, Aoric yelled his prognosis. It could not be a draw! Overwrought by events he had difficulty being impartial, or pretending to be so, and his statement boomed, "This is a sham! Whoever heard of such a thing?—a professional lancer killed by woman. A giant, mind you!" He worked his jaw, eyes wider than the Danube, "But it has no bearing, one way or the other. She is not a king's table companion and the Mordwine wins by default."

"What?" cried Stefan, his arms flying, "Nay can a deadamon win!"

"I think the brikan-meister is correct," admitted the Squinter.

Aoric glared at his son. For once the seed of his loins had spoken intelligently... yet only in contradiction. He puffed and shook his walking stick, "Well, they had no champion to begin with. He never showed up, and they still lose."

Jumping to his feet, Selenas wheeled to the Arians in the crowd, "Bring blankets quick! And a wagon!"

Frit knelt to Thulia, pressuring a palm to her wound, his mind locked frozen. His eyes watered, hands quivering, no control over them or his thoughts. *What if she dies?* Only once before had the notion struck his mind, for he was too young to remember his mother's death and too childish to lament his father. And he knew this day was far worse than the one in Transylvania with Selenas dying upon the road.

He wanted to take her wounds, no matter how bad, how deep, and heap them upon himself, a surrogate who could bleed and die in her stead. Yet the thought was a fractured wish; and plunging back to the real world, Frit caught her left hand as it clenched in pain. Her other arm moved not at all! *My brother's God help her. She's all broken inside.*

Chapter 14: Not Since Penthesilea

That afternoon under the oak, the conservator opened eyes to view the sun one last time. There seemed no reason to cry out, to finally ask for that last sip of water. The taste of it was all he craved, yet why give anyone the satisfaction of seeing him beg? A hard man all his life, there had been no softness in him. Only women were soft, the very reason they were secondary. Fitting that he might die alone, no weeping for him, for he wished not to see or hear it.

After all the months, dragging from one to the next in a stream of nothingness, he would finally reach his simple goal. She knew it, the tainted bitch, yet she left him without a decent word. *I'll not be back*, she said, the filthy whore. He mashed remaining teeth as muscles in his neck tightened. Who else hardened her resolve?—for only he, Pigfoot and no one else, spat on her feet when she burned the mutton, or when she tried to rise above her station. Yes, scorn, the greatest of all lessons; yet she only tolerated him, not a drop of respect. He never asked for affection, yet at the thought of her infidelity his breath came hard and shallow, and he damned well knew she was seeing another man. She was worse than a harlot—an adulteress—and she should burn with her lover swinging from a rope above her.

Repeatedly she cheated on him, even Sesca was not his but the spewing of some noble prick she laid with, out in the bushes or deep in the hay. He had her only once, the nuptial night, yet she dropped the child seven months later. He always stared at Sesca's features, trying to figure which young stud she came from.

Not another man in all three tribes had such a shameless wife! He believed she came as an easy trade, but there was no bargain in promiscuity. Whenever she could, she flaunted herself, lifting a skirt to expose a shapely leg, always wearing wrap-around tunics, never quite cinched in the front, not even in cold weather.

Closing eyes for a moment, he reviewed years with her. She spent too much time away from the house, returning home late, all out of breath. *"I love to ride,"* she always claimed, but it wasn't horses she rode but a hundred hard lances, one after the other. She was a talented flirt, sly in her intrigues, and he could never prove it—not once!—and now it was too damned late. He garnered a mordant grin, like death itself, for he had a few good days in better times. He found a way of putting the wanton whore in her place, slapping her down verbally. *"I gave two geldings to Hempstalk, but you're not worth one."* The first time he said it, she wept. A great day it was, to see tears roll from the Amazon. After awhile she hardened to it, the shameless slut.

Ah, yes. And the family sword. He never used it when he could, for he came not from acclaimed fighters, yet he sealed her grasp from it. More than anything she wanted to wield it, to practice slaying unholy demons... or whatever she dreamt they were. She once claimed, *"Someday I'll protect women from beasts like you."* Too much imagination beneath those mountains. *What right does a woman have to a sword? Let her swing her frigging stick.* He would take his sword to the grave where she could never touch it, his final act of sweet revenge.

Yes indeed, Pigfoot wins. He knew they called him that, all the bastards who thought themselves better than he was. Again his blood boiled, his heart pounding as his face twisted in the anger of a man who made two great errors— marrying her and falling from his horse. Under the shade of the oak, he stared to a far colder place, empty and ready. The conservator's fingers clenched involuntarily, his arm muscles stiffening, hating her and himself to the end.

*   *   *

The healer's arrival at Thiudgards seemed to take forever, the afternoon creeping slow as hot water grew cold, servants reheating it. Frit paced across the house, one way then the other, stepping outside to look down the path and returning along a row of reaching shadows. *The day is fleeting, like sparks of life itself.*

Back in the house, he went beyond the draped partition to the far room where a shuttle rustled in years past, thinking of a woman lost yet never truly grieved. Returning to the bed, he perceived life's finale, that irreversible and empty void. *They are wrong in their assessment. No day is a good day to die.*

Finally Merjands showed up, tall in over-aged countenance, wire-thin with a wispy beard plunging from chin-tip, the strands timeless and streaming to his stomach. His hair reflected the beard, pure white and no shorter as it hung straight along his back. Among his arts he was a lekseis—*one who casts spells upon disease*—a herbalist and balmist, a philosopher's sage, and most profoundly the one Proclaimer of all the gods.

He came through the entrance lugging a satchel hung from a shoulder strap, its leather seams bulging of mysterious nature. When Frit was younger he quizzed upon its contents and the man shrugged, *"Nothing much. Potions and salves. Things that wriggle when placed in water. The usual tripe."* Merjands exuded knowledge of the pontifically wise; and in the past, Frit's own Greek teacher consulted the man upon points of correct grammar; for Merjands knew grand and ancient tongues no longer spoken. Yet above all, he was a healer of mind and flesh; and having ministered to Thulia many times, she spoke fondly of him. *"He's my life-thread guide,"* whatever that meant.

Dropping his staff and satchel next to the bed, Merjands explained, "I have been off on a hermitage trying to find a giving woman, unaware that the younger one would try to patch the world of men. I should have known she was here, not there."

Frit had trouble following the man's gist, and his immediate concern was Thulia. Upon the bed she slipped in and out of consciousness, now wincing in pain. The healer dropped upon its edge, one leg tucked under itself, his other foot upon the floor, with Fritigern kneeling at bedside. When Merjands remarked, "This is going to hurt," his words seemed to float by her like a shadow-lark. Thulia's expression remained unchanged, almost blank; and with a quick sideward glance to Frit, she announced calmly, "I left him to die this morning."

Today was going to be an ending—Pigfoot's or hers. Frit assumed she rode for Hempstalk, Selenas, and the Christians, yet there was more to it. He could sense it. Perhaps even the Amazon had reached that caustic divide where the mind whispers filthy little yearnings, a good day to die.

Leaning to the bed, Merjands began his manipulations, pressing one hand to her shoulder, grabbing her forearm with the other while pulling her arm at the same time. She gasped and blacked out. That part, the most painful, was over, and the healer could work upon the wound unhindered. At the Willows she steeped in sweat. Now her uncle's armor was so tight they couldn't slip it over her head, and Merjands began cutting it from her torso, using a sharp knife until it dulled, then switching to a second blade while slicing through the leather and tunic at the same time. The old man worked the blade carefully between iron scales until her upper body was free from constraint. Taking a good look at the woman, he gasped, "How could she breathe?" Not answering, Frit lifted her torso while the healer pulled the armor from her back, dropping it to the floor.

"No wonder they thought she was Cannabas," the old man observed, "She squashed her bosom to her stomach trying to get that thing on."

The statement passed by the young Balth. He stood back from the bed as the man slathered urine paste upon the puncture, wrapping it with linen strips while muttering softly, "Aryante. Aryante," whispering as if scolding.

Frit had never heard anything like it, "Aryante? What's that? A healing chant?"

"What?" asked the elder man, his eyes snapping from her.

"You were crooning the word *aryante*."

"Oh? Well, so I was. Yes, a chant to ward off evil spirits," and he nodded quickly, "You can never be too careful. Chanting. Superstition. All good stuff in its own way. Positive reinforcement, if you get my gist. Aryante. It works every time. A lot like booga, booga."

"Will she live?" asked Frit in a lower voice.

Merjands cracked thin lips, "Oh, yes. I think the *aryantes* saved her. She had a dislocated shoulder, enough to faint from the pain. The wound is minor although a large bruise. She'll have to wear a sling for a week." Still crouched upon the bed, the old man brushed her cheek with gnarled fingers, much as a swain would. Then he squeezed her hand.

Frit wondered at this step beyond repair, trying to utter something appropriate. "She's a strong woman."

"Rather strong-willed," agreed the healer with his trace of a grin, "The gods make few women like this—not since Penthesilea. Of course, this one killed her Achilles and Penthesilea didn't." He swung from her, leaning to stuff salves and linens back to his leather satchel.

Frit studied his bearing, surprised Merjands would chant shamanistic gibberish, yet impressed by an educated Alan (if that's what he really was). He knew the sage spoke Kohtani Saka as only an Alan could. He also quoted Homer as if once living in the Poet's world; and everyone acknowledged his wisdom. But the Proclaimer had a well hidden past. Through slips of tongue, the Tyrfingi knew he arrived from Issyk-Kul on the eastern steppe, yet he had schooled at Antioch and then taught medicine in the Far East. He arrived in Threisbaurg shortly after Thulia did, his motives vague, *"When the pupil is ready, the Magus arrives."* In a decade's time, he aged not a day, only his cinnabar wagging longer. The Greek surmised that Merjands was at least a centenarian, married "forever" to a wife who died long ago. And he always walked with a staff, never riding a horse. *How strange a man he is.*

Standing tall with his accoutrements, the sage nodded his farewell and departed, opening the latch to greet the curious as a servant almost fell through the doorway. The wise man put a finger to lips, a cautioning "schhh" as he quietly closed the door behind him.

The house of Thiudebalth fell to quietude no louder than an Amazon's breathing, inaudible and barely perceptible. Frit dragged a chair to the bed, studying the woman and bandage, reflecting upon boyhood and a tutor who forced him to read Greek. Penthesilea? *Yes, this one lived.* Merjands was medically proficient, yet Frit held distrust in healers, for they purveyed inexact science. *Strips of linen and stinking pastes. What do they really know?*

Pulling the blanket to her neck, he sat to her again. The physician was right. No other woman could have passed herself off as Old Hempstalk. She rode without peer, the Horse Dancer. Yet there was far more to her, that defiant spirit only the willful had, also a quality in him. Thulia loathed rules, men's rules, defying her uncle until he finally gave up and married her off to Pigfoot. Frit hated to see her go, especially to a man like that. Even back then he knew he loved her. The other things he cared for—fishing for marbled trout, hunting roebuck, or dogging boars—all seemed inane.

He stared at her features, high cheekbones and full lips, a face tanned overly dark, as was her torso, oft stripped to the waist at the barns. The noble and free and unfree alike, all saw what wrought the Amazon above other women. No modesty in her, only pride in a Sarmatian heritage. He reached to her, brushing hair lightly. Such beautiful hair, a true cast of molten bronze—hot enough to burn men to the bone, a superficies of the great flame within—untamable, unquenchable.

She was named for an isle in the Sea of Ice. Legend claimed steam boiled under its glaciers, hot springs welling forth. She was like Ultima Thule, great warmth under a frigid surface. Why couldn't others view it?—manifold beauty unrecognized. He never could keep eyes from her. Now he would watch over her, however long it might take, until she opened those fire-green eyes.

Chapter 15: Spirit of the Bear

Selenas stood reticent in the eve's twilight, wondering why he was summoned to the Alan meeting. The entire tribe, even the young, gathered around a huge cauldron suspended from a tripod. Buckets of mare's milk poured as the fire crackled and children grinned. An older woman added honey, stirring the mixture with an iron ladle, and others nodded as if agreeing she was doing it correctly. Off to one side everyone formed a huge circle, all sitting cross-legged. Rustan motioned Selenas to sit beside him although the grass was cold and damp.

An old noble stepped to center and cleared his throat, surveying those before him. The circle hushed; and when the last murmur ceased he began his speech, "We have asked the Christian priest to participate in this ceremony. Words have fallen to me because the Chief Priest," and he swept a palm toward Ufar Gudja, "claims this eve too emotional and asks me to take his stead."

The older woman stepped through the circle, handing a round-bottomed cup to the old noble. He took it with both hands, raised it to the heavens, lowering it to look directly at Selenas as he cracked a smile, "We have a Goth among us. I am sure he is unfamiliar with our ritual, so I will explain. The cup is wood because it grew from the earth, mother of the deer and Alani. The bottom is round so it must be shared, passing from one person to another. The handle is gold, symbol of nobility and wealth, not in coin but in heritage. And the handle is shaped like Artur—the Bear—who is not a god but a spirit.

When the progenitor became wise, he carried this cup to White Mountain; and there he planted his sword, offering mare's milk and honey to the spirit of the Bear."

Selenas raised a hand, catching the old noble's attention, "Who was the progenitor?"

The noble rolled his eyes and caught Rustan's glance, "He was Alanus, the same Alanus whose blood flows in your wife and son. If you wonder about the deer, know it is the provider, giving us food and sinew. Aye, sinew for bow and string, and for the soul, to trice us up within."

"And the bear?" asked Selenas.

"Our guardian—Protector of the People. A brave warrior is given his name—Artur—if he is selfless and pure of heart. Few have earned it. I know nothing of your Xristos except what I hear, but I think he must be like the Bear, to defeat evil around us. Now I say what Ufar cannot, for this milk is getting cold. This tribal crisis needs the spirit of the Bear to protect us." He stepped forward to Selenas, offering the wooden cup, "If you will accept the Bear, then sip the milk and pass the cup to Rustan who will do the same and pass it on. This sharing of humanness is called the Grail—older than the tribe itself. Where this sharing came from, I do not know. So aged it is. We ask you to accept the Grail and the Bear. Perhaps you cannot understand the significance of this revered cup. You can leave and no one will think the worse."

Selenas took the cup in shaking hands, his emotions welling; and he understood why Ufar could not recount the premise of this sharing. It choked words and made the tallest man shrink beneath the smallest star. This Grail ceremony was exactly like the Eucharist, this wooden cup no less than a chalice. He closed eyes and sipped, passing the vessel to Rustan.

The old noble continued, "When we lived in wagons, the Huns rode from the witches womb to split the proud Alani. Some fled north to forests thick, to hide like fowl from wolves. Others became the Hun's vassals. The rest of us crossed many rivers and came here, pledging ourselves to Thiudebalth and the Tyrfingi, just as the Taifali did long ago. Now Thiudebalth has been replaced by a close-sighted man." He looked to Selenas, "Before you came, the council held a meeting, deciding to remain together if we could find an honorable way to break the foedus. If we split—Christian Alani going, us pagans staying—it would be the end of us. We must again find courage. It still lives! What did we see at the Willows? Such a great ride it was!—for I cannot recall a better one. The champion carried the blood of Alanus. Another Aryante! If it takes a Taifala to remind the Alani of who we are, then she has done a gracious deed."

Rustan entreated the old noble, "How can we remain together? Half are Christians like myself. We must go, the judge's edict."

Raising his hand, the old noble answered, "That is true. But this Christian priest accepted the Bear. If we likewise accept his Xristos, all of us must leave. The Bear will protect us as it always has, and we can remain together. Upon the dawn I shall pack my wagon, as will my son and grandson. Let the spirit of the Bear place us in this new god's hands."

Addressing the seated, Rustan asked, "Well now. How many others are now Christians?"

Tribesmen looked to one another, the women doing likewise; and a hand raised, then a second and third, a fourth and fifth. Selenas was overwhelmed; for such was the show of hands that not a pagan remained in the ranks. Nobody had actually been baptized, a small matter really. It was the hand that counted. Time enough for souls in the future.

Sitting upon a stool at the hearth, Selenas held little Waldrid's hands, raising and lowering his knee as if it were a horse, the boy riding in glee. He thought of the previous eve and Thulia's ride. A lay member brought news while Lilia went down to the stream for water, a relief to hear the Amazon's injury wasn't serious. He smiled to his wife's approach, "Thulia has a small puncture and sore shoulder, the total damage from a giant."

"She rode in God's hands," claimed Lilia, "We should reassess our thoughts, I think. All of us."

"Reassess? What do you mean?"

"I was tainted by rumors—the Trollop of Threisbaurg. I always knew you stayed clear, but she has a decent side, none of us aware of it."

Selenas gave a sheepish smile. "Actually we grew up together, more or less. We simply took different paths." Setting Waldrid to the floor, he added, "She almost did it."

Lilia studied him in silence, then asking, "Did you thank her?"

He tried to find a reason, "For the attempt? Frit offered his resources and she's recuperating. I'll not disturb them."

"Oh? Then perhaps before we leave," she mumbled, sipping water from a bronze cup as she took her place next to him. Lilia watched the coals glow to a yellowish red, the last warmth for many days, and she mused aloud, "Our final morning to sit before the hearth. There are more of us now, an entire tribe."

The statement pierced her husband's thoughts, his own mind on the mounts of central Transylvania and the Gepids who now lived there, a people with a language nearly Gothic. They migrated with the Tyrfingi generations ago when they all came down from Germanic lands. Gepids had lived in the mountains so long they were known as "dark-thought ones," a connotation that bothered Selenas.

He would bargain for land with their chieftain, find some equitable payment. Selenas had cattle, always good for bartering, especially for land of little value to that northern tribe. One man's Hell can be another's paradise. The forests of Transylvania were thick, not enough pasturage for large horse or sheep herds. Superstitions kept people at a distance—stories of dwarves stealing children to work their mines, tales of head-hunting men and gold-guarding griffins. He grinned at the thought of them.

Seeing his expression, Lilia noticed, "You have a fine smile on, my husband."

"I was thinking of childhood monsters. Some adults still believe in them: the one-eyed man and trolls. That sort of thing. They abound in Transylvania."

"You had better pack your sword to protect us," she laughed, catching Waldrid by the arm to pull him too her.

"I think the Good Book will suffice."

They both knew how triumphs occurred through adversity—the trials of Arius, exiled yet returning to kneel before the emperor, delivered from the wilds of Illyricum to found the Church carrying his name. Their own flock grew sizeable, neither of them realizing how large it actually became. Selenas never knew Thulia joined his congregation. She never stepped forward at baptismal, perhaps a member of what he called the "silent fringe."

*   *   *

Holding her daughter's hand, Thulia stood beside damp soil as freemen packed it, her eyes watching shovels thump hard. There seemed a vengeance to it, the way they slammed spades to dirt, as if the man beneath took their hits. Below the knoll, a light wagon stopped, the driver looking their way. He climbed down with difficulty to stand for some time, wiping his forehead, again peering up toward her. He turned to the vehicle, his hands resting upon it. Then he climbed aboard and left. Why did Heldrid favor Pigfoot?

She looked down to Sesca, the little girl watching the men work, no expression upon her face. *What did we do to the child in all those years of hating one another?* mused Thulia in guilt, *He despised me equally for what I was and was not.* Lifting eyes, she studied his sister and her husband as they stood across the grave. *What do they think of me?*

As if hearing the thought, his sister stepped forward, standing upon the very place where he was, hardly after the men finished tamping it. "What will you do now, Thulia?" she inquired, placing a hand to Sesca's head.

"I shall work with the herds as usual."

Yet the husband piped, "The tribes let you do it because he could not. Now they will find someone else." Looking down, he changed the subject, "I'm distressed about his family sword. I know you desired it, but he asked me to bury it with him. A hard man he was, far too hard."

Only then did the sister begin to weep, "I'm sorry, dear, that you and Sesca had to live with bile for so many years. Now it's over." Through tears she knelt to hug the child, then looking up to Thulia, "You need to be alone for awhile. We'll take Sesca for the day."

The Amazon released her daughter, standing rigid as they departed. She held back her own tears, not for him but for herself and her daughter. When they appointed a new conservator, she would have no purpose beyond raising Sesca. As a mother she failed. As a woman she reveled in unchecked promiscuity in youthful years. It all caught up with her. *I love to ride!* Many a time she slid from this lover or that one, *"I need a lance, but you only have a dagger."* Each one kept his secret of shame. Why did she crave it? She knew it wasn't physical but deep inside, a search for something she couldn't explain. The warmth of flesh? A protector in the night?

She rode hundreds—totally out of control!—Euric, Ruteric, Munderic, Bulwer, Andric, her affair with Selenas the longest, yet an unending succession of mutual failure. Each moved to other women, for they could not satisfy the Amazon.

But I'm not a slut! I can control it, she reflected defensively. After all those years, all those men, she ended back where she started—in the arms of Frit. Thulia knew he loved her in his own way, but she could never marry him. He needed a fertile woman, one to produce heirs, certainly not her. Once or twice she tried ending their relationship yet found herself walking that early morning path.

The question came hard, the most difficult ever pondered, *How can I give Frit up? But I must before he asks me to marry him.* Somehow, she would drive him from her, perhaps a little truth about past unions. He would storm off in a fury as any man would. Given time she might eventually forget him, Bad Boy, her morning lancer. Yet it would be an eternity before he would fade from her soul.

Feeling pain, she thought it came from her shoulder and adjusted her right arm in the sling. Taking the ride was a foolish stunt. She tried to save Old Hempstalk's life and help the Christians. Yet she failed, even though toppling the Mordwine. Had she remained upon her horse, no-one would have known she wasn't her uncle and the Christians could have stayed. She referred to the Arians as "them," yet God touched her, even though she remained unbaptized. Thulia felt guiltier than ever! What she did within marriage was unspeakable, wrong by pagan standards, yet she couldn't accept baptism or confess sins to the presbyter. He was Selenas!

Perhaps she took the ride as an act of atonement, the guilt in viewing her daughter. Upon another day she might not have done it, but her uncle would have perished. The act was compounded by Pigfoot, a man who claimed she was worth less than the very gelding she rode at the Willows. *Now the poison bastard is finally dead.* She took a deep breath, releasing it as an extended sigh... for the sword was gone. *Let him carry it to Hades.* He always forbade her to use it, *"Women need a spoon, not a sword,"* and her one chance to protect the good with a real weapon lay under a ton of dirt.

Life would continue; and in a fortnight she would be in the widow's lottery. She would have to stand in the light of probity, "unvarnished truth" as Merjands phrased it. Barren of womb, perceived as worthless, only an eldermon would take her to wife, his future cook. And then a further truth would surface; she couldn't fry an egg without burning it. Beyond Pigfoot, both her uncle and Frit had chewed her culinary massacres; and it seemed that Frit didn't mind, or so he claimed. She grinned a hard one. He would become a reflection of her past. *Never will I have the man I love.*

The freemen departed with shovels upon shoulders, the bastard's sister had taken Sesca, not a soul to see a strong woman bend. All of it—Sesca's muteness, her failure at the Willows, the needed rejection of Frit—came streaming forth. Alone on the hill of the dead, tears finally came, only God to view them.

She stood upon her husband's grave, eyes to black earth below, and she could only think, *You have done your dirty-work... as have I.*

* * *

Sitting upon a log, the magistrate held a willow pole over the brook, his horsehair line sinking to a swirling eddy. Bound to a plank and cured through the summer, the pole was straight. Even with a good rod, the fishing was poor. Something kept stealing the worm from his hook, and he had no idea what it was. *Probably a small perch or dace.* It mattered little. If he caught it he would kill it, pure and simple. Suddenly he got another bite, the black poplar float dipping under the surface. Waiting a long moment, Aoric jerked the rod-tip up, missing the fish again as he stared at an empty hook. "You little son of a bitch," he spat. Raising himself quickly, he threw the rod to the ground, looking for the earthen worm jar. "Little bastard," he mumbled.

"You must have patience," scolded a near-distant voice.

In his tantrum, Aoric never saw the Alan hetmon dismount, not even hearing the horse approach. "Patience?" he snapped, "What I need is a smaller hook. A tiny fish, it is. Too small to even fry!—but if I catch the little shit, I shall have the pleasure of stomping it, squashing it under my heel. Like a bug."

Changing the subject while approaching the magistrate, Rustan explained, "Your servants told me you were here. The Alans are leaving the federation, packing their wagons as we speak."

Aoric's eyebrows raised, "What? The whole tribe? I said only the Christians."

"My people are exactly that, as am I," avowed Rustan, "Did you forget my daughter Lilia was the first one banished? The Alans have decided to keep the tribe intact and accept the new god. In this manner we do not break the foedus. We simply follow your decree."

Standing frozen, Aoric remained speechless for a moment, finally declaring, "But you hold a quarter of our warrior strength and half the cavalry. You cannot leave!"

"Did you think a father forsakes his daughter? We are a caring people and stay together." With that said, he returned to his mount, gathering reins and turning eyes to the judge. Aoric stood mutely, staring at him as he pulled himself to the saddle. Glancing to the sky, Rustan noted, "There are storm clouds up there. It will rain."

"Snow where you're bound," snapped Aoric as he reached for his rod.

Rustan turned his horse, glancing back to the magistrate, "I find the Commandments easy enough to live by. Perhaps others cannot. We shall keep old gods, modify them. We have done no wrong, kept to ourselves. In your decision, you were a poor judge." And then he rode off, leaving Aoric to himself.

Abandoning the worm-jar, the magistrate limped to his wagon, tossing the pole in the bed with a clatter. With a wince, he seated himself. *It must be stopped. They will pay for this.* He urged the team over the knoll, his mind upon retribution. *Every Christian shall be expelled. Punishments will be made. We shall set examples, a drowning or two, perhaps a crucifixion.*

*　　*　　*

Saba's home stood to the wind, foul smoke rising through its peak. Too many people lived in it. Even the unfree enjoyed a better place next to the woods and their lords. *My sisters pick up twigs and branches nobody wants. They tie them in bundles and place them on their heads. They walk a mile back here. Sometimes we burn horse dung. Then we stink.* He stood in his father's house, his mind confused and thinking of all these things, eyes red and watering. His lower lip quivered, and he bit it to keep it from braying. *Other Christians are leaving, but my family must stay.*

His father and youngest sister had a crippling that ran in the family. *They do not walk at all.* With him gone the two oldest sisters would tend the flock when not searching for wood or horse chips. *They work so hard to stay warm, they have little time for spinning wool. And so we have no money for food.* Fritigern made sure they ate meat once a week, hares and birds from the catchermon, but it was too late. *We did not eat well as children, so we grew up bent.*

He turned to the dark wall, hitting his head on the overhead thatching. He wiped his eyes, and turned back to study his parents. His mother was thin, her teeth gone. Sometimes she would remember her name, but mostly she could not. She would stuff wool in a basket, then remove it and ask, "What day is it?" So she passed her time in feebleness, not knowing which day it was. They were upset over his leaving. He was abandoning them at the worst time of the year, the month of Naubaimbar forecasting Jul—cold time. And in early spring, who would help birth the lambs? Some ewes would die!

Saba's father sat at the hearth with hands upon knees, his beard yellow-stained instead of white, his face wrinkled and dark from not washing. A long walk it was down to the well. Saba stood before him, extra clothes all packed in his coat, a few apples in the pockets.

"Where must you go that is better than here?" asked the old man.

"To the Bairgs-ahai," replied Saba.

His father's eyes grew large among all his cracks, his head shaking, "No, my son! You must not go there, for it bids great dangers. Terrible creatures of darkness!"

"But God will protect me. I know he will, and Selenas too."

"He may try, ja. But how can any god fight demons of the forest?"

Saba shifted to his other foot, for he was very nervous, unsure about the world of the Others. "I'm the congregation's lector. I must go." Selenas had squeezed his shoulder, actually touched him, and Saba remembered his words exactly as spoken. He could do that, and then repeat them just right, even when he knew not what they meant. *"It's a God-given gift you have,"* said the preacher, *"To speak gospels without error is amazing, and that's why you shall be my lector."* But Selenas never mentioned the terrors! He said the mountains would be a safe place.

His father shook his head, his expression pleading, "To lose a son to creatures is a heart of woe. What of the gold-guarding griffins, the one-eyed man, and the four-legged ones? How can you run fast enough to escape their grasp?"

"The gold-guarding griffins?" he replied, his eyes wide.

"Aye," said his father, "They line their nests with gold, they do! In their lust they let no man near their treasure. He be a dead man who even ponders it!"

Saba had never thought of that. He would not steal the gold anyway because it was a sin. "You cannot take another man's gold."

Stretching arms wide, the old man cried, "They are not men! They are griffins… with huge beaks and claw-like feet."

"But I would not steal their gold either," declared the shepherd.

"Do you believe the griffins know that?" the old man huffed, "They kill anyone and all, they do! They think everybody wants their gold."

Saba looked at his father, then turned to his mother. She was very busy placing twigs from one pile to another, counting to ten but not beyond it. They would miss him, but what could he do? In his heart he knew his parents could not take the trek. They would die upon the road! They had to stay behind. He stood quietly, studying those who raised him, thinking of his sisters out gathering twigs, and his heart broke in his chest. He shuffled in a circle, peering at this item and that one, the earthenware pitcher chipped, the copper cauldron with its old rivet patch, the wooden spoons and cracked bowls, each one older than he was; for he could not remember when they were new and good. *All these things are my father's house*. It was the only home he knew, yet he had to leave. Saba glanced to the door-crack.

"I must go," he said.

Chapter 16: One Less Mouth

Fritigern helped Selenas carry a chest to the wagon. Both looked to dark clouds, Frit thinking they should spread canvas before things soaked. They had spoken softly while Lilia packed, her mood pensive. *She's scared to death, not brought up for it. Not prepared in any fashion, a child-woman with an uncertain future.* Watching his brother's wife and son, he swore a mental vow. *A time will come when the judge shall no longer rule—a war or calamity, one arriving every generation. Then the tribe will elect a military leader, and a reiks will be raised to the sky on a buckler.*

Frit would bide his time, knowing he needed a few years for maturity. He would ask his brother's god to help him. Yes, God and Xristos. Yet he could not become a Christian. He and those who needed him would lose everything in a purge, as had his brother. Perhaps this new god would frown upon him for it. Perhaps not. When Selenas convalesced at Hospice, Frit spent the fortnight reading the bishop's books, nothing else to do. Older ones were crammed with fabula, worse than Homer, not even well written—Adam and Eve cringing naked for no good reason, women bearing children at a silly age, men who lived to be three hundred. Older than Merjands! But the gospel books gave the life and sayings of the teacher. Xristos was a wise and caring man. After reading every book, he knew something of Arian philosophy, yet could not meet his brother's zeal. There was a guardian of the soul, what Merjands called the Godhead; and Frit believed in a Creator, otherwise he wouldn't exist and the earth he stood upon wouldn't exist either. *So much for God, molding man from mud, like a village idiot.*

He knew some Christians would remain at Threisbaurg to speak of God in secret meetings, the lot of the persecuted, among them Thulia, her religion whatever she wished to make it. Aoric would stay clear of her and Old Hempstalk, for the man's Taifali were now the Tyrfingi's major cavalry. Frit grinned while Selenas pulled the canvas tight. With the conservator gone, he could take Thulia to wife, a strong woman in mind and body, a fertile spouse for a future reiks. As he and his brother tied the canvas over the wagon bed, he made his announcement, "I'm speaking to Old Hempstalk about the widow's lottery. Of course, I'll ask Thulia first."

"Oh?" returned Selenas, eyebrows raised, "Do you think it a wise choice? For the kunja, I mean."

He caught Selenas' implication—she was unrefined. His brother had become righteous on top of being the snob he always was. Frit waved his fist and snarled, "Wise choice? You find God, become an Arian priest, fuck-up the entire kunja, and get banished! Where in hell is your head?—between your ass?"

Selenas backed away from his brother's fist, trying to readdress the subject, "I mean someone younger, the daughter of a godakunds, a man of good high family."

Frit coiled, ready to strike with eye's tight, "Like whom, perchance? Edric's daughter?—lily-white inside and out, nice and vapid? Is that *your* ideal for my wife?"

"No! No! You're right. Thulia is intelligent, perhaps no beauty, but smart. I meant someone who could increase future standing, that's all."

Calming a little, Frit stared to the forest, not really seeing it. *No beauty? She's the most captivating woman I've ever seen!* He swung his gaze back to Selenas, "I knew you'd say that. Any councilor would. But damn it, I love her. I really do! I love this woman with great passion."

"Ah, passion. It has a way of tainting logic," Selenas replied with a patronizing grin, "I keep mine within the Commandments. A little procreation now and then. Lilia is pregnant although she doesn't show yet."

A fine one to profess logic. But he let it drop, smoothing his demeanor, "Congratulations. Procreation has rewards. Thulia and I will try for a child, and now we can do things openly."

"Such as?"

"Well, we can ride together," he professed, smiling at the thought of her horse galloping, a marvelous sight.

"Ah, horse riding," returned Selenas somewhat facetiously, "That is certainly worth marrying Thulia for. Personally, I would not have thought of it."

His brother's humor touched him just right, and he slapped the man's arm. They walked toward a house all but empty, most items in the wagon. The younger brother advised the elder, warning Selenas to continue beyond extreme boundaries of Gothia. A time was coming when not one professed Christian would be safe, he could sense it. *There is going to be a purge, and they'll kill just enough to set an example.*

* * *

Upon the east hill, Athanaric sat in his saddle. Below him upon the road, vehicles moved slowly, noble wagons and client carts. Most of the women and children were riding various conveyances, the freemen and unfree walking. The train passed forever, the true number much higher than first assumed. He expected to see Selenas and a handful of outcasts marching off to wherever, but he never dreamed the full scope of it, a full-fledged migration. *Father never quite envisioned this*, his eyes bugging, *It's not dozens; it's thousands!*

Among them went Lilia, now an object of the past. There would be others. His tastes in women varied; not really physical attraction that made women desirable. No, it was elusiveness, like a hind that smells a hunter's scent, never close enough to kill. Other attributes made women worth coveting—strength, fertility, practicality. And the best, he was sure, were widows who had already borne children. Besides, they had much experience in bed, something he lacked. Not because he wasn't manly, but more of a hesitancy that forever piqued caution. One could never be too careful. There were diseases found in loose women and the unmarried, the type to avoid. No, the best were widows, good clean women of fine character.

Among those worthy of being a wife, he pictured the form of Thulia. She had attributes a manly man could be proud of. Among other things she stood taller than most men, yet not as tall as he was, exactly the way it should be; for a man should never look up to a wife. With her strong build, she could produce many children. And now with the conservator dead, he could make his move, talk to her uncle Hempstalk the hetmon. Athanaric knew she partially disliked him, but once she settled into the marriage she would come around.

She had to be one of the most sought-after widows in recent times, probably good under blankets. Thulia bore the conservator's child and he was an older man. She was swarthy, not fair-skinned, yet she had a stride of confidence.

In his reverie he pictured himself atop the Taifala, for he knew how to do it, having seen his parents in bed when younger. *That's how all those sisters were made. You lay on top and grunt a lot.* He espied them often, late at night while they thought he slept. It was different than watching dogs or horses. Truth was, he couldn't view much of his mother, always deep under the covers, yet he would picture her naked while gratifying himself.

Oh, yes. He liked to watch… very much.

He squinted down to the road again as a totally different thought slammed hard to chest. *I hope Thulia's not in that caravan!* In recollection he couldn't remember anyone mentioning her as a Christian. *After all, a Christian wife would never do. Father would disown me in a heartbeat.* No, Athanaric was almost positive she was a good pagan, even though Old Hempstalk had gone to the services. Yet even Hempstalk was backing his wagon, perhaps a little too old to ride off into the wilderness and start over. Yet the fact remained; a number of those staying with the tribe had gone to hear Selenas preach. They needed watching. A few trusty clients would be able to discover any holdovers within the populace, and they would be banished in the blink of an eye.

As he observed the multitude departing, the Squinter noticed his father's wagon coming up toward him from the opposite direction. Aoric had been out fishing at the brook, a pleasant pastime and a chance to unwind from vagaries of being judge. Heeling his mount, Athanaric rode down to meet him in the road and take a closer look at those leaving. When he got there, the last wagon was beyond Aoric's, the remainder of the march being stragglers, the old and feeble, the unsure who might renounce their god and turn back, plus a few simpletons. Among them he noticed the shepherd wearing a black robe. *Good riddance,* he mused, *One less mouth on the noble dole.*

"They are leaving in droves, Father!" he exclaimed, finally approaching the wagon.

In a black mood, Aoric quipped, "Do you not think I know that? I want a couple of riders following them wherever they go."

"I'll assign two clients to travel in their midst," vowed Athanaric, "Then they can report back when Selenas has reached his destination."

Aoric shook his fist at the train as it faded to the distance, "The Alans went with him, they did! They packed up and left, the whole damned tribe."

"We are lesser for it," noted the Squinter.

The magistrate's eyes burned with hate for the Alans, plus disgust for a son reporting the obvious, "I know that, too! They better go beyond the Caucaland, because we have a new agenda."

Athanaric moved his horse closer to the wagon, "What might it be?"

"I cannot ride any longer, so it falls to you, my son," declared the elder as the first rain droplets fell, "After the beginning of Jul, we shall start a campaign to expel every last Christian in Gothia, first with an example, bring one to trial and public execution. After the rest are given fair warning— ten days notice—you will burn their churches and eliminate Christians who remain. Warn them all from here to the fiefs of the Greutungi, and work your way back with torch and sword."

* * *

She noticed Selenas gripping the prod tight, too tight, bullocks plodding through increasing mud, as if God himself had turned their journey to a trial. Most of the forenoon she sat upon the board next to him, not hearing a sound from his lips, only shouts of a cart or wagon owner to the rear as animals bogged down in the narrow road. Lilia knew the mountains were to her left, although unseen. As they traveled west, the road skirted the base of the peaks. In all, they would cross small rivers, each with a bridge except the last, the Aluta. She had no idea how the last river would be forded, and she sensed Selenas didn't either. That problem would be solved when they came to it—at least seven to ten days in the future, depending on the weather.

They crossed a river at noon, although she had no idea if the sun were overhead or not. Perhaps mid-afternoon. There had been a village, old in its Dacian foundation, a Roman temple stripped of signs of the old gods, yet she had no idea if it was Gothic pagan or Arian. Selenas said nothing, nor did they stop. The torrent fell harder, the wool cloak upon her shoulders feeling all the heavier; and under the cloak, cold droplets trickled down her back.

She watched rain bounce from the top of Waldrid's head as he squirmed around to look at her. His eyes were pleading. Again she twisted to look down the road, back to the Gothia she was leaving. Turning to her husband, she asked, "Did you thank Thulia?" He gave no reply, holding the prod and reins in an iron grip. She pulled his sleeve with her free hand, "Did you ever thank the conservator's wife?"

"I found no chance."

That was all he said, nothing more, no explanation. Certainly he had time to express gratitude for such a brave effort. Lilia sat in deep reflection. *God watched over Thulia's shoulder, protecting her from that evil man. Yet he let her fall from her horse, as if he wished banishment for us Arians. We were not destined to live in Gothia.* She returned her muse to Selenas' not extending appreciation to Thulia. It seemed rude. *The woman risked her life to help us.* Brushing wet hair aside, she studied his grim demeanor, knowing he was seldom this silent. Was his courage vanishing? *No, that's not it.* She found no answer for the longest time. Then it hit her. *He's worried speechless.* They were not travelers. They were exiles! The word rang less heavy in their warm home at Threisbaurg. Now it was entirely different. There was no home. Somehow before dark they had to find clear meadows to circle wagons and carts into a protective laager, the herds rounded up and positioned within the encampment.

The day passed slowly. Waldrid began to bawl after the fourth hour of rain, even worse during a downpour. In retreat she abandoned her husband, taking the boy to crawl under the canvas cover. Laying upon the empty mattress and atop sacks of grain, she tucked legs to stomach, pulling a wet blanket to her neck. Waldrid slept at her side, exhausted from bawling. Never had Lilia seen an uncomfortable trek, and she shuddered in its dampness, unable to find warmth. She thought of days ahead, dangers beyond each curve, the whole thing weighing her spirit. If rain turned to snow, what then? And how could they erect a house if the ground froze? She wiped moisture from her nose with a hand, peering at fading light as it crept along the magnum's sides.

Yes, this is a trial, just as Xristos experienced, as did Peter and Paul, and all the martyrs, even Arius himself. It shall pass, as it always has. Yet she could not stop the tears, only known for what they were by their saltiness.

*   *   *

Saba carried all his possessions, his other trousers, his old coat, all wrapped in a belt too small to wear anymore. He clutched them to his chest, for he did not want to lose them. In his other hand, he held his long shepherd's staff, handy for walking in the rain. Wearing the long robe, he felt proud. *It's woolen and warm, and very black, the robe of a lector.* At first his pace was quick, but walking fast became tiring. Amongst people he had no fear of monsters. After all, everyone was in this trek together, all related in some way. Wagons made ruts in mud and he followed behind. Now and then, someone

176

would smile at him in passing. One noblewoman even spoke to him. "How are you faring, lector?"

What an honor it was to have a person say that! Lector. That's what he was, and he returned, "Very well, my lady. This is a good robe. It has a hood! A gift from God through Selenas."

Oh how she smiled at that, "Oh, yes. A fine robe. You are a good man, Saba."

He was a good man! Her words made him smile, for he thought he was a man of little worth. That is what they always said until he repeated a psalm perfect. The noble lady had a carriage, not a wagon; and pretty soon she and her husband disappeared beyond. After all, he certainly could not keep up with a carriage! The day passed slowly and he thought about the family and sheep left behind. As he walked along, his feet became slower, others moving past him. The ruts became deeper and he was cold beyond wet. Saba wished to have a wagon but he never could afford one, not even an old cart. The road snaked this way and that, trees crowding in, a perfect spot for hungry trolls to grab him. *I shall walk slower and be careful,* he warned himself.

He looked one way, then the other, keeping pace in road-center and away from trees lining both sides. *What of the one-eyed man? This must be where he lives,* thought Saba as he stepped carefully. All the wagons were in the lead and everyone had passed him. He could walk all day but never fast! No, and now he was alone, for they were all up ahead. *I think this is where gold-guarding griffins hide, too. Behind those trees over there. Where are my friends?* He could no longer see them! *My dear God in Heaven, protect this sinner, for he never should have left home.*

Saba thought about his feet. They were slow because they wished to tell him something, and he knew what it was.

These feet wanted him to go home, back to his feeble mother and poor father. He was the only son! And what of his sisters? How could they survive? Some walked poorly, and his father and little sister walked not at all! He was the only good walker, for he could trudge many miles if he knew where he was going. But out here in this place he was lost. They were far ahead now, way down a road to nowhere in particular. It just went up hills and down, curving one way then the other.

Awhile back they passed through a village he had never seen before, so far from home he knew not one person who glared at him. *Perhaps they wanted my robe.* Yet he knew what to do and stared intently at his feet, not looking at strangers or anything they owned. *One never knows what gasts covet, what they wish to protect or even what they think... for they are the Others.* The rain fell harder, his feet sinking deeper in the mud. Pulling the hood tight around his face, he thought of Selenas and the other Arians. They were far more than he could count! *If I turn back, they would never miss one small person. Maybe with God's help I can reach home before dark when all the creatures come out.*

Trees leaned low and mean from the rain's weight, their branches reaching for the innocent, the young and old, and those of no importance. They were hands of the head-hunting man, claws of gold-guarding griffins. *Far worse in Transylvania—monsters of all kinds!* Saba stopped walking, his feet not moving, and he lowered eyes to see them turn around. As he clutched his staff and extra clothes, he looked again at wet feet. They were pointing toward home. And then his feet began walking very fast, as fast as they ever did walk.

Chapter 17: They Were Many

Within the oak grove, the final patches of green poked through autumn's carpet, the horses partaking its rough sweetness, dry hay their future fare. Their owners paced slow, almost touching one another yet apart. The dead quilt beneath their feet seemed far too brittle as each step crushed brown leaves.

"Why? Give me one good reason."

She couldn't look directly at him, distancing herself by a quick stride, "Because I would make a poor wife for a man who might become reiks."

He studied her profile as she stared through the oaks, perhaps to the hill beyond or to a future, a past, "That's not a reason, only a statement, Thulia."

She took one of her famous breaths, grabbing his forearm, *He has to know*, and she said it, "I'm barren, and you would have no sons."

Surprise flashed to Frit's eyes, "You bore Sesca. Could you not have more children?"

Thulia could see the conversation going nowhere, simply back and forth, no end to it, and she had to tell him the blunt truth. "I became pregnant again two years after Sesca," she explained in a hard voice, dropping her hand from his arm, "And he tripped me, kicking me hard for it. I had a miscarriage."

Frit paused in his stride, "Why would he do that?"

"The child was not his," she returned in a cold voice, "And neither was Sesca."

Great surprise came to the young Balth's face, speech eluding him for a moment, "Who's was she?"

She said nothing, again stepping from him, then murmured, "I don't know," the statement an ambiguous way of describing her background. She knew exactly who the father was, but Frit could never find out. She loved him almost beyond reason, but reason had to prevail. Hurting him deeply was the only way to drive him from her. She could see his difficulty visualizing it, a woman not knowing who her child's father was. It was sinking in—the slew of lovers involved, enough to muddle the parentage of her offspring. He always knew she was wayward, but this was unselective beyond lewd.

Frit could not even speak, simply staring across the grove to brown fields. An irony he chose this grove to meet her, where the great gift was created, where fulfillment was born. She toughened her expression, clenching teeth, closing her eyes for a moment and knowing she couldn't give in to tears. Not here. She chose even harder words, assured the statement would truly end it, "They were many. I couldn't keep track of them." It hit him deep, Fritigern knowing he was no more than one in countless string of men.

They stood in silence as he studied the oaks, barren themselves. He was obviously waiting for her to say more, anything. Yet she would not. She wanted him to mull the words proclaimed—*They were many*. Finally he faced her, his expression almost blank, his complexion sallow, "I understand. When not with me, how many other men occupied your spare moments? Five? Ten? It must have been confusing."

She hoped he would say something like it. She earned the remark and it made her anger genuine. With all her strength Thulia brought her arm round in a wide arc, her palm smacking his face with such force the horses jumped from the sound of it, each pacing off a distance. "There!" she spat,

"We're finally through. Do not come near the horse barns or my house, and stay away from my daughter. Understand?"

Frit never bothered to answer. There seemed no need to as Thulia ran to her gelding, jumped to it, and stormed from the grove. *So this is how it ends, vile and coarse.* The woman and horse became infinitely smaller, no bigger than a dot upon rolling fields. He stood frozen and angered, watching her disappear from his life.

*   *   *

They stood beside swift rapids. The road ended at the Flodus Aluta then continuing as little more than a horse path on the other side of the river. Into the sixth day of their journey, the entire train stalled at the river with time being crucial. Land had to be found and cleared. Cabins needed building, and reeds would be required for the thatching, all of it in some nebulous place yet unknown. The old catchermon stood between Selenas and Rustan, a man of uncertain lineage, short and grizzled with wild gray hair, half of it covering his face. He knew less than most men, for he lived feral and alone deep in the woods. To hear their own voices, they shouted above the roar of mad water.

"This is where the dark-thought ones cross," explained the catchermon, "They do it regular-like by horse alone, but me know not their wanderings."

"Are they warlike?" asked the presbyter.

"Nay, but they always carry weapons, for protection they do."

"They have a leader, a chief or king, do they not?" assumed Rustan.

"Aye. Gunter. But me know him not, only his name," the old catchermon smiled through soft lips.

"Then this path leads up to their villages?" Rustan asked.

"Aye, up through Red Tower Pass. They bring amber down from the other side, maybe two days ride. Be a lake up there. Not big but deep it is. Then they go over the high ridge and down to the river that snakes from the Frozen Sea."

"You mean the Vistula?" for even Selenas knew its name—the Vistula, once the avenue of his own people's migration, the link between the far north and the warm south.

"That be the one! Me remembers, now you say it. They be strange folk who come by here once or twice a year. A short man—with hooded eyes!—named You-He, and a darker one called Oxartes. They be traders from the east, Sogdian methinks. Give me coins they do, for hares and things," the old man hinted with a wink.

"They go up into the mountains?"

"Nay. They camp right here and the Gepids bring down amber, maybe for a week each spring and fall. Once the snows come, none but fools hike this path. Too dangerous, for snow buries them alive."

"Have you ever gone up there, to where the Gepids live?" inquired Selenas.

"Nay! Him who goes up shall not come back. There be things up there—the creature of darkness, hunchbacked dwarves, the head-hunting man."

Selenas knew of old wives' tales. Hunchbacked dwarves, indeed. He thanked the old man, giving him a silver coin as Rustan raised eyebrows. The catchermon bowed three times to the presbyter as if he were royalty and then walked alongside stalled vehicles, waving the coin for all to admire. He knew his monetary gain was quite safe, for they were Christians, the whole lot, even the ones who looked fierce.

Lilia sat in the old magnum, keeping Waldrid from climbing down over the side and pondering how the wagon might cross a swollen river. The boy was fearless of height, perhaps thinking the earth softer than it was. She studied her husband and father, wondering what they planned next.

Rustan waded into the river up to his thighs—as if answering his daughter's thoughts—feeling the current pushing him sideways, each step unsteady in its foothold, then turned back shaking his head. "How do we cross it?"

"We fill the ford with rocks to shallow it up." Turning to a client, Selenas asked, "Is my horse ready?" Feigning stout-hearted confidence, he mounted the animal, leaned down to kiss his wife, and began his crossing. He knew the flodus was swollen above normal due to rain; and finding a maximum depth just above the gelding's belly he reached the other side with little difficulty. That, he knew, was the easy part. Somewhere along the path ahead, he had to convince Gunter that the Gepids had more land than they needed.

* * *

The east hill was clipped to the soil, gnawed to the quick by his sheep, its goodness removed until the following spring. The thought of moving his entire flock to the west hill seemed an adventure, a full half mile away. Saba herded them from one hill to the other twice each year, his trusty friends, for sheep were docile except during breeding season. He recalled words from the huge Book as spoken by Selenas. *I shall lead them to new pastures, just as Moses did*, although he knew the distance was far shorter than a forty-year trek. But the analogy seemed perfect, his sheep being his tribe of sorts.

In a way, he felt guilty in abandoning his post as lector, but this was his true element. Yet his parents and some of the other families asked him to speak the Good Word on the Sabbath. He repeated a wonderful story about a camel squeezing itself through the eye of a needle. *That must have been some miracle,* he mused with a grin. He knew the camel story was a parable, for Iesus was showing his own flock just how difficult it is to reach the gates of Heaven, especially if you were a rich man, mean and ornery like a camel. He had never seen a camel, but they were like bulls he supposed, not kindly like sheep. It seemed to him that he himself had a good chance of reaching Heaven, for he always tried to be one with God.

He followed Selenas' teachings to the letter, giving his food to his mother, even though she was too foolish to thank him. Saba gave his extra coat to his crippled sister, for he knew she would shiver when Jul arrived. He did these things not because they were expected from a Christian but because they were the right thing to do. *Someday*, he hoped, *I might sit beside God, perhaps even meet Iesus himself, for what teacher could be greater to learn from?* He looked up from the flock to see a wagon approaching, a fine vehicle with iron tyres. *The magistrate is coming to see me. He has never done that before.* Saba's glance fell to his clothes, the holes in wool trousers, and he hardly felt presentable to greet such an important man. As the magistrate's wagon reached him, Saba smiled but the elder man seemed dour, not a kindly face at all.

"Saba," said Aoric as the vehicle stopped, "You have returned. I thought you went off with *them* for good."

"I did," replied the shepherd, "But who might care for my family and flock? So I came back to do what I must."

"I understand you have spoken Christian sayings to the tribe. Is that true?"

"Oh yes, for they asked me to tell a story or two," Saba admitted, "I do not think they are bad stories, for they speak of loving one another."

"It's not important what you think," claimed the magistrate, his jaw clipping tight, "I gave explicit orders, all Christians banished from these lands. Yet you came back."

"Who might care for my family if I were gone all winter? I have done no wrong."

"But you have... simply by repeating the stories. I'm sorry, Saba. It's not your fault for being endowed worthless. You have always been a polite, simple man of the tribe, but your addled thoughts have fallen to Christian spells, and now you must go."

The shepherd stood motionless for a time, surveying the flock, not looking up to the magistrate. Aoric remained patient, then asked, "Do you understand? You must leave now. Not tomorrow, not the next day." Answered by silence, Aoric's patience dwindled, and he finally snapped, "Look at me. Speak to me!"

Saba met his eyes, his lips quivering. Where would he go?—now that winter was upon the land? He would die out there in the wilderness. He had no idea where Selenas and the people went or which road they took. Yet he mumbled, "Yes. I understand."

*   *   *

They were a tough looking bunch, all Germans in furs, a dagger in every belt, a beard sprouting from each hard-carved face. Even their boots were sewn from fur, then cris-crossed with sinew to keep them over stained-hide trousers. Their tunics hugged drab to muscled frames, and most men had dark hair, few blondes in the lot. They could not or would not smile—as if the gesture might cause cracks—and it was plain to see why they were called "dark-thought ones." To Selenas, the women were conspicuous by total absence, all hiding in bark-roofed cabins, the doors cracked just enough for each one to peer his way. *Why do they hide? And what place is this?*

The entire group stared at him as if he was strange, and perhaps he was to their way of thinking. He was the

Christian Man, standing before them in clothes tinged in whiteness and totally foreign to all they knew. Just before reaching the Gepid village he observed human skulls impaled on poles, the ancient way of displaying executed criminals. They were still living in a rustic past. This place, remote and cruel and far too old, had taken its toll upon the human spirit, a tribe fallen to darkness. He could not save them. If he preached the word of God, they would kill him for it. Simple as that. Hard enough it was to fathom the thoughts of their chieftain.

"What? You think a hundred cows are worth the valley round the lake?" spat Gunter with his head tilted, one eye cocked at Selenas, the other staring toward the sky, then flipping to ponder the earth.

To make a point, several Gepids shook their heads, tipping eyes to trees as if the Goth might be riding on half a horse.

"Well, actually I haven't seen the valley or the lake, and a hundred is just a number to start with."

"Get on your damned horse," cried the Gepid chieftain.

"But I just got here, and you're kicking me out?"

"No. We're going up there. I want you to see what you think you want. Then you can name numbers."

Selenas wished to be sincere in his approach, but the man's eyes were askew and he had difficulty figuring out which one to look at. And it seemed to him—with eyes like that—Gunter would have trouble following a well worn trail, yet he replied, "Very well. You lead the way."

Mounting their horses, they proceeded up a narrow path for a considerable distance, Selenas staring at Gunter, the Gepid doing likewise until he broke silence. "You keep looking at me, don't you. Let me set you straight. My good eye is the left, the other blind. It happened when a Vandal tried to poke my wife. He can't see with either eye. He's dead."

The trail became even narrower, a single horse width, evergreen branches slapping Selenas' face as Gunter continued the lead. It seemed all uphill and Selenas pictured difficulties of getting wagons, even carts, up to the high valley. In dark cover, the land rolled up and down, never flat like parts of Gothia. There were no hills, just mountains as far as he could see. No bird sang. And he felt watched, as if something or someone hid in the undergrowth. He could sense the presence of death, either in the future or past. Not the traditional grim reaper, little room between trees to swing a scythe. No, this was a different kind of death, perhaps unique to the woods around him. A hard world it was, Transylvania, a wilder place than first imagined. *No wonder not a soul wants to live here. It's like the Ripaean Mountains of legend. We'll need to build a road and bring up hay, and we'll have to slaughter animals that cannot be fed.*

These were sobering thoughts to Selenas, to lose so much wealth until gardens and fields displaced the wilderness before him. Reaching a high pass, the Gepid stopped his animal to sweep a hand across the vista. The lake ran narrow, then opened wide as a near sea, towering cliffs bordering east and west, the entire shore covered with virgin spruce and pine. It sparkled emerald green, the outlet brown and becoming lighter where rapids tumbled south. Below the lake, the land swept through a narrow valley.

"There it is," said Gunter, "A useless chunk of land. An old road comes up along the river. You see what it is. No hardwoods left. Not a one. No decent firewood, not since the charcoal man."

Selenas jumped at the words, trying to look unaffected, "Some time past, was it not?"

Gunter eyed him intently, "He who puts it in the wrong hole dies."

The chieftain's comment struck an eerie chord, for it recalled words of the catchermon back at the lower river.

"Just Gepids live up there?" asked Selenas.

"No-one else. Years ago, a man lived near the lake," claimed the old catcher, "Had a crew of axe-men and burners, he did."

"His name?" questioned the presbyter.

"The charcoal man!" and he laughed his toothless way, "Thumped his thing in the wrong hole—and Bang, he was gone just like that. Folks say he was good at thumping holes. She did it, some claim."

"Who?" implored Selenas. Hard to picture such a death.

"A little witch!" the catchermon cackled, "Made him vanish. Still up there, methinks. Searches, he does. Looking for his body... and his thing."

"Christian Man! You up here or down there?"

"What? Oh, I was just thinking."

The chieftain continued, "Down there, a fat horse will starve to death in a fortnight. Junipers, firs, pine, not a field in the whole valley. Take a thousand men to clear it, and then what? Think you can plant it?"

"What do you want for it," asked Selenas.

"Give me ten. Ten cows or pigs," the Gepid demanded, "You want it, Christian Man?—it's yours, but keep to yourselves."

"Just ten? There must be something more you want."

Gunter cocked his head and became specific, "I saw you looking for the women. They are for us, only us. I want you and your kind down there. Keep it in your pants, all of you. No Christian comes near my wife."

Chapter 18: The Upper House

Wind howled across a land of whiteness. The woman trudged a buried road, carrying bread in an osier basket, dark bread and almost flat, baked that morning in the earth-brick oven behind her lord's house. She was a good baker, better than her husband who overcooked the loaves until the crust required a chisel to crack it. Twice each week, the woman distributed bread to other client families, always pleased to hear compliments. She walked briskly, the day cold as snow fell in profusion, blanketing the road. Peaks above her village were peppered with evergreens like stubble on her husband's chin. In Jul time, Transylvania was no place to be.

With a shiver the woman hunkered lower, pulling her chin beneath the coat like a turtle, raw snow stinging her face yet feeling prickly-hot. She followed the road by walking in sled tracks, now almost filled by the blizzard's depth. Some distance ahead she espied a strange man trudging slowly before her. He wore black, the hood of his long garment topped with snow, a crooked staff in hand. Never had she seen such a man. He paced with difficulty, as if wandering in a dream. Then he fell, not moving. Finally, an arm bent and then a leg as he rose to hands and knees, remaining stationary. Long moments passed before he stood to his feet, stumbling forward again.

Soon enough she caught up with him, even her—a woman laboring with twenty pounds of bread. As she passed him, she peered under his hood just to see what kind of man he was. *May the gods be kinder!* she gasped, his eyes blood-red and watery, his long beard untrimmed and covered with ice. His face was unhealthily gaunt; and she knew that under the robe, his frame was far too thin, the sight of him foreign and shocking.

She dropped her basket to the drifts and grabbed his sleeve, "Are you alright? Do you have anything to eat?"

He peered straight to her eyes, like a dog beaten to life's end. His voice was not from this place, but another world, quietly abased, and he croaked, "I have not eaten anything... since I left."

"How many days?" the woman asked.

"Days?" the man questioned back, "It was light, then dark, then light again. The dark times were many," and he held up bony fingers of both hands.

"Where do you go in this cold time?—winter came early here."

"I do not know," he coughed, his voice cracking, "but I want to go to Heaven."

She had never heard of any town called Heaven, for assuredly it had to be far away, and the woman knew he had a long journey ahead. The poor man was starving, freezing to death! Reaching down, she retrieved her basket. Grabbing his cloak again, she ordered, "You come with me and get some warmth and bread."

* * *

Frit lay awake in darkness, her face before him whenever he closed eyes. How many nights had it been since they fought? Ten? Yes, ten. In a few days they would meet for the widow's lottery, the conservator's wife going to whoever stepped forward. He knew exactly who that man would be— the old widower Heldrid, an eldermon and noble of high standing. The previous eve Heldrid came to his house with papers, needing him to sign them as a witness. *"You can read and write. Not many others can, certainly none I can trust to silence. I am dying, Fritigern, and all these years I have loved her. A foolish old man, yes, but I must do this, for it will change her life. Do you understand, my young man?"*

Frit did understand, a gracious gesture from a passing dreamer. *Ah, the World of Dreams. It never quite reaches the real plane.* He knew Heldrid well enough, although the noble's active years eluded him. The man left the tribe to reside in Constantinople, a trader of some repute. Heldrid came back to Gothia an educated man with a Roman wife. In tribal matters the man seldom spoke within the council, but when he did the elders listened.

"I thought I would never find courage to do this. They would all laugh!" Heldrid grasped his wrist with a palsied hand, pressing tight, *"But when your days are all gone? What must you do, if not the right thing?"*

Perhaps the trader's maturity could tame her if he lived long enough. She was too wild, too reckless. Yes Heldrid would be a good husband for her. Better than him, for he knew not what he wanted from life.

Closing eyes again, he envied Selenas. For all of it—the banishment, the trek into Transylvania—his brother had a certain stability, a good wife, a good god. Yet he, Fritigern, had little more than the inheritance of dependent clients. The woman he loved—Oh God, how he loved her!—turned out to be the worse strumpet in three tribes. In hindsight he still yearned for her touch, even after hearing the sordid confession. Amazing what long nights of introspection could do. Her promiscuity was something far behind her, not the Thulia he knew. He would take her back in a heartbeat, just to be with her again. Why did she lay out her past like a dirty blanket? There had to be good reason for it. Perhaps she thought her passions would catch up with her. Yet she spoke the truth—a man who might become reiks could not marry a barren woman. But really, what were his chances of becoming the kunja's military leader?

Eyelids now open, Frit turned to his side, greeting rosy fingers of dawn. They caressed his shutters, driving off another long night. Rolling from his bed, he dressed and went to the wash stand to shave, trimming his moustache. Another day, another chance of meeting her. The world was smaller than most people imagined. Sooner or later, they would cross paths upon the road or at the horse barns. What would he say?

He mulled the thought again, the one creeping from deep within. *Perhaps I need a few months—a few years—to find my real place in the scheme of things.* His brother found it at one year his senior. Frit could strike out upon his own, leave the clients to the head freeman, and cross the Stone Bridge. The world was a wondrous place. He had seen little of it; and perhaps it was time he went south.

What might await him? A junior command in the Roman cavalry? He was a Tyrfingi, federates since the time of Constantine. There were honorable battles to be fought beyond the confines of Gothia, over in Britannia, up in Germania. The only Roman settlement he had visited was Drobeta, no more than a twin fort. Frit had never seen a real city. He could venture to Adrianople, Constantinople… and yes, perhaps even Rome.

*   *   *

In the half-light of dawn, Athanaric headed down the road to the Taifali village, a coat of frost upon the ground, the grass killed flat along path-side. Reaching the trees he dismounted, a ground squirrel running from the sound. He tethered reins to a small birch, walking a short distance to wood's edge.

Chill reached Athanaric's bones, his coat not really warm enough for the season of Jul. He crouched unnoticed by those beyond, hardwoods thick and white, and he waited for Thulia to greet the day. There had to be some sign, a gesture of comment from her lips, to discern her penchant. *If She's not a Christian, I shall marry her. But what if she is?* The thought ran uneasy through his head, *I don't like punishing women, especially such a fine widow. But she'd have to go, the only way to protect the tribe from corruption.*

Then he saw Thulia, her hair shining and well-combed. She wore a dark coat, tresses hugging her back like strands of bronze in the waking sun. *A good color for a Gothic wife, to make sons as strong as the metal itself.* He pushed aside a few branches to get a better look, a limb snapping, the crisp noise seeming louder than it was. Quickly, he leaned back against the birch, closing eyes. *What if she saw me?* He waited, his heart beating loud in his chest, then peered around the birch again. An older Taifali woman came through the village, bucket in hand, just as Thulia came back out. He could even hear their conversation.

"Larisia, you look well today."

"For all the cold? A wonder I can walk, but I'm doing well."

He heard nothing remotely Christian. They would have said, *Good tidings to you,* or something like, *The Lord has blessed this day,* for that's the way Christians talked. Athanaric leaned back in relief. *She is not one of them, just a polite widow of good breeding. A widow!—the best kind—so practiced in bed.* He pictured her under the covers as he rocked upon her softness, producing good Gothic sons, perhaps four or five, for he knew he had it in him. Craning around the birch again, he watched her snatch a bucket and walk with Larisia toward the well. He always had resolve even as a youth; and he vowed, there and then, to let her know his intentions. *I'll ride up to Thulia this very morn and speak my words.* He wiped frost from wet knees and melded with long shadows, disappearing as quietly as he came.

Again upon his horse, he turned to the road as his mount's hooves crunched frosted dirt; and he finally reached her with a nod of recognition, not knowing exactly what to say. She glanced up unsmiling to reset her eyes directly ahead.

He cleverly piqued, "Who shall step forth to claim you?"

"The best kind," she snapped back.

"Oh? Who would that be?"

"Heldridus Constantinus," she prided.

Athanaric assumed he was the only eligible male interested in her. *Heldrid? The man is old enough to be her grandfather!* He worked his mouth several times—"Heldrid? Heldrid!" Somehow, mental confusion allowed his horse to pace beyond her. *Not confusion. Surprise, that's all.* Forced to look back at her, he reined his gelding for a moment as she caught up, "Surely, you jest! How can you seriously think of marrying Heldrid? He's almost dead! It's me you should marry."

"You?" she laughed, "A great lover with a reputation like yours wants to marry me?"

He never knew rumors pinned him as a great lover, for he had no real experience at it. But if Thulia believed it, such a notion gave him a great edge. Aye, he could grunt like the best of them, deep under the blankets. Sitting upright in the saddle and reaching for more height, Athanaric spoke proudly, "You're an upright widow, a pillar of womanhood; and yes, I will speak to your tribal hetmon."

Thulia stopped dead in the road, not quite believing what she heard. The Squinter just heeled his mount forward, passing the morning water brigade, his head in the sky. She watched him go, his pride a little taller than he was. *He always was a fathead*, she mused. Even as a youth he believed himself superior to the common element, never knowing what went on in the horse barns. "What an incredible dunce," she murmured, the expression not caught by her older companion.

"Would you really marry the Squinter?" Larisia piped.

"Are you daft?" blurted Thulia, "He's a strange bird. Everyone knows it."

Larisia waved a hand at his departing figure, Athanaric disappearing round the bend, "But he has power, the future magistrate. Everybody knows that, too. If I were you, I could put up with his oddness."

"Not in his lifetime will he dip his wick in my oil," vowed Thulia, "And besides, Heldrid is a very good catch, if you know what I mean."

"But he's older than my Erich by at least twenty years."

"True, and richer than your Erich by at least a hundred cows, a hundred horses, and a hundred pounds of the good stuff."

"The good stuff?"

"Gold, Larisia. Gold!"

The older woman shook her head, "Gold is a poor match-mate, the twin of avarice. I don't understand why Fritigern hasn't approached your uncle. He must need a good wife; and he's at least your age or near it."

Hearing his name Thulia went silent, increasing pace to leave her companion behind. Larissa sensed a sour chord, rushing to catch up, "I had no idea you disliked Fritigern. You always smiled at him."

Thulia stared ahead, her chin high and stride resolute, "It will become warmer, I think, once the sun comes up."

The freeman stood next to the hearth, watching the black-robed stranger. After a good night's rest in the loft the man shook less, and now he sat eating a barley porridge, dipping black bread, as liquid rolled from his chin. Never had the freeman seen a man so hungry. Once again he would pry for information, hoping to help the man reach his home. What he knew seemed vague. The man's name was Saba, arriving from the south upon ten days walk, evidently looking for a friend of his, Iesus, perhaps a relative, who lived in a town called Heaven. Yet not a soul in his village knew the man or place. He was positive because his good wife had asked every knowledgeable person, including nobles. Upon this second morn, the stranger seemed less confused, perhaps more helpful after rest and food. He squatted at the hearth next to the stranger, "Good afternoon, friend."

Saba turned to him, his mouth open, holding the bread in mid air, then lowering it to the bowl, "Is it after noon? I have slept for more than a night. Have I not?"

"Yes, but you feel better now, eh?"

"I like the food. Very good. My sisters cannot cook this good."

"Where do you live?"

"In Gothia."

"This is the Caucaland, at the base of mountains just above Gothia. Where in Gothia do you come from?

"My family lives in Threisbaurg, the place where the Prahova meets the Ilomata. Do you know Fritigern?"

"Nay, but I know the twin rivers. You walked from there without food or sleep?'

"Yes!" prided Saba, "I headed for the mountains to my other family."

The freeman finally realized where the man came from, evidently trying to reach relatives up in the forest. They had to be very poor to live that far up, and true, this man was poor and also simple. "Where in the mountains? Is the village called Heaven?"

"No," replied Saba, "We all live here in the midjungards, do we not? But Heaven is the upper house. That is where Iesus lives."

"Now I understand. You thought you were dying and would be going to himina-gards where your friend Iesus is."

"Yes! Yes," beamed Saba, "I hungered and was tired, and I thought I would die in the snow."

"Ah, my good man," said the freeman as he patted Saba's shoulder, "The upper house can wait! I will take you back to your family where the twin rivers join."

Chapter 19: Sacrificial Lambs

A fine day in Threisbaurg, blithe as the breeze. Yet somber clouds hung low to the north, brooding over the mountains. *It will snow upon the Bairgs-ahai,* noted Heldridus Constantinus, *but down here?—a fine day to speak for the widow Thulia.*

He clutched reins tight, quite nervous upon this particular ride. Fine was his favorite word. He had a fine one-horse carriage, a light two-wheeler with narrow tyres. Not another man in Gothia had one like it, Gallic-made and carved from dark wood of the Jove-nut tree, then polished with coats of boiled flaxseed oil. He thought himself a fine man, unusually upright in a world of barbarians, a self-made man who treated everyone as the gods claimed he should, although the gods probably didn't exist. *Still no reason to be uncouth, Goth or not.* The notion of one real God, not a bunch of fake ones, seemed logical, good enough for his benevolent mentor, Constantinus Gothicus. In fact he almost became a Christian, the idea of a real afterlife quite alluring. But he feared social stigma. They would shun him, especially the council. His worst fears loomed in the near future: all Gothic Christians without high influence would be hunted, exiled, or even killed.

Now he was tidying up his life, only one last thing to accomplish, an act of beneficence, perhaps a little lechery as a bonus, the perfect entrance to Dreamland. Yes, Dreamland, his greatest hope. He had lived correctly for it, never killing a vanquished foe, never turning from the correct path, always beholding to his word.

Heldrid guided his horse south toward the crossroads, passing the grove of trimmed birch, only another mile to the Taifali village as he headed for the home of Cannabas to barter for Thulia. *I shake like a leaf!* Back when she was fifteen, Heldrid believed he was too old to wed her. Now it mattered not! *It never does when the water-clock dries.* As he rode along, his thoughts ran amuck, for he pictured her before him, first with clothes on, a potent Aphrodite of Cos, and then sans any clothes at all. Every time the naked scene popped into mind, his hands shook all the more, the vision of a robust Venus.

He worked hard all his life, building a fortune in commodities—gold, amber, tin, horses, pork bellies—all fine things of worth. Now he was ready to die a happy man. His heart bothered him every day, once so bad he lost control of his left side for half a year. How many fortnights left? One or two?—perhaps three? Not that many. And Thulia would be his great exit. The prospect of having the Amazon for a wife tolled upon him hard, and they weren't even married yet! Feeling his heart beating too fast, he stopped his carriage in the road; and with a trembling hand he wiped sweat from a clean-shaven face, still supple for a man his age. Yes, a clean man with a clean tongue could get somewhere in this life and perhaps the next. Unlike his son, Heldrid left barbarism behind, studied his Greek and Latin, making something of himself.

Oh, Thulia!—my wondrous young woman. Such thoughts could wreck serious damage, yet he was still a Goth and a brave one; and by the gods, he was going to live long enough to wed her. At Cannabas' house, he would hand over twenty pounds of gold as a gift to the bride—that would do it!—and then another twenty to the Taifali hetmon, just to seal the bargain. Four years ago he rode by the wedding wagon and saw a man too ignorant to even hand her a flower, a woman lost to a cheap bargain. After giving birth, Thulia grew even bigger, "maturing" as they say, induced by motherhood. That's when he discovered how and where she lived. No more than a hovel. He approached the conservator to find a long-legged mare, for he needed a light horse he could train to the carriage; and there she was, naked to the waist and nursing the child. Heldrid gasped in perspiration, *Oh my gods, all that milk spilling from the infant's lips. Flagons of it. Buckets full!*

The pain in his chest became unbearable!—sweat pouring from his face....

"You be all right up there?" a woman's voice cackled.

He focused his mind to where he was, his vehicle in the middle of the north road, his thoughts wandering somewhere huge and soft. Opening eyes and looking down, he viewed an ample freewoman gazing up to him, and he mumbled, "I shall be better in a moment, just as soon as I get to the hetmon's house."

"Ye wants me to drives ya?" And she hoisted herself aboard.

"Yes, if you would. I'll rest a moment and collect my thoughts. That's it. Just turn right toward the river."

Coincidentally (or not), Athanaric rode down the trade road a half-mile behind Heldrid. He wore his best tunic, although a fruitless gesture after donning his coat. Perhaps after arriving at Old Hempstalk's, he could find an excuse to take it off, for he wanted to present his best appearance. *It's not every day a man asks for a widow in marriage, especially such a fertile and virtuous one.*

Reaching the crossroad, he continued east, heading straight for the Taifali village just before the Ilomata. Up ahead he saw the rear of a light vehicle come into view. *If I didn't know better, I'd say that was Heldrid's carriage. By the gods, it is!* He slammed heels to the gelding's ribs, the mount breaking into a gallop. With long strides, his horse reached the vehicle ahead. Pulling sideways at the reins, Athanaric guided his mount into the bushes for a moment, passing the elder Goth's carriage. He had to be careful, the road vending along a hillside with a steep incline. Once upon the road again, he knew he was safe. *I have the lead!*

The long-legged mare spooked as the rider rushed by! Heldrid jerked straight-up, opening eyes to view his foe, having been forewarned on the previous day. *"The son of Aoric also wishes to marry the widow,"* the sawyer's wife proclaimed, *"What shall ye do, old man? Fight him til death?"* And she laughed her saw-toothed grin.

Yes, he would even swing his rusty sword; for his compulsion soared far beyond lust to that great realm of love. In those years, he watched Thulia bloom to the strong woman she was, and he knew she gained through adversity. He had done it himself. The struggle of it, the pain she endured, he knew firsthand; for he had walked from the battlefield into the harder world of Rome. He had a well at the villa with fine tasting water, yet he traveled to the Tyrfingi well just to see her, then bringing gifts she needed. He couldn't give anything to her directly. The conservator would have killed him!—gifts for a man to be used by a woman. When she carried a second child, he donated a sacrificial lamb anonymously. The only way he could help her.

Now, upon a horse before him, this… this ignorant buffoon… would beat him to her! The man had no idea who the real Thulia was, human in her ways yet a woman of strength, destined for some unknown privilege he could neither define nor view. He could only sense it in a link beyond his own future. Heldrid would give her all he had, for no-one else within this midjun-gards deserved more. The magistrate's son was far too young to know the many facets of her soul. Even she could not view them. *I cannot lose her, not now!*

"Please get out!" he commanded the freewoman driving at his side, grabbing the lolly-stick from her.

"What?" she wailed, "This thing be still moving."

"I'm hauling back to a near stop. Jump! For it shall move faster in a moment," his demeanor now aggressive, for his heart felt irascibly stronger.

"Well, that be the thanks me gets for helping an old man," she spat, grabbing the seat as she swung to the ground and lost balance. She landed in the brush, hopefully unhurt as she began rolling down the incline.

May the gods forgive me! I've never done anything like this before. He prodded his mare in newfound vigor, impelling it forward and yelling quite loudly, "Cheat me out of a fine woman, will you? Get out of my way!" Heldrid never said anything like that, either. His deportment was always genteel and constrained. *What is wrong with me?*

Turning back to him, Athanaric returned, "She's mine, you dirty old fart."

"Old fart, am I?" Heldrid screamed as he jabbed the mare hard with the lolly-stick, a front corner of his carriage goosing Athanaric's gelding. The horse veered across a ditch in a flash!—toppling his master into the bushes to roll down the hill behind the simple woman. Heldrid felt like a hero, like a far younger man, virile and immeasurably strong. His heart was fine, for it only palpitated once a day and the bad part was over; and with quick movements, he prodded the long-legged mare to full trot, the horse tearing down the trade road, the village in sight!—the hetmon's house coming into view. He reined to a stop. Glancing back down the road he carefully stepped from the carriage. The young suitor ran toward him, hard and fast, stopping now and then to wipe dried leaves from his clothes. Yet Heldrid had too much of a lead even though the Squinter would soon catch up. He reached under his seat-board with both hands, lifting two hefty bags. *I'm almost there. She's only drawstrings away.*

*   *   *

Someone was banging the door with doubled fists, plus heavy thumping at the same time! *My God, so early in the day. What time is it anyway? Noon?* Deep pain throbbed in the hollows behind his eyes, as Old Hempstalk rushed for the latch, the string inside to keep miscreants out. "Who comes here? This is too early."

"It's Heldrid. Open up."

"No it isn't! It's Athanaric."

Two men at once? He knew why they came, expecting them but not together. As he opened the door, they tried entering simultaneously, each shoving the other, Heldrid's extra bulk winning. In a flash, the man slammed something heavy to Hempstalk's stomach, the hetmon staggering back, clutching sacks with both hands to fall through his table. CRUNCH! Laying on his back upon splinters, he raised his head to study the objects' considerable weight. "Look what you did!" he chided, "Broke my good table. It was an heirloom... to some Roman, back in a town we sacked; let's see, maybe twenty five years ago."

"Buy a new one," said the retired trader.

"I can't afford it," spat Old Hempstalk as he rolled to gain his feet, still holding the leather bags.

"What do you think you've got there. Sacks of rocks?"

"I dunno. What have I got?"

"Twenty pounds of gold in each, enough dead Caesars to tile this floor and all the walls," Heldrid bragged.

With a quick step, Athanaric moved forward, adding, "Well, I brought you something, too."

"What's that?" questioned the hetmon.

"A vintage jug of Falarian wine from Campania. Expensive and rare."

"Then where is it?" Hempstalk demanded.

"Well," admitted the young man, "It broke," and then his voice raised to a squeal, "when this son-of-a-bitch ran me off the road. I would have been here first! First, I say!"

Finding his balance the hetmon sat upon his bed, motioning them to a chair and stool, Athanaric rushing to the chair, a surly curl to lips. As they sat down Old Hempstalk untied the drawstrings to each sack, feeling inside. *Ah, so smooth and heavy, a little lumpy Caesar stamped upon each.* "Let me guess," he purred, "A bag for me and one for my niece, eh?"

Heldrid grinned a jaunty one, for he felt better upon this day than he had in years.

Jumping to his feet, the Squinter slammed a fist to chest, "What about me? I'm younger than he is by fifty years. I can sire children, tons of them. She should be mine."

"I think," said the hetmon rather calmly, "that Thulia should have a say in this. After all, she's the widow."

"That's not how it works!" cried the Squinter.

"This is my house, she's my niece, and this is Heldrid's gold until she makes up her mind."

Wagging his finger at Old Hempstalk, the Squinter warned, "The law says the first man who asks should get the widow's hand."

Hempstalk rose to his feet, setting the sacks upon his bed, "This is not a Tyrfingi matter but a Taifali one, and what I say is law. Thulia alone will make the choice," *and she'll not marry a beady-eyed boob like you.* Then he rubbed his lips— for he was very dry!—smoothed his moustache, and concluded, "I thank you nobles for honoring the worth of a good woman. One of you shall hear from her tomorrow."

*   *   *

Winds swept through hard crags, whisking dust-like snow as a hare ran under a twisted pine, stopping to look back at Selenas under harsh shadows. He caught his breath, air freezing his throat. *Jul in the Bairgs-ahei, yet a beautiful sight,* never viewing anything like it. At sunset the mounts glowed purple-pink, clouds much the same, nights royal blue, as if God might say, *"Here it is. Paradise or Hell, whatever you might build of it."* Half a day the presbyter walked, ever up steep slopes to reach what seemed the top of the world. A far cry from the low valleys of Gothia. He climbed this long way to thank God for good fortune: the friendship of Gunter of the Wandering Eye, the old road cleared in four days by a thousand men, the village that arose from nothing, downed spruce and knotty pine, bark cut to overlap roofs, and all of it done in little over a week. His Lilia, his thoughtful wife, knew exactly what to name it. *"Call it Ascentia—a high place where man can find God."* She was right. It was halfway to Heaven.

He sent every wagon the people owned to Hospice empty, and Wulfilas gave enough hay to feed half the animals for the winter. On their way back the snows came, yet every wagon arrived save two that broke down. Even then, one wagon's parts were used to repair the other.

Never had Selenas heard of such things. These were ultimate blessings, a great gift. The very idea of a gast handing over good land seemed odd in this modern world, yet Gunter did it. A great majestic hand in it, the marvelous touch of God. Assuredly, times would be hard, just the beginning of Jul. Winter would become worse, for the high mounts were forbidding in cold time. Already, they had slaughtered and salted a hundred cows and half the pigs.

He continued plodding upward, knee deep in snow. And finally upon the incline he sat upon a downed tree, its elevation high enough for his purpose. The cabins below appeared as small squares, each brown upon a white floor. Across the valleys beyond, he could view the northern edge of the Carpathians, swinging like a giant hook to form a barrier to the Vistula beyond. The river flowed to the Northern Sea, back to his ancestry—a freedom gained through the worth of a single horse, a clan that sailed from the Misty Isle, the amber-lined Insula Aballum. And now he knew his legacy. A new generation, a Christian one, would grow up here in Ascentia.

The young presbyter gathered his thoughts, cupped his hands, and thanked the Father, the Son, and the Holy Ghost.

* * *

For three days the doe hung from a low tree branch and now Gunter skinned it, drawing his knife in short strokes between skin and flesh. *I should have bartered the land to Christian Man for more cows. More fat on a cow.* Yet at least he had not frightened them away by asking too high a price. He had done well enough. *The Christians will have their use when the time comes. Sacrificial lambs.* And he genuinely smiled to himself, continuing to skin the deer.

He peered up from his rote to see Armenius step from the cabin, the man wrapping his coat tight to winter's chill, then wading through the snow toward the chieftain. *I must be affable to the man. After all, he comes from good blood with three healthy brothers.* And so he nodded to the Gepid noble, "Well now. Was she in good form?"

"A little thin," replied Armenius in a discomposed tone.

"Closer the bone, sweeter the meat," bantered Gunter in an overused expression, adding, "You have two boys, now. Correct?"

"Aye, two. And my wife is pregnant again, perhaps a third son on the way."

Gunter strode through the snow, plowing it before him to reach the noble. He cocked his head, one eye studying Armenius, the other canted to a clear sky, and he drew his blade downward along the man's chest, tight past his stomach, to prod the man's groin. Gunter flashed a fiendish glint, "All I need is one. One male from that useless cunt."

Chapter 20: A Small Black Dot

"Sesca," he asked, "Can you say something to grand-uncle Cannabas?"

The little girl shook her head, yet extended arms to him. In a swoop, the aging Taifalus picked her up and clutched her to chest, continuing his pace into the conservator's house.

Thulia stirred the cauldron of stew, acknowledging his presence with a curt glance, angered at how women were traded—like a leg of lamb or to solve a family problem. She stood straight, arching her back, "Have you bartered me off yet?"

Setting the girl upon a stool, the Taifalus shook his head and raised a finger, going back outside and returning with the leather sacks. At her table he untied the first one, dumping its contents upon the clean wooden surface. "No," he said, "But you have this offer from Heldrid, just as rumors foretold."

She stared at the gold, not having seen that much in one pile.

"It's yours if you accept him as your husband— fourteen hundred solidii, enough to buy a pride of geldings, have what you will." He dropped the other heavy sack next to the empty one, "This would be mine, another twenty pounds."

Thulia glanced at the cauldron, a gift from Heldrid, finally realizing it was given to her, not the conservator. *He had an eye for me even back then.* She raised eyes to meet Old Hempstalk's, "He wants to buy me like a slave. I would be a rich one, though. Have you consented?"

He shook his head in a room as quiet as Sesca herself, "I could not," he admitted, as mist formed in corners of his eyes. "Years ago, I gave away my foster daughter for a pittance and she went to a bad home, all because I could not control her. She was too much, wild in determination, riding like a man, selfish in pride, angry at those who thought themselves above her. It was in her blood, the same blood that traded her away for nothing but two geldings. I was too old, too stubborn in my ways to raise her. This time, it's your choice."

Hempstalk wept before her, rubbing his blue-veined nose, yet not a sip of wine taken that day. A half-smile disappeared as her own tears came, ruining that great perception—*the Amazon does not weep*—and she turned quickly to find two towels upon a rustic cupboard. "I'm sorry," he confessed, "for all the bad years. I thought of killing him more than once, even killing myself."

"That's when you began drinking hard, was it not?"

"Yes," he admitted, "How could I have done such a thing? To sell my own blood to a misanthrope. What kind of man was I?"

"You coveted your neighbor's things."

"I did! I wanted those geldings so much, for they were the best."

"And what now?"

"I told Heldrid you would answer him tomorrow. You can return it if you wish, all of it; for all I want is God and you to forgive me."

Thulia dropped the towel from her eyes, tossing it back to the cupboard. Walking around the table she hugged his bulk, kissing his cheek, "You were human in your wants. To covet a horse is part of us, and I think God forgave you long before either you or I knew he existed."

He nodded with a sheepish grin, motioning her to follow as he departed. She wiped corners of her eyes, passing through the doorway. Outside he stood beside the geldings, each saddled. "A man can only ride one mount at a time," he claimed, "Two horses are more than anyone needs in these peaceful days." Old Hempstalk pulled himself to the saddle, adjusting his position, nodding to the second mount, "Perhaps a Horse Dancer could use this other one."

Then he rode off in a hurry. Thulia watched him depart, tears forming again. He called her a Horse Dancer, the greatest compliment to bestow a rider. She turned to the gift he left behind, running a hand from forehead to muzzle. It stepped a pace closer, nudging her. The horse was symbolic—a beginning and end of a great rift—the white-spotted gelding.

* * *

The Villa Heldridus Constantinus was horseshoe-shaped and built to Roman standards. Six pillars formed a raised portico at an entrance leading to spacious rooms, their hollow walls built from pit-sawn timbers covered with plaster, the entire structure heated by a thermocast within its cellar. She had ridden by it a few times, stopping to admire its splendor—a northern villa and the finest house north of Marcianopolis. Now, she arrived here not so much for herself but for Sesca. Thulia stood one step inside the doorway, his manservant running off to locate the trader. *He's probably lost in here, trying to find his way from one room to another*. Then he entered, his kaftan so blue it glowed like an August night. Seeing her burden, he asked, "Would you like to set them down?"

"Yes," she murmured, for that was all she could think to say.

"Please come sit by the braiser. Perhaps a little broiled beef?" He waved her to an inner room, high-backed Roman chairs circling an iron pit, the smoke rising to a vaulted ceiling. One side was spanned by a huge rectangular table, two long benches running its length, each carved with a miniature frieze of the Parthenon, a continuous line of Greek deities interacting with each other.

She placed the two sacks in a chair and dropped to the next one, her fingers numb from the heft of that much gold, and she announced, "I wanted to see where you live."

"This is it," claimed Heldrid as he moved a chair to face her, "Not very humble and built for my first wife. She grew up in Milan. I'm sorry for not seeing you the past few mornings. I always enjoy the ride to the well, but as of late I have been feeling poorly."

Bypassing pleasantries, she continued, "I'm returning your coin."

"Then you refuse my offer?"

"I refuse your gold," she affirmed, "for I shall not be bought."

"What, then, if I ask you to be my wife without offering gold?" and he leaned toward her chair, his expression curious.

"First I want to know what kind of man you are. Perhaps I'm blunt; we have always talked but polite conversations tell me nothing."

"I am retired, like an old legate. I amassed my coin in bulk commodities—papyrus, furs, coral, even bacon and hams. From my name, you already know I served Constantine after the treaty. He remains in high esteem to many Tyrfingi."

She eyed the contus upon the wall, the bucklers shining bright, turning her gaze back to him, "That's not what I meant. I want to know your secrets, the ones inside this big house."

At that, he smiled, "Ah, secrets. Ask away, and I shall be honest."

"Do you sleep with your female servants? Do you like boys?"

Heldrid seemed taken aback—two questions in one! "No and no. Would you like to ask my staff?"

"Are you cruel to them or your dogs?"

"No. They have the run of the house. There are no Roman whips here, no Roman chains. Rumors float around, do they not?—whispering how pro-Roman I am. The truth? Every emporium along the Danube is open to the Tyrfingi. We are now the most civilized people in the Barbaricon; we can speak and write Latin, we use Roman coins, we buy Roman clothing. There are men who point fingers at me, just as they resented my colleague Thiudebalth. You know who they are. Thiudebalth and I signed a foedus with Constantine that created a fuller way of life. Such is my guilt."

"Are you a Christian?" she asked, studying his eyes to see what he believed in.

He blinked, smiling a moment, "No. That would drive the final nail in my coffin. Yet I do not believe in the old gods, nor do you."

Thulia leaned forward, taking a breath, "You know?"

Heldrid stood to express no surprise, "Ah, my dear Thulia. I know many things about this world, not enough about the next. You are safe here... just like your image," his eyes focusing beyond her.

She twisted in her chair to follow his gaze. Upon the wall stood a goddess painted in muted shades, her figure tall and robust under a tunic's folds, a complexion dark for Greek; and below the tunic, her legs ran bare to the earth. She held a bow in one hand, a greyhound's leash in the other. Thulia stood, shocked!—the face, the skin, the hair, all colored to her likeness.

"Aphrodite," breathed Heldrid as if the painting were sacred, "Praxiteles made two statues. The one unclothed went to Cnidas, the clothed one to Cos. This is an image of Aphrodite of Cos as the Huntress, painted by Julius Africanus.

"But it's me!" she gasped.

"Of course," he chuckled, "The goddess of goddesses." Unsteadily she turned, sitting to the chair, flushed and embarrassed. He continued, "Aphrodite was the patron goddess of Amazons. You should know a few other things. I have a bad heart and shall die in a week or month."

"Then why do you want to marry?"

"I wish to wed only you, not someone else. If you wish not to accept, I will meet death alone. As you see, I have been an admirer of yours for many years. You are a fine woman, far better than you think you are; and *you* are how I wish to die." The old trader turned from the painting, waving at a mosaic table, the magnificent candelabra and cameo vase, rich tapestries under foot, all encompassed in the sweep of his hand, "I have an estranged son excluded from my will. When I die, all of this will be yours whether or not you marry me. I'm not buying—I'm giving."

"People don't do things like this. What do you really want from me?" she demanded, standing to face him.

"Just you. You can pretend if you wish, but I dream of one night, even part of a night, with you as my wife."

"They will talk and I will be perceived as a gold monger."

"And I will be known as a dirty old man. We are alike, then."

She studied his face, looking for that flaw, a hint of the lie, but she could not find it. Nor did she ever see it before. He was always a noble man in every sense of the word. Thulia knew her men although he would be the oldest. He must have been handsome in his day, and he still retained a certain aura, the confidence of experience. She understood him. Heldrid had an obsession, and she was it. How many other men had another man's wife painted on his wall? She could live as a goddess, rough it, make all those sacrifices that goddesses endured. Trying not to laugh or faint, she reseated herself. This marriage would give her daughter stability, perhaps a little healing. That's what Thulia really wanted. Wealth comes in many forms. Parting her lips, she felt too warm, rather weak for an Amazon, and her tongue felt dry. "I will kill you with love," she whispered.

"Ah, my fine woman. What more could a man ask for?"

*   *   *

There are witches. And they hover over men like me. They cackle and wait, ready to do evil things that happen in this world. A curse! What have I done wrong that they so bewitch me? A curse to them all! She was rightfully mine, for I spoke first, yet that damned rich man bought her. He shall die for it!

In time, he knew full well, the witches would be driven back to where they were banished, just like the Christians. He would be a rich man himself… with them gone. Athanaric walked along the brook searching for a deep pool, the new snow's whiteness blinding his eyes. *I squint worse than ever!* A lead curse reposed in his hand, flat and cold and hard. He told the augur what to write upon it, scratched deep by the man's stylus. The curse would last forever, yet Heldrid would not. *He shall die horribly!—for no man crosses me like that.* Athanaric rolled the heavy weight in his fingers, a half pound of venom, as he paced through wet snow, his boots now soaked, his feet numb to the ankle. The brook tumbled forever as rapids, washing white-topped rocks.

Then up ahead he saw it. *A pool!* Hurrying his pace he began to run, the snow so wet he slipped, falling sideways into bowing alders, the chunk of lead flying from his grip. *Damn it all!* Rubbing frozen hands on his coat, Athanaric rose to his feet, afraid to move lest the spot where the curse fell might be covered by footsteps. He turned slowly, ascertaining the probable direction of its flight. Then he took a careful pace, squinting hard, trying to locate the spot where the lead entered the snow. After another pace and another, he saw the hole. Leaning toward his treasure, he pulled it from wetness, the lead now colder than ever. With a wincing squint, he cleaned snow from the curse with a freezing hand. Then he clutched it with an iron grip, following the rapids to quiet water, stepping carefully as he walked down the incline.

This will be deep enough, a quiet pool where no human hand will find it. Here under waters of time, the curse will do its work. For a moment, he studied the incised writing, running a finger over Greek letters. He couldn't write, but he gave the words to the augur slowly. The man scratched them to its surface at the same speed he spoke:

> *A curse on Heldrid the Trader,*
> *who shall meet a terrible death,*
> *who shall gnash his teeth,*
> *and writhe in agony.*

With a quick swing of his arm, Athanaric tossed it. The lead curse splashed far beyond the middle of the pool, almost in the bushes on the other side and lying partially exposed to air. *Shit!* His very soul cried. He shivered to his depths, his hands like ice, and he sneezed. *That's not where I wanted it!*

The curse wasn't totally submerged as instructed by the augur. He was unsure if it would work, but he certainly wasn't going to wade across the pool to fetch it. He was getting the sniffles from what he already did!—a frigging runny nose, probably sick in bed for a whole damned week eating nothing but broth and pea soup.

Yet all the wetness and cold was worth it, for a little bit of air couldn't negate his intent. Heldrid would die the worst death a man possibly could. Athanaric smiled to himself, his teeth chattering. He was unsure of the time required for the curse to accomplish its task, but... *Then she will be mine!—an upstanding woman twice widowed.*

* * *

At path's-end Fritigern turned back, looking at his home one last time. The servants stood in the open doorway, two of the women weeping. He was abandoning them, yet cared for by a foreman; and after all—now they had the entire house to themselves. He was traveling light, a single pack-horse, only one sword, a coat upon his back, and a change of clothes, the fancy ones, just in case he needed to look presentable. First he'd go down to Noviodunum to meet lost relatives. As Frit headed down the road, it seemed fitting to pass the horse barns; and turning up the hill, he pressed the white gelding to a gallop.

Reaching the crest, he passed the other rider coming his way, their tracks no more than an arm's length apart in the snow. He stopped, pulling hard on the reins, and she did likewise. For a time they remained where they were, Thulia thirty feet beyond him and looking down one side of the hill, Frit staring at nothing on the other side. They were taking separate ways, one north and one south. If they were to continue their way, neither would speak to the other, the best course to take. Yet they both turned their mounts at the same time. That bespoke of something unfinished. Neither would admit it, even at sword-point. They both pressed their horses back toward each other with a hint of speed. At last they met again, eye to eye, distanced by a touch of knees. In that brushing touch, momentary and light, he felt her strength. "There is a mountain in Magnesia where iron attracts iron," he proclaimed, not knowing whether to smile or not.

But she did. Thulia grinned at his statement, expanding it, "It must be where talented sluts meet dirty men."

Frit laughed heartily, surveying the woman in her wolf-fur coat, "You look good."

"So do you," she replied, "All clean shaven, mustache trimmed. Can I ride with you for awhile?"

He nodded; and they guided mounts down toward the trade road, riding side by side. Thulia finally asked, "Where are you off to? Constantinople?"

"No, just Noviodunum for starters. Then I'm really not sure. I want to see a little portion of the world."

As they rode, each kept studying the other, not looking ahead or off to either side, a wonder they didn't run over a freeman walking the via. Frit knew she wouldn't ride far with him; and she passed those moments not wanting to let go. They knew each other's thoughts, rare for mortals.

"You'll marry Heldrid tomorrow, eh?"

"Yes. The Squinter's father will officiate."

Frit stopped his horse, and she followed suit. They had ridden together long enough, "What will you do... after?" He wasn't sure she knew what he meant, but Thulia did, "Oh, I'll be rich then. Probably cross the Great River and look up an old lover. Rather good he was."

"What if he wasn't there? Would you search for him?"

"Most likely," she returned.

217

"Strange," he opined, "how it ends but doesn't." He heard no reply, one way or the other. The notion they would ever get back together again was the substance of dreams, both his and hers. There seemed no reality to it. Their lives were ruled by fate—a man born second yet expected to be reiks, a woman barren to give him no sons. There was a bitter taste to fate. Acrid. The same held for the gods. If they existed at all, even his brother's god, they had a strange way of guiding man's destiny. He would ride from it, toss it aside, for the gods or fate trampled his young life, driving lovers to separate paths. Life would look better down the road.

Then Frit heeled his mount ahead.

Now it was her turn. She watched him go until he became a small black dot in the whiteness of it all.

Chapter 21: So Speaks the Pipit

What prompted her to wear it?—a ring of yellow flowers, dried, and paled by copper-bronze, a faded crown for a gold digger. She knew the judge perceived her more like a prostitute than a bride. Heldrid grinned as Aoric wrapped a scarf to joined hands. Thulia couldn't believe she did it, the most shameless performance of her life, and there had been quite a few. The entire community buzzed beyond the trader's villa. At that moment of hesitation, she almost pulled hand from scarf and bolted for the woods! In the past she traded her body for pleasure, but never for wealth; and it seemed she finally got it right, punctuated by a mental giggle. She was giddy, incredibly happy. Heldrid seemed a good man, generous in outlook, although totally obsessed with the idea of sleeping with her. Holding to his thin strand of life, he wished to have it cut in one great night.

She would give it to him. After all, he paid dearly for it. With Aoric's departure, Heldrid turned to his bride, "I'm blessed to have such a fine wife. You are more beautiful than Venus, stronger than Diana, and smarter than Athena. I revere Greek goddesses. They remind me of you."

Thulia smiled pleasantly. She was not beautiful at all, perhaps somewhat "pretty" in a semi-dark room, one with a single candle. As for strength, he got it right, but smart? Well, maybe she was. She married him above the Squinter. She giggled uncontrollably, the idea incredibly jocular.

"I'm happy, too," he affirmed, not having a clue why she stifled the laugh.

As they walked into the reception room, a male servant arrived with a flagon and two unique cups shaped in flowing glass, hand-blown and frosted blue. Setting the accoutrements upon a mosaic table, the man smiled, "Welcome, my lady," and departed to wherever he came from. Heldrid poured the wine while priding, "I had these made in Syria. They remind me of you, graceful in their shape."

She studied them, each large at the top, then sweeping to a thinness in the middle, flaring to a small base. Thulia got the idea, for she was top-heavy. *So this is what he likes—great big brusts.* "Please," he begged, "Take off your coat. This is your home. I keep it quite warm, just like summer. You needn't wear so much."

Oh, God, she mused, *Another Fritigern!—just a lot older.*

*   *   *

Saba's sister crossed fields to reach the tree line by midmorning, the day warmer than those past. New hardwood branches littered the ground, some good oak, others birch or poplar. *They have fallen from the weight of melting snow.* She would carry less fuel home. *The time of Jul when everything becomes more difficult.* Her wool mittens were full of holes, the new ones reserved for the Sabbath, her hands wet and numb. She looked west to blue-haze mountains, knowing the presbyter and his people were trapped in winter's depth. Saba couldn't find them. *They are up there, maybe frozen, eaten by wolves. No good time for Christians.*

Leaning to her work, she began collecting smaller twigs first, a rote beginning in childhood. They would be piled outside her house, the air drying them for a few days; and when broken with an axe, they would burn just right, not too fast or slow. She or one of her sisters would bring them into the hut. *Then Mother can count them before they burn.*

Gathering them into a pile, Saba's sister heard a noise. Looking up she saw the catchermon, trap nooses dangling behind him. She waved, for he was a nice man, giving her family three hares a week. The lords paid for them, the hares not free. Her father would then give the lords wool. Fritigern was the best lord, for he always returned it, saying, *"I have plenty of wool today,"* a good man, but he had gone away to another place.

The catchermon stopped his pace, smiling, "This be a good hare day—warm!—and they hop from their holes looking for juniper."

"I hope you do well," she returned, "For peoples, a good day to live. For hares, a good day to cook." And she laughed at her joke.

"Aye," he agreed, "Better than days past. Without Saba life is harder, eh?"

Nay," she bragged, "Saba is back, he is. Just like a male hound, he went away for a spell. But he is back."

"Well, good thing," noted the catchermon, "This winter be a tough one. Feels it in me bones." Then he was off for the softwood, old growth downed some thirty years past. That's where the hares lived.

*   *   *

The dinner was braised duck with honey-glazed carrots, then sweet breads. He had a good cook, Roman dishes to Gothic taste. After sweet cakes, Heldrid seemed nervous, explaining his bedtime ritual, a sleeping quarters in the villa's right wing, the room lined with manuscripts, "I always read before retiring." As they left the table, he smiled thinly, "Perhaps we should become more familiar with one another. I'll sleep alone until you feel comfortable enough to join me."

He left her at a bedchamber next to his, a room that equaled the size of a house! The dressing table held candelabrae at each side with a giant polished mirror of pure silver, positioned between them and swinging upon a bronze frame. The bed was high, more than two feet above the wooden floor, its backboard carved to a graceful curve. Tucked within its coverlet Sesca slept restlessly, her first night in a strange house. When they ate dinner, the girl walked about the room, staring at this object or that. She had never seen glass or gold.

Thulia studied her daughter for a moment and paced to the six-foot wardrobe. *This is how a queen lives.* Opening the doors, she studied the clothing, new and unworn, dyed smocks and long woolen skirts. Earlier she tested one of the smocks for size. Far too small, it squashed her bosom downward, making her look pregnant.

Heldrid had given her a wedding gift, a green robe from India, gossamer in weft, and what he called a camissia. Before dinner, she scrubbed herself in the bath, a building connected to the villa. Thulia knew the robe would be the key to his great pleasure. Lifting it from the wardrobe, she tossed it next to Sesca, removed her old smock and skirt, her high-cut boots, and walked bare-foot to the bed. Like most of the clothing, the robe seemed small for her size. She picked it up, the material delicate, and she slipped it on. The sash tied high, not at the waist but in Greek fashion, and she had to hoist her bosom.

At the dressing table, she slid to the high-backed chair, peering at the mirror. The robe fit her reputation perfectly—the most indecent thing a woman could wear! Cleavage showed to the sash, her brusts bulging below it. After the initial shock, she grinned broadly while untying the sash, the robe falling to each side. *He bought the biggest globes in the Barbaricon.*

Heldrid was far from the man she yearned for but she could learn to love him, as was the case in most arranged marriages. Yet this one was different; for the husband already loved a woman he considered a goddess, almost bizarre, a man too decent to die so quickly after nuptials. She closed her eyes and sighed. *Not tonight, my spouse.*

* * *

At mid-morning they stood in the smokehouse, his father cutting brown rind of a hanging ham. The second cut produced pink meat, moist and cured for six fortnights. Not offering the slice to his son, the magistrate stuffed it to his mouth, closing eyes to savor it, chewing slowly. "Good," he pronounced. Handing the knife to Athanaric, he turned to sit at the doorstop, his feet in a puddle of melting ice. He stared at the water as his son carved a slice for himself.

To his rear, the Squinter asked, "Must we really do it? I fear no man, not contus or sword, but what will the spirits do?"

"These stories he tells—turning the other cheek and the like—are poison in the apple. Sweet but deadly."

"To kill a man of little worth seems futile," the Squinter declared as he stepped through the entrance to the ground, brushing past his father.

"Better to execute a simpleton than a nobleman. Less repercussion," snapped Aoric, "Twice he came back. Twice! No respect for authority."

"But, Father. There's no honor in it."

Aoric stood, leaning to his walking stick, shaking a hand at his son, "No more about it! His trial before the council will be tonight. In two day's time—what they call the Sabbath—he shall die. I want all to participate, especially the poor, the unfree. They be the ones!—whispering around their fires, thinking this God will give them a better life in the hereafter."

"Most Christians have gone. Those remaining can only be a minority."

Aoric lifted his cane, tapping the Squinter's chest, "Do not believe it! Before you were born, I was a hostage in Constantinople, living in their court. They were building churches in every square! I met him, you know, this Arius who started it all—a crazed old man—and I ate a dinner with that Eusebius of Nicomedia."

"I never knew that," the Squinter blurted.

"I was young, Eusebius himself just a priest, and they tried to convert me," spat the magistrate, "But I held firm because I knew what it was—an abomination!"

The Squinter studied his father's face, seeing him as a youth in a city of Christians. What trials he endured! "Then it begins," he replied.

"Yes. The shepherd as the unfortunate example, then the campaign. After the execution, you will ride to the Christian coven—Hospice—telling Wulfilas to get out. I want them gone before this thing grows into a giant cancer."

* * *

Gothia's snows had thawed, exposing packed grass at the four corners of Threisbaurg, the garden road meeting the north, the trade road passing down from Tyras and vending to the twin Drobetas. A layer of frost permeated the ground, just deep enough to form pools of water at every flat place. The redsmith dropped three bronze stakes from his shoulders, relieved from their heavy burden. And the butcher did likewise with his maul.

"It shall be a poor day to recall," muttered the smith, "I'll not lift a rock or stand here to watch it."

With a tight grip, the smith held the first stake upright to the frozen soil, "Go for it, but if you miss and hit me hands, I'll kill you dead."

The butcher just grunted, for he had the weapon; and with a well-placed swing he slammed the maul. Not much happened.

"Harder!" snapped the redsmith, "I wants to be gone." Ten swings later, the stake punched through frost, finally on its way. With the first in place, the smith grabbed a second stake and stepped two paces. "Six feet apart in a perfect triangle. That's how we put 'em."

They placed the stakes as instructed, the butcher missing his aim but once as the smith cried, "Damn!" As they prepared to go their way, the first cart of rocks arrived, three cartloads all total, a weight of two tons as the smith guessed it. The butcher looked hard at the cart and shook his head, once again muttering, "A bad day in the eyes of the gods, I'll wager."

The redsmith said nothing, pacing down the road to put it all behind him. *I was never here at all*, he vowed, *but hard at me forge all this morn.*

*　*　*

Heldrid and Thulia broke fast at the long table, he at one end, she at the other. A dozen men could have sat at the benches along each side. She had no idea if he was disappointed in the previous eve, for no blushing bride came to his lair. After eating bread cakes, he was off to see how the clients fared. Thulia dressed in work clothes and went for a ride, meeting him again at mid afternoon. He brought her to his bedchamber and located three sheets of vellum tied together with linen cord.

"This is yours, a valuable document," he explained, "If something should happen to me, you must contact the pleader Eugenius Benobus in Durostorum. He handles my affairs. Can you read?"

"Only Latin, but my grammar is atrocious. I'm sorry, but I cannot read Greek."

"Ah!" smiled Heldrid, "This *is* in Latin—modern times, my dear—my dispersal papers as to who gets what, and legally witnessed. Take it. I've sent a copy to Eugenius." He handed the document to her.

She studied the expressions, "fine lady" and "Lady Thulia." Her perception of him enlarged, as she realized he truly respected her; for no man—ever!—had referred to her as a fine lady. It stated his Roman citizenship bestowed by Constantine. He left her everything: the house in Durostorum, his lands in Africa, a villa near Hippo, the home where she stood, and fifty thousand solidii in a counting house at Rome. She was shocked! "Why? she murmured.

"Because I saw a young woman unbridled in determination," he explained, "I was a coward by not asking for your hand back then. After you went to live with that surly man, I loved you for your courage, your beauty, a beauty within yet even more. Old men like myself are intuitive like women. I believe you are destined for great tasks. Great tasks. Something majestic links you to this house, this property."

Thulia's eyes misted as she reached the end of the document. The witness, in clear strokes, proclaimed the son of a reiks—Fritigern. Pushing it to Heldrid, she shook her head, tears finally spilling, "No! You don't really know me. I have done terrible things, ruined my own child!"

Surprised, he returned, "Sesca?"

"Yes. She does not talk… ever."

"Perhaps she is deaf. I thought she was shy."

"She can hear perfectly; she nods but will not speak," claimed Thulia.

"What happened to the poor child to make her this way?"

Thulia told him of the fights, havoc in a girl's life. He knew of her trials. Only a blind man could not view it. As she wept, Heldrid put his arm round her shoulder, setting her down to bed-edge. He would call in doctors, also believing it expedient to pray to the Christian God who alone seemed to heal afflictions. Heldrid placed the will back in her hands, adding his own grit—a son who sailed his separate way, trading in the "wrong commodities." He hinted at a secret from his past, back when he owned ships, a singular task that made him a rich man. And then he admitted the truth. His fantasy— the one great night—was beyond him, now too old and sick to be a virile lover.

She knew that truth months ago. Thulia kissed his cheek and reassured him, "It's the thought that counts." After their talk she bathed for the longest time, knowing this would be the night. He had too few left. That eve they ate dinner with the servants, the long benches filled as Thulia discovered his usual dining habit, for he normally ate with his entire staff. She conversed with Maura the cook, spoke to the thin doorman, even got a short word from Raimond the gruff old agister, all of whom appeared like family.

That night, Thulia again slipped into the green camissia and left the bedchamber. She knocked upon his door, "Heldrid. Are you awake?"

"Yes, my dear. Please come in."

She entered dramatically, inhaling deep as the sash snapped, her attributes plunging as she purred, "I wanted you to see your gift before you fell asleep."

Sitting up in bed, he brushed manuscripts aside, a book with board covers clattering to the floor, his eyes the size of bucklers. "My dear woman," he gasped.

"Would you like a goodnight hug and something soft?"

By noon, the sun beamed warm upon the crossroads, a perfect day for an execution. Many people refused to attend, all at risk of being punished themselves, yet each knew they'd not meet Saba's end.

The cart carrying Saba and his family rolled to a stop, the bullocks eying a huge pile of rocks. Aoric stood upon his wagon, leaning upon his son as Saba was guided to the three bronze stakes. "Let it be known," he began, "that the shepherd was banished, not once but twice, yet he came back. Where is his respect for the law?—for the law guides the community, as the community makes the law. Let this day be remembered, for a man who breaks exile must receive due punishment, and the community shall carry it out."

As the judge sat down in his wagon, Saba was lowered to the stakes, his arms outstretched, legs bound to the third post. A horizontal crucifixion. Long moments passed, the throng standing idle, Saba's family looking to this person or that one, their expressions pleading. Aoric stood, his face twisted, "Do it! Bury him alive, so no more foul stories pass his lips."

The crowd stood silent.

"Get me down!" cried the magistrate, the Squinter helping him to the ground. Without his cane he limped to the rocks; and taking one he carried it the stricken man, dropping it upon his chest. Turning, he pointed to a young man, "Get another!" He wheeled to his son, almost falling, "You too," and he looked to the miller, "Quick about it." In a fury, Aoric yelled, "Those who refuse shall join him."

People came forward slowly at first, taking the rocks, the boulders, and laying them upon the shepherd. Saba turned his head to his father and spoke calmly, "God will not let my soul die."

Those hearing his words were at first stunned. He was a simpleton, yet he had more faith in his God than they did in all of theirs. The mass of rocks and boulders grew higher as the community hurried to quell the nightmare, trying to end his agony. Held upright by two sisters, his crippled father wept, shuddering as the pile of rocks grew upon his son.

Saba winced, for the weight upon his chest almost took his last breath, yet he found the strength, "I go to my father's house."

The man disappeared—his body, legs and arms, under a huge cairn. With him went innocence, flying to a place where a soul might go… the major consensus of those who buried him. In that rightful thought, there was no difference between Christian and pagan. When it was done, the populace stared at Aoric. Taking his prod he forced his wagon through them. Perhaps he knew the truth. The man's death finalized nothing and raised more questions than he could answer.

*   *   *

Merjands arrived at the villa by mid afternoon, his cinnabar longer yet no whiter. Other than that, he remained unchanged and far more talented than the prognosis required. The most telling hint was a slight curl to the deceased's lips, the way cheek muscles remained after life's flight. *A fine passage from this world. Everything was fine with Heldrid, except his heart muscle and probably the other one.*

He shouldered his satchel, grabbed his staff, and took a stroll to pay respects to his pupil, almost feeling like her grandfather. The barn entrance was small, and he ducked to enter the structure. She leaned against a post, studying the white-spotted gelding. As he approached, Thulia turned to face him.

"They said you were out here. A substantial horse," observed Merjands, "Yours?"

"Yes. The symbol of my worth… along with a lesser gelding."

"A beautiful animal. You must be worth a fortune."

She grinned at his humor, raising her chin, "No doubt Emperor Constantius is sending a carriage for me."

The horse barn sat too low, and the healer stooped, looking much like a buzzard yet smiling in return. "How's the shoulder these days?" he questioned, referring to the dislocation.

"Fine. That's what Heldrid oft said. They all think I killed him, correct?"

"No. They believe the truth. He died because his life-thread snapped."

She bent to snatch a piece of straw, toying with it, "He caressed me with loving hands, complimenting my stature. I kissed him good eve and went to my room. That was it. I could have loved him but he went too soon."

"Well, I'll ready him for the sarcophagus. I understand it's been finished for some time. None of this is shocking, you know. I would put it behind you and go on with life. Find a good man, my dear. Like Fritigern was."

Her eyes narrowed, "I'll never marry again. They'll have another lottery, but this woman is going to be long gone."

Merjands stepped closer, squeezing her shoulder to gift his half smile, "Don't say that, Thulia. Your man is out there. A little bird whispered that you were thinking of going up to the Christians after things are settled."

"Oh? What kind of bird was it?" she quipped caustically.

He tugged his cinnabar and scrinched eyes, "A pipit, small and tawny with a clear mind."

"What did it say?"

"It claimed that a certain student had defined probity and knew Threisbaurg held little for her," and he fumbled a hand through his satchel, "What she required, declared the pipit, was a link to heritage; so here is an old akinakes." He handed it to her and added, "The sheath is aged, the leather cracked, and the leg ties are broken, so you must have a girdler make a new one."

Indeed! The sheath was ancient—the dagger forged in a time of giants when griffins roamed the steppe. The blade was flawless, not from iron but steel forged in many drawn twists. Gold inlay snaked the hilt as mirrored griffins, two at the top to form the pommel and two at the bottom to make a grip check. She studied it with eyes wide, knowing its worth. Age could not diminish the hand that made it.

She brushed a hand to the man's cheek, "This is as old as you are. Probity should not be denied or hidden. Where did it come from?"

Merjands was in a quandary, for he could not give her a full accounting. She was not ready to know it. He turned a step, tapped his staff and shrugged a shoulder, "It belonged to a warrior, a woman like yourself who died beneath the Heavenly Mountains. She was a friend, no more than you are; and the time has arrived when you should know part of her."

Thulia gave him a hard eye. *He's being evasive.* "Oh? For what reason? Was she one of your disciples in some past life?"

Merjands seemed nonplused, a rare phenomenon, "The student questions the master? I was her pupil, not the other way around."

"Explain who she was," demanded Thulia, "I have dreams beyond nightmare, enchantments not a part of me or my life. They are your doing, and I want to know whom and where they come from."

"I cannot tell you, my dear. But they arrive not from me. I am only forging the blade. The rest—all the embellishments—the carved hilt and insets, the chasing of the graver, are accomplished by another's hand. Great time is required to complete a sword, to finish it correctly, to make it hard and sharp enough to perform the task required. Study the akinakes and hone it with a red stone. When you go riding, strap it to your leg and it will speak to you. Not until the spring will you leave; and by then you'll have your answer."

"So speaks the pipit?"

He cracked lips to a half smile, "Little birds know more than we think. They keep secrets because they have to, because they are guided by forces beyond control. So too with humanity. Even the master has a master and gods have a God. So firm is the stone of destiny. A chisel cannot mar it, nor can a maul crack its strength. It cannot be questioned or altered. Even when the pupil becomes the master."

Chapter 22: Kill Them All

A week after Heldrid's death, a freeman came up from the Stone Bridge in a cargo wagon, what was known as a magnum. Thulia knew him not. The man arrived with vintage wine—as if a cellar-full were not enough—along with items of silk, a dozen Gallic hams, and three sacks of finely-ground wheat. After climbing from the vehicle, the man came into the villa inquiring, "Pardon, my lady. Are you Thulia?"

"Yes, of course, and you?" she returned, striding from the kitchen, her hands wet. She was not above scrubbing a pan, albeit thankful for Maura's good cooking.

"I'm Culfrit, back from Durostorum. I knew Heldrid would remarry," he acknowledged pleasantly, the snow melting from his boots. Then he added, "Where is he? The trip took longer than expected, bad weather and all. I have a letter from Eugenius."

"I wish not to inform you, but Heldrid… passed over."

He studied her face, his astonished expression falling somber, "Oh. Passed over. As in beyond?"

"Heldrid died a week ago. He's in the crypt out back, and we shall bury him when the ground thaws."

"I'm sorry. He was more than my noble; been driving for him twelve years now. I hope to continue." Not waiting for her response, he reached to his coat and withdrew a letter, "This was for him. I suppose it's for you now. Allow me to take my leave and unload the wagon."

She nodded and Culfrit left somewhat dazed. For a moment she stared at the correspondence, then breaking the wax seal, unfolding it, and beginning to read:

Greetings, Heldridus   from Benobus
To the honorable trader H. Constantinus, prized citizen, friend of Rome. I have reviewed your deposition with utmost scrutiny and cannot execute it. A marriage between citizen and non citizen is not recognized by Imperial courts. If you should expire, the courts will freeze the bullion in the counting house of Sextus Probus; and your son, if still living, will receive a share after taxes. As they are non-portable, the court will extract less from the assets in Africa and Hippo. Your son is still entitled to these properties, including those in Threisbaurg. Time and again, I have asked you to disown your firstborn and adopt a male heir. I hope your health improves. Until you travel here to Durostorum, I remain your faithful servant,
                      Tomas Eugenius Benobus.

Thulia walked to the outer room, falling to a chair by the brazier. Stretching legs before her, she read the letter again and dropped it to the floor. She was an illegal spouse by Roman terms, no better off by Gothic law. In a singular moment, she had lost Heldrid's wealth, even the house she sat in! Her lip quivering, Thulia almost threw the letter to the brazier, changing her mind at the last moment. She might need it in the future. *I'll tuck it with the deposition and his other things*, all in an arka on the floor of her vanity. Within the strongbox Heldrid stashed varied items, aged bills of sale to the Romans and even a fragment of timber wrapped in muslin, a piece from an ancient house, perhaps the house he was born in. At the bottom of the arka were the twenty-pound bags of coin, plus another two bags, all totaling eighty pound-weight.

Thulia stood from the chair, taking a deep breath. In the world around her, men wanted what she had. They always did. She would remain at the villa for as long as possible. They would come when the weather broke, especially the son, and he would hunger for something more than overripe melons. She was poor again. *When wealth fleets, so does influence.* In philosophy she was a Christian, some tribal members aware of it. She hadn't known the shepherd, just his name and how he died. Was her future like his?—pinned to the soil or a burning stake, perhaps ritually drowned in a river? *No way for the Amazon to die.*

Sesca was still in the kitchen "helping" Maura the cook, and Thulia had time on her hands. Leaving the warm brazier behind, she walked down the right wing to her bedchamber, opened her vanity, and placed the letter in the arka. She unwrapped an old fold of linen to expose Heldrid's pitted sword. The only poor thing he left.

After his death, she found the sword leaning in a corner behind the thermocast, in the cellar for years-- *aging like the wine*—probably last used when he rode with Thiudebalth and Old Hempstalk against the Vandals. The sword had rusted inside its wooden scabbard, only freed by several hours of diligent tapping with a hammer. The blade was a mass of brown rust, and Maura suggested soaking it in a tray of olive oil for a day or two. The process worked, only to expose ample pitting. Both edges looked like old Othar's saw teeth, yet it was a sword, more or less—mostly less and seemingly the poorest excuse for a weapon in Threisbaurg, although a cut above a pitchfork.

Taking the pitted sword she slipped on Heldrid's wolf fur coat and walked outside to old snow, dirty, soft and melting. To the rear of the villa, she had a freeman cut a large birch to head height, her new strawman. She began what became a daily rote, finding the sword's balance, learning every inch of the poorly blade, and hacking deep into the standing birch, first one side, then the other, alternating her strokes. *Let them come to the widow if they wish.*

*   *   *

Helena sat in the library clutching the manuscript tight, its pages sewn between thin boards, the vellum flawed with tanner's stain. Yet this one book was more valuable to her than all the gold in the world. She studied her husband as he wrote a letter in haste, then looked to the deacon standing patiently beside Wulfilas. Helena peered up to the lector fidgeting at her side, *Botheus wants to get going,* and her eyes fell to the book again. *It matters not what we lose—this country villa, the furnishings, the Sassanian rugs—but we must save this, the Book of Little Wolf.* Other things, overly temporal and accumulated in their seven years north of the Danube, mattered not. They could be replaced. *Seven years to write it,* she mused with pride, *The most difficult task in the history of the Arian Church. Who would have dreamed a project like this was even possible? He is a great man for it. A gift to his entire people.*

At the table, Wulfilas folded the letter. He grabbed the candle, dropping wax on the document's fold, pressing his ring to it, a letter from the Bishop of Gothia to Emperor Constantius. The deacon would take it to the twin Drobetas, handing it to a ranking officer, not a regular but a man of station. From there, the communication would be carried by officers in the Roman postal service, passed directly from one to the other, until it reached the imperial court at Constantinople. Wulfilas was asking for permission to cross the Stone Bridge and enter the Eastern Empire, not alone or with a wife, but with six thousand Gothic Christians. Never in the history of the Roman state had such a request been granted. Goths could trade at the emporiums, but they could not establish residence south of the river, that liquid divide between civility and the Barbaricon.

The bishop stood from his chair, handing the letter to the deacon, "God speed, and ride like the wind." With a nod the man ran from the library. Helena raised to her feet, holding the volume tight, not wanting to let go.

"The wagons are loaded. We had ten days, now just nine," claimed Wulfilas, "That's it—nine short days for the entire population of Hospice to leave Gothia. Are you ready, my dear?"

She nodded.

"Let Botheus have it. It's the safest course, Helena. We must pass through Tyrfingi towns. The volume will be safer if it's carried northwest to Ascentia."

Almost weeping, Helena offered the volume to the lector, her hands not wanting to release it. Yet they did.

*   *   *

Six days later in Constantinople, the emperor found a suitable place to contemplate. Taking bread to the peristyle, Constantius sat at the edge of a large artificial pond, his bench built upon a raised platform next to water's edge. Rectangular and five feet deep, the pond harbored carp of considerable size, imported from Seleucia by his father, perhaps pilfered from under the very nose of King Shapur, the Sassanian shah.

The emperor tossed another piece of bread to the pond, the fish rolling at the surface, large scales flashing to the sun. *Nothing any greedier than a carp, not particularly great eating, too soft and bony.* He preferred dining upon firm salt water fish, baby tuna or a big anthias, something with tasty dark meat.

He studied the feeding carp. *Much like the masses they are.* As one swam off, so did the rest, all following for no good reason, herd mentality. Constantius thought of the followers of Wulfilas. When he received the bishop's letter, expedience was important, his answer dispatched immediately. No time to mull the situation over! In truth, what was there to decide? Wulfilas needed an answer before the Gothic purge began. Getting wind of the bishop's letter, his Minister of Policy tried to talk him out of it, *"If you let Goths into the empire, it will set a precedent. There will be no stopping them in the future."*

Perhaps the Minister was right, yet the advice was not. What was he to do? Raise state policy above security of the Church? Constantius knew exactly what would happen. Bishop Wulfilas wouldn't cross the Danube without his people, he and Helena perishing at the hands of the Gothic judge and his henchmen. A fine kettle of fish that would be—a leader of the Arian Church and his wife killed by barbarians. Constantius didn't bat an eyelash, for Helena was his third cousin, and her father baptized him! He answered the letter in great haste, dispatched swiftly for the Bridge garrisons at Drobeta by a trustworthy currier. Arian Goths would be admitted into the empire immediately and relocated in the Balkans. True, it set a precedent, yet Constantius believed the situation unique. The chances of similar incidents were slim, and he felt a better man for it. The admission was the correct and only Christian choice.

Alone to his thoughts, he leaned back on the bronze bench, closing eyes and raising his face to the sun, far warmer than the Danube's waters. Snow and ice served but one purpose, used by chefs when forming a tasty jell. He hadn't had a jell for some time, at least a week. *That's what I'll order for cena tonight, a cold main dish made form, ah... let's see...*

---

perhaps anthias. That's it! And artistically shaped jell in the form of a fish.

*   *   *

After the shepherd's execution, Athanaric sent four riders in as many directions, each proclaiming his father's edict. Receiving the orders, one of his riders had asked, "Where's the written proclamation." Athanaric then pondered the question. *Written proclamation?* As a youth, he was curious about writing, caught by the Greek while looking at the brothers' study books. *"I'll tutor you for free," the Greek claimed.* Athanaric knew better. *I'll bet he wanted to bugger me. He must have had something foul in mind, because nothing is free.* He distrusted the man. On his own, he tried learning the alphabet but couldn't concentrate.

Suddenly he snapped from childhood, telling the rider, "There is no written edict. Give it verbally." For the next ten nights he slept lightly, knowing what it would take. If he were fortunate, all the Christians would be gone. It mattered not where. They could go to Hades for all he cared. What if some did not?—especially if great covens remained, huge nests of them, buzzing with talk of their god. One could not bring hundreds of people to trial. He had to use expedience, otherwise this whole thing would take decades to accomplish. Athanaric considered the women and children, the most difficult part. He had only killed men. Of course, he wouldn't actually do it himself but simply say, "Kill them all." Preparing for the purge he rode to a hilltop, always thinking more logically when above other people. Alone and at great height, he practiced verbiage, getting the tone just right, the true ring of Gothic autocracy, "Kill them all." The order was all inclusive—a far less guilty expression than "Kill all the men, women, and children."

Alas, his worst fears came true. Upon this eleventh day, the Christian village at the river Busau was still occupied. With him, Athanaric had a hundred horsemen, all well armed, some quite adept at burning, knowing how to construct good torches, not those quick-burning ones, but real professional torches, lasting until flames licked every house. Now the torches were lit, a whole slew of people running into the church. *At least they're consolidated in one place, easier to burn the entire nest that way.*

They knew their fate, a man running back out, screaming, "You must not burn us! This is a church, holy sanctuary!"

"You were given ten days to leave," replied Athanaric. That sounded correct, truthful and honest in its implication.

"But there are women and children in there," the man bemoaned.

"That is the unfortunate part. If you men used good judgment, your whole coven could have lived happily elsewhere. What are laws? Are they designed to be ignored?" His father couldn't have said it better. The torchers arrived next to his horse, smoke rolling upward, each man ready for the order.

The man looked at the flames and pleaded, "No! We are Catholics."

"Do you think I care?" Athanaric questioned. With a quick movement, he drew his sword and cut the man down. Then he studied his weapon. *What a frigging mess. Spent an entire day polishing it!* He pointed the dripping blade to the church in a squint of authority, "Kill them all… and bring me a rag, a piece of cloth or something."

*   *   *

Safrax entered Selenas' house finding it difficult to close the door. With a foot he brushed the snow back outside, "A stranger is coming. A man."

"A snowman," said Waldrid, jumping from the hearth.

His parents stood, Lilia wondering, "Who would come up here in midwinter?"

Selenas rushed to the door and peeked outside as the rider approached, the nostrils of the man's horse pushing frost with each breath. Without even donning a coat, the presbyter stepped into the storm and plodded through the layer of white, "Botheus! What are you doing here?"

"Freezing to death, pastor!" the lector answered.

"Quick. Come inside. My young brother-in-law will tend to your animal."

Botheus snatched a leather sack from his mount and they both entered the cabin, Safrax going out a moment later to unsaddle and feed the horse. At fireside's warmth, the lector passed the large bag to Selenas, then rolled his hands to flames. "The magistrate of the Tyrfingi killed a shepherd, reputedly a Christian," panted Botheus, beginning his tale, "All of us had ten days to exit Gothic lands. Helena, Wulfilas, and the rest have gone to the Stone Bridge hoping Constantius will admit them into Moesia."

"Helena is related to the emperor. He'll not refuse her or the bishop," answered the presbyter, "Who was the shepherd? Saba? He was my lector."

"Yes, that was his nomen. A simple man, they say. This is for you until we know Wulfilas is safe enough," and he passed the leather sack.

"Poor Saba," cried Lilia, "He was harmless, a good man who trusted in God," then asking about the sack's contents,

"See for yourself, my lady. It has great value."

Sitting with her husband, Lilia watched him withdraw the manuscript. At four months until birthing, she held hands to a stomach just beginning its growth, peering over her husband's shoulder.

"A big book," claimed Waldrid as he reached for it.

Selenas held it higher, finally realizing he would have to stand. They stood together, man and wife, as Selenas turned the pages. He couldn't understand the words, the writing much like Greek, some letters foreign yet not Latin. "This is a strange language," he noted.

Somehow Botheus could smile, cold and tired as he was, even fearing death in the last few days, and he commented, "Strange? Study it closer."

Selenas held the book at an angle so Lilia could see. Then he recognized the word *gudjas*—priests. He looked at other words, the phrases, and suddenly the whole thing fit: *"Now the chief priests and elders, and all the council, sought false witness against Iesus, to put him to death."* He pulled his wife to him, his eyes misting; for the language was Gothic!— the very tongue of his people, of his wife and son. It dated beyond memory to an uncertain place along the Frozen Sea, just an ancient land and people in the dark mist of spoken words. Now the words were before him in a book, the Gospel of Matthew, as a true written language.

* * *

The wind howled outside, as they retired for bed early. Lilia lay awake after little Waldrid and Selenas entered the world of sleep, as she thought of Saba. She was thirsty, perhaps the child in her womb telling her to drink some water. Quietly she slid from the covers, trying not to wake her husband or the boy sleeping between them. She tiptoed to the bucket on the bench, the dirt floor cold to toes. Transylvania's winters were colder than those in the Caucaland or out on the steppes of Walachia. *In a couple of months spring will arrive, mountain flowers blooming.* Winter was the worst time of year. They all smelled of smoke. To get water she chopped ice with an axe, white flesh numbed on a winter washday. The choice of food dwindled, nothing tasty, no fresh vegetables, no eggs or milk, everything a struggle.

She dipped a cup to the bucket and went to the hearth, adding two logs side by side. Lilia sat to a stool, sliding it closer to the fire's warmth, the bottoms of her feet chilled. She mused upon the child she carried, probably another boy. *A daughter would be so pleasant to have. We could do women chores together when she becomes mature enough.*

The picture of Saba snapped back to her senses. *To kill a man like him?—so innocent and pure.* Not a better man walked this earth in God's eyes. This would be a hard time for Gothia's Christians. *Many more shall die, all good people trying to better their lives here in the middle house, preparing themselves for the upper one.*

Yes, things could be worse than here in Transylvania. Selenas seemed worried they might run out of food, yet plenty of onions and turnips were left, the leeks and carrots gone. Salted meats were scarce, but each day another cow froze, butchered upon the spot, its meat distributed. Lilia took another sip, putting a hand to her stomach and the child therein. They would not starve, and she would give birth with flowers in bloom. Ascentia was a good, safe place.

Chapter 23: Wet upon Dirty White

Tuna boats hugged dry to the south shore, owners and oars now idle at a season's end. Days enough for tuna in the summer, when schools passed upon their procreative swim. At the wharf, the Roman trader munched pine-nuts from a rolled papyrus horn. He ducked his head as the ship's boom swung outboard, its cargo destined inland. The chilled vender continued along the stone pier, hawking his product, "Pine nuts for bronze!" as north's chill howled down from the Bosphorus. *Had he owned better intellect,* mused the trader, *the man would have sold Jove-nuts from an iron brazier, a bit warmer on the hands.* Winter wooed Cyzicus.

Two men aboard the Goth's ship scrubbed the deck, bearing their weight to long-handled rods, both guiding lava-rock across the filthy timbers. A third man, probably another slave, dumped salt water from a bucket, wetting the volcanic stones and the area they scrubbed. The excess liquid, green and black, splashed through the scuppers. The Roman trader jumped back as putrid grot spattered on his coat. Carefully, he checked his cone of nuts, fearing a drop of slop—or whatever it was—tainted his snack. Pushing nuts around with a forefinger, he studied each little treasure carefully, peering for the slightest sign of glop. *Missed them,* he determined, feeling safe. Raising his glance, the heavy boom net swung outboard again, this time directly for his head! He crouched fast, stepping a quick pace to the rear. *Don't give a damn about another man's life. All they can view is an awaiting tavern.*

The trader snapped upright, pawed for a nut, and yelled to the boom operators, "Is Scandius Constantinus still aboard?"

One of the seamen turned to the aft cabin, "Scandius! The Tomisian is here."

Moments dragged, the big Goth stepping to the deck to run hands through sandy hair. He waved the seamen off and tightened his tunic. Pacing around the wet deck and both stoners, he pushed the boom net aside; and with a crude curl of lips, addressed the Roman, "Looking for warmth on a day like this?"

The trader studied his bearing. He distrusted the Goth, yet the man had a good eye for flesh, "I need Colchian or Armenian linen and something young for my wife."

Scandius guffawed, "Sailed straight across the abyss from Olbia. Hit Cherson first, never went further east. Too frigging rough. Pontic seas are capping white, some a good eight feet, rough enough to make this miserable cargo puke." He jerked a thumb at the two stoners and their mission of removal, eying the Roman again, "Boy or girl?"

"A girl," replied the trader, glancing aghast at his pine nuts.

"A few, the youngest thirteen, maybe fourteen," the Goth bragged, "Not bad looking and a virgin when I got her."

"Not a harlot, eh?"

"Damn-well believe it! Broke her cherry myself. I can show you the blanket."

The trader knew the Goth's tricks. The blanket's blood could be a year old, Scandius little more than a pirate. "It matters little, one way or the other. Experience has worth. Blonde?"

"And blue-eyed," frowned the Goth, palming his chin, "She's expensive. Not enough fleeing into the Crimea. When the Huns cross the Borythenes, they'll drive more Greutungi and Alans south. By spring, a young one will come cheap... but not now."

"I'll not haggle all day," professed the trader, checking a pine nut carefully before tossing it to his mouth, "Got to reach Nicomedia. A load of vellum."

Scandius gave a sly grin, "Much like bringing papyrus to Byblos."

Better to peddle worth than debauchery, mused the trader, "I won't make a killing, but the trip will pay for the girl and more," then adding, "She must hold attraction for a young woman."

The Goth looked sideways, pulling an earlobe, "A bed maid, eh?" He glanced back to a seaman, "Bring out the youngest Greutunga."

They waited, the trader mumbling, "Sorry about your father. Keen at his trade."

In a flash, the Goth smile vanished, "What about him?"

The trader gaped, assuming Scandius knew. "He died a fortnight ago."

"How?" snapped the Goth.

"In the saddle, they say. A second wife just like mine—passionately young."

The Greutunga was pushed to ship-side, her eyes studying the deck as the Roman trader assessed her features, his front teeth mincing the last pine nut. She was still green, her complexion pasty. The Pontius could roar this time of year. Judging from her countenance, a fresh hint of shame, he supposed she might have been a freeman's daughter. *She'll do.* "Find a warmer coat for her, and name your exorbitant price." The Roman hunkered while the Goth stumped off to find the garment, slipping as he passed the stoners and muttering to himself. *She shan't be living in Hades, a better life than her previous one.* His wife wasn't an ogre; she just liked a good tonguing. The breeze flew damp, and white foam surged against the pier. He crumpled the paper horn, tossed it to the water and tucked hands under armpits. The trading season was over.

*   *   *

Scandius watched the trader guiding the girl along the stone pier. They passed the pine nut vender and almost disappeared along the shoreline, a glimpse of them now and then as they passed between hauled boats. *Good riddance. A frigging weeper.* He reached up, grabbing the empty cargo net as if to steady himself, patting his belt-purse with the other hand. *Forty-five sesterces, and he complained. Less than what a fish dealer gets for a big gray mullet, if it's still alive.*

Peering sideways—as if being watched—Scandius gave a crooked smile, one eye almost closing as he palmed his chin. *Dead, eh? About time he shit the bed. Well now, looks like I've got myself a villa or two, and a new ship. Better than this stinking tub.*

*   *   *

In the fortress riding hall at East Drobeta, the dux galloped his mount for one last circle before slipping from the saddle. He held out the reins to a riparian and strode toward gray light at the hall's entrance, his nine-year-old son leaning against the huge door-frame.

He grinned a big one, "How's the buttocks, a little better? You rode for nearly an hour."

The boy smiled back, "I'm fine, father. Someday I'll lead the cavalry, just like you do."

"That's the spirit. After a few months practice, you'll hardly feel the bouncing and chafing. I think a butt gets calloused from it," and then he caught the approaching aide through a corner of his eye, "No more bad news—the bishop's wife sick in the infirmary, Goths trying to sneak in and buy food, Aoric's henchmen somewhere out there. They'll slaughter these people like lambs, and I cannot lift a finger. So, what's it this time?"

The aide tipped his eyes, coughed through a closed fist, and mumbled, "Well, sir, there are more Goths. They keep arriving. Wagons are lining the road—I dunno—maybe all the way up to Ulmenia."

The dux winced as if stung by a bee, "Damn. Are they blocking egress?"

"Fairly much, I'd say."

"Where's Bishop Wulfilas?"

"Still with his wife or maybe over at the Stone Chapel," the aide claimed, "It's a traffic jam, alright. Why do they not pull off and circle into a laager?"

"Beats me," resigned the dux, nodding for his son to run along, "But I'd guess they have no military men, no caravaneer; in other words, a bunch of displaced farmers without a clue of how to organize. People die that way." He paused, looked up the Via Principalis, shook his head, and motioned for the riparian to bring his horse. "I'm going out there. These people are in for a shit-storm. Look at the sky! Winter is throwing its vengeance, and they have no covers on their wagons. In a big hurry to get to hell out, I guess."

"You'll be needing an interpreter, sir, Shall I summon Cunimund?"

"Cunimund, the stiff-assed signifier? No thanks. I'll just wave and gesture with my hands. At least one of those Arians must know Latin."

"But going out there alone?" quizzed the aide, "Could that not be dangerous?—to yourself, I mean."

"What do you think might happen? A crazed farmer swinging a hoe?" the dux chuckled, "I'll be back within an hour. We need the road cleared."

*   *   *

Outside the East Gate, the road ran straight as an arrow, passing between two low hills upon the steppe of Walachia. The dux tapped heels to his mount, not with any vigor. He was dressed informal, wearing his heaviest trousers, not clean or new but an old pair used for hunting and riding; and his coat was plain brown, as were his boots. Wagons were stalled along both sides of the frozen road, many of them partially in it. Between the wagons and hills, the Goths had built fires; he wasn't sure from what, a general lack of standing or dead wood for miles, and the few pieces left were buried under snow-crust.

People huddled around the fires, and the dux could hear wailing of children. He halted his mount close to one of the campfires and watched a man toss a stool into the flames. Only then—when the hard vision hit him—did he realize what they were doing. These people were burning their furnishings and possessions, prized yet expendable, just to keep from freezing. *My God! They'll be out of fuel by sundown. Then what?* He looked up to the mounts of Transylvania, all capped white, and a gust of wind caught his coat, lifting it from exposed ribs. A number of people, still crouching and rubbing hands to the flames, began staring his way. "Listen up!" he questioned, "Who among you speaks Latin? Spraken linguae Latina?"

A younger man, tall yet slight, raised a hand and stood from the fire, "I do. You are a Roman from the fortress?"

"Yes I am." The dux swept his arm, "I want these wagons moved from the road. We have late traders coming down from Olbia and Tyras, and they need clear passage.

Laager these wagons away from the road. You know, like Gothic armies do."

"We are not warriors," the man shrugged, "How should we know what to do? Some of us can no longer move. We are ill and exhausted. Through endless coldness we have come. We will move the wagons from the road, but a laager we cannot make."

"Do it immediately while there's still daylight and before snowfall. Understand me?"

"You are an officer from their army?" asked the young man, as more people stared. A woman crawled upon her knees, sliding them wet upon dirty white, trying to get closer to warmth as she rewrapped a bawling child in her coat.

The dux paced his horse almost to the fire, peering down to examine the child, a girl of perhaps three years, her face stained from a mixture of tears and dirt, or was it charcoal? Quickly he turned back to the Goth, "Yes. I am an officer. And I want you people to get these damned wagons moving now!" And then he heeled his mount out to the road, stopping in the icy ruts. He reined the horse short; and he sat there, looking straight ahead to the lofty walls of the east fortress, walls that kept all the riffraff from crossing the Stone Bridge to Roman soil. Now away from the Goths' fires, his clothing seemed too thin; and a chill—incessant and demanding—pecked through his coat, no less porous than a sieve used for straining wine. And so he turned back to the fire, his horse at a gallop, until reaching warmth again as the young man turned to face him.

"Move the wagons," the dux repeated, "Then get the children to the East Gate, right over there. We'll be waiting. These children will be housed in large riding halls, one across the bridge in West Drobeta, the other on this side. Every spare military blanket will be requisitioned for them, also hot water. Get a move on it!"

"But how?" pleaded the young man, "They will not let us in. We are outlanders, and our children have not papers."

"Listen up, all of you," commanded the Roman, "I'm the Dux per Dacia Ripensis, the ranking general in the Diocese of Moesia. Above me sits the Emperor, and above him sits God. I want these children inside the fortress before dusk." He looked up to the darkening sky, and readdressed the open mouths, "And dusk may not be far off. I want every child under the age of thirteen out of the elements until word—good or bad—comes up from Constantinople."

*   *   *

The eve took a foul turn at the Noviodunum inn, rather sobering. They all milled about, some talking, a few gesturing toward the man's body. Blood sill oozed from it, running along cracks between floor planks. A carpenter stared it, then proclaiming, "Good tight flooring, holding blood like that. Built like ship's planking."

A portly riverman poked the carpenter's elbow, "A stupid son-of-bitch to reach the age he did. Halfwits usually die early."

"Yup," the carpenter agreed, "Oldest dumb-ass I ever seen."

Awhile back, someone ran out to the soiled-white street looking for the authorities, yelling at the top of his lungs. Two or three dogs began barking, one close to the inn, the others in the distance, all fearing the dark. Then a hound began howling. Finally, the officer arrived, a young lieutenant of the First Jovia stationed at the fort, well-dressed with cheeks shining, for he obviously shaved twice a day.

"You, there!" snapped the officer to a bestubbled man, "You saw everything?"

"Aye, I seen him do it. Stuck him like a pig, he did!" the man laughed.

"It's not jocular," huffed the innkeeper, "He killed me brother. Killed him dead over what? A sword?"

The lieutenant hated assignments like this, investigating petty murders. Turning to the crowd at small and filthy tables, he ordered, "The rest of you find someplace else to bibe your drink." The bestubbled man began to leave, the officer demanding, "You stay. I want two witnesses."

He walked over to the body. The corpse lay face up, eyes and mouth open—still in surprise—a fatal wound just below the rib cage in the man's huge gut. No weapon in sight, blood still pooling on the floor. N*ot exactly a citizen. More like riffraff.* "How did it happen? You first," he said to the innkeeper.

"Young he was, eating stew and having a beer. His sword lay upon the table. Wasn't gonna have no man take his food, if you asks me," he paused, seeing the officer waiting for more, "Well, then. Me brother comes up and grabs the sword. The young man says, '*Return it before I take it back*.'"

"And then?"

"Me brother laughs, '*Why should I? You no longer have a sword.*' He was joking, you know. Making fun."

The bestubbled man piped, "He was serious, and then he asked, '*What's in the purse? Coins? Give it to me and maybe I'll return your sword.*' That be what he said."

"He was funning," retorted the innkeeper, "Just pulling the young Goth's leg."

The lieutenant became more interested, "Money was involved? He was a Goth?"

"Aye, a Goth," the innkeeper nodded, "I can smells 'em a mile away. Leeks."

"He was not!" corrected the bestubbled man, "A Roman. He had a short military cut. His clothes were too good for a Goth's."

"Then what happened?" inquired the officer.

"That man's brother grabbed the purse, he did, waving sword in hand, like he knew how to use it. So the young man jumps up from the table and pulls a dagger from a sheath strapped to his leg."

The lieutenant waited, not hearing much more, "Well? What happened next?"

The innkeeper's eyes grew small and beady, his jaw tightened, "He throws the dagger like in the Hippodrome. Stuck him in deep, and me brother looks at himself and falls. Rolled around a bit, right where he lays."

"That's what happened," agreed the bestubbled man, "Then he grabs what's his and runs out the door. The innkeeper is right. I seen daggers tossed like that in Constantinople, a woman knife thrower—stark naked she was—black hair up to her navel and sprouting round the armpits. Nice, dark paps. The Emperor was at the show, drooled like a fool, his toga soaked with sputum. Probably had a hard-on. Armenian, I think."

The lieutenant fumed in a quandary, "Well, was the killer Gothic, Roman, or Armenian?"

"He was a Goth!" cried the innkeeper, "It's a long river, it is, and them what's Goths cross it in dugout boats. Day and night, they do."

Hearing enough, the lieutenant waved them off. If the young man was a Goth, he's search for him. But it sounded like the victim got exactly what he deserved. Noviodunum was a tough place, a frontier outpost, and men died in every way imaginable, including getting stabbed. But throwing a dagger like in the Hippodrome? Very clever. Certainly not a Goth's style.

*   *   *

The moon arced full overhead. *Probably around midnight*, guessed Frit. He let his freezing mount pace slowly. *No sense in murdering a horse after killing a man.* The road shot straight along a riverine levee, bordered by little gray willows—trees leaning from the burden of mounting ice. Beyond them, mace and sedge lay flat upon frozen peat, the entire marsh seemingly crushed by vehement wind. He had no idea where the next town was. Yet he knew he was moving south, the river less than a mile to his right. *Most likely, I'm heading toward Capidava and Durostorum.*

A woman had cut his hair on the north shore and then he found a fisherman to transport him across the Danube. A thirty-oar ship passed close astern as he stroked the white gelding's neck, the horse more nervous than he was. What could an officer of the Classis Ripae Scythica do? He was simply a Goth heading to an emporium for a day's trade. He knew several islands lay downriver. Upon those isles, he had relatives—Balths—one of them a cousin named Alaviv. Spending five days at Noviodunum, he got no closer to finding Alaviv than he had in the first hour. If seemed as if the man had been swallowed by the marshes.

Now he had to give up the search. Even with a near full moon, the road ran black, as dark as his life seemed. The wind stung his ears, his hands numb upon the reins; and Frit shivered as he hunched low with elbows tucked to sides. The moon had a halo skirting it. *It's going to snow again.* He could have fled southeast toward the port of Tomis but it would have been a dead end. In winter, few ships sailed, either tied to wharves or hauled upon the shore. Only the greedy sailed the Pontic Sea after mid October, mostly slavers. Frit had to head west toward Novae or south for Marcianopolis. South seemed the most inviting—warmer.

He certainly couldn't remain in Noviodunum; they would be looking for him. It wasn't exactly self defense but he wanted his sword back, and the money was crucial. All that he had! He threw the akinakes in desperation, a rote learned when young. He and Thulia oft tossed a knife at a black poplar, first to make it stick in. Then the game became accuracy. Poplar wood was soft, like a fat man's stomach. Thulia would have been proud of him. *Right on target.*

Killing a man on Roman soil would have consequences, the authorities checking into it. He needed to distance himself from the scene in a hurry, no sleep, no food for awhile. Riding through a bitter night, he felt alone, his life on a downward course. He had given up or lost a great deal of what he loved, some of it based on poor decisions. And now he was a fugitive. Frit wondered how Thulia fared. For an infertile woman she found the perfect husband, a man too old to sire children. Trying to set his mind at ease he mused, *She's married to a rich man and a good one, an old friend of my father. Thulia is fine.*

Chapter 24: When We Grow Up

At East Drobeta's Legatenpalast, falling snow made winter look cleaner as the dux stood under the colonnade's roof, checking his uniform for unwanted spots—grease or ink or the like—and waiting for his son and wife. *Ah, the Sabbath,* the one day per week he slipped into his uncomfortable cuirass and officer's tunic, draping a scarlet sagum about his shoulders. *Frankly, I'd rather be hunting,* yet he was expected to attend communion at the Stone Chapel, no getting around it, especially upon this morning. The Gothic Bishop would conduct the Eucharist.

Women! They take forever to dress. He rotated an elbow, then the other, making sure no stains were visible. The tunic was not exactly new, about fifteen years old as he recalled. Suddenly, a rider shot through the palace gateway, galloping full speed across the courtyard. The dux ran into the snowstorm while screaming, "Hey, you! Slow down! This is a domestic area. Servants. Children. And not one of them totally aware of where they're going."

"I'm looking for the fortress commander," the rider offered back.

"Well, you'll run over him in a moment."

"Oh!" returned the rider as he slid from the mount, his footsteps squeaking in the snow, "Sorry about that, sir. I'm with the Postal Service, and this here is from the Emperor. Took twenty seven to get it here," and he fumbled at a large saddle pouch.

"Twenty seven hours?" cried the dux, his eyes bugged wide.

"No, sir. Twenty seven horses, a new one at each station."

"You carried it the entire way from Constantinople to here?"

"I was told to ride the distance; and that's exactly what I did," explained the postal officer as he handed a leather cylinder to the dux who fairly tore at the circular cover, attempting to open it, finally withdrawing the letter to crack its seal. With hands shaking, the dux looked up to see his wife and son walking along the colonnade; and in a mental rush, he twitched, dropping the letter at his feet. *Shit! Call me Grace, any one of the three.* Both he and the postal officer bent to retrieve it at the same time, bumping heads.

"Watch what you're doing!" he snapped, then laughing. "Pardon that remark. I'm at wit's end. Actually, I was at wit's end." He turned to his family, waving the letter like a gladius, "I knew it! All I needed was this." His aide was already over at the Chapel, so he shouted across the courtyard, "Cunimund! Cunimund, get your stiff ass out here!" then turning back to the postal officer, "And you? Get some sleep," and he spun about, "See that third door to the left? That's a guest suite with a deep bed. Scat!"

Cunimund hopped across the courtyard, tucking his shirt and pulling at a boot. He fell! And getting to his feet, he stood erect, unphased, and a lot whiter than he wished to be. The dux rolled his eyes, thanking God that Goths were more prompt than Spaniards, "That's the spirit, Cunimund. Fall in the snow, and present yourself half-dressed to the commander's wife."

The Goth stopped tucking and snapped to attention, "Ja, zur. I mean ne, zur."

"Looks like you were sleeping through the Sabbath. Up late last night? Across the bridge at that swill-hole chasing floozies, eh. Well, snap to it. Find a captain and have him run a maniple through the East Gate. Make it archers. My family and I are required at the church, and I'll hand good news to Bishop Wulfilas and his wife."

"Ja, Kommandar," nodded Cunimund, "Vot shall ve do?—vid der Krvistians, I mean."

"Put riparian archers between them and Ulmenia. Smile at them, slap their shoulders, kiss the girls, and tell them we'll be guiding them into Moesia, the Balkans precisely. They've found a new home. Any of your family out there?"

"Ne, zur. Ve are pagans," resigned Cunimund.

"Oh?" quizzed the dux, "Well, keep your jaw tight on it. They might consider it *sermo rusticus*. And if you see Aoric's boys galloping your way, give them my regrets. A good swift volley's worth."

*   *   *

Aoric rode his wagon in a scowl. Athanaric was off to the east, still campaigning with the torchers while he was strapped with an unexpected visitor. He thought little of the man sitting next to him, *A flesh peddler. One thing to be unfree, but not sold like meat. Not the Tyrfingi way*. The magistrate arrived at Heldrid's, both the widow and Cannabas forewarned and standing at the villa's portico. As Scandius jumped from the wagon, Aoric remained where he sat. "Say what you must," he snapped, uncomfortable in his official duties.

The flesh peddler paced haughtily, addressing the woman and Taifalus, "I'm Scandius Constantinus, the son of Heldrid. As you know, I'm here for what's mine."

"He left it to me," spat Thulia, a deep breath eluding her.

"Perhaps he did in his doddering old age," returned Scandius, "But he was a Roman citizen, as I am. And all of it—the Villa Heldridus Constantinus and everything in it—is legally mine by Roman law."

Aoric spoke forcefully to those below, "This is Threisbaurg, not the Empire, and Gothic law rules here."

Scandius heeled to him, "Gothic law it is, then. What are my rights, old man?"

The magistrate puffed, his eyes flaring large, "Mind your tongue." Then he recited words passed through generations, "His father's chair is his chair. His father's horse is his horse, all property going to the eldest son. The widow keeps her dowry and half the wealth accumulated during the marriage."

Old Hempstalk shook his head, and Thulia stepped past Scandius to address Aoric. Her eyes held a tight rage as she spat, "You're going to let him kick me out of my house? Heldrid left it to me! I have documents."

"Young woman, control your temper," Aoric ordered, "I was hoping for an arrangement between the two of you. What documents?"

"Get them, Thulia," bade Old Hempstalk, "They're legal."

While the widow rushed off, Aoric pondered his predicament. He couldn't read Greek or Latin. Not a word! *What can I do?* He mulled carefully, trying to figure a way to salvage his reputation as a judge and sage. *Ah, ha.* He would pretend, upholding his image of authority and not appear as a barbarian. *May the gods forgive me. She's back!—and wearing a sword! What comes next? Blood on a dead man's door-stoop?* He studied her uncle's face, the man armed and ready to reach for his own weapon. Things could get ugly, a little more than Aoric needed!—Heldrid's son accosted by the Taifali hetmon. *Good enough for a major tribal rift.*

Thulia paced to him in long strides, handing up the parchments. The magistrate set them to his lap, turning each page carefully, for he wished not to break the place where they were bound by linen. From the alphabet, he knew they were written in Latin and signed on the last page by two separate hands. Aoric repositioned them, holding the documents down to Scandius, "Take a look. They're in good Latin and officially witnessed."

* * *

Scandius snatched the packet, flipping pages while studying the writing. *They're in Latin, eh? Well, it's all Greek to me.* He never had an inclination to master languages, much to the consternation of his father. Here and there on the parchments, he could recognize a phrase, probably composed by that sag-assed Iudean lawyer Benobus. Scandius never dealt with Iudeans or Christians. They lugged cerebral impedimentia.

He always knew Benobus searched for a way to cheat him out of the old man's fortune, or at least the bulk of it. Now Scandius had to respond carefully, especially since he had no idea what the magistrate discovered in the document's content. He examined Aoric's face, the way the man looked down at him with disdain, unable to see through the magistrate's expression. *He knows something I don't, the old bastard.* Scandius would proceed with tact, not one of his finer points. He seldom dickered, having chosen a trade not requiring finesse. Slaves brought fixed prices, depending on age, sex, and strength.

All he really wanted was the cream of the estate—his father's gold, portable objects worth trading on the market, perhaps the old fart's prized gelding, at least a better horse than he arrived on. But a farmer he was not. He could pass the villa, its oinkers and sheep or whatever these people cultivated.

Turning eyes from the magistrate, he studied the woman. *The old man always liked the buxom type. Probably can't count beyond her fingers. And what's with the sword?* Scandius knew his rights. He was the first born, the only son. Offering the document back to the widow, he said, "You know its worth. But I think you and I should deal in private."

*　*　*

Away from the magistrate and Old Hempstalk, they stood inside the horse shed, Scandius leering at the white-spotted gelding, "A fine animal. I need a horse like that."

For what? A quick ride to Hell? seethed Thulia. Unsheathing the pitted sword with a metallic swish, she twirled it in a lightning arc, pressing the point to the slaver's neck, "He's mine, also the red-maned mare. I brought them to the marriage." His eyes wide, Scandius lifted his chin as she pushed with more force, hissing, "Oh, yes. It's sharp, and so am I. What did you think?—you'd sail in here and rob a sweet little widow? I can lose some of it and not kill you, or I can kill you right here and keep it all. What's my best option, Flesh Peddler?"

"Wait!" he gurgled, "We can work it out."

She ran the blade along his wind-pipe, just deep enough to create a sting, not quite drawing blood. His mouth gaped as muscles froze back, and beaded pupils strained to view his throat, peering down cross-eyed. If circumstances differed, Thulia could have laughed at his pose, "This pitted sword was your father's and much like you—a poor excuse for what it is. You want it?"

He gave a nearly imperceptible "Nay" as she pulled the blade from him in another circled swing, throwing it across the shed. The weapon revolved but once, its tip driven through a bucket as water showered and staves flew in a clatter! Thulia paced to it, retrieving the sword to run a finger along the jagged edge. Her eyes pierced his, "That could have been your gut, and more than water would have spilled. I'm not some helpless pipit, and you're still alive by God's grace."

"My… my lawyer has contacted Benobus," he stuttered while rubbing a hand to his throat, "Everything will be legally mine, but this farmstead does not suit my lifestyle. I know he kept gold here. How much can you give for this place?"

Thulia tabulated carefully, knowing the man expected every last coin. She had to quote a reasonable figure, "He left five thousand solidii." The slave trader balked as he studied her expression, then dropped his shoulders in resignation. *Close to truth; it must show in my eyes.* She withheld six hundred to raise Sesca and pay for food, "The gold is yours, but I keep this villa, its furnishings, and the livestock."

"Very well," Scandius returned, still fingering his neck.

"Naturally you'll write a receipt of trade witnessed by my uncle and the magistrate."

He shrugged to mumble something as Thulia slipped the saw-toothed blade back to its scabbard, "What was that?"

"I, ah… caught my hand in a ship's block. The running line was moving too fast. My fingers have difficulty in grasping a pen."

She knew his hand was perfectly capable of movement. *He cannot write because he cannot read.* Her voice lightened, "Oh? Well, sometimes accidents happen when people reach for more than they can handle. Either myself or my uncle will pen it, and you can sign it with your personal X. Then we can get along with our lives," and she politely waved him out the doorway.

The boy sat upon a rock at road-edge, his hair curling dark to a ragged coat, his feet placed wide and legs too short. With elbows upon his knees, his chin nestled tight upon raised palms; and then he looked up to see a young horseman slide from his mount. As if recognizing a friend, he stood and leaped over a bucket of water as he ran toward the man. The day was warm, not balmy yet comfortable for Moesia.

"Where am I?" asked the horseman in Greek.

With a gape, the boy replied, "In a road. You're Apollo, are you not?"

"No," chuckled the horseman, running a hand along the white gelding's neck.

"I thought you were Apollo. You look like him with your golden hair. You have his eyes and you ride Apollo's horse."

"No, I'm just a man, a man from the north with a tired mount."

"Oh," the boy sighed, "I was hoping you were Apollo. Then you could make me stronger, cure my mother, and lighten the water. The bucket is too heavy and I no longer want to carry it."

The horseman studied the boy's eyes and small frame, "Sometimes tasks seem burdensome, so we avoid them. Perhaps when we grow up, we can easier face a burden's weight. Tell me—if I were to continue down this road, where might it lead me?"

"To Epirus," claimed the boy.

"Ah, Epirus. And you are going the same way?"

"Yes. I live about a mile further. My mother has a fever and her left eye is shut, so I must carry the water. I think she is dying. Then I shall be alone."

"Let's trade places. I'll carry the bucket and you can ride Apollo's horse," and the horseman reached down, lifting the boy into the white gelding's saddle, "Could not a physician help your mother?" And he plucked the boy's burden and led the horse along the road.

"I think so, but we cannot afford a doctor. We are free but like the unfree. My mother cleans the temple and my father is with the army. He went to Armenia, but that was long ago. I cannot remember him, but mother says that's where he is. He has died or decided not to return, I think."

"Is he a soldier?" asked the horseman, glancing up to the boy.

"No. He loads the mules that carry supplies. They are fighting King Shapur, but they never win."

"Some wars take a long time because the enemy is powerful. He must love you and your mother; and if a man loves someone, he will come back."

"Maybe he loves us not enough and wishes to avoid responsibility."

The horseman offered no answer. And so they continued down the road, the boy riding and the horseman carrying the bucket until they reached the boy's home, a small house built from odd sizes of rock, some jagging this way, others protruding upward or downward, the roof thatched light over heavy poles, the windows few and shuttered. And an aged pen built from salvaged wood contained a goat for curd. The horseman lowered the boy to the road, handing him the bucket. Then he reached inside his coat and the neck of his tunic, working fingers into his purse. He felt around for a little weight. "Here," he said, "You give this solidus to your mother and then run to fetch a doctor. Will you do that?"

The boy stood shocked, even forgetting the bucket's weight, "Yes I will. I thank you, and I will thank you again at worship. You thought you could fool me, but you could not. Only you, and no one else, has gold hair and gold coins and a tall white horse." And then he ran for his home, his short legs raising dust, the water splashing as he shouted, "Mother! Guess who gave me a ride? Apollo! The real breathing Apollo!—not the one at the temple.

Canto Three
FAITH
Anno 349
Six months later

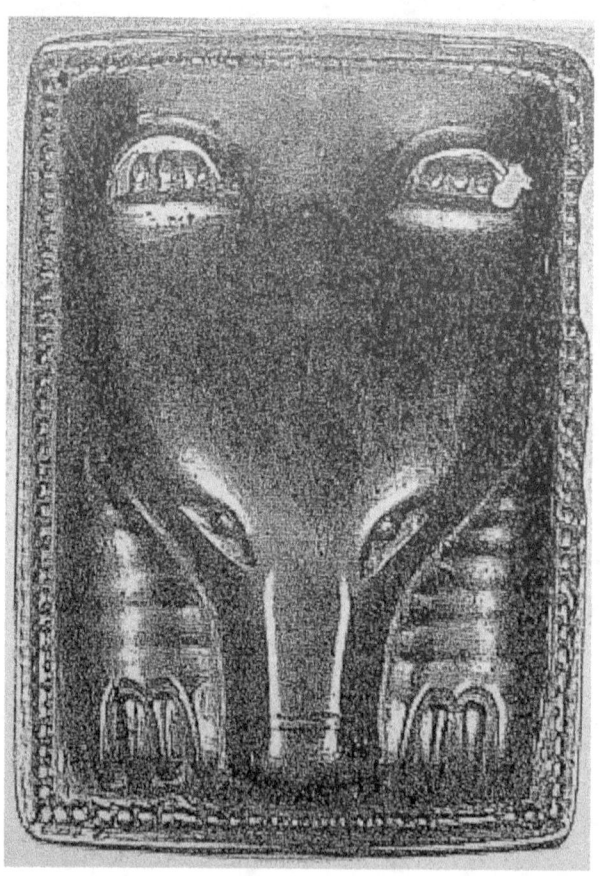

Chapter 25: *Tyrfing the Iron Breaker*

The Kalends of Maius, anno 349

At noon, the tribes conducted the age-old rites of spring, the phallus once again tied upright as the virgin traversed the gardens. Mud season waned as the roads dried, their ruts now being filled by freemen; and Athanaric had decided to take a pleasant ride.

Certainly it would have been pleasant, his intentions honorable, but the widow stood rebuking him. He was taken aback!—always considering himself a pillar of the community. His father was close to retirement, and now he filled the physical functions of magistrate, an important and desirable man. She seemed upset that he even considered a friendly visit! *Odd, what a little bit of wealth can do, change a woman overnight.*

Thulia stood next to her gelding, fitting a bit and harness. "I shall be honest," she continued, "I'm really not interested in your type of man. The best thing you can do is turn your horse around and leave."

She swung from him, dismissing his presence. A freeman brought her saddle as she held the reins to run a hand over the gelding's muzzle. *That's it? Just waving me off like I'm one of the unfree? I'm almost the judge!* He sat straighter in the saddle, his eyes piercing, "My type of man? I'm a decent Goth, a man who adheres to tradition and the law."

Snapping her gaze back to him, she asked, "Would a decent man kill women and children? Tell me. I want to know."

He couldn't find an answer for a moment. What if he had? They deserved their fate and it was his position to eradicate a growing problem. Soon enough he would resume the campaign. The integrity of the kunja depended on it. "I did no more than lance a festering sore."

"By killing Christians?" asked Thulia, "How can you sleep at night?"

"Very well," he retorted, "And in the knowledge I've done good service."

In two long strides, the widow strode to his horse, looking up to his eyes, "It all depends how we view ourselves, doesn't it. I try to have a Christian outlook; and to me you're the festering sore, but I shan't lance you. That would only make one more needless death."

"What?" he balked, "Christian outlook? You're not one of them."

She stepped back a pace, gazing off to somewhere, not directly at him, momentarily silent, then speaking in a low tone, "I guess I am, perhaps a poor excuse for one. It cannot be a secret. Just about everyone knows my views."

Athanaric's eyes widened, his jaw slacking for a moment. *How could an upstanding widow of a good pagan admit to such a thing. She's obviously possessed by some demon to even talk like that.* "You shouldn't speak such words," he returned, "You'll get into trouble."

"What will you do? Crucify me?"

"Well no, but certainly I'm going to send the tribal priests to counsel you. Perhaps they can find the root of your aberration." *The woman has all the signs—combating authority, delusions of righteousness, and foolish enough to admit a stance dictating certain death. A witch or demon has twisted her thoughts. Call me a festering sore? She's completely addled to even think it, let alone claim it.*

Thulia continued to avoid his features, "Please go and don't come back."

Athanaric turned his horse, "Very well. But I don't believe you're thinking straight, Thulia. Priests will arrive the day after tomorrow to conduct a cleansing ceremony, and both tribes will provide witnesses." Then he rode off.

*   *   *

She watched the Squinter gallop down the road to disappear beyond the villa. Her admission was a great mistake, and if she had not been so incensed she never would have said it. The words fell from her lips, too late to retract them; and now she was being tried by priests, not the magistrate. Why? Cleansing ceremonies were given to the possessed—as if she were a diabula, a she-devil—yet she could only stand by her philosophy and admit to being a Christian all over again.

The priests? Thulia knew them both, good men as different as night and day. Ufar Gudja, the chief ceremonial priest, was a meticulous woman-man, never marrying. He dressed himself in spotless clothes; and everything he did was correct and discerning, always clapping his hands three times, loving to watch his assistants run for this and that. He was odd, as they say, but neither mean-spirited nor overly spiritual. Considering himself an artist, Ufar relegated proclamations to old Merjands.

And what of the Proclaimer? He was her confessor, her mystic healer and much like a grandfather. When she first arrived at Threisbaurg, Old Hempstalk sent her to Merjands for counseling. Even later, when troubles choked her spirit, she would sit at Merjands' table as he listened while mixing putrid potions, then offering sound advice. He was from the Far East, the ancient lands of the Alani, no less than a Magus and a disciple of Galen and Plato. And most important, he believed in a deity beyond gods, the Godhead. *Yet he is too wise or stubborn to be a Christian.*

Years ago, both priests knew she held little faith in tribal gods. And now Ufar and Merjands would be her judges. Suddenly, the freeman's voice pierced her thought-train, "Thulia. Your gelding is saddled."

"Oh? Thank you," she returned, her gaze swinging from where Athanaric disappeared, then adding, "I'm sorry but I've changed my mind. After all, I'm a woman. I shall go back to the villa and see how Old Hempstalk fares."

*   *   *

By mid-morning of the second day it seemed darker than pre-dawn as thunder clapped in the distance, creeping down from the oak grove. Old Hempstalk rolled carefully on the lectus, now moved to the villa's anteroom, while Maura the cook fussed over him like a nanny. Thulia stepped back from the main entrance as the rain began, swinging to face her uncle, "How seems the hip this fine morn?"

"I have my good moments and bad ones. This will be the day I toss the crutches and take up the walking stick," and he looked up to Maura, "Teach an old drunk to break his hip. How long has it been?"

"Six weeks, dear," she purred, "And I do believe you can live without another drop."

He chuckled a good one, "I traded drink for a cook, a fine cook. A better man for it," then twisting to the doorway, "Aoric is barking out there. Are they still at field-edge?"

"Most of the witnesses ran into the horse shed. Merjands raised a hand to the sky, Aoric waits stubbornly in his wagon; and it shall not be long before Ufar tippers over to fetch me."

"This is a mock trial and nothing more. They'll not harm you, professed Christian or otherwise, because you're the Taifali hetmon's niece, actually my foster daughter; and for that same reason they cannot touch me, Christian that I am. If they do, the kunja will lose the Taifali—almost its entire heavy cavalry—just as it lost a third when Rustan and his Alans left. The witch hunt will continue beyond Threisbaurg but not here with this family."

Thulia gave a breath of relief. *This family. Yes, we are a family.* "I never thought about it in those terms, but what are they planning?"

"Hokus-pokus," Old Hempstalk professed, "A bold ceremony designed to prove the gods stronger than God. Once that has been established by whatever means Aoric deems legitimate, then our God will be no threat to the tribes."

Thulia peered out the doorway as Ufar came splashing across the villa grounds, puffing as he reached the portico's pillars. He jumped repeatedly in one spot, shaking rain from his brown habit, then catching his breath, "Oh, dread. What a foul day, yet auspicious. We are using the older sword, the one Merjands usually keeps hidden. Breathtaking!—old yet a masterpiece. You should see it planted in the stones; but come to think about it, you will," and he giggled at his statement. "The inner circle is three feet round, perfectly artistic, with rocks piled halfway up the blade, beautiful rocks I found out near the pasturage, all greenish blue, a work of art. The outer circle is six feet from *Tyrfing* who shall be your judge, and Merjands will be the Proclaimer."

"Who is my judge?" asked Thulia, her eyes wide.

"Tyr himself. No-one else. This is the old way, born on the steppe, according to Merjands. Come along, my dear woman, and then we can all go home to a dry hearth," he paused, eyes skyward, "And perhaps a hot cup of spiced wine."

* * *

Thunder boomed closer, almost overhead, as Aoric hid beneath a muslin canvas draped over his wagon seat. Athanaric hunkered tight, his neck short like a turtle's, feet placed firm while halting the wagon's team from bolting through the field.

Thulia stood beyond the outer circle of stones, Ufar at her left side, his woolen robe all the darker from a pelting rain, its folded hood now draped to his nearly hidden face. To her right, Merjands seemed unruffled, his head bare. All the white hairs he possessed lay tight to his skull, and a multitude of liver-spots merged brown through soaken strands. Old Hempstalk leaned upon his new walking stick, Maura's arm around his waist as if she might catch the bulk of a man who hovered at two hundred fifty pound-weight.

Thulia knew most of the witnesses, all standing back at a safe distance, unsure if gods were particular or just haphazard enough to level the whole throng. Among them was Larissa, an old friend from Thulia's days of walking to the community well. The new horse-breaker Russo stood by, having replaced Stefan who moved to Ascentia with the Alans. Other faces known by Thulia seemed overly long with expressions drawn as the storm yanked them down.

In a fury, Aoric jumped to his feet, "What in Hades are we waiting for? It shall not cease, only rain harder. Do you think I enjoy sitting out here in a downpour? I thank my son, my illustrious and weather-wise son, for this fiasco. And why? Because the gods held a draw at the Willows last autumn, no winner, no loser. I want an affirmative exhibit from our tribal gods, a fair and righteous show of their power against this new singular deity."

Merjands turned to face Aoric, eying Thulia before speaking, "Well, then. Let the show begin, as our good magistrate has termed it, although I should point out that the singular God is not particularly new. He has been around for some time, going back to the beginning of the beginning. Tyr will be our judge, his word being first and last. This has been decided by the priesthood; and I should point out that in the past, those unconsecrated, those required to pull *Tyrfing* from the Stones, have failed. Some have died from a failing heart, others blinded, but most have refused to even attempt it, thus admitting guilt."

"What must I do?" pleaded Thulia, raising her voice as the downpour flooded through her kaftan's neck and running down her back.

Suddenly!—like the world's end!—a bolt of lightning slammed to the circle before them, crackling down the sword-hilt and shaft. *Tyrfing* glowed! And the rocks around him fused to a conical stone!

Each man and woman, even a brown dog, caught the acrid scent of brimstone, vaporized sulphur. And steam—or was it smoke?—hissed like a dragon, as half the crowd sprinted to a nebulously safe distance.

"Heavens forbid!" cried Ufar, "Palpitations immense! I have lost my bowels," and he waved a soft wrist before lips, his knees buckling as he sapped to the ground. The assistant priests ran to him, one of them gently slapping his cheek, "Ufar! Are you alive?"

The wagon team bolted, dragging the Squinter as he clutched reins with a death-hold! Picturing himself trampled, he released his grip, falling to mud as the mares galloped for the oak grove, the vehicle slamming through the field while Aoric bounced from the seat, flipping backward to land in the wagon bed and hammered lower with each bounce. "Shit!" he yelled, and then he yelled "Shit" again!

* * *

A slice of time elapsed, heartbeats aflutter coming back to normal rhythm. The crowd closed in, now curious and certainly entertained; for if Aoric wanted a show, he certainly got it. And for whatever reason the rain slacked to a sprinkle. "That was a good one," declared Merjands the All-knowing as he grasped Thulia's arm. "I suppose if you must fetch *Tyrfing*, now is the time to do it."

"But what does this prove?" she wanted to know.

"It's a case of which is stronger. Your one God?—or Tyr, one of many gods."

"My God is," she affirmed.

He smiled a knowing one, "Then you have strong faith. You are gudafaurths—devout. Breathe normally and reach over the inner circle to pull *Tyrfing* from the melted stone. Be careful! It could be hot. You can refuse, but you shall not," and he flipped eyes to the sky, "You are too stubborn, my dear. About as strong-willed as they come."

"Who are *they*?" she wished to know.

"The average Amazon," he winked.

And so it came to be. She stepped into the outer circle, no pains, no heart palpitations, her sight clear enough. With resolve, enhanced by a hint of reckless bravado, perhaps a touch of foolishness, she extended her right hand, grasped the sword's hilt—hot to the touch but not burning hot—and she pulled.

Nothing happened. *It's stuck!* She released her grip and rubbed her hand furiously along her trouser leg. *I'm going to do this one-handed or not at all; otherwise God will think I'm a milksop.* She grabbed the hilt firmer; and gritting teeth, she gave a yank. The sword popped from the stone! She lost her balance, yet regaining it to hold *Tyrfing* high. The witnesses ooed and awed. A rather indistinct murmur followed, and then came the voice of Ufar, now revived and shocked to the core, "Gods above! She had drawn it from melted rock! A divine sign—for Tyr has let her take it."

Even Thulia was shocked! *A most unique sword and a fancy one,* and she stepped back outside the circle, extending the weapon to Merjands, "Here you are, the Sword of Mars."

He shook his head, "Nay, nay. Faith and resolve allowed you to pull it from the stone. Now it's yours," and he turned to the witnesses and proclaimed, "We mortals never expect the unexpected. Yet the gods do, as does the God. And they, in their wisdom, allowed this mortal, this very mortal woman, to touch divine hands. What are we to think?—that Tyr was away on some errand in another part of the word?—or did he, in fact, create the storm itself? I pronounce the sword hers—a most guiltless warrior—as a gift from the gods."

She felt warm in a cool drizzle, her head light upon her shoulders, and she mumbled, "Perhaps I should sit for a moment."

*   *   *

The hay pile cradled Merjands as he sat next to Thulia in the horse shed, the crowd gone and the thunder far to the south. The white-spotted gelding watched them both, his ears cocked to their conversation. She rolled the sword in her hands, examining one side, then the other, green eyes glowing. Never had she seen a weapon like it, absolutely flawless except where the grip-wrapping had burned away. The pommel was topped by a green stone, wide as two thumbs. She passed it to her confidant, still fingering the etching along the blade, "It has an inscription chased along the shaft, but not Latin or Greek. Who etched it?"

"One of several great smiths, my dear. It was forged in the Ili Valley by students of Tzu Chi—the First Master. The blade will cut the hardest iron; and it was given to a great priestess of the Wusun—People of the Crow—now called Alani... the very blood flowing within you. I named the sword the *Iron Breaker* to record its strength, but call it what you wish. The script is Khotani Saka and denotes the Bear—Protector of the People."

The sage felt along blade-edge and fingered the hilt, pulling his cinnabar to finally postulate, "The sword has changed, the grip still aged but the blade has turned to flame-hard blue. Gods create strange things. It was the strongest sword upon the steppe, now infinitely better—not just a weapon but an instrument—a companion for the Amazon in all her travels."

Thulia glowed, "*Tyrfing the Iron Breaker*, a fine name for a great blade. Since childhood, I prayed for a real sword. But this? It came from God, I think," and then she added, "And from you."

"You charge at anything, lancing giants real and perceived, the last one standing after fighting bandits. You are the She-Bear—protector of the people—just as this sword is; and you earned it through more than deeds and by a higher goal. Years ago, Cannabas sent a girl to me because she claimed to be an Amazon," and he chuckled through his half-grin, "She said, *I'm going to protect the people from evil*. How could I rebuke such an ideal... from the one pure heart? And too, I believed as I still do: that something evil happened to you as a child. Even back then, the Godhead was in you. I told Cannabas you were perfectly normal, and he allowed you to do things Amazons were famed for."

"He did?"

"Well, I believe he scolded you, half-heartedly strapped you, but he never discouraged you. He complained yet he created a lancer and the best horse dancer this kunja will ever see."

She leaned and kissed his forehead, "Thank you."

"For what?"

"This wondrous sword."

Merjands rolled to a knee, then to his feet, "It was never mine to give. Only to pass to its rightful Guardian. In a time of crisis, you may lend it to the morally brave, for you are Giver of the Sword. It was forged to save the innocent, to combat evil. You and it are one and the same." He brushed straw from a wet robe, "Heard anything from Fritigern?"

She looked up the mystic, "He's upon some palm-treed shore, eating dates and chasing Aethiopians. He'll not write if he had the chance."

"Fine young man there," winked Merjands while stooping, "Give him a few years."

"I'm perfectly happy the way I am. What did you mean?—*Giver of the Sword*."

The old man ducked his head at the horse shed's entrance, stepping outside. Then he leaned back in, "We saw no average storm. A great battle, my dear. The greatest battle ever fought. And those who were fortunate to see it, to recognize it for what it was, shall recall it through the generations. What you hold is sacred, as was its previous owner. Soon you will be the master, not the pupil, and you will know who she was. It was made in the old style, when her world rolled green. But now the sword is new again, re-forged by the great hand of God. You are its Guardian, as it is yours; and now you shall leave us. Up to the Bairgs-ahei… to your own kind. Aoric fears you and all you stand for; and though he'll not banish you in so many words, your time in Threisbaurg is over."

She jumped to her feet, "How did you know?" then realizing he sensed more than thoughts, "I cannot stay here another fortnight. Much too uncomfortable, for they wish me out of their lives."

"This shall pass, as shall I... in this, the twilight of the gods. You have a new guide—a man of light—no more dark robes. Men like Aoric and myself will find little room in the new world, your world. But remember us, the old order, who do what we must to protect what we built. Remember the steppe and where you came from. Will you do that?"

She looked down to the *Iron Breaker*, again meeting his eyes to nod affirmative, "This belonged to the master who owned the akinakes, both the same age and forged in the days of the Wusun. That I know. But I need more than hints and cannot lose my life-thread guide. Can we continue in the future?"

His expression waxed to tenderness, "It's already here. You outlived a time of giants, with its profane swords and fools for priests. Was the future so hard to gain?"

"No," she admitted, "But it was painful. And why should you scratch me with wisdom and not impart it all?"

"You ask *me* to live in the new world? *Me*—the champion of the old?" He sighed to momentary silence, and then continued, "First I must strengthen Ufar Gudja, if that's possible. Then we shall see, my dear. Perhaps we can meet again... upon the shore of a deep-green lake." And saying all he would, the Proclaimer ducked from view to return to her fleeting past.

Chapter 26: By More than Chance

Thulia sat at the long table, a pile of receipts heaped before her. Throughout the morning, she accumulated Heldrid's bills of sale to the Romans, all going back through a period of twenty years. Most were for horses sold to a place called Capidava, the signatures varying from year to year, and each bill had a red cross stamped at the top. *Why would a man use a cross as his logo if he were not a Christian?*

In the corner of her eye, she caught the cook sweeping by with an armload of clean linen. "Maura, can I ask you a question?"

"Of course, dear. What is it?" and Maura dropped her burden to the far end of the table.

"These bills of sale have a cross on them," and she held out a document.

"Oh, yes," Maura purred, "That's Heldrid's tamga. All his free-ranging stock has that brand. They are separate, you know, from the kunja's horses although they cross pasture."

"But look at the design," implored Thulia.

"Oh, such a sad thing. So many Christians died that way. When I was a child—I am Dacian, you know—they killed many harmless people. He was, let me think, Diocletian. Yes, Emperor Diocletian."

Thulia dropped the bill of sale back to the stack, slouching in the high-backed chair, "But why would Heldrid use the cross for a tamga?"

"I do not know, dear," Maura admitted, "I never thought about it. You know as well as I do that he sympathized with the oppressed. He always used it, even before I came here. But why?—I have no idea. You might ask old Raimund the agister."

Thulia nodded and Maura gathered up the linen, trudging down the villa's right wing. *Evidently changing their sheets*, Thulia grinned to herself; for Old Hempstalk's sheets and Maura's covered the same bed. Then she went back to the documents, trying to grasp the nature of running a self-sustaining estate. Heldrid had additional monies, but she did not; and now she was leaving the villa to her uncle's care.

*   *   *

After cooking pot greens with Sesca, buttered and tasty, Thulia arrived at the oak grove to noon-time shade, the trees green again, their leaves well beyond budding. Dismounting, she walked deep within the grove to where the cabin was. It stood barren and small, the door falling from its leather hinges. To one side lay the wood pile, now rotting with worm holes in each short log.

A great sadness welled in her breast as she paced to the largest oak, a cairn of rocks stacked near it; and she knelt to bless the man below her. Leaning to cold stones, she placed a handful of trumpet-flowers upon them. He was such a poor man, a good man, his essence still in this world; and she recalled the first time she revisited the grave.

Upon her knees she caressed rocks as a black robe blocked the sun. She stood to face him. The sadness in his eyes equaled hers and then they brightened above a barely perceptible smile. "Do not weep for rotting flesh. Let the worms have it," he stated, reaching to her and wiping cheeks with an aged hand.

"What of his soul? Here it remains, trapped upon this earth," and more tears rolled, unquelled.

"Was he not a Bear?" claimed Merjands, his smile now broader.

"Yes. That was his name in the Fenni tongue, but he wanted to stroll among the stars. An Arian priest could help his soul reach them. I'm sure of it."

Merjands' grin vanished in a flash, "There is more to priesthood than the Church and more to a Bear than ascent. Perhaps he rode to Dreamland upon a borrowed mount, to return to this vulgar plane with good things. He may be the essence of a new protector. So the Bear never leaves us but enters another skin. Otherwise, who might be the next Othar?"

Her tears quelled, and she asked, "Dreamland?"

He turned and waved toward the hill, "Come. Let us walk to the horse barns and I shall attempt to explain." They strode from the dark grove as Merjands puffed, "Someday I shall find a better staff, but this aged one has served me well across this known world. Where was I?" and he stopped midstride to fondle his cinnabar, "Ah, yes! Dreamland. Only the righteous, the highest soul, can ride there," and he chuckled, "That leaves me out," and then continued, "Such a journey is beyond himina-gards. Dreamland is where the karman awaits rebirth. Such is the process of Delayed Samsara—the karman in suspension. When the precise recipient is found, the Bear returns again, to enter a correct mind and physicality, to nurture the good and defend it from all things evil, from avarice and lust and all the poor seeds that sprout within us. Christians have ten commandments, but there is only one—always do the morally right. That is your charge, as it was Othar's. And he did it without hesitation."

Thulia returned to the present, still unable to grasp Merjands' gist. Samsara? Dreamland? Seers were an odd lot. Himina-gards seemed easier to comprehend, and she cupped hands to close her eyes, speaking softly, "My Father in himina-gards, blessed be thy name. I plead that you accept the man who lies here. Let him stroll among the stars, his one great wish. He had a pure heart. For the soul of Othar, I pray."

She stood quickly, turning from the rocks. Although he killed a man, Othar could not be in the lower house. He spent his last sighted years in goodness, cutting wood for an entire year to buy a cow, then giving it to the priests for sacrifice. The meat went to the other poor and Othar kept the heart to boil it. He planted a small garden, calling it South Farm; and until his last year he walked a big man, still tall and wide, a wood-cutting Finnermon. He never spoke well, his native tongue too foreign, not like Gothic or Latin or Greek. Then he shrank, his back hunching. On his last day, he wanted to cut wood, probably to hear the sound of it. That's how she found him—at the wood pile, saw in hand.

She wiped a sleeve across cheeks, sopping up the wet and breathing deep. Othar ached for what he did to the Wasteland, killed his own brother to save her life, and he gave her the balsam doll exactly when needed. There had to be a way for the unbaptized to avoid the lower house.

If anyone could help Othar, it would be the presbyter. She would leave upon the morrow, probably a week of traveling with Sesca in tow, and find a new home at Ascentia. *Time to make peace with Selenas*. The resentment was hers, not his, and she was sure he was oblivious to it.

*   *   *

Selenas and Rustan stood at the Aluta admiring the finished bridge, built from huge trees laid across the river. Smaller trees ran crosswise on the span, all bored and pegged—thirty miles below Ascentia, another twenty to Axeville, at forest-edge in the Caucaland. To build the bridge, they pitched tents and made lean-tos, camping at the river for a week. *A fine structure*, mused Rustan, *As good a bridge as any in these rustic parts.* A total of fifty men with axes, bow-saws, and huge wooden mauls, worked each day from dawn to dusk. Four bullock teams and stout rope moved the two trees, the bridge a real accomplishment with the help of God. Easier it would be to travel back and forth to Ascentia. The village would grow.

"What now?" asked Rustan as they stood on the rocks below the bridge.

"We can pack up and go home."

"Good idea. Our wives have lived a long week without us," Rustan beamed, "As we have likewise."

Selenas tossed a small rock to the flodus, "True, but no wife awaits your return. Do you not get lonely?"

Rustan had dug a verbal pit for himself, a stark and immoral truth at the bottom of it; and he was somewhat embarrassed for not being candid with Selenas before. "When I failed to remarry, some folk believed I wished not to bespoil the memory of my wife. That was half a truth. We continue our lives, do we not? Safrax was raised by my woman Valeria, and she is no less than a good wife. She was a Roman slave, you know. Some people remember it, a raid into Moesia now twelve years past."

Selenas appeared mildly surprised, obviously never thinking of Valeria's place in a wifeless household, "Oh. You mean she sleeps with you, then."

"Well, of course," admitted Rustan, "We only have two beds, and she is the mother Safrax never had. We live in sin, but I cannot express any regret for her or myself. If anything, I apologize for laws that forbid us to marry. To me, she is not unfree. Never was. I took her from the Romans for that very reason. Was I wrong to free a slave?—am I still wrong in my judgment of her status? I do not think so, and I'll not have anyone tell me otherwise. He can pronounce, *You are going to Hell for it*, but what would Xristos say?—that I build a third bed and treat her as the Romans did?"

"No. You are correct; a freed woman is far from a slave. And sleeping with women before or beyond marriage is exactly the same. Time holds no factor. And as my father-in-law, you certainly know I have sinned no less than you." He smiled, tipped a gaze toward the bridge, and changed the subject, "Look at that great crew."

Rustan glanced up to men crossing the span with their tools, Safrax among them. The boy was beyond ten, not old enough to be a man or young enough to stay home with the women; and so Rustan brought him along to give Safrax a taste of future manhood. The boy was tall and big-boned, his hair now oriental saffron. He looked down to see his father and Selenas, then pretending to lose his balance.

"Don't fall!" cried Rustan, "You'll break a leg, and the water is cold."

The Aluta ran like ice—even though mid spring—as it tumbled through Red Tower gorge to smoothen upon the steppe before entering the Danube. Rivers and lakes abounded in Transylvania.

The two men looked to each other in satisfaction. One river was conquered, at least after a fashion. A job well done.

* * *

As she returned from the oak grove, Thulia noticed Raimund the agister working in the client's garden. She dropped from the saddle and approached him cautiously, the man known as the estate's curmudgeon; and at the moment he swung a mean-looking shovel. "Hailog, Raimund. Perhaps you can help me," claimed Thulia.

The man peaked at six feet and more, gruff as a badger at seventy years. He weighed her with hard eyes, stabbing his spade to fresh-turned soil. The plot was used by the entire staff, large enough to produce most of the vegetables consumed at the villa. "Horse shit," he snapped through tight-lipped gums.

"What?" she piqued, taken aback.

"Black horse shit," he enlarged.

"I'm sorry, but I cannot understand why you speak to me like that."

"Old black horse shit," he enlarged further.

"Have I trespassed upon your domain?"

"Look, shweety," he growled, "You're standing in old black horse shit."

"Oh! Well, so I am. Sorry about that."

"Shorry for what? Shit on yer boots? It's plenty old, no longer stinks. Last year we grew a squash bigger than a stallion's head. Huge it was. Horse shit. That's the stuff—food of the gods."

"As the agister, Raimund, you oversee the tamga branding," she declared, stepping back from the garden to field-edge, "And so I was wondering why Heldrid chose the cross for its design."

"Course he did," the big man spat, "Got his citizenship from it. Made his coin from it. Got that place in Africa and built this one."

Thulia nodded politely. Turning from the curmudgeon, she gazed across the fields toward the oak grove, mulling Raimund's answer. What is he talking about? She spun around, trying to pry more from him, "When, and from whom? Diocletian?"

"Diocletian? You flying with one wing, shweety?" he huffed, "Constantine and Lady Helena. Twenty years ago."

*   *   *

At mid afternoon, Thulia walked through the birches with Sesca as they picked more pot greens. Then she went back to the stack of papers on the long-table. Maura helped her with geography below the river; and Capidava turned out to be a small equestrian fort between Durostorum and Noviodunum. According to varied sales, Capidava was purchasing thirty to fifty geldings per year. Thulia would have Old Hempstalk assume Heldrid's position by contacting the garrison's present commander. The villa could sell or trade horses for wheat and barley, plus a few incidentals.

Pawing through the papers, Thulia couldn't shake the Heldridian mystery—the cross-shaped tamga. And she strode outside looking for Raimund again. He was obtuse and cranky, yet the man knew more about Heldrid's past than any other person at the villa. She found him in the horse shed mixing fodder. He glanced her way as she entered, then returned to spooning yellow ooze from one bucket to another. "How do you fare this afternoon, Raimund?" she asked cheerfully.

"Mutton fat," he snapped.

"Excuse me?" she returned.

"Mutton fat and barley," and he pointed to the long-legged mare, "This one likes it," then the red-maned mare, "That one hates it," and finally the white-spotted gelding, "That one loves it."

"I'm glad you care for them so well. Tomorrow morning, I'll be taking two of them up to Ascentia with my daughter. I shall not return for some time, perhaps years. But I was wondering about Constantine and his mother. What did Heldrid do for them?"

He stopped stirring the bucket, tilted his head, and barked, "Years? Who will care for them?"

"The horses? Why, I will."

"You feed them poorly. They should stay here."

"Well, I shall not walk. Ascentia is a long ride from here."

Raimund seemed surprised, "It is, eh. How far?"

"A week, perhaps longer."

He almost dropped the bucket!—his jaw aslack, "Too far for a little girl. Why?"

"It's a long ride but we have no choice," she explained, "You see, Raimund, I'm a Christian and this place—Threisbaurg—is a bad place for Christians now."

"Ah!" he nodded, stirring the bucket again, "Now I understand. A hard time for some. That be why you keep asking me about Heldrid and the Constantines, right?"

"Actually, I'm just curious about the cross."

"Cross?" he grunted, "I helped him. Went to the place where Helena found it. Wrapped it in muslin. Put it in a box, a big box. Lugged it to Byblos. Sailed it to Constantinople—new center of the world. Got a piece of it, round here somewhere. Still in the muslin. Sometimes it bleeds or sometimes it heals. Heldrid got a new name, a chunk of Hippo. Got this place. Anything else you need to know, shweety?"

"No," she gasped, her head light and eyes ablur, clutching a stall with both hands so she wouldn't fall. It remained in the arka on the floor of her vanity. *A piece of the True Cross.*

* * *

When she returned to the main villa, Maura greeted her on the portico, excitedly blurting, "The old Magus was here. The tall one with the ash-wood staff. He wanted you to have a traveling mirror, an odd gift."

"A mirror? Where is he?" demanded Thulia, looking for Merjands beyond the pillars. She had been at the horse shed for only a short time; and how could she have missed a man who always walked?

Maura stepped off the portico, looked both ways, and mumbled, "How strange. He was here a moment ago," then turning back, "But the mirror is inside on the table. Not much, judging from the leather case. Rotten and falling apart."

Thulia rushed to the long table, grabbing the case as crumbling scrids of leather fell to the floor. She peeled back the flap, and it broke in her hand as more dried chips sprinkled to her feet. *Thank you, Merjands. It comes from the heart, so it's still special—even though crusted with age.* She had difficulty sliding the mirror from the case, almost stuck within it. Then the fancy edge came into view. She tugged it again as it finally slid free. It was heavy for its size and he had obviously cleaned it with great care, for its surface reflected a bright candescence. She held it by its handle, "It must be gold plated to shine like this. Much nicer than the case," then handing it to Maura.

The cook hefted it, looking at both sides, the mirror finish and the intricate scrolling of crouched stags upon the reverse. Her eyes bulged and her jaw dropped, and she worked her mouth to find words, "Oh, my dear. I'm rather sure this is solid gold, not plated." And she handed it back to Thulia, "It must be very old, judging from its brittle case. It looks Scythian or like something ancient. I know not what a mirror like this is worth! How odd. The old Magus gave it away as if—you know what I mean—it was just an ordinary mirror. Perhaps he had no idea of its value."

Thulia dropped to the bench, confounded by the day's events. She closed eyes, breathing slowly, and looked up to Maura, "He knew. And you just called him a Magus. Why?"

"He must be a Magus to do what he does," shrugged Maura, "How else could an old man come and go without anyone seeing him?"

Thulia mulled the answer and picked up the mirror, "Sesca is still outside with Old Hempstalk. I'll be in my chambers packing." And she left Maura to a cook's duties.

In her room, she placed the three items upon her coverlet—the sword, the akinakes and mirror. She plopped to the bed and studied them. They all belonged to the same person, she was sure of it, each of great age and older than Merjands could possibly be as temporal flesh and blood.

These gifts were not of this earth, not from a world as it presently existed, yet they were real enough. *There IS a Dreamland! He has been conditioning me since childhood as her replacement.* Yet there was even more to it!—the guidance of Othar and Old Hempstalk, even the man of light. And what about Heldrid? All of them were aged men, each sent or placed in her path by some unknown force. Thulia wished to smile but could not find one. *Your destiny is never what you think it is. I was simple and thought my life would be the same.* Falling backward to the coverlet, she rested her eyes but could not gain a wink of sleep, nor would she find it in the coming night. That she knew.

After awhile, she heard Old Hempstalk with Sesca down in the great room. She slid from the bed and rummaged in the wardrobe, rewrapping an artifact so aged and holy that it brought tears from the deepest wellspring. *Truly, it should be with Selenas.* She wiped a forearm across cheeks and placed the muslin in the largest travel sack, then tying it off. Thulia would take no more that her gelding and pack horse could carry—a woman on the road, alone and with a child, nine pounds of solidii, and a gold mirror. If the wrong person knew she carried that much wealth, they'd attempt to take it. During the winter she designed a new armored tunic. Made by a girdler, it was fashioned with heavy leather; and to it she sewed the browned scales from Old Hempstalk's original. Built with three overlapping shoulder tiers, the tunic belted at the torso. *New armor for a new life.* Now she could breathe, for the tunic raised her bosom instead of squashing it, giving fluid movement for swinging a sword.

She would leave Threisbaurg not as a mother in flight, but as the Amazon with the *Iron Breaker's* blue-hard blade. She had lost Merjands. Her fading mentor had vanished in a wink, the one earthly person who knew about her encounter, or was it a vision?—the strange man of light. All of these gifts, these events, came to her by more than chance. She had been conditioned, groomed, for some ultimate purpose. The sword was sacred, an old god giving way to a true one. The akinakes and mirror came from her ancestral past, from some unknown woman who owned weapons, perhaps an actual Amazon. And the wood came from the very timber Xristos died upon.

She felt drained. Never had she considered herself as anyone special except at the horse barns. She had been a poor pagan and even less a Christian, and she was sure that spirituality had nothing in common with the gifts. Yet they were given to her charge.

Why? The answer was inexplicable. She would ask Selenas, a poor substitute for Merjands. As did Selenas and Frit—*my dearest Frit*—she was heading for a world beyond twin rivers, yet what this new world encompassed she did not know.

* * *

Frit sat at a tavern just inside the wall at the Via Flaminia, his gelding at a nearby livery. The commotion outside was near deafening as teamsters prepared wagons for night delivery, large vehicles not allowed on Rome's streets during daylight; and beyond the teams and between them, revelers shouted and laughed, all pleasantly drunk at the end of a fair day in Maius.

A young man at a nearby table noticed his military cut, listening to his inflection through the din. "You're not Roman.

They never drink ale," he proclaimed in a Germanic accent, then adding, "Coupo, give this man another round."

Frit looked up from his mug to study the stranger, obviously an officer though he wore a single wristlet extending up his right arm. It appeared to be pure silver. With the ale coming his way, Frit slid his chair back, standing to the man and speaking louder, "I thank you, sir."

The man's countenance changed, the smile leaving his face, "A Goth?"

"Yes I am. A Tyrfingus from Scythia."

"We're old enemies, then. Opposing Germans," the officer stated. He wiped ale from his upper lip to add a grin, "But the heavens rotate. Change, do they not?"

"And you are?"

"An Asding Vandal."

With some difficulty Frit accepted the ale as the coupo passed it to him. The Asdings killed his father in battle. Many a tribal veteran had scars to remind him of it: Aoric, Heldrid, and Old Hempstalk included. Yet the young officer was correct. The blue vault rolls, expanding time, a previous day chased by night—a day forever gone. Frit shrugged, wanting no part of the past. The stranger was too young to have fought anyone in a battle occurring some ten years ago. "Have a seat," waved Frit, then adding, "I'm not sure Goths are actually Germans. My mother was Carpi. We're bastards—German, Carpi, Dacian, Sarmatian, even Cappadocian."

The Vandal plunked to a stool across from him, the noise of liverymen requiring the man to almost shout, "Then a Goth is a Goth. I'm expecting a friend. Perhaps you should meet him. Ever thought of joining the auxiliary?"

"That's why I'm here in Rome," announced Frit, "My nomen is Fritigern."

"I'm Thaurus. They call me Silver Arm. It hides a scar with too long a story. My friend is a Spaniard—Theodosius—actually my superior in the Tenth Legion Gemina. I assume you can ride well."

Frit grinned a big one, "I was trained for five years by a Taifali cataphract."

Thaurus laughed, "The heavy horse, eh. We don't need lancers in Germania, but there's a dearth of light cavalry. I'm willing to bet Theo will snatch you up. He's a Christian, you know, his only fault."

With a chuckle, Frit admitted, "All of us cannot be perfect. My brother is an Arian presbyter."

The Vandal sat back, raising a brow, "And you?"

"A pagan. But I know some of the Bible, the memorable tales."

"Good," professed Thaurus, "A Bible-reading pagan can't be all bad. Personally, I'm much the same. Vacillating. Meet me at the Cassian Gate by mid-morning if you haven't changed your mind."

"Where will we be headed and who are we fighting?"

"Up to Placentia and Como, then through Brennus Pass. Our destination is the fortress Vindobona on the Danube plains," claimed the Vandal, taking a slug of ale and wiping his lips, "Our foes are the Alemanni, strong and determined, and poorer than field mice. We were all that way once. But you know it's far better to drift with the current than flail against it. Some of us—the Gauls, we Vandals, and you Goths—can view something better than tearing at venison," and he chuckled while sliding the empty mug across the table, motioning to the coupo again. Then he met Frit's eyes, "Ride above the Alemanni. Do not eat the deer and hare. No fat there. Chew the cow and lick pork, quench from the golden pear, and drop a real, honest coin to your purse. Fight well and hard. And when a few years pass, and if you remain alive and earn the right to call yourself 'Flavius,' then marry a woman of substance. Your sons will thank you for it."

Frit knew exactly what Thaurus meant— citizenship, Roman citizenship, the most valuable commodity in the known world.

Chapter 27: The Dark-Thought Ones

Four days before the Ides of Maius

In Vindobona's Praetorium courtyard, Soranus and Theodosius paced slowly before seasoned horsemen and new recruits, all standing at attention six lines deep. Soranus halted before a burly young man, curly haired with a bushy, drooping moustache, "Ah, Antonius. Am I correct?"

"Yes, sir," the man shot back, "Antonius Julius Arvernus. I was in last year's campaign."

"The wild Gaul, eh? I recall you swill your drink. Well, you're a year older, perhaps wiser and know when to bibe and not to." Then he stepped two paces back, "Listen up! For some of you horse soldiers, a welcome back to the Tenth Gemina. For others?—well, we shall see. My name is Junius Soranus, commander of this hell hole. Perhaps I look young, but I can kill you like a seasoned pro. This is my fortress and you are my ultimate toys. Some of you will make errors in judgment, tossed out like rotten cabbage, or—even worse— executed for it. So welcome to the real world, the Imperial Army, the only world you shall live, bleed, and die in."

He took a pace to the right, eying a couple of new faces, then snapped his gaze ahead, "You'll find out quick enough that I'm a Christian; and drinking, whoring, and cheating, do not cut it here at Vindobona. What you do at the front is your own business. Whore wagons will park there; but when gonorrhea climbs up your prick and it refuses to piss, don't come sobbing to me. I'll hear none of it! Understand?"

Flicking a half-hearted wave, he brushed off additional words on morality, "So much for that subject. The Gemina is the largest and best legion on the limes. Our auxiliary cavalry is foremost this side of the Euphrates. The Ala Vindobonisis will again be led by Commander Theodosius, a good Christian. The new ala—probably called the Alemannisis—will be raised by Captain Thaurus, who shall become a good Christian of I'll have his ass on a big fucking stick. Enough said," and he strode back to Theodosius, exchanged whispers, and finished by commanding, "I'll see Fritigern the Goth in my office at noon, no later. Dismissed!"

*   *   *

After the critique by Commander Soranus, each man found something to do, if only repacking gear for the front. Frit went outside the fortress and sauntered past horses grazing in a field no less spacious than a steppe. Each rider in an ala would have access to a second mount, paid from his own wages, and handy if he rode a wounded or tired one. The horses were kept by a corps of stablemen, and the herd was tended by a medicus equorum.

Frit looked skyward to check the sun's height, and walked down to the river. The upper Danube seemed no smaller than it did at the Stone Bridge, rolling lazy as a flat and seemingly current-less body. He watched a naval vessel come downriver, its oars raised and pulled in perfect unison, a smaller boat of the dromon class. It passed, and the Danube fell back to tranquility as a huge fish rolled at the surface!—not ten arm-lengths from him. He could swear it was a trout yet the fish was nearly three feet long, perhaps thirty or forty pound-weight. Not a trout, but a giant that looked like one. Frit squatted, hoping to see it again but the sun neared its peak, and so he strode back to the fortress.

When he entered the Commander's office, the man stood at the window, his back to Frit as if studying a far off occurrence. Soranus turned, his features young and swarthy like a Syrian, his nose beaked and carrying a small white scar. He leaned back against the iron window-frame to speak informally, "Had a chance to examine your new surroundings?"

"Yes, sir," claimed Frit, standing erect, "Checked the mounts and then went down to the river. I saw a trout bigger than any in Gothia. A tough one to catch, even on fifteen-hair line."

"You're a fisherman who saw a huchen, eh? Well, nobody catches them. They spear them," claimed Soranus, stepping to a heaped desk, "Have a seat. Pull up the King's Chair, I call it," and he pointed to a high-backed one against the wall. Frit did as ordered while Soranus slid to his own chair behind the clutter, "I'm a fisherman myself, a Nicomedian, so I fished the Marmara for tuna, some as big as a horse—the ones you never catch. Angled with my brother since childhood. Peter and Andrew fished as brothers. I understand your brother is a churchman, a presbyter?"

"Yes, sir. He has a congregation in a small baurg in Transylvania, but he's not the angler I am. Angling is the highest sport, even above hunting."

"Really," mused the Commander, "Why is that?'

"An angler can toss an unwanted fish back. You know, either too small or the wrong kind; but a hunter?—what lies before him is lifeless, and even the gods cannot revive it."

Soranus leaned forward, his examination intense, "That's an odd philosophy in these parts. Most men up here kill and think little of it, yet you're not a Christian, are you."

Frit squirmed, the chair too spacious, the back too straight, and warmth flushed from his neck to color his cheeks,

"No, sir. I'm not sure what I am at the moment, but no, I'm not a Christian."

Soranus stood again and Frit did likewise, the Commander turning his back again to gaze out the window, "When you boys stopped at the Pass for a show of talent, you flashed a quick sword, also a natural horseman." He turned to face Frit, "Speak three languages, eh? We're shorthanded for the new ala, and I'm starting you as a Decurion in charge of thirty riders, the only recruit starting off as lieutenant. Officially, you're a mercenary, hired by the yearly campaign. Thaurus will be your immediate superior, but Theo rides a horse above. Live up to Theo's expectations and you'll live up to mine. I've heard quite the tale—a young Goth who wheedled his way into the Empire, traveled through Moesia, down to Epirus, up through Illyricum, into Pannonia, down to Rome, and back up here to Pannonia again. That's a journey and a half. What exactly are you searching for?"

Frit got warmer around the neck, "Nothing, sir."

Soranus gave him the hard eye, "Oh? Then what are you running from?

*　　*　　*

Forty miles from the Aluta, as a snake crawls, Ulmenia sat where the trade road followed a brook that never dried in summer, always coursing clear through the meadows. Ulmenians seldom ventured to Threisbaurg or down to the Drobetas, and they certainly stayed clear of Transylvania. They were not totally foolish!—just mostly foolish. Although they were Goths in the general sense, they were actually Carpians who were defeated so long ago their swords became shorter and shorter until they turned into whittling knives. Ulmenia held great stands of ash and birch and larch, and the baurg's famed carvers made bowls and spoons for the Roman trader and who not else. Among elder artisans, the old man—

as he was known—carved pea soup spoons, products of intricate science, famed as just right and always fine and smooth. No blistering the lips. Even You-He and Oxartes bought one each time they passed through.

Now, upon this particular day, the old man sat outside the roadhouse upon a stool when the young man approached. Earlier, the old man had been inside, just to see what the Amazon looked like, more womanish than he expected. He looked up at the young man, then checked his spoon for straightness. By day's-end the spoon would be finished, a good, birchen soup spoon—as smooth as they come—and fetching two asses when sold, maybe three asses if the buyer was entirely foolish.

"Is she still in there?" the young man inquired, sheepishly pointing to the door.

"Yes. Yes. And she has a child. I did not think the Amazon would have a child, for when would she find the time to… Well, you know what I mean."

"True," agreed the young man, "To spend all your days killing evil men leaves few moments for procreation. Is she big and strong?"

"No. I mean yes!" explained the old man in wonderment, "She is like a woman only bigger," and he pinched the knife and spoon between his knees, pushing hands far out in front of his chest.

The young man's eyes grew immensely huge, and he gasped, "No! You are making me a fool."

"It is true. Great big ones! See for yourself."

"What? Go inside?"

"Certainly. She does not bite," the old man claimed, "I went in to look at her and I am still alive, but I have tried to be good and honest all my life. She must be able to tell if a man is good or bad… to slay the bad ones like she does."

"I have been good," the young man affirmed, "You can ask my lord and lady. They always say, *Oh that Mensa, he is good. Never does bad things.*"

"Then she will not slay you," the old man professed, "Go ahead. Go inside."

The young man reached for the door latch yet pulled back. He wiped hands upon his trousers and looked at his fingernails, having washed just in case the stories were real—*"The Amazon is at the roadhouse. She has a real sword and rides a huge horse."* Earlier, he stopped at the livery. Inside, a great horse ate hay. It even looked at him! So he thought, *If this is her horse then she is real, too.* He had never seen an Amazon before, especially one who slew the evil Mordwine. Then she killed a dragon!—and a hundred trolls. Not a single troll was left in the Caucaland. *She is a legend and really real all in one person!*

His fingernails had a dirt under them, but not much. So the young man opened the door and stepped into the roadhouse. Over in one corner, a man drank beer. The man was Walia. He always drank beer. *It is very crowded in here.* Lothar and Gorbanus sat at another table playing their usual board game; and six men stood above them, each nodding at Lothar's skill and wincing when Gorbanus moved his piece. *Lothar is going to win again. He always wins.* Four strangers sat at another table while chewing partridge. They were traders, either headed to or from Olbia and the twin Drobetas. In another corner, a woman and little girl sat eating deer stew. They were the only people in the entire roadhouse! There was no Amazon.

Then he saw the sword lying in the empty chair next to the woman. *Such a sword must be keen-edged—to kill what it did.* But he could not actually see it, just the grip and hilt, its scabbard encased in polished bronze! He gawked at the sword and then the Amazon, for she was gigantic. The old man was right. She looked more like a woman than any other woman he had ever seen! So he went over to ask about the weapon but could not help staring at her bosom. Not wanting her to think he was lecherous—*for she might slay me*—he thought of something to talk about as he noticed the spoon. "Do you like the soup spoon?" he asked.

"Oh, yes. A good spoon," she returned, slurping the stew.

"I carved it," he said proudly, his front teeth protruding beyond his smile.

"Really?" she grinned back, "You carved it all by yourself?"

She is very impressed! "Oh, yes," he puffed, "This is Ulmenia, the spoon and bowl capital of the world. Even the emperor's cook uses our spoons. We make soup spoons, stew spoons, gruel spoons, all different kinds of brusts… I mean spoons." Turning flush, he changed the subject in a hurry, "That is a very long sword. Is it sharp?"

The Amazon was laughing very much, and finally she nodded, "It's *Tyrfing the Iron Breaker*. Sharper than most."

"Did it slay the evil giant?"

"No," she smiled broader, "I used a lance."

"Oh," said the young man in his buck-toothed grin, "Did it slay the dragon?"

She chuckled and replied, "No."

"Did you strangle it with your hands?"

"No."

He could not understand how she killed such a fierce beast, unless—and it seemed entirely possible—so the young man blushed to ask, "Did you smother it in your cleavage?"

She laughed greatly as stew flew from her mouth!— and she began choking. The young man ran quickly to the roadhouse keeper and got a towel, for it seemed a proper move. He wanted to do a good deed! Returning to the Amazon, he offered it to her, "I am sorry, but I have never seen a legend before. Where shall you go next?"

"Up the north road to Transylvania," she said, just as calm as you please.

His mouth gaped wider as he recoiled from the name, staggering back to trip over an empty stool. He stood up quickly and wiped his trousers, looking this way and that, hoping no one had noticed. But they had, for the customers were howling in laughter, slapping their knees, and Gorbanus was rolling on the floor. "The north road? Transylvania?" he gasped, "There are terrible things up there! The dark-thought ones. Hunchbacked dwarves. The creature of darkness."

"Well," she shrugged, grinning again, "I'm going anyway. You must know the stories. I'm fearless."

"Will you slay the one-eyed man or the gold-guarding griffins?" he asked, for there were such things, he knew full well.

She ate a spoonful, laughed once more, and replied, "Perhaps."

*　*　*

Another bear skin for my useless wife, thought Gunter as they walked the path down to his village. Just beyond the outlying cabins, the six Gepids shot the bear. The big animal was first spotted in early spring by his nephew. They baited it, placing food scraps in the same place for a fortnight. Upon this auspicious morn, six arrows flew at first light, the bear running halfway up the mountain before dropping in its tracks. They downed a small poplar, hacked off the branches, and used it for a carrying pole, two men at each end, the bear hanging feet-tied in the middle. The walking was slow, the bear swinging side to side as the pole cut into the warriors' shoulders.

One of them claimed it was three hundred pounds, but it wasn't, Gunter knew. More like two hundred pounds or less. "It will make good soft fur," he claimed in a forced chuckle, "My wife will be more comfortable when she spreads her legs." Not a warrior laughed back. They saw nothing jocular in his wife. *A sorry excuse for a woman.* His arrow missed the bear clean, and they all knew why—he was a one-eyed man even though he had two, and such a man could not use a bow well. He usually missed. Their respect for him dropped another notch; he could sense it. Yet Gunter could still swing an axe with the best of them.

He walked as a worried man, no son to take his place, no external enemy to fight, nothing to keep a midnight coup from slipping a dagger along his throat. Even his wife would not mind. His star was fading. What he needed was a war, a good conflict to rouse warriors behind him again. Even a small war would do. In the meantime he would present the bear to the tribe, a gift that would temporarily placate them, especially all the married women who detested him. Gunter could tell from the way they glared and clicked tongues.

The warriors reached the village, entering the baurg's center where they would skin the animal to distribute the meat and fat. Bear meat was greasy and tasted much like a combination of mutton and beef. The cows bartered by Christian Man were but a fond memory, and now his gift to the tribe would be this bear. As for the animal's fat? Gunter proclaimed, "My wife needs much bear grease for her woman tunnel."

His men found no humor in that statement, either. They stared at him and looked away. A few cabin doors swung to a crack, their wives studying him. The hunting party almost reached Gunter's cabin when its door opened and a young man ran out, holding up trousers as he fled. Not a Gepid had seen him before, not in their village.

Another one! How do they find out? Yet in truth he knew, for tales were told. *"Speak not a word and climb upon her. Keep your mouth shut and she will never know the difference."* The last one was a Vandal. A Vandal! Gunter's face twisted in rage, and he yelled, "Stop him!"

His nephew was good with the bow, drawing back to the corner of his mouth for the release, the arrow sailing into the stranger's back. The unknown man ran a few paces, staggered, and fell face down. Soon enough they stood above the stranger, one warrior kicking him over to face upright, the shaft breaking as he rolled.

"Your name?" gritted Gunter with clenched teeth.

"Euric."

"From the Christian place?"

"Yes."

Gunter had to ask—he needed to know—as nerves around his good eye twitched. His lips compressed to a sardonic grin, "How was she?"

The young man offered no comment, his eyes closed in pain.

Gunter kicked him hard in the ribs, "Was she good? She has had much practice and loves it. She must have been good."

The young man nodded, his eyes still closed.

Quite the unwanted crowd had tasted his spouse, each one now quiet, hollow and sightless. Gunter turned to his nephew, "Give me your sword," then revising, "No. Fetch my axe. It works better."

Chapter 28: A Blink of Innocence

The day turned warm, almost like summer. In the afternoon Selenas cut firewood with his bow-saw, some of it seasoned hardwood, rare and from young trees, the rest being spruce and pine. What he wouldn't burn through the rest of spring, he would use next autumn and into winter. Waldrid walked around the wood pile, picking up a piece and pretending to stack it higher, his reach only three and a half feet above ground.

In the cabin Lilia lay upon the bed, feeling big, her stomach huge as birthing time approached. He mused, *Soon we'll have another gift from God*. Overhead in a cloudless sky, a large bird circled a wide sweep. Selenas thought it was a fish-hawk, for it had some white on it. The bird came from the south on its way north to the Frozen Sea, or perhaps it would stay there in Transylvania. He had seen few fish hawks in Gothia, only along the big river. The hawk chirped a *reee* sound, then flew toward the lake where it circled again. Busy watching the hawk, the presbyter almost failed to notice Gunter's approach. Riding a shaggy horse, the chieftain carried something attached to the end of a pole. Only when the object got closer did Selenas realize it was a human head—Euric's!

Gunter sat expressionless upon his mount, "Keeping warm, Christian Man?" He then slid to the ground, leaned hard, slamming the pole into the soil. "Euric says, gooten-da," claimed Gunter with a brutal laugh, "He dumped his man-juice in my wife. He says she was good." He turned an eye, looked to the head and demanded, "Speak again, Euric!" Then he cocked a glance to Selenas, "What about you? Can you speak?"

Selenas was appalled by the chieftain, the repugnance of the man's deportment. A few people had gathered around, all staring in disbelief. Then the silence was broken by Euric's wife as she screeched at her husband's remains, her hands to her mouth. Lilia ran from the house clutching her ripe stomach as the chieftain scanned the Arians, his gaze falling to her condition.

Gunter stared at Lilia for a moment, patted Euric's head, and returned to the presbyter, "I told you once—He who puts it in the wrong hole dies. You disobeyed, and now the price is ten. Bring them to me. You have one day."

Finding words, the presbyter asked, "Ten? Ten what? Cows?"

"Not cows, fool! Men, women, children. Bring me ten heads."

Selenas recoiled at the words!—his eyes huge and mouth agasp, "I will not! Butcher ten people for want of a man and woman's chastity? Euric was married, too." He stepped to the dead man's wife as she wept upon her knees, dragging Waldrid behind him.

"Not anymore," Gunter snarled, glancing to the widow.

"You're upset, as any man would be. It's a great shock to find your wife with another man, but you don't demand ten lives for promiscuity. I'll not bring you anything. You already have more than required."

The Gepid chieftain said nothing, shaking his head, turning to stare at the people and widow again. He pulled the pole from the earth and jumped back upon his horse. The Ascentians watched him ride slowly, proudly, to the edge of the woodland. Then he vanished to the trees as quietly as he came.

*　*　*

She held Sesca tight to her chest, the child sleeping as she oft did upon the journey. Thulia rode tired, her head nodding for short moments. Not a cart rolled as it might on the trade road. No freeman walked or vendor passed. Nothing but the sound of heart and hoof, the afternoon almost gone. No village or tavern lay ahead for comforts, and still another day's ride to the Caucaland's last settlement before the flodus Aluta.

Then she saw him!—the man of light—the same man as before. He rode fast, coming toward her, his horse silver-white, his scale armor gleaming in the same hue. This time he was easier to see. He held a long spar with a Sarmatian draco, the shaft vertical and cupped to a strap below his saddle. As he approached, Thulia discovered the draco was actually a pennant carrying two Greek letters, alpha and omega, sewn in pure gold.

He stopped before her, turning his horse to block her gelding's path, a steed wild and huge, its eyes black. She still had trouble seeing the man, for his features vanished between movements, his hair white, as was his full and curling beard. His eyes flashed colors of his horse, then burned to the pennant's shade, constantly changing—mirrors of the world around them—and a moustache streamed from his lips to reach his chest. Belted at his waist hung a sword much like hers, so anciently fashioned. He raised an arm to point a finger. "This is the hard road," he vowed, "Few travel it. You can turn from the quest if you wish." His horse pranced sideways as if having other roads to vend, and the man added, "They usually do."

What quest? Who was he?—now dropping his spar to halt her progress. The man seemed old but not aged, and he moved as liquid, much like a spectre. Yet Thulia knew he was real enough yet brighter than human. She had traveled too far to let him stop her; for she had to redeem Othar's soul, save her own, and have Sesca baptized. Although the man showed no evil, Thulia would take no chances. With her free hand she reached for the *Iron Breaker*, drawing it from scabbard to demand, "Who are you?"

"I'm called Michael. Evoke my name and I shall be with you."

She pointed the blade to him, demanding, "Are you a ghost!"

"Part of me, yet no more than the Ghost in you," he answered wryly, then questioning, "You wish to pass?"

Thulia sensed he meant no harm, a spirit-force not of this earth, and she sheathed her weapon, "Shall I ride through you? I have things to do, concerning this world and the next."

He exhaled, "Ah. The next? Let me ask—what is the name of the ride?"

Thulia hesitated. *What links the ride to the next world?* Yet she answered, "Cataphractum gallante."

"Whom does the ride serve?" he demanded.

"It protects the people."

"Ah, the people," he mused, his aged eyes aglow, "That is correct. The ride serves not glory, to heap fame upon prowess. It wins no wagers, but protects those who cannot protect themselves. You helped the one you loved, aided thousands hardly known—riding not for your own welfare but for others. You rode with the spirit of God. Now you have the Sword, and you are asked for even more."

Heaven beyond!—even spirits have heard the tales. More what? Taken aback, Thulia studied his demeanor, the great ardens within his gaze, searing like a blacksmith's forge. Oh yes, she knew her men and the flames they held. He seemed ethereally wise, and she wished the girl in her arms might awaken… just to view him. "Is this some kind of test?" she finally asked.

"The test is ahead," the man claimed, his countenance sobering, "Many perish upon the road you take, nailed along the wayside." And he raised his shaft, allowing her access, "You have come a long way—from spitting at deities, fornicating through the night. In compassion, you took the ride," he said tenderly, "You rode in the light; and now you must save those who walk in darkness. The Lord knew you would not turn from the quest," the man mused, as if he and God discussed her journey on a regular basis. Then he announced, "You may pass."

He reined the steed aside, his eyes following her progress.

How could he know such things? Only God knew! Thulia wasn't frightened but uneasy. He was neither human nor demon. An envoy from another realm? She had scant knowledge of spiritual matters, yet she knew what this man did. He personally conversed with God.

She wished to ask his name again, for she heard it not clearly, foreign sounding, the name of a gast although he spoke perfect Gothic. And what exactly was the quest? She rode by him slowly, studying liquid eyes, passing his silvery whiteness, feeling not Sesca's weight or her own in the saddle. Beyond his presence, Thulia feared to look back. She heard no sound of his departure, yet knew he was no longer there.

* * *

Frit wasn't sure where he was, around thirty miles above the plains of Vindobona and fighting under Commander Theodosius in a warm morning's sun. Soranus was sincere, and he rode as a fresh lieutenant in the auxiliary horse. With Captain Thaurus, he was fighting the Alemanni. He had reached Germania, alright. Not exactly as expected. Germania was mud and blood, far less glorious than Theo proclaimed. *A man could die here, easy enough.* Death took this rider and that one, indiscriminate in choice. Some, the so-called enemy, should never have died at all, the wrong age and gender.

During the first two days, they pushed the Germans beyond a nameless river, a bloody rout. Alemanni had no armor, few helmets, their iron forged to slashing swords and axes. Only a chieftain had a breast-plate or chainmail, the rest wearing leather. Heavy casualties. Then the Germans made themselves scarce, the main body elusive. Thaurus knew it, taking the day to drill new horse. Even Frit did, raw as he was. With signs of life near a stream in a steep ravine, the Spaniard gave word to charge. Frit dug heels to the white gelding with thirty men behind him. Nestled between hills, the brook rushed quick, big enough to harbor minnows, not much else. Ferns fanned a tumble of water suitable to quench a thirst on any other ride.

The Alemanni scattered for cover, running hard to reach the tree line. All but one. She was young, her burden oppressive. He almost reached her before she turned to him. She dropped the bucket, precious water splashing to German soil, and she looked directly at him with no outward expression... yet he could see it.

Her eyes! He had seen them before, stressed and tired and wounded. Needy eyes craving. They spoke to him— unguarded whispers from a fractured moment—eyes of a woman older than her years. *It's in the eyes.* All the pain, disappointment and anger, could be hidden from muscles of the face, even the lips, but not the eyes. Then she fled, reaching the woods before him, vanishing with less than a shadow in the firs.

He hollered, "Alto! Break it off!" His men reined to a stop, all staring at him. Frit glanced back uphill. He knew what came next. Another confrontation, but not with the enemy. Theo charged down at him, the man screaming profanity in Spanish.

"What in hell do you think you're doing?" shouted Theodosius, "We're here to fight Germans. Not sit on a nag and watch them slip back to the forest."

Frit glowered, shrugging shoulders. He turned his horse from wood-edge and brought it back toward the rivulet, its water clear and coursing. The Alemanni women had been dipping buckets, now lying abandoned. Among them were a few children and young girls. He didn't see any men, a sorry flock, their clothes like rags, lives dissolute by ambitions of a recanting chieftain.

Evidently Theo wanted an answer, riding up beside him, "What do you think they looked like?" the man contended, "Civilized Greeks? Were they Alexandrians?"

Frit eyed him again, "They looked like I should've taken them home and given them a bath."

"What's that supposed to mean?" the Spaniard queried.

"Two things," Frit spat, "Pushed back from the river, they can't take a bath. And second, they're all women and children."

"They're Alemanni, damn it!" Theo raged, "Why can't you get it? Either straighten out or take a long ride south."

A few riders went by, all going back up the hill to the infantry. Jumping from his mount at streamside, Frit returned his eyes to Theo, addressing the commander formally, "I thought you were a Christian, sir."

"I am," claimed the Spaniard, "What's that to do with it?"

Frit reached down and picked up the young woman's bucket, "They thirst!—for more than water. And what about all that business about the poor and meek?"

"You're a pagan. How do you know about that?"

Everybody knows! The bucket leaked. Water dripped between staves, droplets bouncing from his boots. Bound with twine, it was a sorry affair. He knew another young woman who had a bucket like it—once no better off than these Alemanni—and Theo couldn't make him cut women and children down. Frit snapped up the commander, "Perhaps I'm a pagan, but I'm also an equite. And I fight men."

The Spaniard stared at him, scrutinizing his composure. He looked toward the remaining riders and yelled, "Fall back! The day is over." Then he glared to Frit again, "You think you're the Great Moral Knight, eh? Well, I think you're a frigging fisher angling for souls."

* * *

The day passed beautiful for Selenas, a morning's rain dried by the sun. Afternoon saw husbandmen tending calves or plowing the community garden. *No phallus or Freyja here.* A fine day it ran, the spring eve producing a perfect sunset, clouds pink across the lake. *God is good*, he mused. He and Lilia invited her father and brother for cena, the fare being broiled trout with tender fern greens stewed with salt pork. Even Waldrid ate heartily, the dinner tasty to all but Safrax who refused the greens even when disguised by grape-must vinegar.

Outside in twilight, beyond the dinner, beyond grateful eyes, ten Gepids ran from the forest, some dressed in skins, others naked above the waist. All carried axes and a few held torches. They ran fast at an even pace.

A freeman ran through the village warning those within; and the people of Ascentia barged out to see their fate.

No time for an Alan cataphract to dig armor from a dust-covered arka, not even time to find sword or buckler beneath his bed. Death arrived too quickly, a whirlwind in a blink of innocence.

Selenas and Rustan believed Gunter would calm down, his anger passing, not expecting a raiding party. As Safrax and the two men ran from the presbyter's house, Selenas shouted back to Lilia, "Stay in there where it's safe!"

Outside, the presbyter and his father-in-law stood before the chieftain, hoping to talk sense into the man. They were totally unprepared. With a swing of his axe, the chieftain downed Selenas, slamming the flat of his blade quick and hard. In his second swing, he knocked Safrax up against the cabin, the boy sliding to unconsciousness. At the same time, another warrior struck Rustan to the ground. They all fell easily.

As Selenas lay bleeding, Gunter spat, "Your time is up. Now I take ten."

"Please," cried Selenas, blood running from his nose as he tried to regain his feet. Gunter grinned, kicked him hard to the head, and he fell to deep darkness...

* * *

Lilia pressed her back to the rear wall, holding Waldrid tight as he bawled. She sensed little time left, knowing how the chieftain stared at her the previous day. Her thoughts tried to amass themselves above screams of the boy. Somehow she knew he would live, too small and worthless a prize for a Gepid. Falling to her knees she yanked Waldrid around to face her. As he cried, Lilia shook him with trembling hands, cupping his face tight, looking to frightened eyes. She gasped, "Mama is going away. She loves you. Now you must mind your father."

She clutched her son tight and thought of undone tasks, words unsaid. Time upon this earth had vanished, yet she wished to thank the Lord for sixteen years. As best she could, Lilia prepared herself for the upper house. Her voice rose above screams of the boy, words from her very soul, spoken verbatim from the Book of Little Wolf—"Atta unsar thu in himinims. Gif to us this daye uns dayly sinteinan. And forgeve us uns trespasses, even as we forgeve oure trespassers. And leade us not unto temptation, but deliver us from evil; For theins is the Kingdom, and the Power, and the Glory, Forever. Amen."

*　*　*

Christians ran from Gunter in panic, all knowing what would come next. This was no raid looking for cattle, wanting grain or coin. He intended revenge and nothing more. The sounds of women were heard first, then weeping of children, as they all tried to escape. Staring down at Christian Man, Gunter shouted to his warriors, "One each! No more." He turned from the man upon the ground, adjusting the position of his axe-head, rotating the handle, his fingers opening and closing until the blade came around to cutting edge. His warriors ran through the fleeing crowd, each choosing their victims. They studied faces, looking for the most frightened.

Gunter's good eye focused upon the cabin entrance. *A flimsy thing. A few boards.* With long strides he ran for it, kicking the door open with his momentum. She was cringing in a corner upon her knees, her arms wrapped tight to the boy, holding him to her huge stomach. The fear in her eyes pleased him. Her hair fell long and dark, her wrists and fingers small. He had noticed her features the previous day.

He leered with a twist of lips. *She carries the child of Christian Man, Useless Man.* Leaping across the cabin, he clutched the boy's coat with his left hand, ripping him from her grasp and raising him high with one arm. He studied the child for a moment, then tossed him to the bed. *Better to kill two for one head! Then Christian Man will remember this day. Forever.*

With a quick swing of his arm, he grabbed her hair. *Dark hair. Just like my wife, yet this one bears a child.* He seethed in envy, his limited gaze piercing hers, his other eye staring sideways to nowhere. Gunter pulled her toward him so quickly she lost her balance. She kicked and screamed as he dragged her from the cabin, bouncing across the door-stoop as he clutched her hair tighter. Her arms flailed as sounds from her throat wailed of agony. *She is a noisy one, but she will be silent soon.* Across the grass they went as he towed her to the wood pile, pressing her head to the presbyter's chopping block.

Now they will keep trousers belted tight.

Chapter 29: Things Unfinished

My Thulia,
Why can't you sleep tonight?
  said the soothing voice.
What is the place where a lonely child never goes,
  not even the bravest?—the woods of Transylvania?
Fear itself—fear alone!—keeps the smart little girl
  from going there.
What, then, lives in your bed of fear?
  to make you wake in the dark of night,
  to sit up quick... yet your lips are sealed.
You know them all, listened well,
  heard their names since childhood days.
Even the fool with his addled brain can name them:
  Yes! The hunchback dwarves, and cackling hag,
  the one-eyed man, and sharp-toothed trolls,
and certainly not least,
  the Other One you saw tonight.
Perhaps you believe he will disappear,
  if you think him gone.
Be stronger. Do not hug the balsam doll.

There it is again! The kindly deep tone of a man.
Thulia snapped upright, eyes wide and peering into the room's
darkness. But the wraith was never there. It only came as a
soothing voice, yet she knew it was guileful.

Many a man could turn a phrase to get what he
wished. She had heard it all at one time or another, much like

315

Selenas, his inflection assuring and warm, each sermon falling to enamored ears. Such was the wraith's tone, a dark shadow leaning to her and whispering honeyed to the point of nausea. The voice belied a dissolute mind, cooing evil from the depths of Hell—the opposite of God—and it always wanted something, to extract a part of her. And that's what made the wraith so fearful.

She felt the lump within the covers, her daughter sleeping soundly; and then she reached to her other side, working a hand beneath the sheet to feel the *Iron Breaker's* blue-hard steel, the sword unsheathed and ready.

The nightmare came once or twice a fortnight; yet the closer she got to Transylvania the more often it appeared. All the creepy things in high mounts—the one-eyed man and sharp-toothed trolls, the creature of darkness or hunchbacked dwarves—were beasts of superstition, were they not? Yet something, terrible and long ago, started it. What happened?—to be forgotten and return as a reoccurring anathema? Usually children's wraiths disappeared at adulthood, or so claimed Merjands as he tugged his cinnabar. He believed the nightmare would go away if she could stabilize her life and find a good "partner."

Upon this night Thulia was in Aqizbaurg— "Axeville"—the last village on the north road before the river Aluta. No-one seemed pleasant, not even the roadhouse keeper, eyeing her with mistrust. Or was it fright? She herself feared no man or god, cold or ice, not water's glide; she was a decent swimmer. Yet she dreaded what lay beyond her bed. The deep woods, the darkness within it, intimidated her—the place called Transylvania.

*   *   *

The morning came chilly, much cooler than the eve before. Clouds rolled low, scratching high hills and leaving damp vapor in their wake. Thaurus could smell it, and he claimed, "North folk call it Dragon's Breath. Creeps from the olden time, back when men were formed from clay."

Frit grinned from his horse over to the Vandal's, "The moisture helped Eve's skin, kept it from drying out."

Thaurus chuckled. Frit knew the Vandal was familiar with Bible stories, but his own humor seemed empty. He wished not to fight anyone—not even a youth with a bone dagger—in a fog like this, "At least we have no sun. The heat would turn Eve to a brick," then giving his toothy grin.

Upon the hill's crest, light cavalry formed to the rear, Theo pushing his horse to the front. When he reached them, the Spaniard looked down to the obscured field, dense gray, thick like smoke. Hidden by fog, and somewhere at the field's far end, the Alemanni leader shouted through the mist.

Turning to Thaurus, the Spaniard asked, "What did he say?"

"*You sleep with your mothers.* Something like that."

Theo eyed Frit, reckoning, "You'll be fighting men this time, Fisher."

Upon this morn, the Roman horse consolidated to a single ala, trying to create a big punch. They knew the Alemanni had been busy, chopping away at something unseen. Thaurus paced his mount to the right flank, Frit to the left, as the Spaniard remained in the center. The draconarius rode to the front, stopping at his commander's side. With everyone in position, Theo turned in his saddle and drew his sword, yelling to his men as they followed suit, "For Roma, for those who died at your side—Ride into Hell!"

As they charged forward, Frit pictured the field in his mind, shaped like a wedge with his end narrower than the Vandal's. He and his men would reach the tree-line on the other side first. Not a comforting thought. The field was a garden once, and the stubble of unpicked turnips and horse-beets remained, all of it freezing during the previous winter. Now it had distinction. Men would die here; and he prayed to be a survivor.

Frit dug heels to the white gelding's ribs, hearing other equites behind him. He turned quick, and a man to his rear faded into nothingness, now a ghost riding through a dank cloud. Glancing left and right, his companions vanished. He was attacking blind. Then he could see something ahead, approaching it fast. *A fence. An angled barrier? No. Sharpened stakes!* He tried reining his mount. *Too late!* The horse jumped, coming down hard, twitching its legs, Frit pitching forward, slamming chest-first into a stake.

He hung there impaled!—his legs limp as he tried moving his arms. He could hardly breathe, unable to inhale; and the pain, at first unperceived, grew and grew larger, flooding and burning from shoulder to chest. Someone—a man!—screamed nearby, another yell of agony out beyond. Again he tried to move, the pain racking.

So this is it! This is how death affirms, creeping further inside, violating life through an evil and phlegmatic crawl. He went to darkness. Then spots of brown flickered, whether his eyes were closed or not—*they seem open*—yet he could not tell if they were truly open or only perceived so; and the brown spots faded through a brighter background—*ah, brighter, much brighter*—then incredibly bright. *Too bright!—for it hurts my eyes;* and then movement, real movement and not spots. And up ahead, someone came through the whiteness, a person, grayish and less white than all around him... *reaching for him....*

"*Is that you, Son?*"

"Father?"

"*Yes, Frit. You came early.*"

He wished to touch another's hand, not his father's. "Where am I?"

Thiudebalth smiled, "In a field, just beyond the other one."

"Is this a death experience or am I dead?"

Thiudebalth raised a hand to heart-height, extending an open palm, "Does it really matter, my good Boy?"

"But I was never good. You must remember… all the deeds I did wrong. I must go back, to things unfinished, uncorrected."

The aura of pleasantness left his father's lips, "Oh, my son. I do not think so."

* * *

Two days after leaving Axeville, the woman of legend reached the flodus Aluta. She clutched her sleeping daughter tight to her stomach, the girl's feet dangling to one side of the saddle. In every community along her journey they knew of the Amazon. Never in her wildest imagination would she have thought of herself a slayer of dragons, a killer of trolls. Every missing person in Gothia or the Caucaland was dragged off by a troll, for they were strong and ate human flesh. Tales claimed she cleaned each cave, secured every bridge. *"She lures them to sunlight and they turn to stone!"* Each fief reigned safe after the Amazon passed through, a certain jocularity to it, many a face surprised she looked like other women. The Mordwine episode grew into fantasy, he at eight feet tall, she at seven, the War of Giants all over again. She was still smiling when she viewed the bridge. Then the smile disappeared.

All the cross-logs had burned away, the two spanning trees a charcoal black. Thulia wondered what caused it. Lightening struck objects near water, growing trees, not downed ones.

Was it accomplished by the hand of man? On her side of the Aluta, no fresh tracks were found. She would hunt for signs on the other side.

Crossing the river wasn't easy, her feet getting wet and also the clothing bag. At one point she wondered if the gelding and mare were swimming or walking on stream-bottom, yet both horses made it. Again she searched for evidence of a guilty party, finding exactly that—horseshoes!—hoof prints of shod mounts, not steppe geldings. *What kind of man rides a soft-hoofed horse?* The perpetrators were not Goths or Alans but northern riders, like Germans or Celts. *Assuredly real enough. No trolls these!*

Thulia had no idea how far she had yet to travel, only knowing the mountain road was lengthy, the peaks a faded green in the distance. *A long way up there.* She imagined what Selenas must have thought, *All the closer to Heaven.* But this Heaven had arsonists, perhaps worse. *Time to wear my armor.* Progressing ever upwards, Thulia could smell a change in the air. As altitude increased, less hardwoods grew. The forest became a tangle of evergreens, all except cedars. There were none. But the smell was unique, a pungent fragrance pinching her nostrils. It seemed refreshing compared to cow manure.

She knew not what awaited beyond each bend, the road narrow, vending upward along mountainside, then reversing, the woods dark even in midday. *"This is the hard road,"* the spirit-man forewarned. Anyone or anything could hide in ambush. Thulia had oiled the *Iron Breaker* with flaxseed oil, a liberal coat, and she could slip it from her scabbard with lightening speed. Yet she was frightened on the comfort of a horse!—the first time in her life. *"The test is ahead,"* the man claimed. She was venturing back to her childhood, her early years spent in these mounts. The basis of fibula was truth, perhaps a reality in her nightmares? Thulia could only think what she wished to avoid—the four-legged ones or some other wraith could actually exist.

Two hours before dark, she found a number of lean-tos, most caved in from previous winters, yet one remained in good condition, their humble inn for the night. She slipped on her armored tunic, and they ate Axeville bread and cured sausage. Sleep came with difficulty, Thulia's eyes snapping open with each forest noise, a gray owl's "who"—who indeed?—or the howl of a distant wolf.

The next day brought them higher, the road steeper, until shadows clawed deep under each tree branch. Then the road edged back toward the river, as the Red Tower stood before them—a mute beacon for the wandering lost—built from brick and a crumbling symbol of Roman greed, once part of a fort that charged tolls to all who traveled through the pass. And here, too, were more log shelters, old and chewn by generations of hungry insects. Thulia wondered at the lack of hardwoods, not an oak or maple, and few were the birch and larch. For an instant, a twinkle in her mind, she viewed men slaving away in some dark glade. Vague faces. Poor men, low and drunk, laughing as they stumbled through a smoky cloud. *Vainamon and the Other One!* Then the forest visage was gone, replaced by a swath of sunlight.

She looked down to quaking hands, clutching her child in a death grip as if she were about to lose the girl to a maelstrom. *The girl tried to scream, to yell for help, but the sweaty rag, the stinking rag, filled her mouth.* Her free hand came to her face, sliding along a cheek, not really her hand but someone else's, a caressing prelude to bestiality; *the Other One*, and she looked to right and left… peering to the woods and knowing the Godless truth. *The wraith is still here, still waiting.*

Spooked and fearful, she would camp here at the ruins, for Ascentia lay another dozen miles above Red Tower Pass. Old bricks were handy, and she placed two of them in the evening's flames. When the bricks were hot, she mixed some flour and water, letting it sizzle as it cooked, Sesca grinning at the thought of eating flat bread from a brick. After she and Sesca supped, Thulia found a small patch of grass for the gelding and mare; and while the horses ate, she cut boughs for the lean-to. Pulling blankets from a pack, she doubled them into a sleeping bed, and the sack of gold became her pillow. Her armored tunic was heavy and chased sleep. With Sesca under an arm, they watched the heavens roll by.

* * *

At some point round the witching hour she sat up straight and wide awake. The phantasm again! *My, Thulia. Why can't you sleep tonight?* She knew this was the place— *where live all the wraiths of the world.* She fell back to adjust her head upon the gold and waited, for they would come upon this night above all others. The sword lay ready beside her under the blanket, cold in its countenance and unable to distinguish one foe from another, ready to slay the perceived or real.

Hours slogged by, her eyes wide in timor as Sesca dreamt in an innocent world. Just before the crack of dawn, Thulia heard the expected. Out in the woods a twig snapped, then another. Yes, they were coming. The footsteps paced toward her cautiously, stopping and advancing. All the creatures in her depths came crawling out, Thulia unsure what caused the sound. It could be anything, a dwarf intent upon stealing her child, a troll hungering to eat them both. The one-eyed man would step carefully in his approach to rape and kill her, leaving her ravished body nude in the brush.

The sound came again!—a quiet rustling of bushes. *They do exist!* She lay frozen for a moment, unable to move. Then her hand crept under the blanket, her touch moving cautiously toward sword-hilt, her eyes following her hand. Another twig snapped! The monster approached with stealth, quietly and slowly, the half-light of dawn fingering through the trees.

Something tapped her foot!

Instinctively recoiling, she viewed a befurred creature squatting before her, a sword propped across his knees. *He's just a man!*—a barbarian and German all in one. He was young and smiling.

"Who be you, woman?" he asked in rough accent, his brows forced low.

She could have replied "Thulia," but didn't. It seemed far more advantageous to say "The Amazon" to a stranger with a blade.

"You are the Amazon?" he quizzed, his expression brightening.

"Want to really find out?" Thulia returned as she came to her feet, pulling the *Iron Breaker* from the blanket, Sesca rolling over and still asleep.

He only grinned, knowing the legend—the hair and bosom, armor and weapon.

"Who are you and what do you want?" she demanded.

The young man answered the second question, "You."

"What? You think I'm going to lay back and open wide?" she snarled while twirling her sword.

"No!" he exclaimed in a whisper, placing a finger to lips and looking out toward the horses, "I want you to kill him... like you slew the giant."

She stepped from the lean-to, eying four more men examining the horses, not sure which one the young German meant. Something told her they wanted the animals, and they were going to kill her to get them. But why was the young man helping her?—if in fact that's what he was doing. "Which one?"

"That one with the biggest axe—Gunter, the one-eyed man. We are Gepids, and he is our chief," he explained.

"Why?"

The young man shrugged, "He is an ebilsmon," offering nothing more.

Gunter looked their way and began walking toward them. He had two eyes for all she could tell. "Who is there?" he barked, "Where does he go?"

"A woman. She is lost, Uncle. Her name I cannot recall."

Reaching them, Gunter spat, "Where do you go woman?"

"Up to the Christian community."

"No," he dictated, "No more Christians. You will have sons and they will have more sons." Turning to his nephew, he ordered, "I told you to kill whomever sleeps here. Do you fear dragon scales?"

The nephew nodded.

"Kill her!" demanded Gunter.

The young man shook his head.

"Then I will. Give me your sword."

"No."

"Give it here or I'll kill you first."

The nephew pulled it from his scabbard, handing it to him. Gunter switched the axe to his left hand and gripped the sword with his right, hauling it outward, turning a glance to examine it.

Instantly, Thulia swung her sword in a quick circle, slamming it fast to the Gepid weapon. The nephew's blade snapped!—flying to the forest. She was shocked. *It can actually break iron!*

Gunter peered to what was left—a hilt with a blade-stub—tossing it aside, "Useless shit." He grinned, adjusting his axe for a doubled grip, hurriedly lifting it with both hands and swinging back for a skull-crushing blow.

Thulia paced firm, raising the *Iron Breaker* with both hands, leaning into the hit when it came. His swing was so powerful it brought her to knees; yet finding strength, she regained her feet. And with a quick swing, her weapon grazed his torso. The chieftain blocked it, as he again struck hard, grunting from his own blow, the handle sheering along her blade's edge, slamming to sword-hilt as the axe snapped. Her blade cut through the shank as if it were sap-wood! Looking at his useless weapon, the Gepid became incensed!—eyes wild in fury as he gawked at the broken handle in his hands. First the sword and now this!—his trusted axe.

Driven back, Thulia again checked her balance, spinning in a circle, heel to toe and bringing her blade up to slice his chest. Gunter leaned back in surprise, gaping at his own blood and sheered coat. His eyes widened. Never had he been wounded by a woman, nor had he seen one dressed in armor.

She sensed recognition in his expression as he realized who she was. He was fighting the Amazon! And she knew a fine truth, taught by Old Hempstalk—*accuracy beats force*—the exact way she slew the Mordwine.

On his next try Gunter lunged in desperation, trying to impale her chest with the broken axe handle, yet deflected by iron scales. She stepped back to swing the blade across his face.

He dropped the axe handle!—screaming like a madman! Instantly he fell to knees, hands covering his left eye as he wailed, "I cannot see. I am a blindamon now!"

Thulia stepped back in horror, looking at the other Gepids, waiting for them to attack. To slay a man in self-defense seemed one thing, yet to blind a man seemed another. She steeped in guilt! The act was accidental, his fate now worse than death. From his shouting, little Sesca awoke and began bawling. "Mother is fine," Thulia managed to sooth her. Where the calm tone came from, she wasn't sure!

The man upon his knees begged, his hands outstretched, "Kill me! Please. I ask you to kill this useless man. He was a great chief, he had a wife! But he had no sons."

From the woods and trees, more Gepids appeared, all running toward her. The young nephew implored, "You must finish what began. He is a blindamon, to live his days in shame, to hear grunts of men upon his wife and not know if they are from the tribe."

She had trouble understanding their morals, or was it a philosophy? What did humping between the sheets have to do with life and death? "I cannot do it," she explained.

"You must!" cried Gunter, "It is your obligation." He reached his hands out, groping for death. Grasping the *Iron Breaker's* blade, he guided the tip, centering it above his shoulder blades for a downward thrust. "Come closer. Stand over me and push hard."

Thulia closed her eyes, tensing muscles as she took the step. Once before, a man begged her to kill him. Back then, she found not the courage. Yet upon this pale dawn, she pushed with all her weight!—then withdrew her blade. Thulia stepped back; and Gunter—the one-eyed man, the head-hunting man—fell limp between her outstretched legs.

The nephew reached toward her and spat, "He was a desperate man. A cruel man. Now we are free of it. Let the Amazon give me her sword."

The Gepids stood in awe upon hearing the name, each glancing to the other. Not altogether sure of the nephew's motives, she finally released the weapon. He stared at it in birthing light, turning the blade to view its blue sheen; and he frowned to ask, "Knicks there are none. What kind of sword *is* this?"

"*Tyrfing the Iron Breaker*—forged by man and re-forged by God in a circle of stone."

"A man should fear it in the right one's hands. I think you are her, for you have done a right thing," he determined. And then gripping the sword mid-blade, he raised it, exclaiming, "Hailog the Amazon! Hailog the *Iron Breaker*!" The warriors did the same, their axes and spears held high, not finding a salute any more original than the nephew's, "Hailog the Amazon!"

She knew they couldn't help it. They were men of the forest.

"It is over. Too many have died for one man's pride," claimed the nephew, "No more villages shall burn. We can go home now."

Chapter 30: A Fallow Garden

He was not the man she knew, but a wretch. His beard grew beyond stubble, untrimmed, and his thin hair flared wild and uncombed. He coughed, and his eyes stared from deep sockets, dark and hollow. The clothes hanging from his shoulders had stains, charcoal mixed with dry blood the color of brown earth. No one could touch him; he recoiled from all. No, he was not the Selenas of her childhood.

"We built him this small cabin," explained Rustan, his voice quavering, "His house was burned and I pulled Waldrid out just in time. He has been this way since... since Lilia died." He turned around, perhaps to view the quarters or weep from his own loss.

The presbyter sat upon a crude bench, staring right through her.

"Selenas?" she said tenderly, "This is Thulia." He seemed not in her world. "Can he speak?" she inquired.

"When he wants to," claimed Rustan, "It comes out as bile." He stood by the doorway, as if hoping not to be there, "We buried the ten in closed caskets, for they were headless— all women, all young and mostly wives. They burned the church. We have tried to hold services by the lake; we have a lector, but he breaks down and sobs while reading the scriptures, then everyone feels uncomfortable and leaves. No less than Satan killed this place. It still reeks of death."

The days after that first one passed slowly. She would try to clean Selenas up but his hands flailed at hers, trying to keep her away. At first she thought he ate nothing, but she

328

found the signs—crumbs, pieces of gristle and small gobs of fat. The bowls remained clean, so he was eating with his hands, like the animal he nearly was.

One day, the fourth or fifth, he spoke in her presence, *"God is the Devil in disguise. He allowed her to die. Damn him and every angel that ever flew."* There was more to it, ramblings of hate, not for the slayer but the deity who abandoned her. That was it—hate, God hate—and the loss of an unborn child had some bearing. Others had viewed death of a spouse, perhaps not in such a brutal manner. Death rode across the earth, taking and taking, cutting down innocence with evil. It took her mother, then her father, even the son from her own womb. No, Selenas was not unique.

How could events turn worse?—riding into a bloody nightmare, not hers but his, the boy's, and Rustan's. She came to Ascentia to forgive Selenas, to have him baptize her and Sesca into God's family. A great irony to it. She wished him to save her soul... but first she had to save his.

Thulia and Sesca moved in with Rustan, his woman Valeria, Safrax, and little Waldrid, finally receiving the full story. The Ascentians counted headless bodies—exactly ten—bone chilling, an act so barbarous it hardly seemed real. Also victims, the relatives lived the nightmare over and over again. Some could not sleep, others waking to the slightest sound, a few like Selenas, but he was the worst. He must have believed it was his fault, the rationale of the overly confident. He led them there, the one who believed God would always be his trusted friend, letting no evil, no scourge, enter the placid realm of Ascentia. Even the name had a connotation of benign happiness. Unrealistic, thought Thulia. The world was still real and God held death high, first with his own Son.

Each day they tried to rebuild something, a cabin or smokehouse; yet instead of applying themselves, the men would sit and roll a hammer or chisel in their hands as if studying it, as if it were strange or incorrect. But the fear?—she could see it, always there in their eyes.

And Selenas? He would self-destruct, perhaps kill himself quick or atrophy in venomous fermentation. She viewed it first-hand in Pigfoot.

Too many days passed. Nobody mourned a loved one forever, and fond memories always replaced bitterness. Life went on; it had to!—humanity's way—yet Selenas remained a rot-worm.

How could she save a man like that? She prayed for him and Waldrid every night, for even the boy had that vapid look of abandonment. Selenas moved about but never left the cabin except to relieve himself, oft squatting by the hearth while tearing pages from the Greek Bible, feeding them one by one to ritual flames. She supposed he was "improving" if the term applied.

*   *   *

The morning arrived crisp, Ascentia's weather colder than the steppes of Gothia. Thulia rolled from the makeshift pallet, wrapping her tunic tight while running to the hearth in bare feet. Everyone was still sleeping. Only in sleep could the ugliness vanish. She plopped to a crude stool and placed two logs upon the embers, then waited and waited. *Come on! Catch afire, damn it! This place is frigging Hell yet it's freezing.* She scrunched her neck, rolled eyes upward, and apologized, *Sorry about that. I'll be a better Christian when the sun rises.* The logs produced smoke and nothing else. She and the children had pallets on one side of the hearth. Beyond it, a huge Sassanian rug hung from timbers, screening them from the bed of Rustan and Valeria. The logs caught, and weak flames hissed to grew stronger.

Thulia had been at Ascentia for well over a fortnight, and she was painfully aware that mountain flowers and grass sprouted late, everything new, short, and light green. During the past afternoon, right after bitching at Selenas and calling him a "shithead," she saw a red stag and two does in the corner of the field down near the lake. They were eating something that grew anew. Spring of the year was reaching prime when all the plants revitalized, and the deer were gorging after a winter of munching spruce buds. The hearth flames sputtered again, and she turned to see if the children were awake. They lay immobile like hearth logs. Leaning, she placed a third log over the two stubborn ones, and then ran to the traveling bag next to her pallet, rummaging for her comb and the fabulous mirror gifted by Merjands.

Back at the hearth-stool, she combed knots from her hair, wincing and discovering what appeared to be a gray one stuck in the antler-bone tines. *A gray hair? God Almighty!— that damned Selenas is driving me to a premature grave.* She clamped her teeth, rolled eyes again and hoped God was busy somewhere else and not hearing her profanity.

With a deft hand, she plucked the hair with two fingers, dropping it to increasing flames. It disappeared in a flashing curl, the evidence gone. She reached to her lap, grabbed the mirror, and checked her handiwork, tilting it sideways to see if more gray hairs were hiding behind her ears. Something moved. Something white behind her. And she angled the mirror to a slight cant, trying to focus upon the image. It was Frit's white gelding!—empty saddled with blood flowing from its chest.

She jumped, turning quickly. The horse was gone, and she could only view a chinked wall in early morning darkness. A great chill—far colder than the morning itself—crept up her spine. Thulia dropped the mirror to her lap, wrapping arms around her torso. Was the mirror evil? An artifact from Hell itself? She thought not, because once before she had seen an image within it, a garden lush with fruits of someone's labor. Rising to her feet, she placed the mirror and comb on the stool, tippered to her boots, and slid out to a cold early dawn. Hopping from one foot to the other, she slipped into her boots, tucking trousers in them, and closing the door behind her.

No. The mirror was not evil; it was a gift from Merjands! It simply showed images that arrived from within her, or maybe they came from inside the mirror itself. She walked down the road to the field, just a pace to keep feet going, for she could not stop. At one point she arrived where she saw the deer, and later she walked near lake-shore. But her mind kept sprinting faster than a horse could gallop, an arrow from a Hun's bow. *He's in trouble! Maybe not dead. No, he's simply wounded. That's it, just wounded because he cannot die and leave me here with his sniveling brother... this smoke-filled wreck of a place, where nothing is right and all is dark, where they all weep like infants and think my strength is sent from God or Xristos, and that I alone must be the mother, the savior, the nightmare queen in a camp gone mad, exactly like the smoking world Othar took me from. I'll not have it! Everything is incorrect. It stinks and smells of death, but I saw it! I did see it—something right—a garden filled with all the things these people need.*

* * *

Frit rubbed his upper chest and shoulder, wincing mildly; for the wound, once seemingly cavernous, was improving. The capsarius, telling over-told and stale jokes, had wrapped a smaller linen bandage than the previous one by half again.

Freshly bandaged, Frit strode from the infirmary to enter a tent equally as large, the officer's mess, to find Thaurus and Theodosius sitting across from each other, not eating but resting.

The conversation's topic was women, three wagon-loads up from Vindobona, all young and eager to earn every sesterce they could. The captain and commander glanced up to him, surprised he was back from the infirmary so soon. Smiling to the Vandal, Theo claimed, "Goths spring alive when the women arrive."

Thaurus laughed as Frit thumped down beside him, "The best looking camp followers I've seen all campaign."

"Aye," agreed Theo, "And young. Tighter than an old whore."

Frit raised his eyes to force a smile, more like a mild grimace. He still felt weak, the wound severing a nerve, leaving his hand numb—luckily not his sword hand. At first the physician gave him up for dead. Long days passed in the hospital tent, men carried in, then carried out, buried in the nearby field of stubble. Halfway through his recovery, he went down to Vindobona for a week's leave. Nothing to do there, so he clipped the tails of the fort's mounts and braided a line heavy enough to catch the uncatchable, a four-foot huchen; and now they called him the Fisher King.

"Look," offered the Spaniard, reaching to his purse, "Why not go over to the whore's tent. The throw is on me."

Thaurus added, "They really are nubile, northern Italians. Nice high breasts, tender thighs. Good looking for the most part."

Frit heard enough, exclaiming, "No! I thank you for the offer but I have no interest in them."

The two officers looked at each other in surprise, quiet for a moment, and then Theo asked, "What? They really are nubile. Honest."

"They're not my type," Frit snapped, "And I'm weak."

A few moments passed before the Spaniard questioned, "Well, then. What exactly is your type?"

He hesitated, trying to find the right description, "I like them soft."

"You mean fat?" asked Theo, his comrade beginning to laugh.

"No, not obese. Slim but a little matronly."

"Oh, God!" cried Theo, "The Fisher's got a thing for Mum."

He always says that, "Oh, God." The man's a philandering Christian. Frit got up and strode hard and fast from the mess tent, for he certainly had no penchant for Mum—she died when he was five or six—his preference not his mother. He stopped midstride before reaching the officer's quarters, deciding to take a walk.

Outside the marching-fort, Frit scrambled up the hill, stepping around downed trees until he reached the crest. Then he paced slowly downhill, across a long flat, until reaching the death zone, the abandoned garden where it happened.

Long mounds of recently turned soil, dark and full of chopped roots, ran parallel to each other. Beneath them lay forty men, all equites, plus the carcasses of twenty horses—one of them being the white gelding.

Fresh seed for a fallow garden. He had no idea which trench held his horse, yet he wished to be here, to give it the respect it deserved. The gelding had been an exemplary mount, trained for more than a charge with swords. It was a cataphract's horse. Old Hempstalk helped him train it until the gelding could pass less than a foot from another mount, until it would charge an unmoving man and not stop short.

Perhaps most important, the horse represented that ardent dream of a boy at the brink of manhood, to be the noble prince, sweep the beauteous maiden off her feet, and ride her to a wondrous castle halfway in the clouds. He knelt to one of the fresh mounds, perhaps the gelding's, perhaps not, fingering the soil and sprinkling it back to an unfeeling earth. *Farewell, old horse.* It wasn't really old, but the dream was—and although each might fade in reality's eye, they would always be there as symbols of all that should be, yet seldom was, correct and worthwhile.

*   *   *

Thulia strolled back from lakeshore with little Waldrid and Sesca. To rest young legs, she had them sit upon large rocks cleared from the garden, positioning herself between them. Afternoon shadows blanketed the garden as if the softwoods wished to return it to a wild state. She was certainly no farmer, yet knew one third of the garden never received enough sunlight, for trees had grown taller along its border. She studied what lay before her even closer. Most of the soil had yet to be tilled, and she was unsure the ploughed area had been planted.

It lies fallow beyond the middle of Maius. What did these Ascentians think?—that the seed fairy would sprinkle a crop for them? Thulia could not believe it! Time, that creeping vine that swallowed all, would refuse food from mouths of a community too wrapped up in sorrow. Long faces would get longer and stomachs would churn. She could not preach to them, she knew full well. But perhaps she might reach them through example.

"Have you ever played farmer?" she asked the children. Both shook heads in a positive no. She paced to garden-center, put hands to hips and declared, "We shall become planters. Will that be fun?" They nodded yes, their faces brightening as they looked to each other; and Thulia added, "All we need is a bullock and plow with a soil-turning thing… and then some seed and starters." She turned one way and another, "And we should remove a few trees for more sunlight and roll more rocks to make the area larger; because the community will grow, just like this garden."

*   *   *

Thulia tapped upon the door again, using a little more force. She could hear feet shuffling within the cabin, and finally the door opened a crack to expose a woman's face, haggard and tight-jawed. "I was wondering if Stefan might be home," Thulia inquired.

"He is," the woman nodded, then turning to an unseen partner in the cabin's near darkness, "Stefan, the Amazon is here." Thulia heard the rustling of bedclothes, then a grunt and another one, and finally quick footsteps. The door opened further as Stefan leaned against the casing while straightening himself and his tunic with a groan. "A faur tyme since me gaze falls to a right wairths queins. Come," and he motioned for her to step in.

"No thank you," she explained, "I have errands to do, but I wanted to stop and express my regrets."

"Aye, I understand. Gutilda was me heart, me soul, right peach o' me eye. Would 'ave wed next month... to a good mon, a fine, fine young mon."

"So Rustan told me," claimed Thulia, reaching to squeeze his hand, "You must have done a little horse-breaking up here. I hope you and your wife feel better... in a few days."

"A small bit. The tamer ones. Nay aulds, but nay a youngermon now. We shall get by."

"Well," she sighed, "I must be off to find a bullock and plow. Plus that thing that rolls the soil. And I'm hoping someone has a decent axe. I think it's time to raise the garden, perhaps enlarge it. Children grow, more are born. Days go by and mouths increase."

"That they do," admitted Stefan, "Have me a boy-child, now eight. Salomon by name."

"Like Solomon in the Bible?"

He shrugged, "Nay. I was a pagan back them. Salomon, as in '*he who uses salt.*' I wanted him to have more than I 'ave."

Thulia eyed him directly, "You have grit. What more could a good man want?" Then she turned upon a heel and headed out toward the road.

She almost reached ten paces before Stefan was striding beside her. He carried an axe, and prided, "Drop a pine in ten cuts, I can. Know a mon's got a bullock and plow." He paused and strode quietly for a moment, then explained, "And that soil-turning *thing* be called a *share*."

Chapter 31: The Creature of Darkness

Thulia headed up the north road from Axeville, fortunate to find extra seed in a small woodcutters' village. She had purchased carrot, squash, and barley seeds. One woman even gave her some apple seeds at no charge or trade. *More than a few years of waiting, there,* she grinned. The people of Axeville seemed much friendlier after discovering she was helping "those poor people," as they termed it.

The Ascentians had worked in the garden beside her, lugging rocks, sticking the furrows, and planting what seeds and starters they had; yet the garden was half again larger than previously. Firs and pines were cut back a hundred feet further. And a community—once steeping in self-pity—had stepped into daylight.

At the Red Tower, she let the white-spotted gelding drink from a rivulet that tumbled to the river while she sat down and ate some curd and a chunk of brown bread. Thulia mulled improvements at Ascentia and all that still needed to be done. The bridge had to be rebuilt, the same with the church. As for Selenas, she was in a quandary, for he was still a rootworm; yet he did get out and about, not speaking to anyone and walking along the lake shore. At first Thulia feared he might fill pockets with rocks and jump in, but evidently the thought never occurred to him; or if it did, he was too much the coward to attempt it. He was never overly bold; and she suspected Lilia prodded him to accomplishment by using female tact. Selenas never was a Fritigern. He was too mindful, too good.

After finishing an early lunch, she dug heels to her mount, passing the turn-off leading up to the Gepid village, and hoping to reach Ascentia before nightfall. *Ah, the Gepids.* She had pieced the entire story together, how it all began and ended with Gunter's obsession with a promiscuous spouse, an intimate experience she lived through first hand.

Less than a mile up the road, she stopped short, for once again curiosity claimed her; yet it was even more, a dark shadow once seen in the gold mirror. What kind of people were the Gepids and how did they live? Like animals?—like Selenas was becoming? She knew they respected her; and as the Amazon she would be safe in entering their village. She had to see for herself. Turning back down the road, she headed for the Gepid horse-path.

*   *   *

At trail's end, she saw the heads. Seventeen in all. Some no more than old skulls, others with tufts of hair in rotting patches. The ten newer ones were enough to make a rat sick, eyes picked out by ravens, jaws slack and lips gone, the teeth grinning at her. One of them was Lilia. That brought a chill to Thulia, even on a late spring day. In composite, they were the legacy of Gunter—the one-eyed man.

She rode into their midst a month after he died, the Gepids running to see the legend. They pointed to *The Iron Breaker*, the laudable weapon that killed their chieftain, talking and gesturing among themselves as the young nephew pushed through them, "Why do you come here, Amazon?"

"Just a visit to see how you fare."

His frown swung a knowing grin, "I think you wish to see how barbarians live," and he swept his arm to the sight before her, "This is the high place where life runs hard. Not enough pasture, not enough seed. People die here... like Gunter's wife."

"Is she dead?"

"She was alive a week ago."

"Do you have room to plant more seed?"

"Yes, but seed we have not," the nephew shrugged.

"Then find an empty pot or sack and I'll give you what I can spare, or you can try killing me for it," and she patted her sword's hilt.

"You would give us seed—the tribe that killed your women?"

"I would give food to a hungry child, for I once hungered."

The warriors eyed one another and cabin doors opened beyond a crack to expose female faces and those of children. The nephew approached closer, speaking with less hostility, "I think the gods know you. I shall not refuse your offer but it must be done through trade. We have amber."

"I have no need for it. Let me see the chieftain's widow, and perhaps I can help her."

A warrior smiled, "With Gunter dead, a new chieftain with a ripe wife has taken his place. Now we are led by Hagen."

Thulia found it difficult to understand them. They were barbarians—much like men from an age now gone, but they were very real. Their ways were backward, their dress primal, as if the forest ruled their lives, and she realized it did. *This is how it was, even with us, when the old gods ruled.* She had ridden back through time, to a life primordial. "Who is Hagen?"

"I am," prided the nephew, "And my wife is big with child. Come if you wish."

She dismounted and the nephew walked her to Gunter's cabin, built low and long, the roof slanting to an angle as thin logs protruded beyond spruce bark. The narrow door was smaller than woman-height, a thin-hewn board swinging on deer-hide hinges. Not a window had been cut into the logs.

"She is in there," explained Hagen, "The creature of darkness. Her real name is Hel."

She answered slowly, "Hell is a place."

The nephew looked at her in wonderment, "Place? No, she is Hel, named for the goddess. It was a fitting name, and so she became Hel."

"You mean she is pretty like a goddess?" quizzed Thulia.

He looked to the ground, studying dry pine needles. Reaching down for a handful, he raised the needles to her, letting them fall from his palm, "What was fresh becomes dead, like the lower house—Hel's realm, the dark place. She never comes out. Thrice each moon Gunter would drag her to the brook and she would bathe. Only then did she see day's light. But now?"

Leaving his side Thulia began walking slowly toward the door, not the long strides of confidence.

"Enter not if it smells of death," Hagen yelled, "We have been waiting to burn it."

*   *   *

Thulia feared little, either through brashness or strength, but this place she feared. Was the woman a witch, or worse? Lifting the latch, she stepped into darkness. After a few moments, her eyes acclimated to nether-light, an eerie place foul with smoke. Yet there was another smell, bear grease and something else, like the scent of woman and man, or the sweat of labor. The walls were empty, their dry bark peeling, some of it on the floor. Not a broom, cupboard, or chair sat within its rankness; only two stools and a fur covered bed. Nothing hung from the rafters, no smoked meats, no osier basket of half-dried vegetables, not a single sign of food. Gunter's house was an empty hovel.

The woman squatted at the hearth, stirring a small cauldron with a long wooden object, not a spoon. Sparse were the flames. Two empty bowls lay beside her, perhaps once containing sustenance. She wore a long wool robe, thick fur at the end of each sleeve. Glancing up at Thulia, her expression seemed blank, not surprised or welcoming; and when she stood, the robe fell open to expose her body. She was small and bone thin, the robe sliding from emaciated shoulders to crumple upon the dirt floor. Perhaps thirty years old, she had wild black hair, and her limbs were delicate like those of girl, yet her breasts sat flat. She was unwashed with patches of bear oil and charcoal producing a coat of filth.

Other than a fire's glow, the cabin remained dark, not a lamp in it. Standing naked before Thulia, she murmured, "You are not a man. Why are you here?"

"I came to see Hel, the widow of Gunter."

"His widow I am. But not another man shall have me. It is over." She reached to the cauldron, pulling the object from the oil. Only then did Thulia recognize it—a hardwood phallus!—shining smooth and dripping bear grease to the hearth. Weak flames sputtered as the widow turned and walked to the far dark corner, reclining upon the bed as Thulia followed.

She lay to a pile of furs, all skins of bears and wolves. Spreading legs, she guided the phallus, working it deep, oil dripping as she began a chant, "God of manhood, break the blockage."

She repeated the words mechanically, again and again. And she arched hips in desperation, her leg muscles twitching from the strain. What was left of her life fell to exhaustion, spent from a want of viands; and she forced her gaze to meet

Thulia's and tried catching her breath, "The god finds no pleasure. Gives no cure."

Thulia stood shocked in the shadows!—for the woman appeared lost in aberration. From the smell and sight before her, Thulia's stomach churned, and she almost retched.

"Men no longer come here," the widow mumbled as she withdrew the phallus, clutching it to her emaciated chest. Her eyes seemed unable to focus, "Not for two fortnights... since he died."

A great fear rushed from deep within as Thulia retreated from the sight before her. *Is this the ultimate craving? The last whimper of self destruction?* In this pathetic shell of womanhood she could see her own compulsion when younger. The only difference was self control. *She is almost dead—killing herself!*

*   *   *

Thulia could not think straight as she stumbled backward over something. She was standing in the hearth!— flames licking her boots! Terrified, she sprang from the coals and ran for the door, confused by countless shadows, colorless shades that hid escape; and it was so lightless she could not find the latch, her fingers sliding along rough wood in a desperate and hurried search, feeling their way along the door crack as her heart battered her chest, ever louder, ever faster, a tambour of unmetered fear. There it was!—the door latch! And running into the freedom of a filtered sun, she had trouble breathing, almost retching again as she bumped into the young chieftain.

He held her shoulders for a moment, studying her fright, "Now you know. She is the creature of darkness they fear in the valleys, not sure what she is."

Not finding her breath, Thulia gasped, "What is she?"

"A woman and her god," explained Hagen, "To be the chieftain's wife and not birth a son?—not even a girl-child. She was a virgin when married. He thought it might be himself so he made them come, one at a time, every man of Gepid blood. Me included. No other man was allowed. The four Quadi, the Vandals and that Christian? Stuck their heads on a pole. Killed them all to keep the bloodline clean... but there was no blood to save."

"There's more to it," returned the Amazon, "She has a phallus, huge in size."

"The god Feda? She must open the blockage with him, make a passage for the man-juice to enter her womb. Quadro-anno she has tried. She is barren and shall die that way."

"Four years? No wonder she is mad!"

"Not crazy," he corrected her, "Desperate. No one wants to starve to death."

"What will happen?"

"See her now? Few men brought her food. They said, *She is not worth a dog-leg*. Sometimes they gave her a chewed bone to satisfy themselves. But now she is like the dead."

Thulia implored, "Why is she abandoned?"

"The old ones guide us. They say, *Leave her be. Let her die. She is not a woman but a Thing*. Her days are gone, her bones like tent poles through canvas."

"How old is she?"

Hagen thought for a moment, counting his fingers, "She is twenty two years, come the winter."

Twenty one! The woman looked far beyond her age, perhaps not mad after all, but desperate beyond reason. She was the cause of great sin, of burnings and killings. Yet Hel was the original victim. Thulia stared back to the cabin, the woman dying within. *A prisoner of folklore and ignorance. The world thinks a woman worthless if she cannot bear a child.* In Hel's trials, she was jolted to the core, seeing herself—for she once prayed to the phallus. There was no option, for she could not leave the woman to starve, "What would happen," she asked in a steadier voice, "If I were to remove her from that place?"

He rolled a pine needle between fingers, studying it, then meeting her eyes, "Take her. I wish her not to die. The old ones are wrong in their judgment." Then Hagen turned back to the cabin, his voice almost inaudible, "I, too, want to do things that are right. We will bury the heads."

*   *   *

The day went. And came the night with a rap upon timbers. Rustan opened the presbyter's door to find Thulia and a shadow before him. He looked into Hel's face, and his jaw dropped. The young woman realized he was shocked by her appearance, and she looked up to Thulia, "I had no mirror. But I was not ugly... before."

"You are still beautiful inside," the Amazon assured her, "You just need some fleshing out and a bath."

The Alan hetmon stepped out through the doorway, speaking to Thulia in a subdued tone, "Selenas is inside writing a letter of resignation to Bishop Wulfilas. Who is this?" and he seemed to be fumbling for more words.

"Gunter's widow. I'm taking her in there," declared Thulia as she waved an article wrapped in wool, "I want him to see her and this. Would you remain outside until the door opens again?"

Rustan nodded, and she entered with Hel. Selenas sat with his back to her at a table crude and built from hewn logs, a candle before him as he scribbled upon papyrus. Hearing someone enter, he failed to turn around. She went to him, peering down at his chore, and she asked, "Do you still think this is Hell on earth?"

He refused to comment.

"Answer me!" she demanded.

He looked up to her, his eyes red with dark circles beneath them, his demeanor expressionless, "Yes."

"Would you like to see what Hell really looks like?" Thulia gritted.

"What do you mean?"

"Turn around, Goody Boy, and take a real look at pain," she ordered while using a childhood expression.

Upon hearing it, he stood and faced the room. Thulia walked back to Hel and led her toward him, stopping short. She wanted him to get the full view, watching his eyes grow. In a mild note she addressed the Gepid widow, "You can drop your robe, if you wish. Let Christian Man see you—the beautiful woman you once were. Let him view the bride of Gunter."

Uncertain, Hel paused. She studied the man before her and returned her glace to Thulia. Then she let the robe fall slowly from the bones of her shoulders, catching the garment for a moment with her elbows. Finally Hel let it drop to the earthen floor.

Selenas backed away, stopping only when the table hindered further retreat, his expression shock, for he gaped aghast at a living skeleton nude and covered with filth. Hel stepped toward him, hands outstretched. Wide eyed, he could only shake his head, mouth open yet unable to find words.

"Yes, Goody Boy. This is the real Hel. She has not eaten for weeks, and for the past four years she's been raped by hundreds. Yet she still wants to live."

His eyes followed her limbs until he stared at the floor.

Thulia hugged the widow, asking the presbyter, "Can you find something pleasant to say… like, *How are you, Hel?*"

His glance raised to look at the woman again, her loose flesh and empty breasts, the bulging joints upon stick-like limbs.

Thulia reached him in two long strides, swiping his face with the back of a hand, "Speak! How do you believe she is? More fortunate than you? I would think you two have much in common. You're a widower, she's a widow, both of you abandoned by a god. This is her god Feda," she declared, slapping the wrapped bundle to his hands.

He looked down as trembling fingers unfolded the wrapping. And seeing the hardwood phallus, he dropped it!— the instrument bouncing upon the floor, rolling to stop at Hel's feet. Quickly, urgently, she bent down and grabbed it, clutching it to her chest as if it were a newborn child.

"She's unable to conceive, Selenas. The priests gave her that *thing*. She still has a thread of hope, clings to it. Do you think the god Feda will give her fertility is she continues to work ardently?"

All the gods and God himself could not starve hope, the one emotion that binds the soul. He could see it before him, viewing it first hand, yet it flickered far too dim. "My, Lord!" he gasped, "Who could possibly have known? We must find some decent clothes, something for this woman to eat, and she needs to bathe." He stepped forward and retrieved her robe, fitting it around her while guiding Hel to the table. And he spoke delicately from the heart, "Please sit. We have beef and winter squash, some fresh bread and eggs." He even questioned, "Do you drink milk?"

And with a swift hand, he brushed the letter and ink aside.

Canto Four
DIGNITY
Anno 352
Three years later

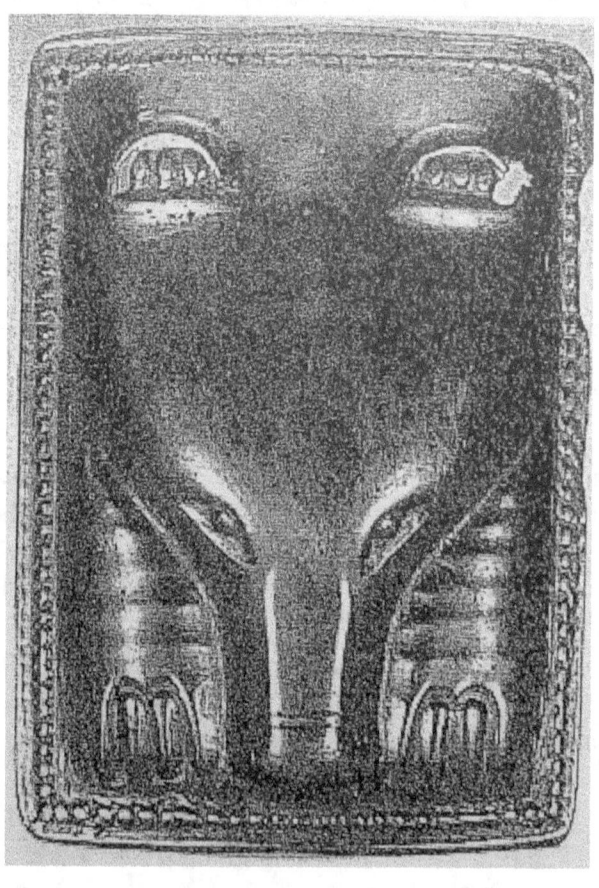

Chapter 32: Just Us Squirrels

Good men were scarce. Seasoned warriors—the fathers, grandfathers and uncles—were gone, and the battle fell to the blood of youth. Bark roofs crackled; and the stench of burning furs (or was it charred flesh?) caught in the hairs of Frit's nose. It scraped the roof of his mouth and tainted his lungs. Flames leapt higher from Alemanni huts too crude for permanent structures, a town now abandoned. The villagers fled west toward Bavaria along time-worn paths, following the major body of menfolk—Germans in retreat. Stragglers remained, coming back in groups of six or eight plus a few horsemen.

A shout erupted again, coming from dense firs beyond the village. Frit wheeled his mount around, guiding it toward the ruckus, and entered the cover by raising his sword-arm to shield his face, the heavy boughs slapping him as he reached a swampy clearing. Dropping his arm, he met two Alemanni riders face-on!—both spearmen intent on skewering a Roman prize. He reined the mount hard to the left and deflected the first spear as his horse trampled a dead equite's body. *Another good man gone.* The second rider punched his weapon hard to Frit's ribs, almost piercing his chainmail. Thinking quick, Frit leaned back from the German's thrust, falling from his horse to land in soft peat moss.

Instantly, he rolled to his feet and remounted!—the riders now coming at him from opposite directions, swamp muck flying from hooves, as they leveled spears for a final head-on stab. He waited. He waited longer. *The last moment.*

NOW. Again he lurched from his horse, dropping face-down to bog-moss—*Shit. I'm soaking wet*—as the Germans skewered each other!

Frit stood in a hurry, his legs deep in black ooze as his mount ran off in terror, frightened to the core. Disturbed from millennial rest, swamp muck stank of rot and sulfur; and both Germans were on the ground, one apparently dead. *They're killing each other today.*

The second Alemannus came to his knees, feeling his own ribs as blood soaked through a filthy shirt. Possibly sixteen, more like fourteen, the warrior reached down and grasped his spear with both hands, pointing at Frit and backing slowly, each step creating a *shwerp... shwerp... shwerp.*

"Scat!" yelled Frit in German, raising his sword at the same time. The young horseman backed further, *shwerp-shwerp-shwerp*, then turned and ran for higher ground. *He'll not be back.* Frit stepped to the second rider, the man lying prone in peat moss. He knelt and rolled the German to his back, *Another young one, too young. Hope he had a sincere god.* With his free hand, Frit picked up the dead man's weapon, examining it. Like most Alemanni spears, it had no iron tip, just a whittled point hardened by flames. He pushed it upright, deep in the muck, and stood to his feet. He sighed and turned to find his horse.

*   *   *

Junius Soranus rode through the east side of the village looking for Thaurus or Frit, wondering where both ala captains were. He reined to a halt, seeing one of his equites sitting on a crude outdoor bench, a rag around his outer thigh and his head to accepting palms. *A hard day for some, a hard campaign for all, but I think we've just about whipped their lean German ass.* He cleared his throat and quizzed, "Mergovius, you gonna make it?"

The horseman sat erect, trying to stand, "Yes, sir. Lost my horse. Got a puncture in my upper leg."

"Good man. Hang in there. The medics and capisari are here. Seen either captain?"

"Thaurus took a spear first thing, sir. He left horizontal, but I hear he'll make it. Haven't seen the Fisher. He was on the west side, chasing them through the swamp. Should be alright, though. The captain swings a killer sword."

"That he does," grinned Soranus as he spurred his mount forward. He reached the other side of the village as Frit stepped from wood-edge into sunlight. The Goth stuck his sword to the soil, unwrapped his sagum and snapped it like a wet blanket while slamming muck-covered feet to the ground. Soranus watched the man's antics for a moment, then shot, "How goes the battle, Fisher King?"

"A mucky frigging mess, and my horse ran off," Frit snapped, then looking up, "Oh! It's you, sir. Fought two in the marsh, one dead, the other running. Thaurus is down and I have no idea how many we've lost."

"Thaurus will live, a tough Vandal there. I'm up here at the marching-camp for a couple of days. Want us to push harder, to the limit. Get a count of the downed, and I'll see you at officer's mess tonight. Got something special for you boys—an amphora of Falarian wine straight from the ash hillside of Vesuvius. Good shit. Older than most of the Alemanni we're fighting." Then Soranus turned his mount, swinging his gaze back, "Received a note from Theo. He's living high off the hog at Trier. Wiping the Emperor's ass, I guess."

* * *

An hour later, one of the ala's horsemen claimed "Seventeen" while counting downed riders. The skirmish went like those of the past three years, gender hard to define with men looking like women, their hair long, only nobles wearing top-knots. Fortunately most never viewed a razor.

"Son of a bitch," spat Frit, his sword still unsheathed as he addressed the horseman, "Seventeen? No more than two hundred against us." He reined his new mount around to face the rider, "How many dead?"

"Half, sir."

"What in Hell is half of an odd number?"

"Eight found; nine when Gallus Avitus is recovered," the man returned, "The wagon went off full. Didn't see his body, but there's his mount."

Frit turned about, his eyes falling to the empty horse. Shaking his head, he ran the blade along his new mount's withers, cleaning off mud and blood, then sliding it to scabbard, another fine day in Hell. Seeing movement, he snapped his glance toward the nearest hut. Avitus sauntered for his mount, re-buckling sword belt. In an instant, Frit dropped from the saddle, striding fast to the Gaul, "What were you doing in there?"

"Who, me?" Avitus stammered, "I was, ah… relieving myself."

"Show me."

"But, Fisher, it stinks."

Frit snapped, "Get back in there," then turning to the mounted rider, "If he comes out before I do, kill him. Make it nine; understand?"

"Yes, sir," noted the rider.

Frit entered the hut with Avitus, the interior swathed in sunlight from a wall partially destroyed. A young woman retreated to the far side, unable to step back further, hands to thighs as blood trickled down a leg. Her cheeks were streaked from weeping, and her eyes held fright. *Relieving himself? I suppose that's one way of expressing it. Most likely, she thinks I want sloppy seconds.*

Avitus had filthy habits, now finally caught. With a fast shove, Frit pushed him to the wall, almost through it, "Remove your sword belt and drop your trousers. Then stand at attention… or so help me, I'll feed you to the scalpers." The Gaul followed orders as Frit studied the woman—striking in lack of beauty—short with full cheeks, her teeth protruding. *Like a damned squirrel.* He asked in German, "Did he take your worth?" *What a coat!—sewn from a hundred mangy hares.*

She nodded ya, mouth twitching, hands moving to her face, shaking as she began weeping again. Spinning to Avitus, Frit reached to the dirt floor and slid the Gaul's sword from its scabbard. He pushed the hilt to the girl. She grabbed it, sobbing even worse, and held the weapon with both hands. *Amazing. The man raped a tree squirrel.* "Take his worth, woman," he urged in German again, "Grab his privates and slice them off. Do it! It's called Revenge."

"No! I beg!" cried the Gaul, his eyes wide as trousers hugged his ankles.

"Whack them off," Frit ordered again. She released her grip, dropping the sword to the floor as hands returned to full cheeks. *She can't even think straight.* Frit grabbed the cabin's center post, leaning to it, his fingers playing with smooth pine… almost casually, a little get-together in mid-war, the rapist, the victim, and a man in the middle. His glance moved from the girl to the Gaul and back again. *Who's the barbarian? Her? Him? Me?* He shook his head, trying hard not to grin, knowing she never would have done it, just a spoil of war and truly spoiled, practically worthless and plainer than biscuit. *Not much left to bargain with.*

Reaching under his chainmail, Frit fingered his purse, fumbling for a couple of gold coins. He dropped them to her hand, "Your dowry. Now find a widower or marry for love. Understand?"

She nodded.

"Get along now. Your people are heading west."

The girl scurried from the hut. Frit watched her exit. *Another screwed-up thrush, tainted in the head.* He turned to Avitus, "Only us squirrels know what happened here. Pull up your trousers, pick up your weapon and follow me out." Frit stepped to daylight, now two riders waiting. Within moments, the Gaul came from the hut, revolving sword belt to position. Turning to Avitus, he spoke curtly, "You owe me coin. Square up with the quartermaster. Did I state rules of my ala in your presence?"

"Yes you did, sir."

"I like to sleep at night, so you'll be leaving the unit. I'll not ride with rapists or men who might hate me for what I think. This ala is like a ship, three hundred men with one captain. Tomorrow you'll return to Vindobona and find another unit. Damned lucky to have something to piss with. You know that?"

"I do, sir," murmured Avitus.

"You have talent, a good horseman, fair with the sword. For your thoughts, I'm faster with a blade than you are, and I sleep light. A little self control might help, although most captains tolerate what I don't. Let Fortuna guide your career." Frit waved the Gaul off, turning to the horsemen, a thumb to the hut, "Go ahead and burn it. The squirrels have departed... taking their nuts."

With a few strides, Frit reached his horse to remount it. He rode for village center to survey the burning, a cool day in Germania. Around him, huts crackled beneath the flames, their heat warming his face. Little for the men to pillage. The Alemanni didn't own much. At least he got rid of the Gaul, five skirmishes before caught in the act. As senior captain, he had rules, sacking yes, but not rape. Now on his third campaign in Germania, he saw little difference between Imperials and barbarians. His men were cleaner, better outfitted, yet the same mindset. *"Man was not born God's next of kin for imitating vileness of beasts."* Xristos the teacher? No. It came from Pliny the Elder. He despised reading when young, yet he remembered the quote, perhaps not verbatim.

Frit closed his eyes, the thatching and pine radiating more heat. *A fine one you are.* Evidently mankind elevated himself rather slowly. As for the Rule of Rape? In his mind he pictured a girl, perhaps eight or nine years of age, hearing the words of Othar when he was too young to know what they meant, *"Took her bloma, he did. Like a lynx eats its own young."*

The Fisher? A wonder Soranus didn't accuse him of being soft on the enemy. Frit always loved women, one in particular. Yet he wasn't the moral gallantus of three years ago, perhaps time to end his education. He had become callous, dispassionate in humor, his mind stripped of everything noble. Empathy escaped him. By another campaign, he would be one of Pliny's vile beasts. Never did he dream of a perfect world like his brother, yet he once had a better view of battle's honor. Fabula! Victory was seeing a girl deflowered, men collecting Alemanni bronze for a redsmith's trade, a stack of blood-stained furs sold for wine. They tossed dignity to dirt, animals once men, now pawing through their own waste, trying to regain their loss. One of his riders—a man dubbed Wolfbane—took German scalps, kept them in a birchen box, counting them like acorns. He disappeared south, escorted to a special ward known as Galen's Head House. Glory was plague no better than a horde of Huns.

Who wins? Just us squirrels.

The burning huts cast a fine glow. He recalled his father's words, the reiks' broad hand upon his shoulder, the warmth of it, *"Do the right thing, and the gods will know you've done it."* In his youth, the right thing was too difficult a task. Easier it was to avoid it. With lids still closed, Frit reviewed his progress. He had been taught by a Greek, now speaking four languages, his speech cryptic, the rhetoric clear, concise. He flashed a long-sword of Sarmatian design, and with lightening speed. Frit was noted for it, the fastest blade north of the limes. A fair combination—mind, tongue, and iron.

He acquired grit needed in the coming world, having lived the glory defining Rome, dark under marble's gloss, no less evil than the woods of Transylvania. He was an ebilsmon riding in disguise.

Enough of it. Rumors were flying, the Alemanni ready to walk beneath the Imperial yoke. If the campaign ended before autumn, he would call it a lesson in human nature and head back for Threisbaurg. Back to so-called barbarians... and that naughty Christian. The mere thought of her, all that softness under hardness, wrought more heat than a burning village.

"Captain!" someone yelled.

"What is it?" he returned, eyes snapping open.

"Your sagum's on fire!"

He looked down at his filthy cape, a plate-sized hole burning. With a quick hand, Frit unsnapped his fibula, the garment dropping to the ground. A battle won, a day not lost. The truth? He was poorer in purse yet richer in tenet.

Chapter 33: A Tribal Heirloom

Selenas viewed deer tracks at his feet, the forest musty after a rain. The path ran old and worn deep, long before he walked it, the soil bare in places as tree roots raised to catch his stride. He was unsure where the three years went, flying by like an eagle, only winters long. Now an early summer filled high ground with minuscule, blue flowers, delicate and beauteous, much like Hel.

She reminded him of Lilia, the same dark hair and eyes, an innocence that held firm through all she endured. The will to live, to be of worth, coursed deep within her, brushing away fingers of death. Never had more abuse been done to a woman. She suffered beyond trial, indeed Hell.

As he walked to the nearby brook, Selenas stopped to adjust his tunic. He wished to appear a handsome man, clean and neat before her. She lived in the cabin built for Thulia and her daughter, a gift from him and Rustan. He never saw Hel enough. She was reclusive, perhaps shy toward men through her background. What did they think of her past?—a communal receptacle, a woman who laid with hundreds. Not one a lover, he knew that.

When did the grief pass? A year ago? At some point it did, roughly about the time he noticed Hel in a different light. She sprang back stronger, like a flower crushed beneath a boot, reaching back to the sun above. The weight of health wrapped around those bones, and then came the half-smile. She never smiled broadly, just a hint of teeth, but it was there more and more.

Selenas hurried his pace, for he hadn't seen Hel in a week. She was doing well tending the gardens with Thulia. To him the act seemed below her, freewoman's work. She had noble blood, once married to a chieftain. Yet he knew nothing of her family, the subject of Gepids not within her speech. She was more or less an adopted Goth; for it was the Gothic way, and hardly a Goth could claim a particular tribe as his or her ancestors.

Voices filtered through the forest ahead, a woman's being the loudest, a coarse laugh. *Probably Thulia. She's the type.* He entered the clearing at the brook, its pool three feet deep if that. They greeted him, Rustan, Safrax, Thulia... and Hel. She wore summer green, a pale linen smock cinched around her narrow waist, a skirt the same color. *Right from the same dye lot. Clothes of a freewoman.* As if the others didn't exist he spoke directly to her, trying to look virile, not really sure what virility looked like; and so he blushed as he spoke, "Good day, Hel. You look wondrous." She did!

Hel also reddened—her head tilting downward, eyes lowering—and she spoke not a thing. Yet there it was! That diminutive smile. Then they all began talking about this and that, with the exception of Safrax who probably wished he was somewhere else. Finally the moment came, the one they all waited for. Selenas waded into the pool, outstretching his hand. Hel grabbed it, still flushed, stepping in water up to her thighs. He knew she had been instructed by Thulia to make all the right moves.

She knelt, immersed to shoulder blades. Then it happened. He feared to touch her, yet he had to. *I need to use force. What might this do to her? Will she forever shy from my touch?* Everyone waited, eying each other. He felt extremely self-conscious, their stares making his discomfort all the worse. Hel looked up to him with those beautiful eyes and she took his right hand, placing it upon her head. Not a word she said. So he pushed, dipping her to the pool and withdrawing his hand quickly. She returned upright and waited. "I baptize thee Hel, in the name of the Father, the Son, and the Holy Ghost."

She stood upright and he blushed all the more as her nipples pushed through wetness. They begged, pleaded to be touched.

Never had he been so nonplused, slowing his pace on the way back to the village, the rest of the baptismal party moving ahead. Thulia stepped off the path and waited for him. *Another confrontation.* As he reached her, she piqued, "What happened back there?"

"I don't know," he answered.

"You couldn't touch her, could you," she stated bluntly.

He repeated himself like an idiot, "I don't know."

"Do you think her a leper?" spat Thulia.

"No! Not that at all," he admitted, "I simply froze."

*   *   *

Fritigern rode down from the hill with a few dozen of his men, shouts of jubilation to their rear, a sight better than screaming Alemanni. This was it, finished, the final battle of the Germania campaign. It ended early, a big ruddy chieftain waving a white flag—not his underwear; they didn't wear a thing under their trousers except their thing.

Once through the marching camp's gates, Frit noticed blood on his hands but not his for a change. *First to the big bascauda to wash it off, then to the baths.* He needed a cold soak to remove the deeper grit, the innocuous smell of war. Somehow, he was still alive, his third term of enlistment over. Never again! Frit wanted to see a little more of life, a few more rolls in the sack, quaff a few good beers, and eat a giant chunk of meat, preferably beef. He knew the roll in the sack part was out, not with the women hanging around camp. Each looked like she needed a good meal or had eaten too many, nothing mid between, and not a busty redhead in the bunch. Too particular, he found not one desirable woman during his entire time in Germania.

After three years of almost getting killed twice a week, he didn't give a damn about anything beyond life itself. Life was good!—time enough for theory later. *Do you elevate, descend, or rot?*

The last two weeks went by without a battle, only skirmishes. It was over and he literally had plans—drawn up by a drunken architect in Saveria, a little squiggly but readable. He caught Thaurus eyeing them late one afternoon, the Vandal abashed, *"Trading a good career for what? A coupo?"*

Frit never pictured it like that, replying, *"What's wrong with a tavern? Good company, food, and drink. All I need is a bawdy wench."* He had the coin and time to build it, far beyond a tavern and huge in scope. Before joining the auxiliary, he never finished anything. Well, no more. This was an extremely serious project, yet Thaurus had shaken his head, *"A waste of talent. You've accomplished in three years what took me five. Soranus is trying to convince the Magister Militum to raise us to junior legate. You know what that means—Flavian blessing. We'll be Romans."*

"No, we'll be a Vandal and Goth in fancy clothes," chuckled Frit, *"I'll believe to promotion when I see it, but this is something I've planned for years."*

Frit wasn't the letter writing type, yet months ago he fired one off to Old Hempstalk. The man answered with good news. Thulia was a widow—Again!—and now living at Ascentia. Time to go home.

Inside the camp he slid from the saddle with the horse still moving. He almost lost his balance; and trying to walk, he found himself striding bow-legged. He washed hands quickly. *Things to pack. Not much. A bunch of ratty clothes.*

In twenty long strides, he reached the officer's tent, falling on his back to the bunk, near exhaustion but still in one piece. In a moment he would bathe, but first he had to think about the Horse Dancer. Leaning sideways he reached under the bunk, feeling for the cloth bag, finding it with his fingers. He loosened tie strings, shaking the bag over his stomach as the little artifice dropped out, along with a half dozen fish-hooks. It wasn't big. He raised it to shadowed daylight, the tent too dark to view true color, a marvelous little horse riding halfway around the world. It came from the land of Qin and had seen a few sights. Old it was, yet shining like new and almost the color of Thulia's eyes. He closed his own to view her, the fire of her hair, that lascivious tongue.

Frit was no gambler, never tossed a die, yet he conceived the most speculative venture of his life. The idea of love over lust seemed anomalous, no other explanation for his plan. He tossed the carved horse in his palm, catching it a few times, then dropped it and the hooks back in the bag. Swinging his feet to the tent floor, he pulled the strings and stood.

The journey held dangers. He would travel south to Vindobona and downriver to Intercisa, then re-cross the flodus and head straight for Gothia through the Barbaricon. Most of it would be Vandal country, old enemies, yet he had fortune on his side—a letter of passage from a Vandal prince, Thaurus the Silver Arm.

*   *   *

Late afternoon remained bright upon Threisbaurg's east hill, not a cloud in the sky as fifty warriors knelt, one by one, before *Tyrfing* to make the blood sign. Once blessed, they would relieve Athanaric's weary torchers in the Christian purge. Aoric stood off to the circle's side, leaning upon his cane, mashing teeth and vexed to the pith. The consecration was lessened by kneeling to what he considered a debased god.

Tyrfing was not the same, shorter and of different workmanship than the older one. The magistrate glared at the two priests as they blessed the horsemen. Merjands and Ufar were guilty of subterfuge, giving the tribe's best sword to that Taifala who called herself an Amazon. *Just handing it over!— like an inferior weapon not worth keeping*.

He turned to leave then decided he'd avoided the subject far too long, spinning around upon his good leg to face the guilty, "This ritual is a sham. An empty sham. Look at that sword!—a disgraceful replacement for the one we had."

Ufar was taken aback, "It was forged by the Chalybes, great smiths of renown. It's still *Tyrfing*. The sword represents the god."

"It does not," snapped Aoric, "This is a piss-poor substitute for the good one. Piss-poor! You two gave the real *Tyrfing* to a woman who should have continued using a stick. A stick is a woman's weapon."

"You were there and saw it," claimed Merjands, "The gods allowed her to pull it from the stone. Even the lightening was a divine sign. The sword was hers."

"I saw nothing. I was no longer there and bouncing across a field in a runaway wagon. All I know is this: the best sword we had is in the hands of a Christian—the very cult we fight against! You could have given her this one, made at lesser cost," and he pointed his cane at it, "But you handed over the best of the two." Aoric took a breath, for he was working himself into a thither!—and he shook his walking stick at them, wishing it were the better sword and wanting to strike them down, "That sword was superior. It had red and green jewels! You know full well the gods had nothing to do with it, not one damned thing; and it was you two who gave away a tribal heirloom."

Merjands raised a finger, "The sword was never owned by any tribe. It belonged to Aryante, the High Warrior Priestess. She had Alani blood, as does Thulia."

Aoric screamed in furor, "Aryante? She is nothing but legend. A legend I say! How could a woman who never existed own a sword? It was used for Tyrfingi rites! Everything used in religious ceremony belongs to the kunja, not the priests. Do not argue! I want that sword restored; and I'll not stand here one more time and watch good men profane themselves before a mediocre blade. Never again! The real *Tyrfing* will be returned, one way or the other. We shall get it back, and that is a cold, hard fact."

* * *

At day's end, Safrax and Enoc paddled Rustan's log canoe for the eastern shore, the shadows long as the water surface cooled. Not a breath of wind, the lake glassed like a bronze mirror, and every tree's reflection lay upon it as a reverse painting. Paddling at the stern, Safrax glanced down at the trout upon the canoe's sole, a huge fish at four or five pounds, the biggest trout he'd ever caught; and he could not recall his father catching one larger.

Yet it came at a price, a stark and unsaid fact he was absorbing. You paid a price for everything. In catching the trout, he cracked the tip of his father's rod; and although it could be wrapped or spliced, the rod would never be the same. It was an old one, made by Fritigern and hauled up from Threisbaurg when they were banished. Back in Gothia, Rustan usually fished with Frit because they had the same philosophy and penchant. Most nobles were staunch hunters, not anglers, each keeping a pack of keen-nosed hounds. His father fished with Selenas a few times, but Safrax remembered the comments. *"He drives me crazy—always jerking his rod before a fish swallows the bait; then he gets bored, never checks the bait and angles with a bare hook. Frit is the fisher. Patience and tact, my son, and quick reflexes—attributes of a great angler and warrior."*

That's what Safrax wanted to be, the ultimate warrior, a real cataphract. He watched Enoc paddling at the bow. Enoc possessed strength but not patience, and he was slow in setting a hook. Yet Enoc had stealth, which Safrax assumed could be an attribute if applied correctly, but Enoc used it underhandedly.

They reached a fingered ledge along the shore as Enoc jumped from the bow, not attempting to steady the canoe while Safrax grabbed the rod and fish to cat-walk along the narrow craft's center. Hopping to the rock, Safrax strode up the ledge to place the rod and prize upon the boulder where Thulia always sat at lakeside. Then they guided the canoe along the shallows until reaching forest edge. Rustan wanted the craft hauled into the woods and turned over, protecting it from rain and unwanted users. Sliding the canoe up from the shore, they finally reached the tree line, Enoc grunting, "This is good enough. Let's flip it."

"No," demanded Safrax, "Only half of it is concealed. We need to drag it all the way under the trees." Enoc glared hard, a surly tilt to his chin; and they tugged it well into the pines, heaved it over, and stowed the paddles underneath.

As they stepped back from the boat, something moved through the pines, a dark shadow in fading dusk. It moved again!—slipping behind another tree, yet totally quiet as if it weighed less than a barley-corn. Both Enoc and Safrax froze where they stood, not moving a muscle for the longest moments, each waiting, for what they knew not.

Safrax knew trolls and dwarves were nothing but superstition, not really scary. But ghosts were a different matter. If the Holy Ghost existed, then so did bad ones; and the evilest ghosts hid in the woods until dusk. It was best and braver to pretend they never existed at all, and Safrax breathed, "It was a roebuck, I think."

Enoc fingered his mouth, his eyes wide, "The ground is hard, the twigs brittle. A roebuck would have made some noise."

"What was it then?" murmured Safrax, "The Gepid axe-man, way down here?"

"Let's get out of here," bleated Enoc in a whisper, "You know who—and he wants what he no longer has."

"A body?"

"Yes. Either yours or mine."

Safrax nodded. The axe-man left bloody corpses, like his sister Lilia; but when people disappeared, it wasn't the axe-man who snatched them. It was someone else, and no one said his name aloud. *You can only think it. A demon of what he was.* Of all the terrors in the woods, he was inescapably real because he was once a real man, tangible flesh and blood that vanished.

In deep shadows, in places wild, nothing could protect them, not even the Great Bear or God himself! Yet if Safrax and Enoc could reach the field, they'd be safe... because the charcoal man never skulked—never grabbed you—out in the open. And they ran from the pines faster than a whirlwind.

Chapter 34: Well, Maybe I Will

An hour after dawn, Thulia walked up from water's-edge and sat upon her favored boulder. She came down to the lake almost every morning before going to the garden because it gave her solace, a friendly place the sun hit first upon its daily rise. Ripples lapping the lake's shore always murmured, as if telling secrets. The lake was her castle. It held a richness that only nature could provide. She stretched legs outward, crossing one foot over the other while fingers fidgeted in her lap.

Earlier when she arose at dawn, Thulia busied herself with morning ritual, pulling trousers from beneath the mattress, smooth and unwrinkled, slipping them on, wrapping herself with an old kaftan, and combing her hair. Again—even though it happened infrequently—she viewed a sober vision in the ancient mirror. It was far worse than Frit's gelding, for what she saw was an aftermath of a battle in this very field. She viewed the dead. Some were almost naked, Germanic warriors; and she knew exactly who they were. Gepids. The others wore armor, some of them appearing as cataphracts. They were Alans and Goths. The mirror's portent was the future, not the past, and many lay dead. The Gepids were going to attack Ascentia again, but exactly when she knew not.

She sat confused, unable to perceive the mirror as good or evil. Did it simply predict? She thought not, because it also gave visions of the past, not great events but small slices of former life. Could she trust it? That was her quandary, for she wished not to cry wolf, to alarm the Ascentians by predicting a horrible cataclysm that might or might not befall them.

Yet she could not dismiss the vision. It was too real and people were going to die, the same people who fashioned themselves after God. The only difference was all the flaws. She reviewed the mirror's curse; yet if it could also save lives, then it was a blessing. *Perhaps then, I am blessed.* The sun arced higher and Thulia knew it was time to meet Hel at the garden. She arose, took a deep breath and walked up through the field. As she strode along, Thulia felt better, her heart slightly lighter. *I shall think of something pleasant, like getting laid by Frit. That damned mirror never shows what I really want.*

*   *   *

The garden ran along a slope, sunlight now warming it, as it did most of the day. Peas were ready for picking, plump and green, despite a lack of rain. Within long rows, Thulia and Hel carried osier baskets, snipping fat pods, leaving thin ones for a few more days. They worked separate rows, yet their timing matched pace. "Why do you not remarry?" asked Hel, the question out of nowhere.

Thulia was taken aback, unable to find a quick answer. She couldn't tell the truth—she was barren and no virile man would have her. Their afflictions were identical, Hel's much worse from what she endured. To even speak the word seemed incomprehensible, so she said, "I need no man. I'm well off. My husband was rich," close to truth, at least a third of it.

Hel accepted the answer, "Why does Selenas not remarry?"

"I'm not exactly sure. Perhaps he wishes not to."

Hel remained silent for a spell, finally saying, "He touches me."

Thulia hardened, "Where? Is he taking liberties with you?"

Hel gave her little smile, "No. I mean in here," and she put hand to chest, "I think he is shy."

"Certainly he's no shyer than you," Thulia guffawed, "You don't say three words a day, except to me."

"I have an accent."

"What does an accent have to do with it?"

"When they hear it, they must think of Gunter and those he killed. So I do not talk very much."

Hel's statement reached Thulia's depths, speechless herself for a moment, yet she found a reply, "You cannot carry another person's guilt, Hel. It will only make you less a woman than you are."

They continued picking peas, Thulia gaining speed, at first wondering why Hel fell behind. She then believed Hel was lost in thought, the conversation's topic unusual. Remarrying? Neither she nor Hel would find a man willing to wed a barren woman, not up here in Ascentia.

Then if finally hit Thulia—Hel was interested in Selenas, a natural reaction to kindness, for he doted on her, making sure she had comforts. *Just like Heldrid!* Standing straight and placing hands to hips, Thulia looked over to the Gepid. Selenas reciprocated! Yet a man afraid to touch her. *His reason is fear of rejection.* To him, Hel suffered more pawing than a woman received in a hundred lifetimes, not wanting to be touched again. But he was wrong. In the first years after Hel arrived, he put a hand here or there upon her, but only as a friend. *Now it's different,* grinned Thulia, *He wants a good grope. A little bit of lust in that touch.* He had to know how Hel felt about him, and she—Thulia the matchmaker—would tell him. And she had a far more important subject to discuss.

She found the time and place. He was in the new church, perhaps not the best location to discuss lust, but the church would do. Selenas stood at the lectern slipping blue flowers between pages he would use on the Sabbath.

"I finally realized why you froze at Hel's baptism," she declared.

"Oh?" he mumbled while looking up from the Bible, "Why did I?"

"You can touch her as a friend but you're scared to death as a lover."

"Lover?" he retorted, "I sympathize with her, that's all."

"Really. I'll bet you'd like to sympathize her right into bed."

He blushed dark crimson, his jaw working. Thulia loved to see men squirm. *He can't even speak!* She laughed and informed him, "Hel thinks you're quite the man. She's sweet on you, Selenas, and if I were you I'd not let a hot one get away." Then Thulia backed a step.

He swallowed a couple of times, "Thanks for the intuition. You have a good heart, Thulia. When I first became presbyter I really couldn't understand you. Back then you were overly physical and I was too spiritual. Things have a way of smoothing out."

Thulia stepped to him and cupped the back of his neck, pulling him to kiss that balding forehead. After releasing him, Selenas admitted, "By the way, I still think you're crude."

"I am, and damned proud of it because everyone knows where I stand," and then she sobered, "I try to say it like I see it. And I can tell you this—the Gepids are up to something. I can sense it; and if I were you and Rustan, I

---

would figure out a method of first alert, some kind of warning signal and a little watchfulness every hour of the day."

He worked his mouth to find words, "Well I assumed we were safe. We have better weapons. Better armor."

"Under the bed? Is that where they keep armor and weapons? And where might the lances be?"

"Up overhead in the horse sheds," he stammered, then adding with a nod, "Yes. I see your point. We're not prepared even though we should be. Perhaps watch towers with smoke pots."

She cracked a smile, "Not a bad idea, for a presbyter." And then she turned heel and left him to small blue flowers and building towers. Off in the distance, down in the valleys of the Caucaland, the Amazon still rode through legend, flashing *The Iron Breaker* or lancing evils of the world. But the real Thulia was different. She pulled weeds, patched torn lives, and taught leaders how to lead.

*   *   *

As children of roughly the same age do, Waldrid and Sesca played together, their games simple ones of childhood: hide and seek, that sort of thing. Sometimes they waded knee-deep in the brook, thinking they might spear a fish with a sharpened stick. The dace were always too small (or the spear too big), and the trout darted upstream far too fast. On this particular summer day, Waldrid and Sesca found a wicker fish trap at the tail of a pool. They knew who it belonged to—the old catchermon, the same man who caught gray partridge and hares with other kinds of traps.

What was in the trap?—a big trout that swam up from the lake? "The catchermon will never know if we peek inside," claimed Waldrid.

We shouldn't touch it, thought Sesca while shrugging her shoulders, not saying a thing because she never did.

Then Waldrid added, "If I pull up the trap, you'll not tell one person, anyway, because you're dumb."

Her eyes narrowed to slits, for he was mean to say such a thing. She was smarter than he was, because boys were dumber than girls, actually quite stupid. In fact, they were stupider than stupid, and Waldrid was the stupidest boy she had ever seen!

Waldrid grabbed the line, pulling the trap onto the bank. It was shaped like a long cone, willow slats woven around cherry hoops; and Sesca could see a lonely minnow inside. He heaved the trap back in the stream and snotted, "It had a giant trout in it! You didn't see it, but I did... because girls can't see fish like boys can."

She glared at him again, her eyes now closed to tiny slits. The trap splashed water, getting her face wet, and she wanted to kick Waldrid hard, but he skipped down the path to leave her standing there. He was the meanest, dumbest boy she had ever met, except for Causas the bowyer's son, who once shot her in the butt with an arrow, a toy arrow but it hurt. Sesca peered into the brook, noticing the trap wasn't exactly where the catchermon had placed it. And Waldrid took off, leaving both fish spears for her to carry. She grabbed them and ran after him, finally catching up. He tried to grab his spear from her, but she pulled it away, shaking her head "no."

"Give it back!" he demanded.

Sesca shook her head again because they were her spears now.

"I want my fish spear. It belongs to me, not to some dumb girl who never speaks!" he shouted, "You're no fun to go spearing with. You never talk."

I can talk if I want to, she fancied, still keeping the shaft from him.

"The reason you don't talk is... because," he claimed.

Because what? She demanded, sticking out her tongue.

"Because you can't talk," he declared, his mouth forming a pout.

I can too! she thought back, her eyes and nose sqrinching.

"If you really could talk, you would," he proclaimed, forcing corners of his mouth even further down.

Well, maybe I will! Her expression taunted.

"I'll be old and dead before YOU talk. Then you'll be sorry!" he blurted.

"No I won't!" she yelled back, "And here's your stupid spear."

They walked down the path as usual, doing children things, Waldrid talking and Sesca talking back. He was such a dumb snot, and she thought it hardly possible that he would ever become old and dead. Only old dead people were that way. But just in case, she would talk to him now. Then when he was old and dead he would know she actually could.

*   *   *

Vindobona lay upon the southern side of the Danube, the river coursing slow through an open plain large enough to be a steppe. Through its ideal location, the fortress was a harborage for more than the Classis Pannonia, a touch of civilization in the wild west and boasting a large settlement and marketplace beyond stone walls. Vindobona was growing, and someday it would be a city, but not a city for Frit. He had other plans.

He passed through the north gate and headed down the Via Principalis to finally enter the courtyard at the Fortress Hall. As he slid from his saddle, a riparian ran toward him, the man knowing who he was, "Captain Fritigern. Welcome back from the front," then extending a helping hand, "Let me stall your horse. The commander is expecting you."

"Oh? What have I done this time?"

"Nothing, sir," chortled the soldier, "He should be back in a few moments. You can grab a bite in the officer's mess or wait in his office."

"My ass burns, so I'll opt for the mess." Frit turned upon a heel and met the eyes of Junius Soranus as the man paced briskly toward him.

"Frit, my good man. How goes the battle?" piqued the fortress commander as he extended an arm for a wrist clasp.

"Worry not, sir. The Alemanni will be bold enough next spring. It's a tradition. They remember not a year of peace in two hundred."

Soranus flicked a grin, "Not that battle. The one in your head. Between empathy and duty."

"Duty lost. I'm out of here after I receive riding papers."

"Now, now! Let's not be hasty." Soranus turned abruptly, motioning to follow as he strode into his office. Frit tagged behind as the man dropped to his heaped desk, "Pull up the King's Chair and relieve those restless feet of yours. I've serious business to discuss."

Frit reached for the chair, its feet squealing upon shale, so he picked it up and dropped it before the man's desk yet remained standing. "Sit," demanded Soranus, and Frit sat. The commander pawed through a pile of paperwork, tossing this or that across a mound of disorder, and finally exclaimed, "Ah, here it is. Do you know what I have?"

"I assume it's my Foederati discharge, sir," claimed Frit as he slid to the chair, perching stiffly.

"Part of it," Soranus noted, tapping the rolled document to an open palm. He leaned forward, "I reviewed the

Acta Militaria, gleaning three years of your volunteer service. Centenarius in one year, then captain by the second, full ala commander by your third. What should I think?"

"Well, sir, any decent officer advances," claimed Frit.

Soranus raised a brow, "Bullshit. Not at that rate. And that's despite a few run-ins with Theodosius in the beginning. The man posted a negative report on you... and then two weeks later, he tried to pull it from the record. What was that all about?"

"A difference of moral opinion. Worked it out, man to man."

Soranus laughed, tapping the scroll again, "And you became known as the Fisher, eh? Well, I saw your point—and you know well enough I'm a Christian—but Theo's report could not be erased; the Acta is a permanent record with no measure for changes after the fact. That said, I can note subsequent reports were more than favorable." He leaned back in his chair and flipped the document to Frit, "Not your standard riding papers. Go ahead. Open them. They're signed by the Dux per Pannonia Prima and the Magister Militum of the Diocese."

Frit unrolled the document, reading the recommendation slowly as his face flushed.

Soranus grinned a big one, "Advancement to full commander is seldom given to three year veterans, especially volunteers. Officially you are, or were, a mercenary. As a tribune, you would have a new assignment, most likely down in Gaul—the Bagaduae are up to old tricks, robbing the rich and giving to themselves. This is a wondrous opportunity, both for you and this army. We need men of ability and sound judgment with the patience and pluck of fishermen, a rare combination in these modern times.

The commander stood from his desk, tapping it, "What am I to think when an officer comes down from the front wounded in the shoulder yet braids a line to catch a huchen? You did it! What was it?—forty pounds on fifteen hairs, certainly enough to elevate you to the status of Fisher King. I ate my words and the fish was sweet to the bone. Think about it. At the rate you're going, in two years you would be a full legate. The Emperor will bestow Flavian citizenship, and you can marry any woman in the empire. We find wives from the equite and senatorial classes for high commanders."

A new world at my feet, the opportunity of a lifetime. Frit slumped forward, letting the recommendation curl back to original shape. This was concrete—no gambling for a woman who might or might not recall a wistful dream. *How can a sane man refuse it?*

Chapter 35: A War of the Gods

Ascentia's new church had been finished for almost two years, yet certain embellishments required a modicum of time. Upon this afternoon, Rustan and Stefan installed a larger cross behind the altar, a cross not hewn from pine but straight-grained oak polished with liberal coats of flax-seed oil. With the cross in place, they scooped up shavings and moved their tools out to the entrance. Modifying the door-jam they would hang a fancy oiled door, much like those found at the Stone Chapel in East Drobeta or the Cathedral of Marcianopolis, neither of which had actually been seen by Rustan yet he was positive this new door would swing as a testament to the glory of Xristos and the Durostorum artisan who made it.

Rustan glanced around, looking for their "assistants," Safrax and Enoc. Not seeing them, he assumed they had run off someplace, probably bored and searching for the more exciting. The boys played together since early childhood, but as of late they quarreled more often. *Probably due to the awkward transition from boyhood to manhood.* He was proud of Safrax, the boy growing to an honest and morally astute young man; and somehow when the time was correct, he would find a position for his son within the Arian Church. Rustan had grown up as a warrior upon the steppe. *You came from the earth and fell back to it, and that encompassed a man's life.* He saw a better world in the Church and wanted Safrax to have it.

They removed the old door, and Stefan growled, "Hinge-cut be rait too shallow, ains me be the uns'll daepen it," and he squatted with a grunt, pawed through his tools and looked up, "Have ye seen me whittle-knife, ay?"

* * *

Thulia walked the garden rows, the soil loose underfoot. Squashes were still finger-sized due to lack of rain, the summer dryer than usual, and vegetables ripened slowly. Hearing a scuffle, she snapped an eye to the road to find Safrax and Enoc in a bout of fisticuffs. They swiped mean blows—for boys!—as Safrax hammered Enoc to the ground.

She ran toward them, Enoc regaining his feet and bawling, "He broke my nose!" Then he turned heel and ran.

Reaching Safrax, she put hands to hips and demanded, "What was that all about, young buck?"

Rubbing the knuckles of his right hand, the boy replied, "Nothing."

"I want more than that," she insisted, "Why were you fighting?"

He looked down, scuffing a foot in road dust, "Selenas was off in the woods. Father and Stefan were working in the church. And Enoc and I watched them for awhile, and then we left."

She glared at him, noticing his cut lip, "That's hardly an explanation. I want to know why you broke Enoc's nose."

"I'm not a tattle-tale."

"Oh? Then you would let someone do wrong and turn an eye from it?"

"I did not turn an eye. I saw the transgression and tried to correct it... by having the guilty right his wrong."

Thulia broke to a smile, "You have a bloody lip. I shall ask no more. And I think you have lost a friend."

Safrax looked down to the road and took a long stride, reaching to retrieve an object. She watched him wipe it on his tunic to remove grit. It was Stefan's whittle-knife. Trying to make him feel better, she added, "Go down to the brook and wash your lip with cold water. Then you can return the knife. You threw a good punch, a regular warrior."

He straightened, reaching full height—almost as tall as she was!—"Not a warrior. A heavy horseman, if I could find someone not fearing to teach me. My father would not approve."

"A cataphract, eh? And Rustan wants you to be something else, is that it?"

He looked straight to her eye, like someone beyond his thirteenth year, "I have not heard of a scripture condemning soldiers. God and the saints aid those who fight the right cause. Saint Michael—the oldest saint, the highest saint—was a soldier."

"Michael?" she gasped, recognizing the name of the man of light.

"Yes, the Archangel Michael. You know—Michael of the Sword."

*　*　*

No, thought Selenas, *Too limited a vantage point. The next hill rises higher.* He walked through heavy cover as fallen trees barred his way, some large as he skirted around them until reaching the next hill's crest. *Much better.* Selenas moved to his right, then left; and taking his axe he chopped a mark to four trees.

In that spot he would have an observation tower overlook the path vending north. Below the village, Rustan would build another one near the road heading south. Ascentians would man them, able to see anyone's approach, Gepids or otherwise. Never again would they be taken by surprise. He wondered why he hadn't thought of it himself. *I'm not much of a strategist*, he mused in fading daylight.

Although peace now reigned, wars began through strange circumstances... like Gunter's obsession with a bloodline.

Somehow the afternoon fell to dusk with Selenas still out in the woods. Too late to visit Hel. He was surprised at Thulia's announcement. After what Hel went through, he assumed she might be emotionally damaged for life, yet one would never know it when viewing her beguiling smile.

Working his way back toward Ascentia, the forest loomed darker, a time of day when fantasy's trolls left caves in search of human flesh. The community's children had adopted a newer wraith, the axe-man, Gunter's ghost. Yet children and common folk believed in a far worse spectre—the charcoal man—a ghost lurking in the darkest glades, a tortured spirit of what once was, still looking for his body... and his *thing*. Selenas heard the tale from several adults, including the old catchermon and Gunter. *Thumped his thing in the wrong hole,* the connotation implicit. Was the charcoal man killed for a sexual crime, just like Gunter's male victims? And he vanished *in a puff.* How bizarre, the idea of it, as if something unknown had taken revenge, righting some terrible wrong.

The charcoal man was shapeless, totally nebulous, of all phantasms the most frightening, an unseen spirit destined to wander the forest in a desperate search. Common folk who remembered the incident claimed he was *killed by a little witch.* What was she? How did she do it? The charcoal man's death—how it really happened—mattered little now. Only his legacy pertained. In low mountain valleys, he wandered in morning's fog; and at dusk he crept from tree to tree, always well hidden, but sometimes you could hear him, the snap of a branch not made by a deer or wolf.

Selenas heard it just then! The snap of a twig, then total silence. He waited for the sound again, trying to ascertain its direction. How could a person fight off something so evil and formless? Yet he knew better. *The charcoal man is just a tale... extending from some real and strange event. Nothing more.* Fiction or not, the thought made woodlands spooky, and he found himself walking a quick pace.

Finally he stepped from the tree line to the field, patches of blue flowers here and there. The glow of a sinking sun upon him, Selenas felt safe again, for God lived in the light. God was the light! He surveyed the late summer bloom, knowing exactly what he'd done, a victim of procrastination. A stronger man would have picked the flowers at his feet earlier in the afternoon and brought them to the Gepid widow. He was putting it off, knowing exactly why. Fear of rejection, fear of a subject no one discussed. Fertility. Or the lack of it. That was it in nut-shell. He wished a rich fruitful marriage, not in the sense of procreation but pleasure in the act, wanting to caress her so bad he could taste her, thinking how healthy she looked. The vision of Hel when he first saw her faded, a new woman emerging.

But what of Hel? What did that many men do to her mind? His own view of it, a subjugation lasting for years, could not be untainted. What would their true relationship be?

* * *

The sun tucked itself in another part of the sphere, birds went to limbs of hosts, and the fields around Ascentia fell to a warm and placid eve. With some reluctance children went to their beds, actually their parent's beds as well. In Thulia's cabin Hel slept alone, perhaps still enjoying the luxury of it.

Thulia lay awake, scratching mental notes of everything relative to the village. She had become a mother hen, tidying everyone's life, never dreaming she would be in such a capacity a few years ago. She believed she had almost come to terms with herself, only a few loose ends remaining, as she closed eyes to reflect advice from her elder mentor.

Merjands' house was a special place, tiny and built from wattle. When visiting, she always wondered at the knowledge hidden within its circular walls. Sitting in its smallness she had learned to read Latin and refused to study Greek. The house held cupboards of earthen jars with cork stoppers, manuscripts of rolled papyrus, a copy of Plato and another of Zoroaster the seer of Vishtapa. More than not, Merjands sat at his table grinding poultice in a mortar, and it usually stank. She would perch opposite him, elbows to the table, chin propped upon hands. In their discussions, she was truthful and he always mulled before answering.

"You have no mirror, do you Thulia," he stated.

She shook her head.

"Well, someday you'll have a mirror, perhaps a fine one; but for now a pool of water will do," he avowed, wincing at the potion's stench, "Take a good look at yourself. You'll find a young woman of worth. You have more than a big bosom; you're intelligent, thoughtful, and graceful in carriage."

Then she brought up the subject of infertility.

"Do you think you're lesser for it in the Godhead's eye? What about men? Can you believe every male upon this globe was placed here to sire children?"

She nodded yes.

"Thulia!" Merjands gasped, "There are men who cannot sire progeny, not old men like me but young seemingly-virile bucks. Fertility and virility are like the boogie man, haunting you until you accept yourself for what you are." He sniffed the potion, rolling his eyes, "Mandrake. A little something for you to try."

"What am I?" she wanted to know.

"You're an Amazon in search of happiness, that's all," he chuckled, *"Perhaps unique for being an Amazon in these modern times, but certes not alone in your affliction."*

Then she mentioned her compulsion, giving numbers, a little embarrassed.

"Ah, a legion of lovers," nodded Merjands, placing the bowl and pestle to the table, *"Even you must know it's your outward—your physical—expression of the search."*

She prepared to leave, feeling better about herself, and he fingered his white cinnabar, adding as he always did, "Keep looking for your man, don't give up! He's out there. The world is a big place."

In her own corner of the night, the world of Ascentia seemed far too small. Potential men were a scarce commodity like a tangy Gallic ham. She looked across the cabin toward Hel's bed, wondering if the young Gepid remained awake. *If she's really sleeping she's a lucky woman.* Did Hel have nightmares too? Often, late at night, she could hear the woman moaning. Finally turning upon her side, Thulia found Sesca's lips, her finger running along the child's mouth. *Thank you, Lord, for letting her speak.* She knew Waldrid had much to do with it, the two of them arriving home laughing together. What a fine day it was!

She rolled to her back. Again she reviewed mother hen problems, wondering if Hel would shrink from a lover's touch, but for her? *The real touch is somewhere on the other side of the world.* She yearned for him every night, perhaps because it was night. The wraith would come and Frit pushed it away. He was the dream fighting the nightmare; and if he ever returned, she would be in a quandary. At night she wanted to ride him to her grave, yet during the day she disclaimed him, gone from her mind to wherever he rode off to. Like the nightmare, she knew the dream was fantasy. Days were the real world—a garden to tend, Frit's unrealistic brother to shepherd, along with all the other lost people in the wilderness—little time to think of Thulia the woman.

Her mind kept running and running, like a wolf frightened by hounds. In a quick move, she swung her feet to the floor, reaching for a smock on the stool.

* * *

Stars glittered as a million eyes, winking to her above the lake's shore; and water lapped far down the fingered ledges from lack of rain. Thulia sat with her back to the field upon a boulder still warm from the day's sun. When confronted by sleeplessness or some daytime bane, she could gain solace from calming waters. If not at the gardens, she could be found sitting upon the boulder at lake-edge; and oft enough, some Ascentians joked about her living there or owning it, as if it were her rock alone.

She mulled through half a moon's arc, pondering Safrax's statement. For a boy, he carried thorough knowledge of scriptures—drilled into him by his father and Selenas—and he answered a question haunting her for over three years. Who was the man of light? Like Michael's appearance, each important event of her life came for a purpose and extended back to childhood, long before she became a Christian. She needed to talk to someone no less wise than Merjands, a bishop or patriarch, but circumstance could only give her Selenas, the ethereal and faltering priest.

* * *

The morning arrived warm and cloudy. Perhaps it might rain, and the garden certainly needed it, for the drought affected crops from Scythia to Illyricum. Ascentians would not want for sustenance, but what of others?—the Eastern Alans, the Greutungi, Gepids, Tyrfingi, and Taifali.

While Hel picked thin beans, Thulia dragged Selenas into her cabin, announcing tongue-in-cheek, "I'm sorry for interrupting your busy schedule, but I need counsel, actually needing it for some time." Hastily she fell to knees, retrieving the wool and muslin wraps from beneath her bed, jumping to her feet, "Please sit on my bed. You should be sitting for this."

Puzzled, Selenas did as asked, for he was good at following women's orders. She plopped to her stool in front of him, placed the items in her lap, and took an extra deep breath, "Do not think of me as a cracked jug or rowing with one oar, as they say, but I must tell someone about happenstance. I wouldn't be surprised if these things happened to a good Christian," and she almost giggled, "But evidently good Christians were too far away so they fell to me." He nodded in agreement—a little faster than she wished—and continued to sit.

Thulia unwrapped the wool, removed the sword, and handed it to him, "Go ahead. Pull it from the scabbard." He did as asked, examining it. And she continued, "It's been under my bed for three years. It had no scabbard, so I use an old one that was Heldrid's, a little short… for some things are found a little short, yes?" He didn't agree so quickly, and she continued, "The sword has no rust, not even a finger-print on the blade. True, the Wusun made folded-steel as good as the Qin, but all steel rusts. Look at the grip. Originally it was wrapped with twine but most of it burned, so I removed what was left because the great age was covered up."

"This is the weapon you slew Gunter with, correct?" Selenas returned, "The sword known as *Tyrfing*."

"Yes and no," she explained, "The shaft is newer—re-forged by God. That is what I truly believe. Witnesses were there, but they only saw an outward manifestation. I think the word is correct, is it not?"

Selenas pinned his eyes to hers, nodded to study her for a moment, "What did you see?"

"The same thing everyone else saw, a thunder storm, but it was different because in my mind I asked God to vanquish Tyr and the tribal deities. That thunderstorm was a great battle—a war of the gods—fighting it out before us. And then the lightening bolt. Who is the vanquisher, God's trusted soldier? I just found out from Safrax."

The presbyter mulled for a moment, "The Archangel Michael."

"Yes," claimed Thulia, now excited, "It was Saint Michael who defeated Tyr, and the sword changed into this one. Merjands noticed it first, the original grip with its aged patina and the unblemished blade, as if two worlds collided and then fused. This sword belonged to someone very special; I don't know her name yet, but she was like me. A woman warrior who lived a long time ago. She blessed me. And when I spoke with Michael upon the north road, he said, *'Now you have the sword,'* like he was involved all along. He wrenched it from Tyr and helped Merjands give it to me… to protect the people."

His eyes grew to the size of bucklers, his jaw to chest, yet he composed himself, "YOU spoke with the Archangel Michael?"

"Of course," she nodded, "He told me to invoke his name, like before a battle or duel, I guess, but I was too awed and could not remember such a foreign nomen. I just knew him as the man of light. You should see him! He has a moustache that hangs to his chest. He glows!"

"Ah, the glowing man of light," agreed Selenas, rising carefully to hand the sword back to her.

"Wait!" she jumped, pushing him back down, "There is more."

He looked to right and left, eying the doorway, obviously wishing he was elsewhere.

Thulia dropped to the stool again, "I know this is hard to believe, especially for a priest, but these things are truth. This sword is waiting, I think. Waiting to do more for the people. Now go ahead, put it on the bed."

He placed it at his side while she unwrapped the muslin, "This was in Heldrid's arka. He found success and citizenship through it." She leaned to Selenas, handing it to him, "Be careful, very delicate. Sometimes it bleeds. But touch it and hold it for a moment, and feel the life that remains there."

Again he did as ordered, and his expression changed—his eyes starting to water—and Thulia could tell he knew exactly what it was.

"Yes," she informed him in a whisper, "I spoke with a man who accompanied Heldrid twenty five years ago—to the Holy Sepulcher—a member of the crew hired to guard and transport it. They traveled with Saint Helena and brought the cross to Emperor Constantine. This is not my imagination, either. This is very real, a piece of the cross that Xristos died upon. And when you touch it you can feel his soul. I wanted to give it to you at the right moment, and I think this is it."

She paused, seeing the emotion upon his face, waiting for his eyes to meet hers again, "I was the worst of the worst, and I'm still a hard-nosed bitch. I sin in big doses, dream of sinning, and will sin again... especially if the right opportunity comes along. And so I must ask—why did these things come to *me*?"

Chapter 36: Squinting to the Sun

A month after leaving Vindobona, Frit led a train of vehicles northwest, heading for Ulmenia from Threisbaurg. He shook his head with a broad grin, *Sorry, Soranus. Not a sane man at all.*

In the past few weeks, Vindobona faded to his rear as he led twenty veterans through Pannonia, most still calling him "the Fisher King," a unique epithet in a world of hunters. At the fortress of Intercisa he found a Roman plumber, a handy artisan he thought. Below Intercisa they crossed the river on a twenty-oared dromon and entered the Great Western Steppe. From there he traveled east, traversing Iron Gate Pass and heading straight across Walachia for Gothia and the Twin Rivers.

At Threisbaurg, Frit acquired the best artisans obtainable, men suitable for a unique project: stone masons, mud daubers, and carpenters. Now he was headed for Ascentia; and with him traveled a thousand clients, the wagons bouncing heavily along the trade road, all loaded to capacity.

Up ahead one of his veterans rode hastily back toward him, reining his mount to a stop, all out of breath, "The torchers are coming! Less than two miles away."

"What?" spat Frit, "We have no quarrel with them, or they with us."

"We're still in their jurisdiction, sir, and they ride fast."

"Go along the train and have the men grab weapons and bucklers, but don't pant so much. We have a perfect right to exit Gothia."

"Yes, sir," the horseman breathed, riding down the wagon train.

Frit jumped to the ground, leaning across the wagon bed and rummaging for chainmail. *Son of bitch! We've got quite the defense—a few vets, and then freemen with clubs and wooden shields. At least they have guts.* In Germania he never wore cataphract armor, yet his chainmail seemed a good start, better than iron scale, tight links crimped by a special tool. Someday all heavy horsemen would wear it. Frit pushed items aside, opening the chest to find the mask of death. It rightfully belonged to the Horse Dancer. He tossed it back, looking for his ridged helm with its red horsehair crest and hinged cheek-pieces. *A little Romanish looking, but it'll do.*

"Bring up my war horse, not the new one!" he yelled to a couple of men running his way, both of them with him back in Germania.

"Fisher," a man quizzed, "What do you think you're doing?"

"He wants a fight, does he?" spat Frit, "Then let him taste dirt."

"Who?" the vet returned.

"The Squinter, the beady eyes of his father's loins."

They looked to the road ahead, torchers closing at full gallop. Frit turned to his clients, each one eying him nervously. They were farmers for the most part, the rest artisans. He flashed teeth, "What's the problem? Not ready to greet the earth? Stand tough, hold your place, and stare them in the eye without blinking. I need that horse."

"It's coming," claimed the nearest client.

The brown gelding arrived as he ducked his head, working the chainmail over shoulders, arms, and torso; and then he leaned to strap iron greaves and pulled himself into the saddle, "Line up five men deep to my rear. I need a weapon."

The column of torchers stopped at a hundred paces, their own leader moving ahead to shout, "Turn back now or I'll use force."

Frit paced his mount until both men faced each other in mid-road. He studied the close-spaced eyes, the sober expression glaring at him. For as long as he could remember Frit tried to understand the man, especially in their youth. Attempting to befriend the Squinter, he invited him to a special Greek dinner. He was serving olives and grapes. Grapes!—and the frigging jerk refused to come. Finally he asked, "Do we look like Christians? Are we waving a cross?"

"You're exiting Gothia with tribal treasures," huffed Athanaric, "I heard about it yesterday while returning from Ulmenia."

"What in hell are you talking about?" declared Frit.

"You have wagonloads of furnishings, old pieces of nobility, freemen who belong to the kunja. You take the best blacksmith, the only stone-mason, take them... just like a common thief."

Frit fingered his chin and stared at the Squinter, "You always were a shithead. They're my freemen and families, and I can hire whom I wish, go where I please, and you can't stop me."

"Shithead?" cried Athanaric, all in a thither, "I certainly *can* stop you. Right here and now."

Frit's smile vanished, "Really." He twisted in the saddle to yell back toward clients, "Somebody bring a contus."

"Wait!" shouted the Squinter, eyes large for his habit, "I have no lance. Didn't bring one on campaign."

Frit raised an eyebrow, turning back to his wagons, "Delay that. Make it a spatha. A sharp one might be best, and grab my officer's helm." He swung to his opponent again, "*Hairus duce*—sword to sword on horseback. The winner has clear passage. Fair enough?"

The Squinter squinted. They reined mounts around, Frit returning to the wagons for his sword and helm, both carried through the Germanic wars, the sword longer than most, its blade honed to razor edge.

* * *

Athanaric waited, drawing sword from scabbard, the same trusty weapon used to slay evil Christians. He smiled in satisfaction while tying his spangenhelm's chin strap. At last he had a chance to humble one of the brothers; and the pleasure of it crept high upon his neck, almost turning him giddy. *He has been with the Romans... Those wanton degenerates with their short little swords and fancy language, with their stupid sandals and silly togas, tripping over themselves and puking on slaves.* Oh, yes. He knew about Romans.

With Frit riding back toward him, the Squinter bethought a concrete fact, *He who strikes first wins*, and he pushed ahead!—slashing hard with his blade, attempting to surprise his foe, yet his move struck cold steel. *What? Frit blocked the swing!* Before he could turn his mount, the son of Thiudebalth was upon him; yet he met the man's swing, taking the blow at mid-blade.

His sword remained high as Frit slashed again, ripping the blade across Athanaric's left arm—*right through my leather tunic!*—then swinging around to slice the back of his sword hand. Athanaric recoiled as Frit struck again, slamming his helm and snapping a side-hinge.

Losing his balance, the Squinter fell from his mount, hitting the road hard as a sound in his ear roared like a river. He couldn't understand it! *No man is this fast.* Getting to a knee, he surveyed his arm and hand, both wounded. *May the gods help me! I'm bleeding to death!* He looked up to see Frit standing before him. *When did the man dismount?* He couldn't recall it. He fumbled for his weapon, but Frit pushed his blade into his tunic—*again?*—driving him to the ground a second time.

Where did my sword go? He was befuddled in slight confusion—no, not confusion, because he, Athanaric the son of Aoric, could never actually fall to bewilderment, certainly not a future magistrate. *I have simply lost a small amount of composure. It happens to anyone when totally surprised. No! Not totally surprised, more like mildly taken aback, in fact just marginally nonplused for the shortest of instants.* And so only appearing confused, he peered around to find his sword directly under Frit's foot. It would be difficult to pick it up, in fact impossible, so he lay there squinting to the sun, his mouth open.

"I don't think you stopped me," claimed Frit, lifting a boot from Athanaric's weapon.

He sat upright to clutch wounds with both hands, trying to stop the bleeding, his head still ringing, "Where did you learn to fight like that?"

"Against big Germans with heavy axes." Then Frit yelled back to the women, "Bring some bandages and bind him up... and we'll be on our way.

"You're a thief," Athanaric spat.

"I have what's mine," Frit resolved.

"What about Heldrid's?"

"Not Heldrid's. Thulia's," Frit corrected him.

Athanaric had the man dead to rights, "Thulia's, then... but not yours. So you're no better than a common thief," and then he squealed, "A thief, I say!" He rolled to his side and then to knees, finally gaining his feet, "First she steals the Sword of Tyr, and now you leave with ill-begotten booty. You're just like *them*, to meet a bad end... up there with all the rest... eaten by trolls or your head on a post. I know what happened to Selenas and his wife. Good riddance to you and every one of your kind."

There! He said it—the undeniable truth. Athanaric felt better for it. He was not fast like Frit, nor as experienced in militaria, but he had ceaseless determination for the long road. He knew he wouldn't bleed to death, possibly own a few scars to remember this day. Far from losing, he had won. He called a thief what he was.

* * *

Frit waited while two client wives bound the Squinter up. What did the man mean about Selenas and his wife? As for Thulia? She would never steal anything, a totally honest woman. *In fact, a little too honest.* He had broken no tribal laws and everything taken was his father's and his, plus furnishings Old Hempstalk gave him to bring up to Thulia.

He knew Aoric resented him deeply for it, but he was far from the first noble to leave the Twin Rivers. The magistrate's limited foresight and poor decisions had weakened the kunja, splitting the alliance. With sparse news from clients, Frit had no idea what happened in Threisbaurg during the past three years. But he knew those years were not good ones.

Chapter 37: The Wayward Brother

He never was a fisherman, the pastime Fritigern's, yet Selenas tried his hand at it. He cut the pole in mid spring, and it hadn't fully cured. No life to it. Selenas borrowed a hook from Rustan, small enough for trout but they weren't biting. Fishing was just an excuse, really. A form of getting away to think about Hel. After Thulia spoke to him in the church, the summer passed as he found this project and that, each keeping him busy, his way of avoidance. Now autumn's leaves would soon turn to marvelous color and birds were winging their way to Asia Minor or Africa.

He had to confront his real problem—a marriage had to be more than togetherness, more than procreation, especially when the act itself was hollow. Hel was a beautiful and desirable woman. What matter if she couldn't bear a child if no offspring were needed? He had Waldrid, a gift from Lilia. Selenas sat at the brook, angling not for fish but an answer. If he betook Hel for wife, she would expect love in its most human form, that unique intimacy when two bodies became one. At least he hoped she did. That's what he wanted, even though it didn't quite fit the letter of the Scriptures. The basic precept of wedlock was procreation, begetting all those Abrahams and Josephs. What of a young yet barren widow?— destined to not remarry, to live alone the rest of her days? An ugly notion, unfair to women and love.

He would be finer a Christian if following the words of Paul or John, but perhaps they had poor relationships with their wives. Yet scriptures could be interpreted by individual presbyters, not loosely but with a certain leeway, and he almost laughed, his outlook rationalizing potential sin yet hardly believing he and Hel would burn in Hell for it.

His mind was settled. Jumping to his feet, Selenas swung the line from the stream, cut the hook and stuffed it in his belt purse, then leaned the pole against an alder to abandon it. *If Hel wants me, she must expect all of me.*

Beyond the tree line he entered the field of blue flowers, now faded with petals tinged brown. *A hard search it'll be to find a glass-full.* Stooping at first, then falling to knees, Selenas began his chore, rejecting most, crawling through the field until he had twenty of the best. *Good enough. Time is fleeting.*

Selenas ran for his cabin to rummage for a small purple glass. He found it! The flowers just fit, water spilling as he rushed outside and along the row of humble abodes lining the road. *I'm sprinting like a swain, incredibly nervous!* He reached Thulia's cabin in fifty long strides, little water left in the glass but the flowers still there; and by the time his knuckles rapped on the door, he was panting like a dying hound. *I'm making a fool of myself. Perhaps I should make my escape before someone answers.*

Too late! The door opened and Thulia stood there, at first surprised, then laughing, "There's someone to see you, Hel."

He backed off, still having a slight chance to run. Too late again! There she was. Hel stood for a moment, arms wrapped to her torso, and then she swung an arm to the log bench in front of the cabin, "Would you like to sit? You are out of breath."

All he could do was nod. They sat, and she adjusted her position to almost touch him, placing hands upon her skirt. Selenas cupped the glass before him, resting it on his knees.

"It's a pleasant day," he noted, trying to think of something to say.

"Yes," she returned, her lips curling slightly, "People can always talk about the weather because it forever changes… although it has been a dry summer."

"I thought I'd stop by and see how you were."

"Do you always run to visit people?" she asked curiously.

How did she know? Selenas couldn't continue beating around the bush, and he blurted, "I got my first wife pregnant before we were actually wed."

Hel seemed to have difficulty understanding his line of thought and asked, "What of your second wife?"

"Did I say *first wife*?"

"Yes. So you had a second wife?"

Selenas found his tongue tied in knots as thoughts came out incorrectly, "I mean my first wife was pregnant and you are not."

"I know," Hel admitted, "I'm infertile."

"That is true," he agreed, "But it doesn't mean I love you any less than I did her." Then he passed the blue flowers, "These are for you."

"Thank you," Hel smiled, "Am I your second wife?"

"Yes," he replied, puzzled at his and her choice of words.

Hel sat quietly holding the flowers in her lap, studying them, finally announcing, "You are a thoughtful husband… to bring his second wife flowers."

* * *

After Selenas proposed to Hel (if that's what it was), the young woman slept fitfully or not at all. In the cabin's darkness, Thulia could hear her tossing and turning into the night. She remained awake for several hours herself, musing upon the turn of events. Everybody in Ascentia had someone to share moments with, yet she didn't, except with Hel and a mother-daughter relationship. Sesca talked a joyous wonder. Improved circumstances reached everyone except the Amazon. She pinched money, never spending it for anything beyond necessities. It had to last for food, eventually for Sesca's dowry. Thulia bought nothing new, her clothing old and worn.

She had no idea where her personal life was going, not a man interested in her, perhaps intimidated by a bold carriage and independent spirit. In better days, men rode for miles for a short throw. Back then she wasn't overly tanned; no raven-foot wrinkles creeping from her eyes. Now she was beyond prime—the Matron Thulia at the age of twenty three. Despite what Merjands claimed, she believed her features were not overly attractive. She was too swarthy, her appearance far below the flawless beauty of Hel. Pretty women—even infertile ones—had a chance to find a new husband, a new life. Turning to face Hel, she listened carefully. The Gepid was finally sleeping.

* * *

The thin man peered through mid-morning sunlight at the lower observation tower, tapping the rotund man's shoulder, "Look, Rodric! A whole army!"

Turning from his bread and cheese ball, Rodric gazed across tree tops as his eyes followed the lower road's meandering; and sure enough, he saw mounted horses. "We're being attacked," he snecked, a unique sound issuing from men shaped like bears, then adding, "Get down the ladder and run to warn the people."

"Me?" exclaimed the thin man, trying to sound quiet, "I fear height! I can get up here but I fear to climb back down."

"Well, I can't do it!" retorted the Bear in the same hushed voice, not wanting the attackers to hear, "I'm fat and cannot run. It takes forever for me to climb up and down this damned thing."

"For heaven's sake, Rodric, they're almost here!" the thin man's voice raised to a shriek.

Studying the attackers again, the Bear saw carts and wagons following mounted leaders. "Forget it," he snecked in relief, "They're refugees. Carts, women and children. Wonder what they have for food?" Then he went back to eating his bread, having finished the cheese in one quick sneck.

"Good," the thin man mumbled, "Neither of us have to climb down this rickety affair until relieved."

People were still coming to Ascentia although most Christians had fled to Moesia. Both men waited. The column of vehicles slammed up the road, a few men pushing a heavy wagon over the washout just below the tower. Whenever a thunder storm passed, rain made the rut deeper. Once above the bad spot, the group continued up the narrow via until the lead wagon rumbled below the tower. The rotund man shaded eyes with cheesy fingers and yelled down, "Is that you, Fritigern?"

"Rodric! How do you fare?" the Balth shouted back from the wagon.

"Put a little weight on," the Bear admitted, "What brings you and yours up here?"

"I'm not going to live in a community run by that asshole," Frit yelled back.

"Who?" shouted Rodric.

"Athanaric!"

*   *   *

The morning dew evaporated to a warm sun, and Waldrid was out playing with Sesca. With the children occupied, Thulia and Hel worked the garden, pulling weeds, choosing a few carrots and onions while checking progress of stunted leeks. That seemed to be Thulia's forenoon plan, not much else to do. As they worked together, Hel made her announcement, "I think Selenas eats not well at all. For dinner, he must have better food. I shall move over there this afternoon, for I am his second wife."

With the sun high, they returned to their cabin to find something to nibble on, carrot slices dipped in cider vinegar. After lunch, Thulia watched Hel gather her few possessions, a skirt and blouse, a peplos, and two smocks. There seemed poignancy to it, Hel's things wrapped in a single article of clothing. A freewoman had more.

Thulia made no attempt to stop her. What was the point in it? The Gepid and Selenas weren't actually married but they had no practical reason to live apart. She watched Hel tie her clothes into a bundle, finally stepping to the Gepid and hugging her. "I'm happy for you," she smiled.

Hel nodded, standing before her for a time, perhaps apprehensive about her first night with Selenas.

"Are you worried?" Thulia asked, woman to woman.

Hel clutched her clothes, "About sleeping with him?"

"Yes," returned Thulia, her soul reaching out.

A sad smile came to Hel's lips, "I have had plenty of practice."

Then Hel left, the door closing slowly, quietly behind her. Thulia seemed alone in life, sitting to a stool at the hearth. A fire hadn't been kindled in months. *I suppose I could scoop ashes and clean it. Autumn will be here soon enough*—her circumstance and future. No more Mordwines or Gunters to slay, the last troll beheaded, dwarves keeping their distance. How could life turn out this way? She felt another black mood rising. More and more often they came, mostly from reflection as life's joys became hollow and her goals withered. As of late, the moods settled like bad food or drink. *Cleaning ashes! A fine chore for the defender of the people*; for the *Iron Breaker* hid under her bed waiting for an indistinct future.

She heard shouting outside where the sun might brighten a heart; and jumping to her feet Thulia rushed out to see what caused the excitement. Standing before her cabin, she watched people milling around as a column of Tyrfingi came up the road. She recognized those on foot, her heart leaping. Frit's clients!

Thulia stared at the lead wagon, a fancy one. There he was, Fritigern!—waving to bystanders. He was reentering her life after three long years, coming to Ascentia like a hero, like he had conquered the whole damned world... and riding the best wagon Heldrid bequeathed her. *What a presumptuous bastard!*

Seeing her, Frit gleamed an expansive grin, "Thulia! How does life treat you?"

How did life treat her? *I wear rags and live in a shack!—dig in a frigging garden, raise a child by myself and trice up an entire village. Look at him, the son-of-a-bitch. What gave him the right to purloin my wagon?* Obviously he assumed she and everything she owned was now his! But he was terribly mistaken. "Who said you could use my wagon?" she yelled back in a peak of ire.

Frit's smile vanished as he shot back, "I borrowed it from Old Hempstalk. He offered it."

"Well, it wasn't his to lend," she screamed, "It's mine and I want it returned. I'm living up here in a hovel! I get by with nothing, and I'll not see you riding around in one of the finest things I own. Do you understand?"

He reined to a stop, his countenance seething as he spat, "I certainly do. You're looking vicious but healthy. Just as soon as I empty this thing out, I'll return it to you," prodding the team to a start while adding, "I guess we all change. You turned into a total bitch."

She watched him go, his back to her as he continued up the road. Finally he disappeared around the bend. In a rage she flew around, kicking the bench in front of the cabin. How could she have done it?—chased off the only man she ever loved!

He was right. She *was* a total bitch.

* * *

When the commotion erupted, Selenas was at the horse shed braiding a new set of reins, the leather greasy and supple, his mind still in a quandary. Hel just showed up, saying, *"We are husband and wife, and cannot live apart. I must prepare a good meal for you and Waldrid. Change the sheet."* He wondered about the sheet part. They had yet to be married and he was the presbyter. What would people think? Especially Rodric's mother, the old crone, as righteous a woman as ever lived. He certainly couldn't turn Hel away! Incredibly nervous, Selenas pictured himself impotent and her lying there like a cadaver. What a frigging mess.

Then he looked up to see Frit!—his confessor arriving after too long a hiatus and leaping from a fancy wagon. *He looks like the King of the World!* Selenas dropped unfinished reins, running to his long lost brother, hugging the man. They spoke of this and that, Selenas finally tricing courage to inform him about Lilia's death as Frit stood motionless, his face paling. Selenas confessed even more, "I lost my way from the good path. We all did. Then Thulia arrived and began enlarging the gardens. Men went to the plow and women plucked rocks from the furrows. With the soil ready, Thulia demanded, *Plant new seeds here.* Do you understand?"

Frit's eyes followed the road from whence he came, his voice calm, "Her project pulled thoughts from death, salvaging the community."

"As if sent by an angel," Selenas claimed, "But I should warn you. She has delusions about a sacred sword given to her by the Archangel Michael. Other than that she seems perfectly normal. You know—combative, crude, the usual." They strode from the wagon, one receiving a terse history of Ascentia plus a dinner invitation, the other hearing about Germania. "I'll inform Hel," explained Selenas, "We're not quite married yet, nuptials impossible to perform. I can't marry myself to her. We'll just live in sin until Wulfilas signs the proxy. After all, we're mature adults."

"Ah, good thinking, bad reasoning," Frit winked, "Nothing like a little lechery. I thought I was the wayward brother."

* * *

"Four bowls are hardly more than three," she admitted, her little smile there. Selenas couldn't tell if it was genuine or forced, the difference between an awkward night and an incredibly awkward one, his vision of the eve asunder.

Hel laid out dinner while one of Frit's freemen brought the wagon over to Thulia. No confrontation expected, the man wasn't the one who borrowed it. The meal—lamb and carrots stewed together—went smoothly, politely. Then Frit produced the artifact from its cloth bag, placing it upon the rough table. Waldrid ran over to gawk at it, knowing it was delicate. Boys weren't allowed to touch that sort of thing; and besides, he didn't want to anyway. "That's girl stuff," he gagged, returning to his project of carving a sword from a pine limb.

"I was wondering," claimed Frit, "If you or Hel might take this little horse over to Thulia in a day or two. I'll be heading off in the morning."

"To where?" asked Selenas, "Why can't you give it to her yourself?"

"Thulia and I aren't speaking to each other. I don't know what's wrong with her; something up her butt, and unfortunately I called her a total bitch. I'm just going a mile or so from here to the north slopes. I want to build on a rise."

Hel rolled the little horse in her fingers, finally perceiving, "This is not glass. It's rock and most beautiful, with one small flaw."

"It's jade from the land of Qin," Frit explained, "I didn't know it had a flaw. I thought it was perfect; paid a fortune for it in Epirus."

Hel's eyes widened, "You have been all the way to Epirus?" then observing, "The flaw is on the chest, noticeable in the lamp-light."

Selenas chuckled, Frit and Hel not seeing the humor in it, so he noted, "A flaw in the chest? Get it?"

Frit became defensive, "Well, I happen to like Thulia's build. I see no flaw in it."

Hel changed the subject tactfully, "Oh, Epirus. They make axe- heads there, and armor too."

Selenas was impressed. She knew about Epirus. He didn't.

Hel returned the jade horse to Frit, and he explained, "I've been far beyond Epirus—to Illyricum and Italia, and finally up to Pannonia. I fought Alemanni for three years, wounded twice, almost dying the first time. I suppose I've changed."

"In what way?" asked Selenas.

"I consider life a precious commodity. Perhaps I'm a little coarser now, using language spoken at the front, and I don't give a damn about much and know exactly what I want."

Hel studied his face, handsome behind its flare of passion, "What do you want?"

"Not much beyond what comes with the flaw."

Chapter 38: In the Wasteland

With Frit and clients beyond her sight, Thulia had stormed through the doorway, booting her stool across the cabin. How could a man forsake her all these years? She wanted him to feel her anguish, to grab him and press his chest to hers, to enmesh with him, not tenderly but in a violent gesture of what? Passion? No, not passion. Anger!

Now she rode from those who saw her make a fool of pride. She wanted to kill, not herself or him, not anyone really, but something. She reined her gelding to a halt a few miles below Ascentia. Leaving her mount, she unsheathed the *Iron Breaker*… unbidden for too long a time.

"God in heaven!" she screamed, "Why did you put me upon this orb to be such a foolish bitch?" With raging strides she left roadside toward a patch of alders, raising the weapon. Thulia gripped it tight with both hands; and with all the strength she possessed, she swung at an alder, shearing the tree in a single stroke, and she killed another one, and another. She stopped mid-swing! *This was once a road.* Alders lined a stream between two hills, clearly delineating taller trees surrounding them. Men cleared this path long ago, now choked by second growth. But who? The Quadi?—for they once lived near-about. Her anger vanished, replaced by curiosity as she walked further into the woods, following the overgrown road. The sun was setting as she reached the top of a hummock. Shifting the sword to her left hand, she wiped sweat from her brow. And she gasped!

Before her eyes, the land rolled up both slopes as far as sight could see—all of it nearly barren as if some giant thing, an evil monster, had eaten all the hardwoods. *It's like the aftermath of a great war!*

Stumps hugged soil, cut to the quick, old and covered with moss. New growth, young firs more than head-high, could not blot the damage. *Who could have done such a thing? They killed an entire forest.* Yet no structures remained, not even rotting cabins. Ahead and off to stream-side, Thulia found the mound, walking swiftly to it. She skirted its height until reaching the other side, the mound hollow, as if dug away by a huge bear. *No. An explosion.* Approaching it she found short timbers packed within, and sooty black. *Still here after all these years. The charcoal burners!*

She knew this place, knew it far too well, aiding in its destruction. Thulia raised *Tyrfing*, not seeing it… only an axe in a small hand. *All the others were men, sometimes six or seven—mostly young and poor—upwards to twenty or more in a good season. Only two seemed old, the brothers Fenni, both hardly able to speak Gothic, their accents thick with each faltering word.*

Thulia closed her eyes to see the carnage. *When it rained, smoke hugged the land like dragon's breath, a stink to it. A cutter came and went as a ghost, oft scaring her in his workplace. The burning lasted for weeks on end, the stench permeating every weft of clothing. While the mound burned, each man chopped halfway through an oak or maple and moved to the next tree. Othar and Vainamon arrived with a two-man saw, cutting from the other side until the tree toppled, crashing through live branches, snapping life from the next victim—fresh fodder for a new mound.*

She recalled Othar's pride in North Farm as he spun tales of reindeer people, men with barrel-stave shoes trudging on "white feathers." He and the youngermen "slew" the forest, Othar claimed. *"Not a wren to find a limb to nest on. An empty place!—empty like us who destroy it. Burned away, ja... like a Wasteland."* He had coined the phrase. It vanished as wagons left thrice a month, rumbling down to the Caucaland and Gothia beyond, selling charcoal for a pittance.

Chill crept her spine as she viewed the scene before her, the exact spot where it happened!—where the charcoal man vanished from her life. Or did he? Something, his essence, a token, a finger part, crept between her legs.

Darkness would find her in no time at all, and what then? What lurked out here in the Wasteland? His ghost still searching for his body?—wanting revenge for a disturbed child's thought? Seeing the place where he died brought memories back. At last she knew. *HE is the Other, the nightmare's voice!*

She raised her sword again, pointing to a phantom, screaming to an unwanted past, "Burn in Hell where you belong!" *You cannot touch me now, you son of a whore.*

She knew the secret to her darkest nights—exploding before her!—so potent she dropped the *Iron Breaker.* Almost dark, and he was out there waiting, his voice kindly, *My Thulia, why can't you sleep tonight?*

A quaking hand reached to soil, groping for her weapon, her gaze riveted to shadows as fingers gripped the hilt. Thulia turned from the Wasteland with quick strides, past young trees between stumps, not even noticing them, pacing faster to leave it all behind.

Then she began running!

But her legs could not carry her fast enough.

*   *   *

Twilight glowed above the lake, clouds deep purple. Frit and young Waldrid settled for the night in the cabin; and

Hel took two blankets from the chest, one soft wool, the other linen. The night was clear, a half moon climbing through miniature lights. She spread the linen blanket at field-edge, the second one rolled as a large pillow. Selenas was incredibly nervous as she reclined, extending a hand to him as he settled beside her. "This is a beautiful night for our first together," she surmised, "I cannot count that high. There are so many stars in the sky."

"Even more than I can count," he assured her.

She stared to the heavens, "They are actually big, and God lives among them. He has good company too," she wished her husband to know, "We are insignificant, for even trees rise above us."

He had never heard beauty of voice like that. *It comes from graced thought. Her mind works silent, in great depth, seldom expressed.* Selenas was humbled by it. Speechless. Every Sabbath he gave a sermon, spoke to hundreds during the week, yet now he found a reply difficult. He was a little man shrunk by a cosmos far larger than imagined. At the extremity of it, the actual beginning, there was a God. As presbyter he was still but a man, prone to all the mistakes, to greed, ambition, the ultimate fear of death. The woman beside him sensed God easier than he could. Hel's mind had that unique ability to fathom abstracts, to see beyond this temporal world. He saw the trees while she viewed the other side of the universe. Dropping his eyes from the sky, he beheld his illegal wife.

She reached to his hand, squeezing it, "You can kiss me if you wish."

Upon one elbow he leaned to meet her lips, at first no more than flesh brushing flesh. She wrapped hands around his head, pressing him to her, finding his tongue with hers. Moments went by as he discovered they were breathing heavily, both coming up for a little air. Hel rose to her knees before him and worked her smock up over her head, Selenas jumping to help her.

In the moonlight she appeared trim and fragile, younger than twenty four years. She retained a nubile figure even as she aged; and Selenas was enraptured, his blood coursing to the right place. Hel was absolutely beautiful, not over-ripe like Thulia.

"It would be best if you removed your trousers," she noted casually.

His face flushed a little, and he felt like a boy as he met her request. A lover's practiced words, so frequently murmured to Lilia, were caught in his throat; and all the verbal eloquence, the memorized flatteries, seemed shallow and ingenuine. Not for Hel's ears. He could only mumble, "I love you."

She gave a half smile, saying even less, "I know."

As they knelt to each other, she stated warmly, "This is the body of Hel. Like her soul, it has been reborn—the only Hel you can see. This is for you, my husband, as you are for me. I think we will be very happy."

* * *

My Thulia,
You jumped from sleep again,
said the remembered wraith.

She bolted upright and sweating, yet he remained, *the man of the voice!* Sitting awake, she could see him. He came back when she discovered the place where it happened—out in the Wasteland. In the yurt, they slept upon separate pallets. He worked each day building mounds of timber, and she helped him. But in darkness he helped himself... to his wine and more.

The first time it happened she thought he was the boogie man who lived beneath her pallet, only feared upon dark nights with no moon or stars. At first he had no voice at all; and then he arrived once a week, even more, to finally speak, *"You have your mother's eyes, your mother's lips."* She knew it was wrong, as did Othar, *"A demon guides an ebilsmon."*

His fingernails were black around the edges, the flesh beneath his trousers white, and his words were always soothing, *"Nothing but a dream."* He crushed her, pumping hard until he gasped and then returned to his own pallet. She would lay there, legs apart, too frightened to weep or move. The pain was less the second time, even less the third, until she only wondered what pleasure he found in her. Alone she studied her girlhood, trying to understand his penchant.

At night he was gentle, but in daylight he used the "thumper," a hardwood stick tucked in the rear of his belt. She knew it well enough, having felt its sting for manifold infractions of men's rules. *"You do not dump wine from men's cups." "You do not put salamanders in men's coats." "You do not laugh in men's faces."* Her sins against men were legion!—and the charcoal thumper led a lively existence.

Vainamon knew what the charcoal man did, and he seethed in envy. One day, he caught her alone at the brook and bound her hands with hempen rope, then stuffing the rag in her mouth. It tasted of sweat and snot, and she gagged while he guided himself deeper. He laughed with grunts, as eyes rolled back and muscles of his neck bulged; and he snarled, *"All you have left are your brusts. Speak to anyone, and I will slice them off."* She believed him, for he was meaner than her father. After Vainamon got her, she always carried an axe to keep bad people away.

One day a charcoal mound stopped burning and began to cool. She backed from the dust and earth, watching her father climb its mass to lie upon it. He listened carefully, straddling it as he did her. A correctly burning mound whispered deep inside, wedding a slow hiss to an internal roar, the mound saying, *I am fine, a healthy burn.* Spread-eagle upon the mound, the charcoal man heard nothing, she could tell because he reached to the rear of his belt and pulled out the thumper, pressing an ear to the mound, first moving to the right and then left. He was listening for the "dead spot" where the fire had died under packed soil. The mound needed an air vent to re-flame its depths. She watched him raise the thumper, recalling its sting and each welt upon her butt, sometimes her arms, but never her face. And she said to herself, *"I wish he would go away."*

He poked the thumper hard, piercing the mound. And in a wink of thought, the coal gas exploded! A dark cloud belched to the sky, the blast hitting her like a falling oak! Dirt and soot rained, and a great noise blew her ten feet to the rear. He was gone!—a wish fulfilled in the wink of an eye.

She caused him to disappear just like that! Thulia regained her feet, looking at legs and hands, checking her hair. She was all there! Even the charcoal man had not truly vanished. She could still feel him... a whimper in the breeze and so feeble and lost he would never—never!—thump her again. Yes. Some of him remained on her smock and face, little scrids of red and pink and black. She brushed her cheek, lowering her hand to rub a thumb to finger. He was greasy and gummy, very moist and warm, much warmer and softer than he ever was in life. He was a good charcoal man now. She wiped his essence upon the linen, blending him with all his other parts.

Inside her head she heard a constant ring as each bell rang non-stop until they all became one. Othar came running with eyes wide, his mouth making movements; and he kept talking while waving arms. She tried her best to smile. He was very concerned!—and she wished to lay his fears aside, "He is gone now. I made him disappear," yet she could not hear the words. Then Vainamon arrived. Old Othar peeled the smock from her, tossing it to the fire, and took her to the stream. As the Finnermon bathed her, Vainamon stared while slavering, wiping lips and repeating the same words over and over, unheard yet known well enough, "She is a woman, ja?" for he wanted her again, trying to turn his brother into the same beast he was. Othar pulled his knife and hissed words she could only surmise, as Vainamon turned livid with hate.

When she was clean, Othar had her wear his new tunic. She liked its comfort, that wondrous feel of pure linen. Several days later when he remembered it, Othar retrieved her woolen smock from her father's oaken arka. It felt scratchy and no longer fit her. She refused to wear it, preferring the tunic. Someday she would be an Amazon and protect good people with a mighty sword. Amazons were strong and they wore tunics all the time. If she were an Amazon, nobody could force her to do anything. No more men's rules.

Thulia pressed a hand to Sesca's shoulder, the girl sleeping in a child's night. Again she closed eyes. All of them except Othar wanted what she had. She carried a wealth no man could steal!—a big, little girl who knew exactly what men wanted, Venus at the age of ten, and a child who perceived the ultimate truth. No matter how many tasted it, her great wealth would always remain warm, inviting, and soft... in the hard world of men.

She fell back to roll upon her side, Sesca breathing quietly. *I was barely older than my daughter!*

He was *the Other One*, Transylvania's sickest wraith, who drank every coin earned and spawned her as his darkest product. He became just a whisper, lived in her head night after night, haunting her as he did in life, the remaining tincture of a demon. The spring after he died, she was old enough to wonder what pleasure might be hers, exposing herself to Threisbaurg's boys, hoping they were old enough. The first one was so naïve he never knew she was considerably used.

She lay in her past knowing the riddle's answer, all of it returning when she found the overgrown road. Vainamon was gone, but the charcoal man was still out there. Even Satan refused his soul. *Such are the mountains, the darkest woods, where creep all the wraiths of the world*. She was a product of the Wasteland. Now she could tell them all—the child-stealing dwarves and sharp-toothed trolls, even the boogie man— *Sorry! Papa got me first.*

Chapter 39: Wild Skins & Somber Trousers

Frit hadn't attempted to see her since arriving. *If he did, I'd apologize, and he better do the same. Call me a total bitch? Who in hell does he think he is?* Thulia looked beyond the gardens and up the road. Rumor claimed he was building a home for himself, a couple of day's work, half a week? She knew full well he didn't come all the way to Ascentia to build a house. She would see him soon enough and was willing to bet he'd ride down to sniff her out by the end of the day. Morning passed to noontime. Noon went by, and the sun set low in the sky. One by one, the women left the gardens to return home and cook dinner. As Thulia prepared to leave, she saw Hel walking her way. They met at garden-edge, Hel all smiles.

"Last night Selenas and I slept under the stars. They were so beautiful."

"Really," piped Thulia, more than a little jealous.

"Yes. The night was a gift from Selenas, but look!" and she produced a cloth bag.

Thulia opened it, pulling out the little horse, "He gave you this, too?"

"No!" grinned Hel, "A gift to you from Fritigern."

A present from Frit? We just had an argument. He still loves me!—but where is he? The day is almost over.

"He found it in Epirus, but it comes from the Orient, I know," Hel was sure.

Thulia hefted the artifact, knowing it was expensive. She studied the rounded form smoothed to a polish, a green crystal sheen. It served no real purpose, not hollow to hold something. *Just to wonder at, I suppose.* It's the same colored stone that tops the *Iron Breaker*!

"It's carved from jade, Thulia," Hel gasped, "Surely it is the most beautiful horse in the world."

It was absolutely stunning. He knew how much she loved horses. They were her whole life, other than men. And the men part was over. "This is a work of art. I expected to see Frit by now, but he must have things to do."

"He almost died, you know, three years in the Alemanni wars. He was a captain of many horsemen."

"So that's where he's been. Off chasing death."

"I must go and prepare dinner for Selenas and Waldrid," explained Hel, "Fritigern will see you soon, I'm sure." She turned to leave.

"Hel," Thulia implored, "Are you happy?"

The illegal bride glanced back, a larger smile than usual, "Oh, yes. We get along."

She watched the Gepid cross the garden and stroll up the road. *The night was a gift from Selenas, eh?* A different way of saying it, her happiness for Hel tinged with envy. *We get along.* She was sure they got more than along, out under the stars. She arched her back and headed for the cabin. If Waldrid was home, so was Sesca and just as hungry. As she walked along, she thought of Frit building a house. He didn't seem the type, and she assumed he would have his freemen raise it. Then he could find time to visit. *But people do change. He isn't going to come. The day is over.*

* * *

Frit sat upon an adzed slab affixed to tree stumps, the men drinking ale as they surveyed a day's accomplishment. The morning was spent building cabins for client families, every man dropping trees, shaving shingles and doors. In a day or two, the cabins would be finished. By afternoon, a hundred additional trees fell for the big structure, perhaps one tenth of those needed. In the meantime, the men pitched yurts and two military tents, peaked and rectangular, temporary sleeping quarters. Soon enough, word would spread he was building something larger than a house. The structure would be the colossus of Ascentia, surpassing Heldrid's in size.

As they studied the plans now and then, the freemen would ask, "What is it?" and Frit would answer, "A big tavern. Big enough for the Fisher King."

While carpenters debarked logs, stone masons began hauling shale and granite from wherever they could find it, some of the best rock coming from near the lake. Half the trees were felled below the site, giving Frit a panoramic view. Esthetics were not part of a Goth's sphere, but he wanted something good to look at—his whole driving modus, and he would get it or die trying. Whatever it took! To Frit she was the best looking, most attractively built woman he had ever seen... and evidently a bigger bitch than ever. She always had that in her, going back to days when he fell from the training horse and she taunted him. Now he could ride better than Thulia with eyes closed, even when sleeping. He'd done that before, awakening with a German arrow in his calf, only a shot's length from the battle line.

When clearing began, he issued orders, a proclamation carried verbally to all those in Ascentia—*"Villagers are forbidden to set foot on the site until the project is finished, especially the widow Thulia."* That would do it! She would dwell upon it, probably fume like Vesuvius, but the ban would kindle the desired effect and she would arrive because she wasn't supposed to.

He was ready this time. Whatever Thulia thought she could slap out, verbally or physically, he could return with the same candor and speed. This was the final showdown—taming the Amazon. He snapped to his feet and went to the ale barrel before it emptied, one more draught before calling it a day. His legs would spasm in knots upon this eve, and muscles would ache in the morning. So be it. The price of love and lechery. He had no idea how long the project would take, the enormity of it beyond a man's ken. Frit needed time to make the place look like what it was, time to work up a libido the size of the structure itself. In the slyest manner, he planted two seeds, each working on Thulia's basic temperament—the jade horse and the ban from coming here.

* * *

Another day without rain. Not that it matters; for it's too damned late, the growing season over. Aoric limped through the Tyrfingi crop, pushing wheat stalks aside with his cane, the fronds stunted at half the length of normal... half the seed.

He had walked through the gardens, examining squash, turnips, and beets, the leaves chewed by bugs unseen, and the produce small and thin. Freyja and Freyr, Tyrfing and Thor, all the deities frowned; and in their anger they had punished the entire tribe—*a blight upon the land*.

He walked no further. Leaning to his walking stick, Aoric turned about and headed back toward his wagon. With a tight jaw he fumed in consternation, for he had been too lax, a judge who avoided judgment. *Well, no more! They shall pay for this.* Three years of bad crops, three years of frolicking—or whatever they did—up in that dark pasture. They had taken the Sword, then stealing the stone mason, the blacksmith, all the talented artisans, and leaving Threisbaurg with the culls.

The crop confirmed it. Christians were the worst plague to ever befall the earth, far worse than locusts. Aoric knew the guilty by name—Selenas, Rustan, Thulia, and

Fritigern—each one a thief and weakening the kunja. *They shall pay for this. We shall have the Sword and artisans returned. And perhaps then, when harmony and correct ritual are restored, the gods will again bless us.*

*   *   *

An entire week passed, vanishing before her. Thulia couldn't believe it! Why did he not come off the mountain? Was Frit balmy, perhaps head-damaged on the battlefield; for things like that happened, the man forever changed. Whatever he was up to, Frit was not letting her back into his life, and she became more apprehensive each new day, wondering if she had lost him forever. Perhaps she did three years ago, although their parting seemed to hint of a remaining flame.

The whole thing affected her to the core. She was turning into a harpy, chastising Sesca or Waldrid for the smallest infractions. They were just being children. Her friends noticed it, cultivating that expression on their faces—*"Come on, Thulia. Nothing is that bad."* But it was! Her personal life was a void, nothing to do except weed the damned garden, burn another meal, or sulk like a rootworm. Hours at her lakeside boulder held little solace—it no longer shined—and every night she sat at the hearth rolling the jade horse in fingers to study it. *Why did he give it to me as a suitor would, then not bother to follow up the gesture?*

Then she would slide *Tyrfing* from under the bed, comparing the pommel-stone with the Serican horse. There had to be a connection, some link beyond chance that could wed the two items. She wished it was love.

Examining the jade horse and sword became a ritual between tucking Sesca to bed and stepping outside. Yet even viewing stars wrought envy; for what Hel and Selenas had?—she would never find. Ascentians were calling her "the widow Thulia." Selenas or Hel would never say it, but others did; and at first she viewed it as harmless, but lately the term jabbed her the wrong way, implying she was no longer alluring. She pictured her future, perhaps becoming like Rodric's mother with tits to her thighs.

She had health, even fame and a sweet daughter, but little else. Frit had renewed her dream of love. Yet as close as he now lived, and obviously with no other woman in his life, he was avoiding her. Thulia felt a sudden chill. The nights were cooling, and soon she would kindle the hearth. The other fire, Fritigern's, she knew not how to spark. *Let him be. Evidently what he wants and what I am are two different things.* She certainly would not ride up there and beg him to take her back.

Leaving the empty hearth, Thulia went to her bed, slipping into it quietly, not wishing to awaken Sesca. She lay silent, her eyes closed to another long night in the realm of the desolate.

*   *   *

Mid-day's sun felt less warm, and a breeze swept down from the mountains, buffeting trees as they seemingly tried to straighten themselves, only to be pressured again. Along the road, the first downed leaves of the poplar rushed before the wind, their movement like the flight of scared brown mice. A little early, autumn's chill pierced deep into the sinew of Transylvania.

In its age the road now held ruts worn by all the feet and wheels of nearly half a decade. Waldrid and Sesca ran along its length, each rolling iron hoops with a stick, the hoops from a broken barrel. The adults watched them in front of Selenas' cabin; and with the pretense of inviting Thulia to lunch, the presbyter wished to talk with her. Something beyond trials of daily life pulled at her soul, he was sure; and even Hel commented on it, a woman sparse on words.

Standing before them, Thulia seemed distant, her mind troubled. She would watch the children, then look north to the mountains as if expecting a ghost to fly down from lofty peaks.

What was up there to affect her? Selenas believed her troubles seated in Frit, not a day passing without an acrid comment. *"What's that bastard doing up there? We were friends,"* she claimed on one occasion. *"We exchanged harsh words but anger passes, does it not?"* she remarked upon another day.

Thulia was deeply troubled, more than ever. She had been brusque for as long as he could remember, a combativeness going back to their childhood. Now she became worse, not a civil word uttered. She spent too much time in the gardens, just as she did at the horse barns in a former life. He tried to make light of it once. *"You're a compulsive weed picker,"* he mistakenly quipped. And she retorted, *"I can damned well do as I please!"*

It was just a joke!—yet she became defensive beyond reason. He looked up, the children running back their way as Sesca's hoop bounced from the road into the field. Waldrid stopped his own toy from rolling and waited for her. Then they continued along the ruts, running toward the adults.

"They love the hoops," smiled Hel.

Thulia remained silent, her mood dark.

In age and temperament Waldrid and Sesca seemed so close, and Selenas believed his son was responsible for Sesca speaking again. The children were good for each other. "Waldrid and Sesca play so well together," he piped.

Thulia looked at him like he uttered blasphemy and snapped, "Children who play together oft end up sleeping together."

The comment was crude, out of place and uncalled for, and Selenas asked, "What exactly does that mean?"

Thulia huffed, "Of course they get along. Certainly *you* should know! Sesca is his half sister."

Selenas stood shocked!—his mouth agape, his wife looking at him. Silence permeated, not a word could he find. *What would make her say that?*

The silence ended when Thulia spat, "Can you possibly think Pigfoot was her father? I was pregnant two months before I married him."

Hel fumbled for his hand as he studied the Amazon, finally exclaiming, "Thulia! This is hardly the time or place to bring an accusation like that up. And how can you be…"

She cut him short as her expression quailed, "Be what? Sure? There were no others in that last year. And if you think they'll grow up to wed each other, you're sadly mistaken." Her mouth twitched as she began sobbing, "And the second time? You sired a boy. He killed my only son!—he might as well have killed me." Thulia put a hand to eyes and nose, wiping away admission, working her lips to express more but could not. She simply stormed off.

Selenas stood frozen, aware of sowing the wildest of seeds. He stared straight ahead viewing his past as his wife's grip tightened. Several times he tried breaking the relationship, yet she was so incredibly practiced. All the others were reserved, good noble virgins, and Thulia was there for the giving. Then he met Lilia, and Thulia became the past. Feeling small and dirty, he looked down to Hel's eyes, knowing she viewed him in a darker light. He could only speak softly, "I'm truly sorry you had to learn something like this in such a crude manner."

She studied his face, her eyes beginning to mist, "You forgave my past. Do you think I can do any less?"

He hugged her for all she was and she returned the embrace willingly, tightly. Selenas smelled the fragrance of her hair, aware she was clean to the soul.

*   *   *

Thulia paced not far down the road when the Gepids barged from the forest on horseback. They dressed in wild skins and somber trousers, no less fierce than old gods wished; and they gripped long spears, not the length of lances but long enough to push through a running victim, to enter a woman's back and exit her chest. And each Gepid had an axe tucked to belt, its blade sharpened upon stones plucked from desolate soil.

They did not smile—balancing their weapons!—half turning toward her, the other half galloping for Selenas and Hel. Thulia instinctively reached for her flawless blade, but the *Iron Breaker* was in her cabin... hiding under the bed.

She and Ascentia stood defenseless, unprepared. And they were back!

Chapter 40: Ten Black Feathers

Thulia ran between riders, heading back to Hel and Selenas. The Gepids reined to a halt before them; and the chieftain—Gunter's nephew—slammed his spear to the ground. It remained upright in Ascentian soil, as a single black feather tied to the shaft fluttered in noon-day wind. Selenas pulled Hel closer as if to shield her, and Thulia stepped forward resolute, "Why are you here?"

"We are ten to replace ten," claimed the nephew, "We shall not see this day's end. The shaman told us long ago when the heads were staked—*The crime shall be cleansed by the blood of ten.* This is the old way. Perhaps new men, Christian men, cannot understand." He looked down with a tight smile, "Is that you, Hel?"

"Yes, Hagen. It is me."

"You look like you did when sixteen," and he pinned eyes back to Thulia, "Is this the Amazon's family?"

"Yes it is," she declared, knowing they were family despite her fevered outburst.

He addressed Selenas, "You have warriors with armor. Is that not true?"

"Yes we have, but I do not understand."

"We have seen your warriors practice with long spears. If they own armor, let them wear it," affirmed Hagen, "Men are coming, perhaps an hour, perhaps two. They have come up the Prahova from Saltsbaurg, but they are Tyrfingi from the twin rivers. We have watched them for two days, and now we know. They are coming here."

Women and children were sequestered in the church, Sesca with them. Thulia stumbled from her cabin, trying to cinch the armor's buckles along her ribs, realizing she had either gained weight or her bosom was bigger. *How much larger can it get? Oh! I almost forgot my sword!* And she ran back inside, plucking it from her bed.

At the horse sheds, freemen were saddling mounts and pulling lances from overhead rafters. Rustan and his Alan cataphracts donned spangenhelms and armored tunics, a few so aged they were fashioned with bronze scales. The Gothic nobles would ride as light horsemen, yet all, Goths and Alans alike, ran about in thither. Rodric—too large to do anything—checked contus shafts, running chubby fingers along their length. Thulia could only recall Merjands' wry remark—*You never expect the unexpected.*

And who shall lead us? Rustan had not fought a battle since the Vandal war, and Selenas had trouble enough being a presbyter, not a military leader and he never was. Certainly she would not lead them, having only fought one on one; and besides, she was a woman. Nonplussed, she ran down the road toward the shed, tugging at her armor and juggling her sword-belt. And she almost ran into someone on horseback. *A Roman! No, it's Frit.*

He peered down, shaking her helm in his right hand. *The mask of death! I left it with Old Hempstalk.* And then he announced, "Get yourself in order, and grab this. You'll need it," then adding, "At last, a perfect chance to vent that hostility of yours."

"What hostility?" she snapped, buckling the sword belt and sliding the scabbard to her left hip, "I was not hostile. Just marshalling fact." She reached up, tearing the helmet from his grasp, "Who shall lead us? You or Rustan?"

"You will," he shot back, giving her a sharp eye, "Is that *Tyrfing the Iron Breaker?* Slayer of countless trolls and dwarves? Certainly you have the wherewithal."

"Not me. Trolls are a man's charge, not a woman's."

"What about Penthesilea? Or Tomyris, queen of the Alans? You have no less dignity that they did. These people respect you," and he pointed to Safrax running toward them with her gelding, "So buckle up, get on your mount, and become a leader."

I have dignity? Thulia fitted her helm, took a slightly restricted breath, and tried to calm herself by asking an inane question, "What happened to your white horse?"

"It died in good service. This brown one carried me through the rest of the wars."

"When it perished from the chest wound, you were injured?"

His eyes tightened as he held silence.

She knew he would give no answer, "I'm fortunate you lived, as are these people. You will help me lead them?"

"Evidently I cannot retire. The Gepids have ridden back to the forest looking for the Tyrfingi's approach. In the meantime we can muster in the field below the garden. It's cleared straight to lakeshore, not a bad place to make a stand."

"Thank you," and she turned to Safrax, taking the white-spotted gelding's reins, "You stay at the Church with those who cannot ride."

"But I want to fight. I'm big as a man and ride better than most."

"No," she insisted, "Protect the women and children and help Selenas."

He nodded with a down-turned lip, shot his gaze to the woods, and asked, "Why do the ten Gepids wish to die?"

"They don't wish to. It's a matter of honor, their way of righting a wrong. We can do nothing about it except thank them for their grace."

* * *

The Squinter caught another branch in the face, his mount shying from it. This was the worst ride he could recall—crossing the Prahova twice, hacking tree limbs along the old horse-path, splashing through swamps—but at least the mosquitoes had succumbed to cool nights. Ahead of him, the Saltsbaurg guide rode cautiously, their pace slowing as they approached the Christian village. The guide was Dacian. And the vengeance of Tyrfingi gods, the pluck of Tyrfingi might, meant nothing to him. He just counted sesterces.

Further down the column, Munderic kept riders in order, a determined young man who began riding with torchers in last year's campaign. Suddenly the Dacian guide stopped and raised a hand, motioning Athanaric to ride up beside him. The man leaned to whisper, "I saw movement, a rider on a horse. They know."

"They know what?"

"That we are here."

"Yes, of course, but where are we?"

"The road is just ahead. Less than half a mile, I think. It matters little to be quiet now, but I'll not speak the first loud word. You will have to form up in the open," and the Dacian swung his horse around, his eyes wide, "I bid you well." And he rode quickly to the rear.

* * *

Hagen and his men rode hard, turning their horses from the road into the field. He halted before Thulia, Rustan, and Frit, looking beyond them toward the lake. Fifty cataphracts straddled mounts, some of their horses with caparisons; and each man held a lance to the sky. Another fifty horsemen, less armored, carried long-swords, horse bows, and circular bucklers painted with the Bear. "These are all your warriors," he quizzed.

"The men on foot are at the church," explained Thulia.

"Then you are outnumbered," sighed Hagen, "They have a hundred times three, maybe more. The forest is thick. Hard to count. They will be here in a quarter hour."

Thulia glanced to Frit. He rolled eyes, shook his head, and mumbled, "Just about average, I guess. Three to one. But fear not. We have the advantage." And he removed his Roman helmet, handing it to Rustan, "Let's trade headgear. A little subterfuge might work. Stay here with Thulia and the light horse," tilting his head to Stefan and the light cavalry, "Line them in the woods on both sides of the field, but let them be seen." As they reined about, Frit asked, "Where's the draconarius?" A young horseman rode forward, the Alan wind-sock flying high behind him. Frit ordered, "It's a blustery day. Let the archers see the dragon at all times. They'll need it to figure wind direction; so if you get hit, forget the wound until passing the draco to another man." The draconarius nodded as the Gepids formed-up to face the coming foe.

"Alright. Heavy horse come with me to the other side of the road. Stay under cover, no talking, no noise." The cataphracts followed him up the field, as Frit tied Rustan's helm strap, digging heels to the brown gelding.

Hagan pushed his mount close to Thulia's, "When this day is done, you must gather the feathers—all ten—and bring them back to my people."

*　　*　　*

The Squinter and his riders stopped short. Below them in a narrow field, a dozen Christians could be seen. He called a halt as Munderic came riding back down the road. "Up ahead is the town and some gardens," claimed the young man, "And further up the road, there's a church with many town-folk. They have bucklers and spears, but most carry pitchforks."

With a grin the Squinter led Munderic into the field. He avowed, "We shall burn the church later, burn this place and every Christian in it. See the riders near the shore?" Munderic nodded, and the Squinter continued, "The one in the Roman helmet is Fritigern, a thief. Beside him is the woman Thulia, another thief. Look closer and you will see a glint of weapons in the forest to each side of them. Such an old trick, yet it matters little. We have them with backs to the lake."

"Who are the riders with them?" wondered Munderic as they reined to a halt.

"Their best men, I think," returned Athanaric, "This place has not been good to them, for they wear skins and rags. Fear not. We shall put an end to their misery and feed them to the soil." Reaching far enough into the field, he turned an eye back to his Tyrfingi, "Line up five columns deep! We have them trapped."

* * *

"Light horse, advance!" shouted Rustan, "A single line across the field, no holes. Archers stay put until they advance, then ride to both flanks and give them what you've got." The Alan archers held position and the Goths rode from the woods, forming up as Hagen returned to his men in the front line.

"What can I do? Beseeched Thulia, for she knew nothing about soldiering.

"Take the lead with me and Hagen's men, but first give us an invocation, something to stir the soul."

An invocation? She had no idea what to say, for such things were for Selenas. Thulia spun her mount around, as did the draconarius, and she fumbled for words. Then she drew the *Iron Breaker*, held it high, and shouted, "This is more than a battle! It holds our future. If we lose today there will be no tomorrow for us and Xristos in this land. The light of God will die, as will our children. In the name of Saint Michael!—defend the people!"

The horsemen raised weapons, cheering themselves on. They advanced, first at a trot and then a gallop, the Gepids in the lead.

*   *   *

"Slahan fiands!" yelled the Squinter. As the Tyrfingi rushed ahead, he fell back to the very edge of the front line. *"Be judicious, my son,"* his father always said. At a slow gallop, the distance closed, a hundred paces, fifty paces, twenty five. And then he heard a ruckus to his rear. Craning his neck, he looked back to see a mass of heavy horse closing distance. The cataphracts balanced lances with both hands, ready for the strike! *Where did they come from?* Then came the shuddering, the grinding crunch, the snap of splintering ash!—*they're downing our rear.* "Hold the line!" he screamed, then repeating it, "Hold the damned line!"

He tipped his gaze forward, meeting a front of warriors. No helmets, no armor of any kind, and nearly bare-chested. They brandished thick-shafted spears, big as man's wrist, thrusting and stabbing, then using them like clubs while screaming at the top of their lungs. *They are crazed. More than crazed!*

Behind the mad warriors came a mass of light horse, just like the Tyrfingi except Christians. *But these can skirmish.* He could not recall actually fighting Christians. They usually ran. And then he saw her!—with her massive bosom and stolen sword, and all that tawdry red hair. He could not fathom why he ever wanted to marry her! And she wore armor just like a man. *"No good will come of it,"* claimed his sire more than once.

Arrows began showering from beyond both flanks! He ducked, but a second one pierced his tunic between scales, hanging there and wobbling as he rode. Athanaric plucked it, knowing he was not seriously wounded. And then another crazed warrior charged at him!

Father was right. They are killing us!

* * *

To the Squinter's rear, Frit wheeled his mount in a hurry, blocking a Tyrfingi thrust and then slashing the man's sword arm. He spun his horse to another Goth poised to take a swing, but the man was impaled by an Alan contus, flying from his saddle to the trampled field. He looked left and right, back to the cataphract, nodded his thanks, and again swung to the melee.

This was a tough battle, too confusing. Exactly who was friend or foe?—not a uniform in the bunch, and every man looked like the other. The only exception was the thick, scaled, armor of the heavy Alan horse.

Tipping his gaze to the front, Frit could see his Roman helmet, knowing his aged fishing partner was still alive. He scanned the fray, trying to find Thulia, looking at each barrel-chested rider. And then he saw her!—with the great mask of death. She swung a mean sword, no matter whom she thought she got it from. *Do not die on me! Not now, not after all the shit I'm going though.*

And suddenly a rider pummeled him with a good one, right on Rustan's spangenhelm. "Don't dent the fucking thing!" he yelled. The Tyrfingus paid no heed, slamming his sword in a downward swing; and Frit, now in the angry mode, let the man have a good one on his own helm. With a grunt, the man dropped his sword and toppled from his mount. Frit looked down, "I said don't dent it. Listen up next time, if there is one."

The field was emptying, only two or three dozen Tyrfingi left in the saddle as the cataphracts downed numbers. Thulia glanced around, looking for Frit but not seeing him. She dug heels hard, pushing the gelding ahead to reach another of Athanaric's men, an elder noble with a drooping moustache. He looked her way, and she quipped, "Are you not a little old for this?"

He lowered his weapon, gave a hard stare, and returned, "Not yet. But I'll not strike the sword you wield."

"I will!" yelled a rider at the man's rear. He raised his weapon to full swing, gripping it with both hands and leaving his torso unprotected. She rode past swiftly and slashed hard across his ribs, shearing his leather armor. "Right through my tunic!" he growled, checking his wound as he galloped for the road.

She pulled the reins hard to the left, turned the gelding in midstride, as a Tyrfingi came at her with a vengeance, blood in his eyes; and then he was knocked from his horse by a well-aimed arrow. At the same time, she took a hard jolt to her shoulder. Still clutching her weapon yet unable to remain in the saddle, she fell to the matted field. Gaining her feet, Thulia faced the bloody-eyed one, the arrow in his upper arm as he thrust his sword like a dagger, jabbing it hard to her chest. Instantly, she kneed him in the groin, as hard a kick as she could muster, and the man crumpled to the ground, his legs raised to fetal position.

Again she turned with legs planted firm and ready. The field was all but cleared, with the Squinter screaming, "Retreat! Fall back!" Another Tyrfingus, perhaps second in command, took up the call. They were riding or running back toward the road. Some Tyrfingi led horses of the downed, and others gave shoulders to injured cousins and brothers. Swords were sheathed, and bows tucked to leather cases. Less than an hour lapsed and it was over.

*   *   *

Frit watched the Tyrfingi gallop down the road, heading straight for Axeville and the safe baurgs of Gothia. *They'll not be back this year.* He rode up to Rustan, slipped off the man's helmet and shrugged, "Got a little dented. Sorry about that."

Rustan did likewise, flipping the captain's helm to him, "Nothing that a hammer-man can't fix."

"How fares Thulia? Took a tumble, I guess."

"She'll be fine. A tough woman there, but I need not tell you that," deemed Rustan, "I heard about your argument, or whatever it was." He sighed, gazing across the carnage, "I'll take a closer head count. At least thirty widows... the hardest part. Looks like Athanaric charged us to bury his dead. Didn't see any of Hempstalk's boys; I think they sat it out. About halfway through, I caught Safrax in the middle of it and believe he downed a few. Shooed him off, and tonight he'll get a thrashing."

"He's a little big for that. You'll not touch his hide. My bet is Old Hempstalk kept the Taifali out of it for two good reasons—an Amazon and God. Well, I should run along and see how my brother is doing. I thought perhaps the Tyrfingi would quit earlier, but the Squinter had a bug up his ass." Frit shook his head, tapped his helmet with a finger, and peered across the field, "I understand her imagination swells keen... but all in all, a fine woman there."

"You mean about Saint Michael? Well, I happen to believe her. No harm in it, and if it's true then God blessed her." He paused, riveting eyes to Frit's, "Not long ago we Alans worshiped the Bear, our ancestral protector. Sometimes when I look at her, I see it—not just in her physical build or carriage but in another way; and I think, *She protects us as Artia.* If the Bear has returned, we must accept it for what it is. A bear is brave yet crude. It often growls—and that's Thulia's essence."

*   *   *

Men lay upon the field in profusion, mostly Tyrfingi and Christian Goths. All the Gepids were down—the fact a given, known before the battle started. The heavy horse held their own, armored enough to roll from the hits. Thulia looked across the dead, both men and horses; and all the hay lay flat and streaked with blood. *So this is war. This is what Frit went through in Pannonia, fighting day after day, week after week in the killing fields. A wonder he's still a moral man.*

She paced slowly along the field, passing Rustan who now carried his own helmet. Both of them were doing the same thing and neither found a comment. She counted nine Gepids, some hardly recognizable as human, only distinguished by their bare torsos.

Finally, in a corner of her eye, she saw Hagen the nephew, Hagen the young chieftain. He crawled with one arm, holding innards with the other, and weaving a red trail behind him. Thulia ran to him, jumping over bodies and a dead horse, falling to knees at his side. Hardly noticing her, he reached for his spear. She grabbed it for him, placing it in his hands.

He rolled to his side, fingering the black feather hanging from the shaft. She leaned to him. With a quick pull, he snapped the quill, raising it to her, "They are from the raven, the good bird of death." He convulsed, his eyes rolling back as his mouth twisted to a grisly pall; and then he came back from where he almost went, "Take them to the tribe. Ten black feathers. Important."

"I will. You have a wife, do you not?" she knew full well.

"And two sons," he tried to grin, "Brave... like their father."

Blood dripped to the feather. Not his blood. "You are wounded," he breathed. For a moment he stared at her, then beyond her, to that hallowed place where the brave go.

Chapter 41: A Semblance of Propriety

Thulia sat at Rustan's table as his woman removed the stitches. "You will have a scar," Valeria claimed, "But you are young, it will disappear, and they will be flawless again."

"Flawless?" guffawed Thulia, "They haven't been flawless since I was twelve!"

"I mean the flesh, dear," explained Valeria, "Think of them as an advantage. If they were smaller, you would have been stabbed in the heart, too good a heart to cease beating."

"It's not a good heart," asserted Thulia, "I shamed Selenas in front of Hel and drove Frit from me. Not a good heart at all."

The door swung open as Safrax entered. With feigned nonchalance he walked past the table and pulled a bow from under his pallet. "I need to practice." He strode by them again, his eyes glued to Thulia's wound, his mouth agawk as he departed.

"The right one looks just like this one!" she yelled to the closed door, then wrapping her tunic and tying the sash.

Valeria blushed to a deep shade, "He's just curious, almost a man. At least he thinks himself a man."

"He can slaver like a man," huffed Thulia as she stood to squeeze Valeria's upper arm, "You have the hands of patience." The woman blushed again and tipped an acknowledgement.

Thulia stepped outside, finding Rustan greasing a saddle draped across a timber. Bare-chested, he wore old trousers, for grease hardly washed from clothing. Looking up as she approached, he mumbled, "My saddle was getting a little dry. I should grease it more often."

She watched him for a moment, finally commenting, "We forget some duties in favor of others. It's our way."

"As humans?" he looked up wryly.

"As humans, parents, and Christians. Safrax is off to flex the bow. Who teaches him?"

Rustan stopped wiping, leaned to the saddle with both hands and gave a hard look, "No one. He practices without my blessing. I have hopes that in a few years he might go down to Nicopolis and study under Bishop Wulfilas."

"Oh. I see," nodded Thulia, turning to leave. She paced a step and turned around, "So he teaches himself, perhaps because he has a certain penchant or talent, even a modicum of intelligence, and might be aware that our community has been attacked twice in three years... and that maybe the next time it happens more than thirty men or ten women will fall to the blade, and perhaps he values his own life and the life of others to the point he must teach himself to be a man."

Rustan snapped straight, his shoulders back while shaking a finger in the direction Safrax went, "You charge me with not attending my own son? Is that it? God has plans for him, and they do not include the ways of the heathen."

"God has plans?—or are they yours? Ten heathens died for his life and the lives of our women and children, and you have the gall to insult them. I tell you what I shall do. I plan to build a mound of rocks—a tumulus—over their common grave," and she thrust her hands forward, "And I shall do it alone and with these, and then I will erect a timber straight to the heavens... because God does not forsake men who died for others, heathens or otherwise. And perhaps you should go to the church and thank him for the Gepids' grace.

Without their warning and aid, this community would no longer exist." Then she stomped for the road.

"Wait!" he shouted while rushing toward her, "I spoke wanting and without thinking. You are correct. Good men, heathens included, do not burn in Hell. Allow me to help with the tumulus, and perhaps we could have Selenas give a eulogy."

Her expression softened, "And what about Safrax?"

"What about him?"

"I could teach him arts of self defense, perhaps a few others as well. Prepare them physically and internally for a life where violence befalls them."

Rustan stepped back sober, "I'm too ardent a Christian and forget where we come from. And yes, I have neglected my charge as hetmon of this branch of the Alans. He can use my sword, but it he dings it I shall flay his hide. Will you instruct him in lancing and the ride?"

"All that I know," she replied, "And if a young woman learns among them, then all the better. Such are the *'old ways,'* a master once said." Preparation was the key. She had misinterpreted the mirror's image, but danger came and would come again.

* * *

The mountain brook tumbled as tannic-white cataracts edged by rock, collecting as a dark pool, the water neither brown nor green but a combination of both, a liquid reflection of oak leaves and old ferns. In its course, the brook streamed downward through a ravine to splay wide and slow as it approached Ascentia. In the lower section, the brook held more life—small trout and myriads of dace—and too, it formed a larger pool where the Ascentians bathed. Frit knelt high above them at the upper pool, washing volcanic cement from his hands and arms.

In the Great Room, as he called it, he assisted the stone mason in placing cut rock in an eight-foot circle, two feet tall and a massive hearth when the cement cured. The structure abuilt at a decent pace, considering all involved. Nearly finished, the Great Room's table was fittingly huge, its top planks bound together by fish glue and rubbed to a fine smoothness by Pontic shark-skin. At the moment, its carpenter was applying the first coat of flaxseed oil.

Frit stood from the brook and shook water from his arms. From where he was, he could just view a few cabins and the lake. Somewhere down there, probably in her passing garden, Thulia fumed in fine style. Before the battle she was curt, and he wondered how she knew his white gelding died of a chest wound. He never spoke of Pannonia to anyone. Evidently she carried intuition he was unaware of. But patience wasn't her forte; and he knew she was close to snapping. Soon she would saddle that prize of hers and ride up to his den of curiosity. And the structure was almost completed and looked exactly correct.

*   *   *

The harvest was over with the exception of leeks and Thulia stood in the garden to straighten her back and rub her chest. The wound had almost healed, the stitches removed, and it itched. And perhaps the wound she gave Selenas and Hel was curing.

What a thing to say!—a long held combination of anger and resentment. A few days after the battle, she apologized, but it couldn't retract her words. Although she tried not to, she still bore animosity toward Selenas. At one time he claimed he'd marry her; and upon the eve she planned to tell him she was pregnant he never showed up. He had discovered Lilia. She became his vulgar past, good enough in the hay but not pure enough to wed. Then he skulked back into her life with Lilia huge with Waldrid. She let him, humping in late-winter snow—and he got her pregnant again! The man was balding, the perennial falterer, yet he sired children at the drop of a seed.

Back then, Frit was too young and she needed what Selenas could provide, a halfway decent sword and a little tenderness. She never loved Selenas yet almost bore him two children. He was always Goody Boy. A decade followed before she could look at him in a better light. Yet even then, she exploded in fit of rage and tears. Some Amazon she was!

Thulia's thoughts returned to the love of her life and all the whispers: *"He's forbidden Thulia to go near the place."* Even during the battle Frit avoided her, fighting the Tyrfingi at the other end of the field.

A fortnight had passed, and she remained a poison bitch, the worst Christian in Ascentia, not saying one decent word in the length of a given day. *It's time to give him a piece of my mind.* She'd feel better after a confrontation. She wasn't going up there to apologize, not on her life!—yet she wanted to know where she stood in his odd life. Some people thought the man balmy, an acorn or two loose. A tavern in an Arian community? How many travelers would arrive at a dead end on a mountain?

Her mind was wound up, her legs gritted with garden dust, and she needed to cleanse herself to the core, a long cold bath in the pool. She left the leeks behind, trudged resolute to her cabin, and plucked her canvas clothes bag from the corner, searching for an appropriate outfit to wear.

She knew Frit's tastes, a lot like hers, something off-color and eminently vulgar. That's why they were soul mates. Thulia was a little rusty at it—her old slutty walk of life—yet she still had the spirit of lust within her. Somehow she would rekindle it. All she needed was a catalyst. She would ask God for a sign, some kind of messenger in her great time of need.

*   *   *

Safrax stood naked at the lower pool staring at a chunk of soap. He was invited to sup with Selenas and Hel, but his father ordered him to bathe first. Hel was a good cook, and he was tired of the same old Valeria food. Yet he also knew the brook was cold, not wanting to step in. Hearing someone approach, he turned to see Thulia coming down the path. She stopped short, laying a linen towel next to his clothes on the tree branch everybody used.

"Going in or coming out?" she snapped in a nettled tone, her gaze surveying tree-tops.

"I must take a bath, but the water is chilly," he admitted, hands covering his privates.

"Perhaps," she remarked brusquely, turning from him to find a stump and loosening boot ties, "People either bathe or stink like sheep. Get on with it. I'm in a hurry."

"Bathe with a woman?" he gulped, "I cannot do that!"

Thulia frowned, glancing to him, "Are you not thirteen, Safrax?"

"More than thirteen," he bragged, for he was.

"Then act your age. It's only water," she huffed, standing to remove her tunic, her expression dour, "And keep your gaze to yourself."

What could he do? Thulia seemed to be in a great rush, and she was taking her clothes off! In a flash he jumped into the deepest part of the pool, bruising the soles of his feet. It was freezing!—and Safrax was in agony, gasping from the chill as he sat to hurriedly soap himself, his eyes stinging even with eyes closed.

After flushing soap, he opened his eyes to see if they still burned, and he gazed in shock—*she's right here, and the pool is much too small!* She sat at the shallow end, her upper torso above water, not actually facing him, but he could finally view what he yearned to see the day Valeria removed Thulia's stitches. To him, she was not a regular person, but the Amazon who carried the world's greatest sword. She was chosen for the deeds she did because she had a man's strength… *but certes not a man's body.*

Thulia scrubbed herself until noticing his stare, glaring toward him, "Your eyes and mouth are open," she snapped, "Have you not seen a woman before?"

"Never like you," he admitted as he flushed deep red.

* * *

She shifted her body, trying to turn her back to Safrax, glancing his way as she continued washing. *The boy is rude, staring like an idiot. People have bathed in this brook for years and most have a semblance of propriety.* She wondered what he was thinking. *He's grinning, the little shit. Well, not really little, but still a shit.* Suddenly she realized the whole thing was rather comical. Ten years ago she would have bathed with her feet touching his, flaunting her charms for all their worth; and they were worth a fortune in the eyes of Heldrid, not to mention a countless multitude of mostly nameless yet not forgotten studs, and others like Stefan the horsebreaker, a true maven of the ultimate female form. Oh yes, she had her admirers.

In that distant past, she conveyed consummate charms, and perhaps she still had them! Safrax seemed rather young to show interest in her type of body, yet he certainly did. She peeked toward him again. *He's leering just like Frit at his age.* He leaned forward pretending to wash his feet while craning his neck, the sun infusing his hair to bright crocus as his eyes flicked her way. She moved sideways a little, giving him a colossal profile. *God forgive me for being a tease.*

Safrax washed slowly—as slow as he could!—wanting the moments to last, for they were becoming increasingly memorable. Thulia no longer had that irritated look and he felt less guilty about staring. She glanced his way again, raising her chin to claim, "This is how real women are built. Now you know."

"I certainly do," he admitted. Wanting to be polite, he added, "Thank you for showing me."

Thulia tossed her hair back with a quick tilt, continuing to soap herself while studying him closely. She ran her tongue along upper lip, wetting it thoroughly, "When I was your age I was an exhibitionist... long before we needed fig leaves."

Safrax wasn't sure what an exhibitionist was. He scrubbed even slower, enjoying the sight. In a quick move she rose to kneel before him, suds rolling down her thighs as she rinsed herself. In a flash she stood erect and arched her back. "There," she grinned proudly, "You've finally viewed a real woman's anatomy. It's a sin, but a small one."

He received a complete education in a single bath! With eyes still wide, he stopped gaping to courteously reply, "You're just like Venus."

She quickly returned, "Not quite. Venus doesn't get back-aches from the weight of her tits." Turning from him, she glanced back, "I hear you did well in battle. Do you still wish to become a cataphract?"

"That's my calling, I think. My Alan blood."

Leaving the pool, Thulia twisted around, "I spoke to your father. He thought I could give you a few pointers on lancing. Stefan knows trick riding, and perhaps Frit can teach swordsmanship. You're quite the man now, Safrax."

"I am?" he asked, not really sure what she meant. He had to be sixteen to be a man in the tribe's eyes.

"Oh, yes," she assured him, grinning all the more, "You've got a good stiffy on. I'll wager you could hang a coat on it."

*   *   *

At home, Thulia combed her hair until fingers cramped, yet she was ecstatic! Safrax turned into a fine adolescent, very polite and still sitting in the pool as she dressed and left. She hadn't done anything like that in years—very enlightening for both of them—and she glowed. *I still have attraction!*

She wore the most indecent skirt she could find, showing calves to the knee. Worst of all, she would mount her gelding with it. Riding required trousers, not flesh to saddle. Thulia had the longest legs of any woman in Ascentia, shapely with ankles thin and her thighs still lean. Frit always said, *"You have graceful legs,"* and the skirt would display them best. The day warmed fast, a time of year known as "Scythian summer." Everyone would be active outdoors when she rode through the village, all getting an eyeful, yet the skirt was only half of it.

Thulia found an old work tunic. It wrapped around her like a kaftan with no toggles to pop, yet the material was so worn she could see her fingers through it. For years she hadn't worn a belt, the lack of it hiding her bosom, but now she had to dress Fritigern style. Cinching a wide belt round her waist, she pulled the tunic loose enough to show a deep swath of flesh without revealing the scar. *Now that's what I call cleavage.* The old tunic seemed smaller than she remembered. In reality her bosom was bigger than it was three years ago, heavier and far lower than she wished. *If he liked them when they were bad, he'll really love them now*, she mused, adjusting her gold mirror as she sat at the table. The expression upon the young Alan's face said it all. She even looked good to an adolescent!

The episode at the pool gave her new-found hope. She reached to the table and picked up the glass vial of unguent. Only once had she worn perfume—for Heldrid, the man who gave it to her. Pulling the stopper, she pressed a finger around the rim, shaking the contents. *"It's Saracen jasmine mixed with ambergris. A gift for my goddess."*

Thulia rubbed a finger to thumb, bringing them to her nose, an exotic scent much like the flower itself, sweet and pungent both at once. Yes, given with love from Heldrid, the only man who truly adored her and all her flaws. She thought of him for long moments, sitting quietly at her table, a table so incredibly crude; and she leaned to it, running fingers over its rough surface carefully and lightly, avoiding splinters. Then she grasped the table-edge, squeezing hard... trying to hold back tears. *If only Frit could love me like you did.*

Enough of that!—dreams born in girlhood and best forgotten. She tipped the vial twice and stoppered it, applying a dab of jasmine behind each ear. *Probably enough to mask the scent of rut.* Love would be a finer stance, the most graced of emotions, yet her quest always wrought failure. *Well, Thulia dearest, rut will have to suffice, and that's the reality of it.* Certainly, the time was right for a good long rut. She would square-up with Xristos later... if she could ever commit the sin. *Make it multi-sins, maybe three or four wild rides.* Frit would reach great excitement, she was sure, for her bosom would bounce further than ever before.

She jumped from the stool, hearing her heart beat. *It's slamming through my rib cage, for he's only a mile away!* Thulia took several deep breaths, hoping the tunic held together until Frit ripped it from her. *It's old and expendable, ripe for a good shredding.* She could picture it torn from her, falling gossamer to the wild pucker-brush, and she felt giddy and appealing for the first time in far too long. Reaching down, she grabbed the mirror for one last look, checking her prodigious overhang and grinning broadly, finally admitting the truth, *I love acting like a slut.*

Tossing the mirror to the table, she raised a foot to the stool, checking her form. *Safrax called me Venus!* Swinging her leg to the floor, she stood erect, chin slightly raised; and a great, deep breath swept away years of indicting comments. The widow Thulia? Not upon the east's boundless steppe or the mystic mews of marbled Rome, nor the brightest glories of Alexandria, did another widow look like this.

Yes, indeed. The widow Thulia—queen of the garden, mother hen of lost souls, and keeper of the sword—had far more exotic talents.

Chapter 42: A Flame in the Hearth

Rodric pawed through the pork barrel in the salt shed, looking much like his informal signum, for he even had dark hair on the back of his hands; and he breathed heavily, sneck, sneck, like a feeding bear. A stockade enclosed the crude structure at wood edge, built to keep the other bears out. Barrels held salt pork, and hewn planks sagged from the weight of smoked hams. Leaning to a barrel with his huge gut squashed against it, he snecked away. He wasn't agile, not like a few years ago. Well actually, the Bear was always rotund but now he carried even more bulk.

His weight problem hindered all he did, even his fondest dreams. Rodric always wanted to ask the widow Thulia to marry him. He wasn't wealthy or well built, but he dreamt that she might say yes. She seemed lonely; and as of late, she became increasingly brusque. *Thulia needs a good man*, he mused, although aware he was not her type. She wasn't into bears.

His friend the thin man poked his head through the doorway, "You heard about the widow Thulia?

Rodric jumped! He was just thinking about her. *Maybe I'm telepathetic.* "No," he returned while lifting a chunk of fatback from the salt, "What about her?"

"She straddled her horse and went up to Frit's tavern."

"What do you suppose that means?" piqued the Bear, wiping salt from the pork and sniffing it. Sneck, sneck.

"A big confrontation if you ask me," the thin man claimed.

"She bring the Sword?" inquired Rodric as he dropped the chunk back in the barrel, smelly green stuff on it.

The thin man peered at his friend, his eyes to slits, "I don't think it's *that* kind of clash. She was dressed like a harlot."

"What was she wearing?" the Bear asked over his shoulder, fingering through the barrel to sniff another chunk.

"It was awesome!" the thin man gasped, "A skirt worn last when she was in her early teens and much too short. Imagine wearing a skirt while riding a horse?"

"That was it? Just a skirt?"

"Of course not, you idiot," retorted the thin man, "She had the thinnest linen tunic a woman could wear without being naked. Egyptian linen, I think. And it was belted, showing nipples the size of Jove-nuts!"

The Bear tossed the chunk back, turning around, "And I missed it."

"Well," snapped his friend, "If you weren't in here playing with your pork, you would've caught the greatest show ever seen in Ascentia."

* * *

When she arrived at the building site, a freeman stopped her progress, calling to Fritigern. He strode down the path, sans shirt, chisel in hand. "What's the fracas?" he demanded, then discovering who the trespasser was. "It's alright. Let her dismount."

Thulia slid from the gelding, her buttocks chafed. Yet she did her best to look attractive, a deep breath for starters. After Frit reached her, she noticed all the tree stumps to arch a leg on. Like the old days, she could hike the skirt up to thighs in some pretense. *Flash him a little womanhood*, an old ploy that always worked. "I understand I wasn't allowed up here until the tavern is finished," she cooed ever so smooth while giving her best grin, "But I had to see the progress."

"Good," he returned with a genuine smile, "There's a flame in the hearth. I figured you'd show up. When something's forbidden, you want it all the more."

"Oh, really," she huffed, "So you think you know my every thought?" He let her statement pass, probably assuming she was entering one of her defensive moods. *I guess I was!— and he caught it, as if reading my mind.*

Dismissing the crew, Frit gave them the rest of the day off; and in moments the site emptied, just the two of them left. As they walked up the path she finally saw the building some distance above. A strange design for a tavern, it loomed forty feet to the sky.

He walked in the lead and seemed more commanding than remembered. In former relationships, she was the one in charge. She felt slightly ill at ease with Frit having the upper hand, conducting himself as if he knew her next move. Thulia commented politely, "Did I ever thank you for the jade horse? If not, I certainly do."

"Had your name on it," he claimed, swinging around to face her, a far more handsome man than a few years back. When dismounting she saw his tunic draped across a stump, and he left it there, leading the way bare-chested. His arms and torso were tanned, wood chips upon his trousers. She stared at his chest and the ripple of muscled ribs; and his jaw seemed more squared, his gray eyes sharper. *Strange. I don't recall him looking this good.*

* * *

She looks hotter than a hearth in Jul and better built than ever. Folks never figured Transylvania harbored monsters like hers.

Frit initiated his strategy to wear Thulia ragged—drain her mental reserve and run those beautiful legs to exhaustion. He knew, for the first time in his life, he had her exactly where he wanted, for the Amazon was vexed beyond reason, dressed like a floozy and totally out of control. Her actions and demeanor reminded him of the old days, absolutely shameless and flaunting every charm she had. *Just like behind the hay pile.* She still had it in her, that wonderful touch of obscenity, *the queen of smut.* Following his every step, she was out of breath and eyeing him like choice beef.

He was in prime shape. Three years in the cavalry built him up, not to mention tree felling and shale hauling—his arms toned, his chest thicker, more muscled. Seeing him bare-chested, Thulia panted like a doe in heat. She stopped again to retie a boot lace. He simply waited, keeping his distance.

Ten paces further, she wiped her forehead with the back of a dramatic hand, staring intently while parting the top of her wrap-around tunic, showing a little cleavage. He pretended not to notice. His reserve was driving her to crass desperation; and he wondered how far she would go to seduce him, hoping for a real show. Sooner or later she would do something so raw it would make a prostitute blush. *You're a licentious woman, Thulia my love. A woman after my heart... and what not else. And I'm going to best you at your own game.*

*   *   *

At the same moment, life continued far below mountain paths.

The day seemed balmy for early autumn, and You-He rode slower than he wanted, his Sogdian kaftan ruffled by the breeze. Back at Ulmenia, the old spoon carver claimed he and Oxartes could now cross the Aluta upon a rebuilt bridge; and what's more, some Goth was finishing a big tavern up in Ascentia.

The mounts of Transylvania finally seemed accessible, making the amber trade all the easier, quicker, and more comfortable. You-He thought about his wife in Kashgar. She was comfortable, a Caucasian woman of the Yue-qi. He was tired of no comforts, wallowing across the Pontic Sea, traveling the stark trade road from Tyras to Ulmenia with its simple people and dark roadhouse. *Ah! Comforts very good!*

Gone were the days when he and his partner had to pitch a tent at riverside and bide their time. They waited and waited, that misanthrope Gunter bringing down amber when he pleased, not an hour or day quicker. The trade always took two weeks minimum with no comforts, no good wife, no rice—only hazel grouse or hares purchased from the catchermon, and the grouse were always too small to eat. You-He turned in his saddle, looking back toward his string of pack mules, his partner dallying behind them. "What you do! You too slow," he yelled.

Oxartes waved his comment off, "I had to relieve myself. I'll catch up in a moment."

"We must be quick. Very quick," You-He commanded.

The Sogdian retorted, "What's the hurry? We can't make it up into the hills for at least three or four days. We'll be sleeping in the old tent."

"I tell you many times. No like tent!" exclaimed the Serican, "Too small. Too uncomfortable. You-He want big tavern."

Yes, he could picture it, a giant Gothic tavern, and he wanted to get there very fast. Such a place would have a tub to bathe in, decent food, and a soft straw bed. *And big blonde women! Big Gothic women, so comfortable. Ah, with big Gothic thighs. Ohh!*

The thought of spending a night at the river grew tight in his chest. In the past, he lay there—*no sleep! Ulmenians tell wild stories, terrible things! Monsters all sizes, some one eye, others four leg. They might get this man!—Drag You-He away to horrible, uncomfortable death.* "Oxartes!" he yelled back.

"What now?" snapped the Sogdian.

"You bring curved sword?"

"Of course," Oxartes retorted, "Are you worried. All the monsters are dead now, slain by the Amazon."

"No," the Serican explained, "You-He not worried. He brave. Just wonder if bring sword… maybe for peeling apple."

*   *   *

What's going on? He was leading her through half of Transylvania! *Perhaps Frit is balmy.* Thulia was trying harder than ever to get him to look at her but he increased his lead, striding at a quick pace. She was worn out, her legs killing her! "Hold it a moment," she pleaded, "Walking a mountain-side gives a woman hot flashes." She loosened the front of her tunic a little more, showing deeper cleavage. He didn't seem to notice, and she was really beginning to worry. She thought he'd make a grope for her a half hour ago—perhaps a stand-up quickie in the bushes—but it never materialized. Perhaps he was injured in a skirmish and lost his manhood, now a eunuch. *Dear God in Heaven, I pray his lance is what it was. Thank you, Amen. Oh yes, and forgive me for what I'm about to do… if I ever get the chance.*

Another hundred yards up the path Thulia was ready to scream, and she *really was* hot and incredibly frustrated. "Wait! It's getting even warmer up here," she complained. As he turned around, she took the deepest breath she could, spreading her tunic to the longest cleavage ever exposed; for she paled the Moors, even Aethiopians! This was the ultimate tasteless adjustment, even revealing her scar. If she parted the material further, her bosom would spill out.

Do you have any idea what you're doing to me! her thoughts screamed, *For God's sake, man, tear my clothes off!*

Frit simply ambled on, turning from the main path to a smaller one until they came to a horse barn. Taking her inside, he pointed to a gelding, "It's new and not yet a warhorse, but much like the one I rode in the old days. I just wanted you to see it. It's slightly off-white, but still white."

She was beginning to think rumors were true. He seemed addled, perhaps a bad axe blow to the head in Pannonia. *Who gives a damn about a horse? That's not what I came for!*

*   *   *

The old crone cackled in outrage, spittle dripping from corners of her mouth, "I tell you, she was indecent! Christian women do not dress like that." She sprayed fluid as she spoke, warts on her nose bright purple, eyes wild as her deep jaw worked to find the next sentence.

Selenas looked to the mountain from his doorway, gazing back to the aged basket-maker as Hel peered from the rear. *Well, I'll be damned*, he mused. Yet he asked, "She rode through the village like that?"

"In a skirt!" cried the old crone, wiping saliva away, "If Heldiga or Heldigard showed that much flesh, I'd pull the latch-string, lock 'em out! This is a Christian community, pastor."

Every time she said pastor, spittle flew. Through the seasons he tried to duck, but never knew when the word would strike. Always without warning. At the moment he was in a quandary, none of his business what a woman wore, although it sounded like Thulia had gone a little overboard. He turned to his wife, "Perhaps we should step outside, Hel."

They left Waldrid and Sesca to their studies, both children at the table learning basics of writing. Not the kind of gossip youngsters should hear. Once they were outside, the old crone spat, "That's not all! She wore a tunic showing everything. Everything!" Working herself to thither, she slavered even louder, spit drooling from her chin and soaking her smock, "This is not Durostorum, pastor! We have a proper community here. I want you to do something about it. Other women will start dressing like harlots, and where will we be? Sodom and Gomorrah?"

The presbyter wiped a sleeve across his face. What could he do? "Thulia doesn't usually wear clothes like that. Not that I can recall," he explained.

The old crone became enraged all the more, her voice now hysterical, "You don't understand! He bosom was slamming up and down!—all the men watching, thinking dirty thoughts," and she tore at her smock, pulling it high, "See these! Well, hers are far worse. Gigantic and no higher! A disgrace beyond all civility." Realizing she went too far, the old crone worked her smock back down to stand there red in the face. "Well," she sputtered, "See what happens? It's a contagion. She started it!—and before long this entire village will go straight to Hell."

* * *

They finally reached the huge building, its entrance a granite arch with double doors, both with intricately carved crickets to welcome a visitor, one door holed for a large key. Frit opened it, Thulia stepping through first. She stood in an ante room no smaller than the largest cabin in Ascentia, with knee-high benches lining its walls and another set of double doors at the far end.

"This is the mud room," he explained casually.

Thulia gawked at it. *Mud room for whom? A giant?* Knowing she had him cornered, the Amazon raised a foot to a bench, arching her leg to its ultimate form. *He always liked long limbs.* Showing flesh well above the knee, she complained, "What a walk. See the scratches from the underbrush? Look!—abrasions all the way to my thighs." And in desperation, she hiked the skirt to the bronze sheen of poorly hidden womanhood.

"Nice legs, Thulia. Weathered the seasons well, perhaps a scratch or two." Frit leaned to casually pat an inner thigh, his fingers almost there but not quite.

That's it? No grope? And she slammed her foot back to the floor in total disgust.

Upon reaching the second entry, he swung a door open for her, the inner room huge. Flat shale stretched out before her, sweeping beyond upright posts hewn massive in strength. A central hearth burned eight feet round, and she could actually feel the heat where she stood, the smoke rising forty feet to an eight-sided roof, a perfect octagonal exit in its center.

"The Great Room, my banquet hall," Frit noted, "Perhaps we can have dinner later."

"Think it's big enough for us?" she returned.

Upon the walls hung bucklers, swords, and pair of crossed lances, not true ones but light practice lances just like they used in youth. A table circled at twelve feet round, bright and smooth; and the room loomed beyond massive doors leading to God knows where? Never had she seen anything like it—as if stemming wild from childhood fantasy.

"A round table?" she gasped, for it was totally different than Heldrid's traditional long-bench.

He grinned broadly, "Should there be disparity between host or wife, friend or gast, Christian or pagan? No one sits at this table's head," then priding, "Well, what do you think of the place?"

"It looks like some king's abode," she gasped in awe, wanting to see the rest of it. And then it stuck her—just like lightening hit the sword! "This is a frigging castle!"

He strode to the round table, picking up a bronze key, tossing it to her. "The key is yours, along with the rest of it. You saw my white horse, so both requirements have been met."

"What requirements?" she asked, not getting his drift.

He sat upon the table, legs dangling, sweeping his arm to encompass the room, "It has a name—Castra Ascentia—a castle built halfway up a mountain. There you have it."

"Have what? I really don't understand you, Frit."

He jumped down and paced to her, speaking clearly, *"The man I marry shall ride a white horse and live in a castle halfway up a mountain.* Your exact words. Repeated oft enough, were they not?"

Her countenance darkening, she replied, "We've been through this before. The answer is no."

"Did you not say it?" he demanded, his own voice hardening.

"We were no more than children, just a romantic allusion."

"You were certainly woman enough back then and I was no younger than Safrax is now. And a woman's word and a man's actions should be respected," he claimed, grasping her shoulders.

"Don't you touch me," she demanded as she stepped back.

He strode firm toward the hearth. In a flash!—he swung partially to her, "What will you do about it? Kick me in the groin?"

"Don't be foolish."

"Only my future wife sleeps here," he growled with a sideward glance, pointing to her hand, "You hold the key. Not me. The door is unlocked and you can leave, for I'll not hold you to the past. But you'll not walk, and both of us know it."

She stared at it, looking back to the man.

Frit paced back to her, his tone commanding, "You came up here searching for a one night stand? It doesn't work that way. Not anymore. You're going to end up in a permanent and proper bed with one man—final—and you're not Amazon enough to stop me. This is it, Thulia!—no more excuses."

"I'm barren and not going to remarry," she insisted with another pace to the rear, her voice wavering in a resolve no stronger than the statement itself.

"Well, I don't give a damn about fertility. Waldrid can take up my father's banner, but that's not the real point."

"What is?"

He reached to her, slowly running a finger down her cleavage, his incomparable touch. Frit pulled back, eying her intently, "It's about you and me. Nothing else. You'd better leave if you wish to remain the good Christian widow, for I'll not touch a woman who'll not be my spouse."

She felt exhausted and totally drained, not knowing which statement to answer, "I cannot."

"Cannot what?" he demanded, blood coursing in his veins, yet a voice solid and controlled, "I'm the man for you, Thulia. I have not one redeeming quality. I like cheap beer, bad tits, and riding 'til my ass chafes. I hate reading and small children, they get on my nerves, and I even let women slap me around." He tucked a finger beneath her chin, tipping it as if studying an artifact, "And look at yourself—blunter than a pounded post, crass and overbuilt, about as lewd as they come and you slap men around. We're the perfect match."

He was correct!—yet making the statement sound ludicrous. No man knew and loved her like he did. She lived in a cabin and he replaced it with a castle. From childhood he was her destiny—the Prince and the Slut.

With shaking hands, she unbuckled the belt, setting herself free. The tunic fell open, her treasure finally released as it plunged to natural form. She found herself panting again, her heart slamming in her chest. Thulia tilted her head back, tongue moistening upper lip... just like the good old days... and she would play the game to the hilt, lance with him to the end, and hoping the end never came. She backed another step, bumping into the table, trying to keep a straight face, "You... you... bullheaded wastrel. Your image is flawed."

"Really," he grinned, slipping a hand around her waist, pulling her to him.

She could hardly breathe! Yet she managed to whisper, "You've got the touch and tongue, the finest lance I ever dueled with, and you're honest."

He offered no answer, meeting her lips with his, pressing with a hunger unfulfilled in a long war's span. Her own tongue chased his in circles, both light-headed as they searched for all that was soft and hard. They fell backward upon the round table, so incredibly smooth they slipped to its center while tearing at this belt and that one, tossing every stitch of clothes to warm shale as hands found keys to old dreams.

"Pardon my urgent haste," he mumbled, "But I cannot wait."

"For what?" she purred back, "A light lunch? Or the *proper bed*?"

Chapter 43: A Giving Woman

After the Ascentians discovered Frit's big structure was actually a castle, Rodric decided to build a real tavern, his sisters employed as wenches, every tavern needing a wench, especially a Gothic one. He knew tavern rumors had spread all the way to Ulmenia and beyond. His mother wasn't too thrilled about the enterprise, yet she tolerated it because it would give Heldiga and Heldigard employment beyond basket-making. The twins were upstanding Gothic women, a little heavy like himself. *Well, to be honest, they put a full-grown bear to shame.*

The rotund man built his tavern using every freeman he had, finished in three days. Of course the roof was none too tight and you could see through the walls; and should it ever rain (a distinct possibility), everyone would be uncomfortable. When the place made a little coin, Rodric would undertake improvements. He was realistic in hiring the thin man as tavern-keeper, knowing his friend wouldn't eat the profits.

The tavern was finished just in time. With the last bench shaved smooth, a pack train of mules came to a stop just before dusk. You-He and Oxartes slid from their mounts, quite sore and tired, evidently not impressed. Rodric conceded that the place was smaller than original rumor claimed—not exactly the size of a castle. Yet he was a fine host in their welcome.

"This Gothic tavern?" snapped You-He, "Look more like pig sty."

"I'll have the shavings and bark removed in no time," claimed the Bear.

"Well, it's better than a tent," grinned Oxartes to his partner.

"Ah, so. Very true," the Serican agreed, "But where big Gothic women with big Gothic thighs?"

Rodric was amazed the news spread so quick! He only hired his sisters that afternoon; and he proclaimed, "Oh, they're inside."

*   *   *

Thulia awoke next to Frit, the bed roomy and soft, a six foot cadurcum stuffed over-full. Beyond their chamber, the sun rose between mountains to their east, the early light piercing open shutters to stab the woolen coverlet. She prodded Frit to awaken him; for he was a little tired after a marathon performance, a lancer extraordinaire. She wasn't sure of the actual number of days, three she thought, a little sore herself, making up for lost years as they rutted like a buck and doe. Fluffing a pillow she reached back to pull it higher, sitting to view her big mirror across the bedchamber. Frit transported wagon-loads of her belongings up from Threisbaurg, even her wardrobe closet, the other furnishings from the house of Thiudebalth, an operation well planned from start to finish. Its immensity was a gesture of great love—an entire furnished castle—yet he would never have a son to inherit it.

She shook Frit again. All he could do was mumble, "What?"

"I've been lying awake thinking, and I've changed my mind. I see no reason to marry. After all, you've got me anyway."

He rolled over and sat up straight, "What? To quote you—*We've been through this before.*"

"Well, I'm not. They'll expect me to have a child, whispering behind my back."

"Thulia! If we don't marry, they'll whisper even more. You're living in sin."

She hadn't thought of that. He was right, but she couldn't let him win. So she quipped, "Let them think what they will."

"What's wrong with you this morning?" he asked while jumping from the bed to grab his clothes from the chair.

"After Heldrid died, I vowed not to remarry. With me, wedlock doesn't seem to work, but affairs usually do. Sorry."

He stood over her with brows furrowed and hands on hips, "Sorry? You'll be damned sorry you ever said it," and he stormed from the bedchamber.

She arose to her wardrobe and dressed, slipping on a tunic and trousers. Thulia assumed he'd be less upset. They always had arguments but the look on his face spelled fury. She didn't want to lose him again. He was her man!—all she ever dreamed of. Yet she justified her decision, *He'll get over it. What more can he want? He's got the Amazon and her legendary rack.*

Time passed and she went to the kitchen, rummaging for something morning-ish, porridge or something like it. All she found was beef—salted beef, dried beef, and beef fresh and bloody. *Where's the woman food? Not a thing to make porridge with. A cupboard full of meat. A woman cannot survive on beef alone.* She slammed the doors, *Men! They eat like wolves.* Taking a brimstone match, she struck it on the Roman stove, warming up the sliding grill with dry hardwood. *Well, it's better than Pigfoot's salt mutton.* She was famished, not eating much of anything for the past several days, burning a lot of energy. Standing before the grill, she tossed a cut of beef to it… waiting and waiting. *Done enough*, she figured.

Thulia had finished eating half the charred slab, a little raw in the middle, when Frit entered the kitchen with sword in hand. Prodding her, he ordered, "Alright, stand up!" As she jumped to feet, he poked the blade to her butt, "Get out front and mount your horse."

"Why should I?" she retorted, yet walking for the mount and feeling her rump to see if he drew blood. He was acting balmy again! Was he throwing her out?

*   *   *

Morning came early for Rodric as he removed excess material from around the tavern. He wanted the Sogdian traders to see the place looking better after their night's rest. With the last pine chips dumped in the woods, he looked up to see Frit and the Amazon riding toward him, something unusual about it. How often did any man hold the reins of her horse? Not that he could recall.

Thulia looked dour, Rodric hearing her demand, "Where do you think you're taking me?"

The rotund man caught no answer as he rushed to the road, snecking away in short gasps. Reaching them, he proclaimed, "A fine morning, Fritigern, Thulia. Where you headed this early?"

Frit snapped, "I'm ending an illustrious widow's career."

"No you're not!" cried Thulia.

Frit stopped his mount in its tracks, swinging to pierce with iron eyes, "Jump down and flee. I'll not chase you. Never again!"

She sat tall, glaring back; and Rodric knew he stepped into a mighty argument. Both seemed incensed over none of his business. He searched for the right words, hoping they'd continue their quarrel beyond his tavern, yet wishing they'd end it, "I hope your day ends better than it begins."

"It will for me," snapped Frit, "As for her? She will lose something dear."

Thulia flicked eyes to the rotund man, raising her chin defiantly, adding a pout for dramatic effect, "I'll never speak to him again! Take note of it, Rodric—the last words he'll ever hear from these lips."

*   *   *

Arriving at the presbyter's house, Frit slammed his sword-butt to the door, causing a racket until Hel opened it. Then he stabbed Thulia in the rump again, forcing her inside. *I'll not do it,* she vowed, now furious. Selenas jumped from the table, breakfast upon his chin and mouth agape. Waldrid and Sesca sat where they were, evidently too hungry to fear the weapon. Rushing around Frit and Thulia, Hel scurried to her husband's side.

Frit spat, "Marry us. Not tomorrow or a moment from now—but right NOW!"

"Don't you dare!" shouted Thulia, "He's daft and I'm not speaking to him."

Selenas paced forward, trying to sound brotherly, "We all should calm down. Time enough for nuptials—and this is not it, or the right place. Perhaps a church might be more appropriate."

"Now," ordered Frit, jamming the sword to Thulia's butt again.

Snapping straight from the prod, she declared to herself, *If he thinks I'll ever sleep with him again, he's got a surprise coming.* Both children smiled at her between spoonfuls of something, probably the porridge she wanted earlier. *What's so funny?*

Hel moved to the fore and grasped her husband's arm, "I think you should do it, dear. This can be an informal wedding."

Selenas studied her, then his brother, mumbling, "Do you Fritigern, son of Thiudebalth, take this woman as your wife?"

"I certainly do!" Frit huffed, "If I don't take her, who in Hell else will?—and for little good and mostly worse, or whatever it is. This mind changing business is going to stop right here and now. You can inform her for me, since we're no longer on speaking terms."

Selenas kept a straight face, "Do you, Thulia, daughter of Rusus, take this man as your husband?"

"No!" she barked, "Never in a million years," the sword prodding her again, "Well, maybe," the prod becoming more forceful, "Alright! Yes, damn it, but not a word will I utter to him. Ever! Tell him that."

Waldrid and Sesca looked to each other, not hearing that kind of language every day. Hel giggled and Selenas grinned broader.

Stepping from sword-point, Thulia remained indignant, finally huffing, "What's so comical? The man forced me to marry him, the wretched cur."

Frit grabbed Thulia's shoulder and swung her to him, slapping the sword hilt in her hand. "Go ahead. Tell her she can kill me for my great mistake! What did I do?—married the biggest bitch north of the Bridge."

Thulia glanced to the sword in her hand, "Is this legal? Are we really married?"

"Quite," prided Selenas, "Hel is the official witness."

Silence ensued, the children still sitting. Then Thulia looked straight to Frit's eyes and took a huge breath, "Yes I am. You can tell him I'm the biggest bitch this side of Aethiopia. If I were any smaller, he wouldn't have married me."

* * *

The weather held warm, now a week beyond their fiery wedding. Two freemen carried a log down the path, both eyeing Thulia while stumbling. Not many women felled trees. She swung her axe accurately, hoping to fell two more pines before noon, her goal being twenty a day.

After Selenas told Frit to kiss the reluctant bride, she fought him off in a fine show. When they kissed, it was fantastic! *"I'm still not going to speak to him,"* she claimed, wiping lips with a deft tongue, *"Unless he kisses me like that again."* She always let him win. On the way to Selenas' cabin, she could have jumped from the saddle at any time. Better it was to feign anger, keep Frit a little worried by a taste of her spirit. He liked to argue too, never abusively, even the sword prods carefully jabbed. They were good at, pretending to confute each other. Finally she had her pigheaded man.

With a dozen additional swings, chips flew until the pine cracked at the stump and began its fall. Stepping back, she leaned to axe-handle as the tree toppled slowly, ripping branches from other pines as it crashed to the brush. Letting the axe drop, Thulia felt her waist and stomach, *Just like I was before birthing Sesca,* back to trim, an awesome body for a twenty-three-year-old mother.

Walking a few paces, she found the tenth pine and began cuts at knee level, one swing downward, the next coming up from a low angle. She felt a pride unknown for many years, the freemen of Castra Ascentia watching a woman perform man's work. The axe bit hard, with chips flying from each swing. She was born for it, a pride not found in a garden or before the hearth, never a decent cook and she could burn anything to a crisp. Nor did she learn how to spin or weave, all beyond her world. Such talents were not her forte. Through her besotted mentor and singular parent, she became a warrior by nature, good with a sword and better with the lance. She had

Old Hempstalk to thank for her formative years. He wrought the Amazon.

At the felled pine, bow-saw men began trimming branches, turning out another log. With the castle almost completed, they were building a palisade to encompass the compound. *One more tree before Frit and I meet at the bath for noon interlude.*

*   *   *

The sun reached the day's high point, and Frit stood outside the palisade surveying an encircling trench designed like those at Durostorum and Vindobona. The entire Christian population would find protection within its walls. *Almost time for the interlude.* At last he tamed the Amazon, yet he knew she would never be entirely tamed; and it seemed fitting, for he wished not to lose the Thulia of his dreams. Her unbridled spirit—that great burning flame—was not always easy to deal with, yet he loved her grit and physical prowess. She could swing an axe with the best, a talent learned from the charcoal man, the full story a true nightmare. In their collective, her many trials would have destroyed a weaker woman.

And he knew why she balked at wedding him. She felt incomplete, satisfied with a role as his lover yet feeling inadequate as a wife. Frit wondered who could alleviate her guilt of infertility, her elusive sense of worth. Usually this sort of problem fell to an understanding tribal priest like Merjands, a man steeped in ethereal knowledge. He raised his eyes from Thulia to the sky, *Why didn't I think of it before?*

*   *   *

Soon bitter winds would push snow through door cracks, hardwoods now void of foliage; and the Sabbath held a frost as Selenas and Hel stood outside the church, the laity departing after services and saying good-tide. On the other side of the doorway Frit stood proudly, his arm tight around

Thulia's waist. This was his baptismal day, a veteran of war yet a moral man, and now a member of the Gothic Church. She looked up to him with a warm smile. *Yes, she does,* mused Selenas, *Thulia looks up to him. He has her under control... more or less. Perhaps it's his bearing honed in Pannonia.*

When the last parishioner left, Thulia went back into the church, his brother nodding to Selenas. Hel and Frit discussed the children as he went to meet Thulia near the altar. She looked stunning with a skirt to ankles and a wool smock under a light coat. *A pretty woman, more so than in her youth.*

One of the servants brought Sesca down to his house several times a week and the girl usually slept over. When grown, she would look like Thulia, hopefully not quite so busty. He would stand by what he said—Sesca and Waldrid were good for each other, both living through dark traumas.

At the altar, he acknowledged Thulia yet noticed the troubled expression, "We want you and Frit to come down for dinner this week. Do you need something?"

"Yes," she stated frankly, "A confession."

"What have I done?" Selenas winced.

"I mean my confession to the Lord," she admitted sheepishly.

In surprise, he moaned, "That could take a long time."

"Then let's get in over with. I want to set things straight."

In his capacity of presbyter, Selenas found two stools and they faced each other before the altar, seemingly appropriate. "Go ahead, God is listening," his voice shaky, knowing he was buried somewhere in the coming dissertation.

"Well," she began, her arms wrapped around knees, "I have slept with, I don't know, maybe a hundred boys and men. Maybe two hundred. I forget their names and never bothered to count."

"Quite some time in the past?"

"Yes, of course," she admitted, "Then I had a child beyond wedlock and conceived another one. God knows the father."

"He certainly does," Selenas agreed, his face reddening, "But that was also in the past. He forgives old sins and true repentance in the wink of an eye."

"It was quite some time ago," she affirmed, hesitating a moment, "I've never told my husband the identity of Sesca's father."

"More than a month ago, over dinner, a certain presbyter told your future husband who Sesca's sire was. Between mistakes, Sesca's father tries to be a good man."

Thulia reached to his hand, squeezing it, a glow to her smile, "I suppose what I really want to confess is... I cannot give my husband a child. I dwell upon it, and it makes me feel useless."

Of all presbyters, he knew what she and her husband lived with. "Do you think the Lord views you as useless? You?—who have slain giants, faced evil with goodness, saved lives from the axe of death and sword of repression? Each of us has worth in the Lord's eyes. Some women bear children, some contribute in other ways."

The presbyter sat in guilt, once using her for his gratification, promising to wed her and then abandoning her for a nubile. Back then, he was self-centered, immature, and she was forced into a life with a misanthrope. *Ah, the trials of Thulia. I was one of them.* Had he counted months, he would have known Sesca was his daughter, yet Thulia never mentioned pregnancy as leverage. He took and Thulia gave. She salvaged his soul after Lilia's death, and then brought Hel to his life. Thulia used Sesca to pull Waldrid out of his own shell after his mother's violent end. By finishing the gardens, she replanted hope, driving off the muse of death. She restored the Lord's grace upon them all!

How can she not know her merit? He reached for her hand, "God gave you the gift of giving, Thulia. You always were a giving woman. Even as a girl you gave willingly—honest to your very essence. You gave to a selfish young man who never appreciated who you were, and you rescued him in his darkest hour. You give... and by giving and expecting nothing in return you receive God's blessing. To the Lord you have great worth."

She must have known it was true, for Thulia wrought a big grin as tears formed at the same time. They arose from the stools. He hugged her tight, and she wept upon his sacramental robe... as he did on her shoulder.

*   *   *

Castra Ascentia seemed quiet, the servants cleaning the other nine rooms, especially Sesca's bedchamber. Frit was forever giving the girl something new, increasing her room's clutter. In the kitchen, Thulia stood at the Roman stove, stuffing more firewood under the grill as her daughter stood tip-toe on a stool, curious about this and that. *Maybe this whitefish needs to cook faster. It seems too soft.*

"Is Frit my father now?" asked Sesca, peering to the broiling fish, its skin sticking to the grill as its aroma filled the room.

"Would you like him to be?"

"Oh, yes. I like Frit. He tells funny stories and smiles a lot. He's going to give me a mare when I'm big enough to ride. That's what he said. He'll be my *pater* now. That's what the Romans say. I can spell it—*Pe Ay Tee Ee Rr—pater*. Who is my real father, anyway? The conservator? He could not have been my father because he never smiled. Never."

My God! Thulia chuckled, *Talk about talking! She runs along at thirty miles an hour, faster than a horse,* and she began laughing, for her daughter seemed to be making up for all the years of saying nothing. She tried flipping the whitefish, but it fell apart as flakes dropped to the fire below. *I should have boiled it... but it's too late now.*

Frit was down in Ulmenia, gone for a few days. While there, he would purchase new spoons, for she burned most of what they had. They burst into flames like kindling! *Why would anyone make spoons from wood?—you have to be an Ulmenian, I guess.* Spoon-makers were a simple bunch, especially the younger one. She turned from the grill, grasping Sesca to sit her down on the stool, "I cannot name your real father. It might hurt you, or maybe him, and I would rather see us all happy."

"Does he know?" Sesca quizzed.

"Oh, yes, and he loves you very much."

"Is he Frit?"

Thulia stood in a quandary, the fish burning and Sesca not leaving well-enough alone! She tried scraping the whitefish from the grill into a pan, more of it falling to the coals as the spoon caught afire. *What got the child on this tangent, anyway!* She blew on the spoon to put out the flames, then answered, "No, not Frit, although your mother wanted him to be... and he did too. Do you understand, my sweet?"

"Certainly," replied Sesca, kicking her legs back and forth, wanting to stand back up again, "He's my father now, and I always call him Papa, anyway. But who was my father when I was in your tummy?"

Thulia gave up, squatting to grab the child's flying limbs, "Your real father is Selenas."

Sesca stopped moving her legs, her eyes big, "No! Selenas is my uncle. He's not my father, too."

"He really is, but say nothing until I get a chance to tell him you know. Will you do that?"

"Yes," grinned Sesca, "But this is very mixed up. Selenas is my father but I call him uncle. And Frit is my uncle but I call him *Papa*."

Canto Five
FORGIVENESS
Anno 360
Eight years later

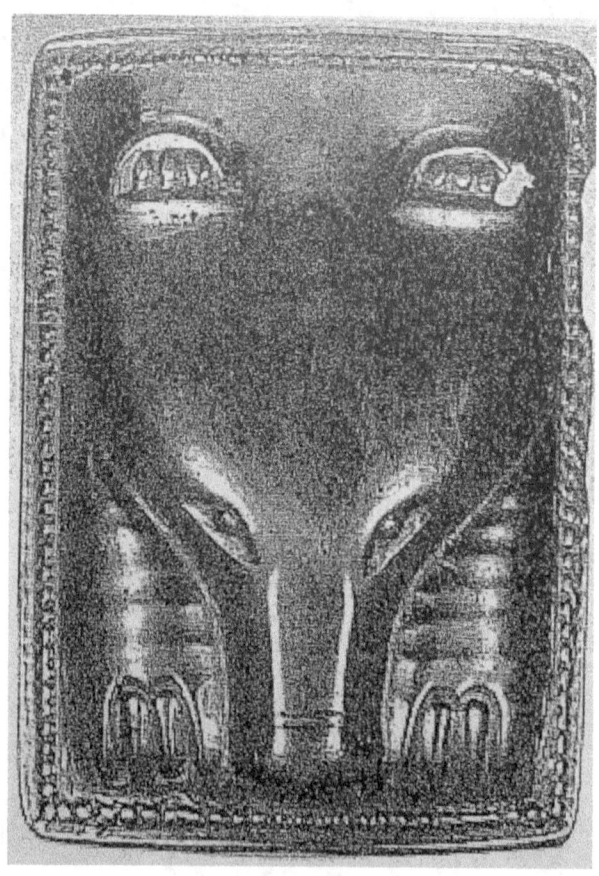

Chapter 44: The Earth Stone

The late afternoon seemed boring to Rodric; and his tavern—now known as the Bear's Den—was much too empty. And then, in a door's sweep, the old man entered. He appeared no more aged than recalled through a lapse of fifteen years. *What's he doing here in Ascentia?* Rodric waddled out from behind his thermospodium, abandoning his stew to welcome a potential and revered guest. "Mine Goten himinims," he sputtered, "Merjands! Wonders never cease. I assumed the Proclaimer *went around the bend*, as they say."

Adjusting his satchel, and with a rise of his staff, the sage announced, "Ah, to be eternally old?—a blessing and a curse. What a journey, strenuous for these aged legs."

"Welcome to the Bairgs-ahei," Rodric puffed, "Please sit at the long-bench and let me take your walking stick. New is it not?

"New to me. I found it in my path. It was dropped, I think, by a fleeing god or perhaps a blind soothsayer who found his sight," and he passed it to the innkeeper while dropping to the bench.

"Oh, it's a fine staff," gasped Rodric, "Deftly carved and topped with a quartzen orb. I cannot recall another like it."

"Stellar is the word, exceedingly rare—an Earth Stone to heal the Mother's womb. With all the years packed upon me, I cannot remember one finer. If memory serves untarnished, Nero had a crystal of like size, only rose-colored. He would view the games through it, for it magnified each trifling event and raised mere cuts to expansive gore. Do I smell venison?"

"Yes you do. I have a few bowls left. Not much fat there, but tasty; for I use herbs and pepper to bring it up to fame. No better stew will be found in these mounts," and he wheezed his way back to the thermospodium, sliding the crock's cover aside and ladled three goodly scoops to a perfect Ulmenian bowl, questioning, "What brings you up here? More than the blooms of Junius, I'll wager."

Merjands cracked a half-smile, adjusting his black robe to tuck his cinnabar between knees, "I was wondering, perchance, if there might be a woman hereabouts… who sits upon a rock at a deep-green lake."

"Robust?"

"Oh, quite. And strong-willed."

"You'll find her at the lake until sundown, then at Castra Ascentia a mile up the road. She's the Fisher King's wife. You remember Fritigern?"

*   *   *

Ah, yes! Fritigern the patient angler, an Apollo for this temporal world, mused the old sage, his smile far broader than usual. After all the hints, the subliminal plantings, the urgings and goading, the blatant implorements!—she married the correct man. *Oh how I love it when a dream sprouts wings.*

*   *   *

Thulia sat at the lectus watching hearth-smoke ascend in long, gray curls. They wisped upward to the octagonal exit, as Sesca reposed behind her, now a graceful young woman serene in sleep. Selenas was down at Constantinople with Bishop Wulfilas at the Arian Council, and the rest of Ascentia's able-bodied men were out in the forest clearing a road with Frit overseeing construction. The Black Huns were moving westward, having ravaged Caspia and now the Alans northeast of the Crimea. The Greutungi would be next in their path; and eventually the Huns would reach Tyrfingi Gothia. Frit's new road would be an escape route onto the Great Western Steppe in Pannonia.

With the castle quiet, and being more or less alone, Thulia found a marbled jar of honey in the kitchen, and now her index finger was all sticky from using it as her impromptu spoon. She licked it again, savoring a sweetness missed in childhood. In awhile Thulia would awaken Sesca. *Better in her bed than here on the couch. Thank you, Lord, for a fine daughter.*

Moonlight angled down to where she was; and in a pensive mood she mused upon her other child, the flames blurred as she viewed her past.

In a dark wood she knelt before the Augur's Stone, his tools upon it, both old and carried down from a land beyond the Amber Shore. No less than heaven's stars had seen their victims. The iron blade curved sharp beneath a gold-wired grip, and the bronze hook carried an antler handle, yellow-brown from unknown age. Ufar carried the fatted lamb to the Stone, placing it gently; and in one quick swipe the augur ran his knife across its throat. She watched blood puddle on the stone to run along a groove, dripping to the bronze bascauda upon the ground. Earlier, Merjands came to the horse barns looking for her, his cinnabar wisping in the wind.

"But who gave the fatted lamb?" she had asked.

He withheld the donor's name, simply claiming, "An eldermon, my dear."

"Why?" she wished to know.

"You are in your third term, so a concerned elder offered the lamb."

At the grove, Ufar carried the bascauda to where she knelt, Thulia unwrapping her tunic, pulling it aside. She raised her bosom as Ufar's finger dipped to the blood. He drew the sign across her swollen navel—a circle, a phallus, and another circle—the mark of a boy-child; and he raised his arms toward the sky, "Let this woman who has dropped a daughter bring forth a son. Let the tribe increase. For this we ask the Fructifier." Ufar avoided Freyja's name for fear of bespoiling his incantation. Freyja knew who she was. He returned to the stone, setting the bascauda next to the sacrifice. The augur opened the lamb's cavity, poking this way and that with his bronze hook, pulling at the entrails until they spilled to the altar's surface. He stared intently, checking for signs, and smiled broadly, "It shall be a boy-child. Blessed be the Fructifier and all her children."

Thulia was overjoyed as she walked home, discovering that Pigfoot had arrived from the horse barns early, sitting upon his stool and sullen. He stood to demand, "What is that?"

"A fatted lamb," she replied curtly, "I shall broil it for you on the spit."

"Where did it come from?"

"I was summoned before the augur. An eldermon donated it as the sacrifice."

"An eldermon?" he spat, "It was given by your lover, was it not? I married a tramp who humiliates me before the priests."

Thulia avoided an argument, placing the lamb to the table, "I'll get firewood. By the time your sister brings Sesca home, we shall eat lamb."

"It's tainted by the seed of another man!" he yelled, "I'll not take a bite of it."

She walked from him and went outside, leaning to the woodpile. Her fingers twitched as she held her distended belly, grasping pieces of kindling with her free hand. Then she went back through the open doorway....

*　　*　　*

"He tripped me... too dark inside to see him... and then he kicked and kicked."

"The man took bloody revenge, did he not?" sighed Merjands, "You have three broken ribs and lost your child. My heart aches far less than yours. To lose a son?" He knew the answer, at a loss for words. *The old healer wrapped the fetus in linen, placing it in a basin, then knelt beside her, brushing a hand across her forehead.* "The bleeding has stopped and bruises will heal, yet things like this can destroy more than the child, the very mother herself. I want you to stop by my house, not for instruction but simply to talk. I listen tolerably well, ask nothing in return-- only that you feel better up here," *and he tapped his temple.*

Thulia wept, yet nodded yes.

"I profess not to be a doctor of the head," *he admitted,* "But if a man or woman goes from my house feeling better about some great cataclysm, then I am better for it." *He paused, gifting his benign smile,* "So, I want you to visit more often. Will you do that for yourself?"

She nodded yes again.

Then he added, "I believe not so much in the old gods as I do in the Godhead. You have no concept of who you really are, blessed by the highest ideal—your desire to protect those who cannot defend themselves—a far higher quest than guarding the land. You are guided by the Godhead. Do you understand?"

She really didn't, nodding as if she did.

He stood, cradled the basin, and stepped to the door. Merjands turned back, arching a thumb to the world outside, "That man ran off to the horse barns claiming he had the *perfect right to do this. He believes in revenge, nothing else, certainly not the Godhead, so he will destroy himself. Do not fall to hate and die from it." And he left, closing the door quietly.*

*   *   *

Sesca was snoring and a little heavy to carry. Thulia would let her sleep on the lectus. Standing, she reached over and placed another log in the hearth, then sitting again to dip honey and eye flames in remembrance, a boy-child dead and her only chance to have a son. No doubt the eldermon was Heldrid; and his concern for her—the fatted lamb—drove Pigfoot to murder, love creating hate. She hoped the Lord would deliver his soul from where it burned, for he was aided to the lower house by her infidelity. Her gaze followed the shaft of moonlight upward… to where God stood in judgment, master of all that is. She knew his great truth, no longer bitter and finally accepting her barren womb. The calamities of life were as much her fault as not. *You reap what you sow.* At last, she could forgive those who trespassed against her, the first man weak in flesh, raping his own daughter, the second unable to understand why she wasn't a virgin.

The trek from the horse barns was a difficult one. She received help along the way, from Merjands and Saint Michael. *"God knew you would not turn from the quest."* She should have known what the quest was! She had coined it— protecting those who could not protect themselves—helping those who walked in darkness. Thulia viewed the quest's true span, a slow discovery of herself, painful at times.

Yet old joys still welled. Once a week she went to the wardrobe, retrieving the old wrap-around tunic, along with the wide belt and obscene skirt. She would sit before her big mirror, savoring the moments, adjusting her cleavage just right, that precise expression of sluttiness. Then she would jounce before Frit, confronting him with an outrageous statement, huffing the deepest breaths her lungs could hold. The servants always vanished, and Sesca rolled eyes huge, *"Mother! How can you speak like that?—and look at yourself!"* Frit would always drop whatever he was doing, find an appropriate comment, *"Your mother is acting like a slut again. I'll have to teach her a thing or two."* He never could. She already knew every lewd trick invented by womankind. She was an artist!

Sitting beside the hearth Thulia pondered Sesca's features, voluptuous for her age and soon to marry the son of Enos, a good Christian. Sesca was now a bishop's daughter, the Arian Council making Ascentia the second bishopric of the Gothic Church and elevating Saba to sainthood. Imagine that!—Bishop Selenas and Saint Saba the Shepherd. Life had changed, and she thought not of herself as the Amazon but as a teacher. Safrax was her first student; and so far she had instructed over a hundred young men in the art of horsemanship and lancing, including Salomon the horsebreaker's son. Old Hempstalk's knowledge was being passed on, and the *Iron Breaker* now carved posts yet remained sharp and ready.

Ah, Safrax, the rebellious son. Two years ago he was slated to attend the Arian seminary in Nicopolis and wed Sesca when she came of age, yet he balked at a profession and marriage arranged by Rustan and Selenas. Thulia grinned a big one, for Safrax chased his own dream, riding off with sword and contus… to live some exotic tale. He went east on a horse like hers, riding with Stefan and Salomon, all three going back to their roots—to the great steppes of the Greutungi, Alans, and Huns. *You take care of yourself, out there in the big world.*

During the past summer, she rode her own white-spotted gelding, knowing it would soon pass over… to wherever horses went. And throughout the winter, she had been terribly ill, losing weight and her complexion pasty. Frit was so worried he went to church and prayed. She never dreamed he would enter a church alone, even though a baptized Christian—*all by himself!*—almost a miracle. She felt better during early spring, back to her old self, with frequent *interludes* to keep in shape. Now she was having a relapse, a woman problem, missing her monthly twice. *Perhaps it shall pass. After all, there's always next month.* She felt too young to become a matron, only thirty one. Certainly she wasn't pregnant, infertile for so many years. No, it was some sort of illness, usually at its worst each morning.

Each morning... almost without fail. I feel good at night, like right now. Thulia peered up along the moonlight's shaft, her eyes wide and mouth aslack. *Oh, my God!* What was the number of the psalm? She was the parish deaconess and couldn't remember it... something about the Lord giveth, and the Lord taketh, obviously backwards. Blessing go and come! It seemed to her, he was giving again—*My dear God, I'm pregnant!*

And then a voice rang from the entrance hall, "Hailog, thein! Is this the Gryll Castle?"

Merjands! She jumped so quick she almost dropped the honey, twisting toward the mud room.

"It's just me, so fear not," he added, moving toward her in tired strides.

Thulia clutched the jar to chest, her speech elusive as she worked her mouth. He seemed exactly as remembered, not a day older... nor was his smile. Dropping a shoulder, he slid his burden from it. Things tinkled within the satchel. All those mysterious potions. He took slow strides, laying his staff at hearth-edge. And he sat before her to enjoin, "Please reseat yourself. I've had quite the journey, walked the distance, horses not designed for the thin-of-build."

She sat back to the lectus, still clutching the honey, voiceless, and he continued with a broader grin, "You look stunning tonight in that blue dress. It becomes the beauty you hold. This is uncomfortable; hurts an elder man's bones. May I sit at your side?"

"Yes, of course. But what are you doing here? The Gryll castle?"

He stood from the hearth stones, brushed his butt with a quick hand, and plopped beside her, craning his neck to check on Sesca, then admitting, "I thought it time for a change... as did Athanaric, who mistrusts my every word, for truth is a bitter root to swallow. And of course, I wanted to see how you were doing with the gifts. You have a welcoming cricket carved on the doors—a *gryll* in Latin—so this must be the Gryll Castle."

She looked him square in the eye, for she could handle men of the earthly type, "I had not heard the expression before. The gifts? I figured out the mirror soon enough, and the *Iron Breaker* cuts exceedingly well. The akinakes connects me to her. I found out from Rustan who she was, and I know they all belonged to her. But why did you pass them to me?"

"If I told you the truth, you would consider me mad. Let us sleep on it, and perhaps tomorrow when my mind is fresher." Merjands patted her wrist to stand abruptly, "It's late and I must find a moonlight glade to rest in."

Thulia jumped to her feet, "You skirt an overdue issue, and I'll not have you leave and vanish again." She grabbed a lamp from the candelabra and plucked his satchel, pulling him from the Great Room, nearly dragging him down a hall to enter a doorway.

Setting the lamp upon a stand, she dropped his satchel to a chair and purred, "This can be your bedchamber and what not else—your herbal den and private balm-works. Stay here to continue my guidance; and tomorrow I want an honest answer. Be the mentor you always were."

"You would like that?" and then he added, "Perhaps for awhile. I'm not getting any younger, and besides, I've never lived in a castle."

She rolled back the coverlet, kissed his cheek, and mumbled, "You should know I'm pregnant again."

"Of course you are. I found the Earth Stone about two months ago," he explained, collapsing upon the bed to lay supine, his feet still upon the floor.

She let the comment pass; yet trembling she reached down, swinging his legs to higher comfort. And then she left him to his eve, returning light-headed to Sesca. *The Earth Stone, mythical and never found.* Yet he retrieved it, now attached to the apex of his staff. This marvel was Merjands' shining gift! She reseated herself quietly, thinking of how similar he was to Saint Michael, exactly the same age and features, although the Proclaimer was far the thinner. Were they brothers immortal?

No. Just coincidence. Yet she knew Merjands came to Ascentia for reasons beyond healing; and the best move was to sit back down and thank God for abstruse old men... and to finger the last swipe of honey.

Chapter 45: The Prophecy of Merjands

Merjands peered from the bedchamber doorway and glanced up the hall. He was unsure how long he slept, obviously long enough that someone had washed his robe and folded it carefully upon the high-backed chair. His satchel and staff were tucked in a corner. The room seemed immense, and he measured its length with eight paces. Twenty four feet—six feet larger than the hut he abandoned in Threisbaurg... just before Athanaric torched it. He stepped into the hall and walked toward the nearest expanse. When he reached the Great Room, a young woman looked up from wiping the huge table and shrieked.

Rushing through a doorway, an impressive noble in a spotless tunic greeted him, "Ah, Merjands. You're up and about," he grinned broadly, "Good thing. We were about ready to hire the coffin-maker."

"Fritigern! Is that you?" blurted the seer, having not seen the Balth for a decade.

"The last time I looked at one of my wife's mirrors. Step into the kitchen and see the fish before they're broiled." Frit turned around and headed back through the doorway. Merjands followed, discovering an amazing room, high-ceiled with shelves and cupboards lining the walls, a brick stove at one end and covered with an iron grating. He gawked at it, tugging his cinnabar, and then noticed two wondrous trout on the cutting table, still moist and rainbow-sheened.

Frit cocked a thumb toward the fish, "Caught them early this morning with Rustan. He missed a bigger one when his line broke. Sapped him to a bad mood. These two will be our lunch. Ever had a meal cooked by Thulia?" he asked with a straight face.

Merjands pondered for a moment, "No, I don't believe I have."

"Really missed something. It's called *charcoal*. She received the knack from her father. In the blood. See those spoons over there?" And Frit pointed to a bundle lying upon a shelf.

"Quite the utensils," replied the seer, unsure of their significance.

"Last week I bought a new supply. Carved by a buck-toothed Ulmenian, rather talented but simple-minded. Thulia burns two or three a week—right up in flames! Smokes up the whole kitchen. That's why I'll save you the experience and cook these trout myself. How you feeling? Hungry?"

"Actually, come to think of it, I do seem to have an appetite," and he eyed the trout again, then inquiring, "Where is Thulia?"

"Down at the lake. Where else?" quipped Frit, adding a quick, "Good to see you in the land of the living."

"Well, thank you. Perhaps I shall take a walk and stretch my legs."

"Not a bad idea. They're about due."

* * *

Frit watched Merjands leave, studying the door as it closed behind him. No coffin had been readied for the old seer, just a joke; and besides, it would have been an odd one, overly long and thin. *Another timeless Seth or Saint Michael, think what you will.*

He walked back to the kitchen and stood before the trout, mulling abstractions. Two fish. How Christian they reposed before him. Yes indeed, the Fisher King, far above a hunter in a world changing faster than anyone wanted. After all the years he finally accepted the Church. But within it, there was a special place for women. They stood aside, apart from men, relegated to lesser status. *Like plebes or the unfree.*

He stood quiet, running a finger along one of the trout, colors fading to an increasing shade of gray. Steppe ways held a dying tradition: honor in its oldest form, courage not to turn a cheek but fight back for what was correct. There would be no more Thulias. She was the final Amazon, last of her kind. *Just like Merjands.*

*   *   *

Thulia knelt and placed flowers upon the cairn, arranging them to look their best. She stood back up to find Merjands coming toward her. He walked with a staff, but his pace was spry for a man his age. *Amazing what a little sleep will do.* In another few strides, he reached the tumulus and studied her handiwork, his eyes following the hewn post as it rose straight to the sky. She broke the silence, "It's a memoriam of sorts, I guess. Stefan the horsebreaker carved the timber, and all of us piled rocks."

"A large axis mundi," he noted, pointing to the carving on the post, "X marks the spot. A burial?"

"His name was Hagen, along with nine others. They were pagans and a cross seemed incorrect, so this timber connects them to their gods."

"They must have been special men, for a people to build such a fine marker."

Thulia knelt and straightened a flower, then snapped upright, "They were martyrs. Brave men. There are others, men from our village, over at the edge of the field," and she gave a smile from the heart, "I'm glad to see you up and about. You gained a little sleep but lost a secret."

Merjands seemed perplexed, "What do you mean, my dear?"

"It's past mid Junius," she grinned, "You slept just like a winter bear. We checked your heartbeat and it was like a tortoise. Now I know what you do when vanishing for weeks. No wonder you never age. Come," she commanded, "And take a stroll down to the shore. We can sit on my shining boulder and have an honest talk."

He appeared taken aback, "Have you become the master?"

They paced along the path, and she admitted, "No. You're still the master and always will be. But this is beyond tomorrow, and the answer is overdue. What connects me to Aryante?" Sitting to her perch, she patted the warm stone.

He dropped and commented, "A hard seat for a man with no meat on his bones."

"Good. Nice and uncomfortable, the way it should be for a change. Tell me about her. The truth, no avoidances."

Merjands remained wordless for longer moments than wished, and finally he began, "She lived at Issyk-Kul, the warm lake below the Tien Shan. The lake was her palace where a soul could meet the seven gods. She could ride like the wind and use that sword with precision, but she was not the lancer you are. She had no bulk, slight of build, yet she carried herself like a great warrior. But those things, prowess and courage, could not equal her spirit. When she died they built a kurgan for her, like White Mountain, layers of rock, then clay, then soil, layer upon layer until the mundi towered to the stars. She became a legend and then a myth, the High Warrior Priestess." He stopped to close his eyes.

She waited for more, then spoke clearly, "I prepare warriors for battle or the great journey. I see the past and future; and part of me dies when a good man perishes. I rebuke sloth and praise God. Rustan claims she did likewise."

"Exactly as you do. She was the preceptor, carrying each gift you received: the sword, akinakes, and mirror. Her essence is in them; and the truth you search for is yourself—Thulia Aryante Artia—'*Giver of the Sword,*' the She-Bear, teacher of young bucks and builder of mounds for the morally pure."

"Merjands! That's impossible," she huffed.

"What? That you're Aryante? Sometimes when you buy a Samos jug, the potter's fingerprint is hardened in the glaze. Have you not seen one?"

"Yes. Impressed before the jug was fired in the kiln."

"The glaze was still wet, much like we are unfinished when children. The print shows up more clearly when the jug is finished. In people the same thing happens. The fingerprint comes from the maker, the ancestor's blood. I am reasonably sure it imprints in our brain," and he tapped his temple, "We inherit all the things that cannot be seen until we are finished—just like the fingerprint on the Samos jug. The gifts helped bring Aryante to the surface and create the person you are."

"Then she was my ancestor," Thulia acknowledged.

"She was. For hundreds of years she lived in Dreamland, awaiting the flight of *samsara*—waiting to be the ripened you or herself again. Rather abstruse, or seemingly so. She was in you before you were born. The progression began in a wayward child, first wielding an axe, then a stick, and finally a sword."

"Hundreds of years?" cried Thulia, standing with a start, pointing a hard finger. *Did he just reveal his age? He must have known her.* Yet some secrets were best kept, and she posed a different question, "Why me? There must be thousands of good Alanic women out there," and she waved a hand beyond the field.

"Well, yes there are. Good women, all of them. But this whole thing was preordained." He shook his head in wonder, cracking a tight-lipped smile, "Do you think it odd that you mastered lancing from the best cataphract in three tribes, or that you married the Fisher King, the one ethical man for this age? You might have wed Selenas or Athanaric, but you did not."

She frowned at that one, believing it incredulous to even hint she might have married Athanaric, then laughed uncontrollably as she plopped back down beside him. *Such an incredible jerk.*

"Oh? What am I? A preposterous liar? Well then, it shall be no coincidence that Fritigern will join the Dragon Men of Safrax and Alatheus in a correct battle for all time. The son in your womb shall become the *Ufar Pandracon*, and your grandson will ride as the last Great Bear, known for all times as Artur. Upon a far western isle, he will protect his people from a pagan host."

Merjands sat straighter and gave her a stern eye, "And that is the truth. Unchangeable, unquestionable, until the last hawk spreads wings to a falling sky."

Thulia sat frozen. She knew one thing for certain—he was the Proclaimer, his one modus above teaching and healing. She had to believe him, "So that's the Prophecy of Merjands, is it?"

"Well, I guess it is," he shrugged, "If I had been cautious, I never would have blurted it out like a nanny-goat. But I did, so it stands and nothing can change it. Not the Buddha or a Magus can alter the preordained."

"So my son becomes Chief Dragon Man. And my grandson will ride as the Protector," and she scrinched eyes while examining his, "Like the Bear on a Grail cup or a Taifali shield?"

"They shall be extensions of you and Fritigern. Protectors of the People."

She could hardly fathom it, a line of descendants appointed to the same task, yet far off in a distant future… *and who is Alatheus?* Looking up, she deliberately changed the subject, "Oh, look! Here comes Rustan," quickly swinging a finger toward the path leading from the road.

Merjands twisted around, watching the Alan hetmon approach, "He seems in a foul mood, the way he trudges with a tight jaw."

Thulia waited until Rustan reached her shining boulder and looked to the sky, "What a marvelous sun. How was the fishing this morning?"

Rustan tipped his chin to Merjands, then eyed Thulia, "How was the fishing? I lost the largest trout of my life. That's how it was. Then your *marvelous sun* rose high enough to put the fish down. And when I got home, I discovered I'd left the bait horn in the log-boat. I'm coming back to fetch it—the only one I have—because that *marvelous son* of mine… whom you counseled," and he spat the words, "dropped the other horn overboard two years ago. Any more questions?"

"No," replied Thulia in a murmur.

"Good! Enjoy the damned sun," he snapped, then nodded to Merjands again, gave Thulia the evil eye, and stomped for the lakeshore.

Quietude enveloped the field until a meadow lark broke silence. Merjands fingered his cinnabar and postulated, "Well, I would say the man holds a grudge towards his son and you."

"Oh, it will pass, I hope. His son the Safrax of your prediction—was the best lancer I coached, also a real swordsman. Rustan had great plans for him, arranging studies with Bishop Wulfilas."

"But Safrax went his own course," postulated the seer.

"He bought a horse exactly like mine, a white-spotted gelding; and then he and the horsebreaker packed up and headed back to the great steppe, back to the days when we lived in wagons. I couldn't stop him, nor did I wish to."

"Ah," sighed Merjands, "He had a dream and awoke to follow it. I know someone else like that."

She understood exactly what he meant, squeezing his wrist in the same fashion he always squeezed hers.

* * *

The iron men raised camp two miles east of Maracanda, having survived a hard ride across Caspia from Lake Maotis. In skirmishes with Hunnic raiders, the lancers suffered almost fifty casualties. The contract number with the Sassanian king—three hundred cataphracts—had always been fifty short and new they rode even lighter.

In the distance, camels brayed along the trade road to the Stone Tower. The breeze seemed balmy as Safrax stepped from his hot praetorium to meet King Shapur's envoy. He gave a positive stride, holding himself erect knowing he'd be half a head taller than any Persian, and he tried to look uncommonly pleasant. Sliding from a well-groomed horse, the envoy stood between rows of tents, his expression sour as if smelling dung, wiping his nose with a silk scarf.

"Hailog, thein," greeted Safrax, "A Gothic expression, but we have Alans... and hopefully Huns."

"Huns?" the man quizzed with drawn lips, "Huns do not ride for Sassania. They are unclean, uncivilized to put it mildly. You must be Framander Safrax."

"Yes I am," the Alan nodded, "Framander Alatheus is not here at the moment but he shall return from Lake Issyk in a few days," *if he's not dead.*

"Issyk-Kul is a long and dangerous ride," claimed the Persian, "I'm Spahbad Ipcar Buran, diplomat for the Shah. We did not expect, what?—two hundred heavy horse? Where are the rest?" Before Safrax could answer, he quizzed, "And where is the Qash ka-i? I must see it."

"The Qash ka-i?" swallowed Safrax while hooking a finger under his armor's neck guard.

"Yes, the pale horse with a white star upon its forehead. That is good luck, the Qash ka-i, a very rare marking," and for the first time the man tried to smile.

"Oh. My white-spotted gelding. We shall get it for you, but please have some Spanish wine."

The Persian's countenance warmed as he purred, "Ah, Spanish wine. Even our caravans do not carry such luxury. Tart on the back of the tongue. Very good, especially with brazed lamb."

With a flare of hand, Safrax stepped to the praetorium's entrance to roll back the flap. They entered to the smell of new muslin, the canvas but a week old. At the rear, a slight and grizzled man bowed three times, waving the Spahbad to a campaign chair. Ipcar Buran felt the seat for dirt, smoothed his kaftan, and dropped to a dignified pose as he accepted the Syrian glass, sniffing it with closed eyes, then snapping them open to pronounce, "Ambrosia. And I see you have a most seasoned servant."

Safrax cracked a full grin, "Well actually he's not my servant but an old friend. This is Stefan the horsebreaker, a little scarred from early days yet possessed with many talents."

"Ah, I see," claimed Ipcar Buran, nodding to the man and taking a sip, "Now I shall make myself a fool, because you know, I have heard you were trained by... that you actually knew... the Amazon," and he reddened to a bright hue, shaking his head, "Such a titillating legend all Sassania whispers."

"You heard correctly. She instructed me in my youth, taught me lancing and the horse dance, as Stefan can attest."

The horsebreaker puckered lips to roll his eyes.

"Then it's true—you are the one who replaced the Amazon and now rides the Qash ka-i. Such a man is favored by the Magi. I bring tidings from Ctesiphon; the Shah is in perfect health and guided by the wisdom of Zoroaster. And I have good news, fine news. All is quiet here in Sogdiana, the people happily subjugated, and now we cross the Indu Kush. Our Lord, the great Shapur, consulted the Knowing Ones and they pronounced the twenty-fifth day of the eighth month as most auspicious for a new beginning."

"Eight weeks from now?" gulped Safrax while eying Stefan, knowing they were a hundred riders shy and yet to be trained, having no idea if his partner was dead or alive. Stefan tipped his head and arched a thumb rearward, "Farqithan meins, begettin thein Qash ka-i," then backing slowly to a fortuitous exit.

"Correct," noted Ipcar Buran, "Naturally, your cataphracts will charge as our wings with Royal Savaran in the middle. They require glory, an old Persian family. We do not expect Kushans to give much resistance; they have been conquered twice already. Malcontents, I would guess," and he leaned to the folding table, eying a parchment, "What is this? A tamga?"

"Yes, a design I've been toying with," claimed Safrax, feeling even warmer around the neck, "A dragon, just like our dracos."

490

Ipcar Buran took a last sip of wine, set his glass to the table, and stood looking up to the Alan, "How oriental. You must call yourselves the Dragon Men. Yes, that would be a perfect name for great warriors. The Savaran and Dragon Men. It even rhymes! And now I must see the Qash ka-i."

* * *

Alatheus spiked his draco to dry soil a quarter mile from the Hunnic camp. To his left, a mud-brick hut lay forlorn, its roof caved in, and the door long gone. He arched a leg over his saddle, dropping the reins of his extra mount to let it feed upon range grass. Before him, just beyond a solitary hill, the expanse of Lake Issyk filled the horizon as an endless sea. Hunnic yurts spotted the shoreline. Soon enough, they would come to inspect him up close and kill him, to let his bones lay white on red earth. *Did I live a wild life? I hope I did.*

He wiped his brow in the heat of a desperate act, for he and Safrax needed what the Huns had, not their women although he was a far better lover than a killer, but their talents with the compound bow. A Hun could shoot a foe in the eye at eighty paces, a good shot at any distance. After what seemed forever, a group of Black Huns left their camp to gallop toward him. Alatheus shifted in the saddle and removed his spangenhelm to wipe the leather liner, then refitting it to tie the chin strap. From all appearances, he seemed ready for battle, his ox-hide tunic a study in metal plate.

The riders stopped ten paces short, their mid-aged leader inquiring in Gothic, "Quisten ja? Why seek you the witch's womb? Or do you look for the Old Man?"

Alatheus breathed in relief and sat less stiffly, for the Hun knew old tales and projected humor. "I have come for your talents," then asking, "What Old Man?'

With a shrug, the Hun nodded to the abandoned hut, "Tales they tell of he who lived there. He came and went in

491

times now gone, tall and thin, old as the sun. He was the Awaiter."

Cocking his eyes to the hut, Alatheus quizzed, "The Awaiter?"

"Aye. People say he foresaw the return of his Teacher. She is buried in that kurgan," and the Hun jerked a thumb toward the solitary hill, grinning broadly, "They say he was always old, for no one remembered him young. Then one day he went back to the gods. What need you from these people?"

"I came to ask one hundred men to accept an honest task."

"You think you can find a hundred honest Huns?" The man grunted, tossed arms to the sky, and swung back to those behind him. They all guffawed.

"I'm serious in my offer; and how did you know I'm a Goth?" piqued Alatheus, removing his helm to again wipe his brow, "You can kill me for my horses or ride with me to high adventure."

"You wear armor of Epthalites or Qin, but they do not have your complexion or Greutungi accent. You, I think, are newer—what they call an iron man. Take heed. You speak to Ondin, the One Who Sees Beyond Days. Tell him of high adventure."

Alatheus was fairly surprised, "You're a shaman, then? A tribal priest?"

"Nay," claimed Ondin, "My mother would not let them have me so I became bow-legged like the rest. She was an Alana, and I have her nose," he tapped its bridge, "So I have blood of the Teacher," and he tipped his head toward the kurgan, "She was Aryante, my ancestor, and she speaks when I listen. We lived with the Alani, sometimes the Greutungi, for my clan traded horses. You are a long way from home."

"My partner and I ride for King Shapur but we need a hundred good archers to fight on the other side of the Kush— the high mountains to the south—men with keen eyes and talented fingers. The pay is good, four asses a day whether fighting or not, plus high man gets two gold Kaisers for each battle," and then Alatheus refitted his helm.

"Ah, an honest trade," sighed Ondin, "Perhaps I might join you, and there will be others. Come. Eat some herring and clean yourself in the Warm Lake. I think a bathing Goth might attract many young women. But if you take one for the night, she becomes your wife."

"What if I shoo her out before the dawn?"

"Ah ha!" exclaimed Ondin, "You are like a wise and crafty thief, careful in what you pluck. Then you must choose another for the next night... until you find the one that suits your taste."

I'm going to live, after all. And live it well. Alatheus guided his mount forward with a genuine grin; for recruiting a hundred Huns would take some time, at least four or five nights, perhaps even longer. And he dug heels to ride past the hut of the Awaiter, past the hill of the Teacher and hidden world of Dreamland—riding to to his own undreamed future.

About the Author

A.J. Campbell is a writer-artist-historian specializing in Eurasian and angling history. He has written internationally since 1978, and is a member of Legio III Cyrenaica and the Roman Army Talk Forum. Campbell is also a reproduction ancient-arms designer and Certified Archery Instructor in steppe bowmanship. He lives in Maine, USA, Planet Earth. Heaven can wait.